LESLIE HALLIWELL

Return to Shangri-La

GRAFTON BOOKS
A Division of the Collins Publishing Group

LONDON GLASGOW
TORONTO SYDNEY AUCKLAND

Grafton Books
A Division of the Collins Publishing Group
8 Grafton Street, London W1X 3LA

A Grafton Paperback Original 1987

ISBN 0-586-07081-8

Printed and bound in Great Britain by
Collins, Glasgow

Set in Times

'The inspiration for this book comes from *Lost Horizon* by James Hilton. An agreement has been reached with the owners of copyright for the inclusion of the name SHANGRI-LA in the title.'

The concept of a remote Utopian community in the Himalayas became famous throughout the world when James Hilton published *Lost Horizon* in 1933. Fifty years later, two chance acquaintances in the Californian desert find reason to believe that the celebrated story may have had a basis in truth. A trail of danger, detection and excitement leads them from a flooded canyon in Death Valley back to the London blitz of 1940; from the spurious glamour of Hollywood to a peaceful island off the Pembrokeshire coast; and finally by an obscure Asian route to a discovery which changes their lives and could even affect the future of the world. This is a unique flight of fancy which intrigues and entertains while leaving the reader with more than a little food for thought.

By the same author

Halliwell's Film Guide
Halliwell's Hundred
Halliwell's Harvest
Halliwell's Filmgoer's Companion
Halliwell's Television Companion (with Philip Purser)
The Filmgoer's Book of Quotes
The Clapperboard Book of the Cinema (with Graham Murray)
Mountain of Dreams
Seats in All Parts
The Dead That Walk
Double Take and Fade Away
The Ghost of Sherlock Holmes

Contents

1

Nicholas Brent's Narrative (1980)

'A DISTASTE FOR THE MODERN ACHIEVEMENTS OF MANKIND'

My strange story, which finds its climax among the remoter mountain fastnesses of Asia, begins in California, America's lotus land for the world weary. Not however in the soulless suburbs of Los Angeles, where bored sun-seekers curl up and die by the million, but in a prehistoric showplace called Death Valley. By official record one of the hottest and least hospitable places on earth, Death Valley has been sufficiently tamed for the purposes of certain kinds of tourist: in air-conditioned four-wheel-drives they flock to it for the pleasure of pitting their strength and daring against its implacable power and majestic indifference, or simply for the pleasure of wallowing in its glory. In Death Valley a man feels very small. Small; puny; utterly insignificant against the spectacular and extraordinary forces of nature, which with water alone can in time carve passageways through ancient rock, or with a single volcanic eruption scatter through the air a cubic mile of that same rock and have it fall again as a thick black tar covering for the bleak earth five miles around.

If the tale I have to tell reads like sensational literature, that can't be helped. Things turned out in the way they did, though not by my design: in a sense, I was propelled along a remote and broken road like tumbleweed in the wind. Oh, I do admit that for a fifty-one-year-old I was a little jaundiced: I badly needed a star to steer by, and the concept of Shangri-La amply filled that requirement, whether in the long run it proved to be fact or fiction. The pieces began to fit when I found clues to Shangri-La in Death Valley, long one of my favourite places; but I could not have suspected when I began to follow the trail that they would lead me to a revelation only slightly less important to our history than what the three wise men found in the inn at Bethlehem.

Now, the time has come for me to share my knowledge with a troubled world.

On that warm spring day in the desert, the day when the strangest events of my life began to form a coherent pattern, Shangri-La had no more than a foothold in my thoughts. Because she wanted me to, and because I usually did what she wanted, I had taken Elizabeth's startling theory with a pinch of seriousness, but I always stressed my suspicion that she was placing far too much credence in a wild surmise by her father, who had disappeared and very probably died in pursuit of it. Sir Arthur of course had been a man to respect, nobody's fool at all; but at a certain age even great leaders of men tend to get bees in their bonnets, and I was rather afraid that Elizabeth's current enthusiasm might at last have the effect of showing up her father as a credulous simpleton. What else could press and public be expected to say if we revealed that he had taken a small exploring party into the eastern Himalayas, determined to find a secret Utopian valley which the world supposed to be a figment of popular fiction?

When I finally reached Death Valley that evening, and found myself once again coasting down the last long slope into Stovepipe Wells, there were more pressing matters on my mind, problems which even the sudden warm comfort of the desert air could not instantly solve. First, the nagging suspicion that physically I was falling apart, that I might even be in the grip of a terminal illness. Second, and rather ironic in the circumstances, the growing conviction that someone that afternoon had tried to push me over a cliff. Oh, I have to admit that at that point I was just a little crazy. Hardly manic, you understand, but not too far from the end of my tether. Pressure of work I'd long learned to cope with, but just recently I'd begun to doubt the value of what I was doing, had often doubted in fact the value of life itself. That sort of blue melancholy usually afflicts me in its most violent form when I've been flying for more than ten hours, and it's even worse when the jet lag strikes. On the evening of which I speak, both conditions were fulfilled. You know the feeling: eyelids like curtain weights, and an inability to concentrate on even the simplest actions. You're more likely to be humming the Warsaw Concerto than I Got Rhythm, if only because it's slower. Warlock says now that when he first made himself known to me I seemed remarkably cool, but I was always known for my poker face. Inside, I must have been a mess of shattered nerves and depression, even though the doubts and excitements had scarcely started. I'd never heard of Dr Pavel Lorenz, nor of Ralph Abel, and I saw Simon Battersby no more than twice a year, which was fine by me. Yet all of them came to figure very largely in what followed, and in less than pleasant ways which I could not possibly have predicted.

I suppose it was largely my own idea that I might have one foot in the grave. Certainly the Wimpole Street man had hummed and harrumphed at the result of my X-rays and barium meal, and there was nothing at all comforting about the way he had put me down for 'a few other tests', none of them specified. But he did say that there was no *immediate* danger, and added that of course I could go on my ten-day business trip to California, but no stressful situations, please, and no smoking if possible, and as little drink as I could possibly manage. I said that if I stuck to his regime, perhaps the shock to my system would cure what ailed me. It wasn't much of a joke, and it didn't raise much of a smile.

The oddest coincidence in my story is that Death Valley should figure so largely in it. On my business trips over twenty years I must have been there for half a dozen weekends without deriving from it the slightest significance beyond feelings of awe and enjoyment. To me it isn't at all the doom-laden place which its name indicates, rather the perfect setting for a triumphant organ voluntary or the Sermon on the Mount. My early afternoon, before I reached the valley proper, had been spent on a magnificent crag called Agureberry Point, six thousand feet above the sandy floor. I'd made straight for the desert from Los Angeles airport, intending a totally relaxed weekend as a preparation for business; but there had been an overnight stop and a long lie-in, so it was nearly two in the afternoon when, after negotiating a long series of hairpin bends through the Panamints, I turned my wheels off the Emigrant Pass blacktop to follow the sign which tells you in no uncertain terms that it's six miles of rough going to the point. Actually cars can make it with no great difficulty, but the surface is washboarded gravel and dust, so they sometimes come back with a few scars. The trail winds past the site of a prospectors' ghost town called Harrisburg: when the sun casts the right shadows you can just about make out where the main street was. Then the route starts to climb, through a canyon lined with giant boulders, towards the crest of the range. You may see a couple of wild *burros* (that's Spanish for donkey). You'll certainly pass a few stands of cactus. Then, pretty soon after you emerge from the narrows, there's a sign on the right telling you that Trail Canyon is closed: that's the one down which jeeps once lurched and zigzagged all the way to the floor of Death Valley itself.

I've always regretted not bringing a four-wheel-drive during the years before storms and landslides obliterated the descent. A mile further on, two of those abominable, authority-provided pink toilets tell the traveller that he has arrived at the first official tourist overlook, an immense distance above the barren desert, with the cultivated date oasis of Furnace Creek a small green square just discernible through the heat haze. I didn't get out, because I knew from previous visits that the higher car park gives an even better panorama. I had just dropped into low gear for the steep and slightly hairy climb when I became aware of the little orange Mustang moving into view in my rear mirror. It seemed familiar. Obviously it must have been close on my tail all the way from the main road; but hadn't it also pulled in, three hours earlier, as I left the Red Mountain gas station? And what matter if it had?

The familiar climb up that final slope was treacherous today. On the right, I kept as close as I could to a rock face: that was because, on my left, parts of the trail had crumbled and fallen away, leaving a vertiginous boulder-strewn drop to a gully five hundred feet below. I manoeuvred nimbly enough, and never even touched the loose parts with my wheels; but I noticed with wry amusement that the man in the Mustang was more than a little nervous. He stopped altogether at one point, then did his best to inch his way precisely over my tracks. Luckily there was nothing coming down, or we'd both have had to back off, and he wouldn't have liked that at all. At last I pulled into the empty parking space with its freshly painted sign (Elevation: 6428 feet), and was out of my Range Rover, looking for the footpath, before the Mustang rounded the high rocks and came to a halt with what sounded very much like a sigh of relief.

I took with me almost as an afterthought Elizabeth's

copy of *Lost Horizon*. For April, it was hot up there – a while had passed since I'd been so close to the sun – but a light west wind kept the air fresh and balmy. The short signposted track is a source of absolute wonderment. It leads one, perhaps two, hundred yards along a shoulder of mountain to a point where there is an almost completely circular panorama. The Panamints rise behind you, but away round to the left you see Mount Whitney, always snow-capped and at sixteen thousand feet the highest point in North America. Along the intervening hundred miles the hills gradually decrease in stature until Tucki Mountain, to the north of your vantage point but below it, drops abruptly into Death Valley at Stovepipe Wells, which stands exactly at sea level. The valley runs north to south, away to your right past Telescope Peak, and before the scene melts into haze you may, on a good day, pick out Badwater with its salt pools (and more pink toilets). That, at minus 284 feet, is the lowest point in the western hemisphere, and its actual rockbed is thousands of feet lower still, covered with a thick blanket of silt from the surrounding peaks. In every direction the view from Aguereberry Point is staggeringly prehistoric, and the mountain air provides a constant stimulus to the sense of adventure. When I felt I had taken in as much as I could, I pottered for a while about the high rocks, counting the varieties of tiny desert flower which thrive astonishingly in every niche, despite being so small that the naked eye needs a little training to spot them. Then I found a clump of rock which formed an angle likely to serve the purpose of a deckchair. It did so most admirably, and I spent a quarter of an hour stretched out in it, idly browsing through *Lost Horizon* and finally settling on the passage which details the kidnapped party's first glimpse of the sheltered Valley of Blue Moon, an incredible blessing to the eyes after a mysterious and alarming flight, a crash, and half a day's breathtaking trudge up a snowy mountain.

> The floor of the valley, hazily distant, welcomed the eye with greenness; sheltered from winds, and surveyed rather than dominated by the lamasery, it looked to Conway a delightfully favoured place, though if it were inhabited its community must be completely isolated by the lofty and sheerly unscalable ranges on the further side.

Glancing down from my own viewpoint, I idly deduced that any real Shangri-La, if it existed, had to be a good deal above sea level, though not perhaps quite so high as my present elevation, which must invite a good deal of winter discomfort. Then I smiled to myself at my momentary acceptance of the myth, and closed the book in my lap. My eyelids drooped of their own volition, and I spent an indefinite time, perhaps seconds but more likely several minutes, stretched out in perfect bliss. Then a cloud passing over the sun made me open my eyes, and I realized with slight embarrassment that an American family was standing nearby, enjoying a quiet chuckle at my recumbent posture. A pre-teenage boy was, moreover, clicking a camera in my direction; but to take umbrage would have been churlish, so I simply nodded as cheerfully as I could.

After an enjoyable stretch I pulled myself to my feet, left the book on the rock and turned around, so that my back was to the main drop, a yawning chasm with spiky pinnacles at its base. I was, in fact, close to the edge of an almost vertical scree: if I'd missed my footing I could well have slithered and bounced the best part of a thousand feet, and survival would have been unlikely. About to move forward and upward to a safer place, I suddenly spotted (because the sun glinted on the frames of his dark spectacles) a strange roly-poly-looking little man who seemed to be almost crouching in the shadow of one of the higher pinnacles between myself and the track. Although I had not waited in the car park to have an encouraging word with the owner of the Mustang, I had to presume that this was he. Not much of his face could be seen because he wore, against the sun, some sort of dark green Homburg. There was no doubt, however, of his moustache – so luxuriant that I could only think of it in the old-fashioned plural, as moustaches. He was clothed in a pale khaki safari suit with a dark tie, all of which seemed a shade formal in the circumstances; personally, I hadn't thought of wearing a tie since leaving London. The impression he made against the mountainside was in fact so bizarre that I could not avoid staring at him rather rudely for several moments. Then I stretched out my arms in a gesture of appreciation of the landscape; but he did not respond. I had taken two or three careful steps up the scree towards him before he rose silently to his feet and came forward.

I could not swear in court as to precisely what happened next, or rather as to why it happened. *My* motive was to regain the track; his remained unclear. The little man – for I doubt whether he was more than an inch over five feet – came down towards me, picking his way with one delicate step after another. His face was still obscured even when no more than ten feet separated us, but I had a good sight of his polished brown shoes. I assumed that his intention was to share my approval of the view from the chair rock; I suppose that's still a tenable explanation, though I have to consider it unlikely. Anyway, his left foot appeared to stumble, perhaps on a loose rock, then to my horror he was hurtling down towards me, apparently out of control. Without even glancing behind me I knew the likely choice of consequence: he would either push me over the precipice and save himself, or take me with him. (It seemed less than probable that he would miss me altogether and take the plunge alone.) A split second was all I had in which to make a judgement and take action. I braced my legs as firmly as I could, thrust my arms hard forward with palms upraised, and took the full force of his onrush. My elbows cracked, and I still went backwards, in a kind of slide through the shale. Then I felt my ankle give way. Clumsily my body crumpled on to the sharp stones, and I caught a whiff of perfume as the almost weightless body of the little man shot over my head with a despairing wail. I heard him hit the ground behind me and skid away. Then I scrambled painfully to my feet, instinctively closing my ears and eyes against what seemed to be inevitable.

The first thing I saw was blood; but it was only a smear on the right hand of the stranger, the right hand which clutched desperately at a pointed outcrop just above the place where the cliff became vertical. He must have grabbed at it as he sailed past it face first, then twisted his body and hung on. The American family had hurried back at the sound of his scream, and within seconds somebody in a red shirt had the unfortunate man by both wrists. Heavy echoing footsteps heralded other rescuers: a burly fellow was helping me to safety as I tried to explain what happened. The moustachioed little man was drawn gently up the rock slope and lain carefully on his back at my feet, apparently suffering nothing worse than a few scrapes and scratches to his person and one gigantic tear to his suit. My first instinct was to laugh, for his green hat was still in place. He must have fixed it with glue.

Consternation does not last long. Five minutes later we were all on our separate ways and the situation of moments before seemed totally unreal. Somebody offered Band-aids, but strictly speaking they weren't necessary just then, clean water being the first priority. The man in the red shirt told the man with moustaches that he should head straight for the ranger station and check that no bones were broken; but he was wasting his time, for the little fellow appeared to speak no English. He simply kept nodding, as though to reassure us all, and once gestured at me with what might possibly have been an apology. But he avoided my eyes.

Back at the car park, I spread lip salve, the only preparation I had with me, over my scratched palms, then carefully pulled on the cheap white gloves which the hire firm had thoughtfully provided for use while tyre changing or doing any other rough jobs which might prove necessary. My ankle seemed not to be strained after all; I was more out of breath than anything. The red-shirted man shook his head and fanned himself with a guidebook as we watched the orange Mustang trundle slowly downhill towards the distant toilets, then turn right and disappear into the canyon. I shook hands with all present, and followed suit. It wasn't until half an hour later, when I had regained the blacktop, that the mists of shock cleared, and the recent events re-enacted themselves in my mind. When they did, I found I couldn't be absolutely certain that what had happened was accidental. If not, the plan had gone sadly wrong; but I thought again of the careful feet in the brown shoes, and was forced to wonder whether, right up to the instant of skidding past me, little Mr Moustaches hadn't intended simply to push me over the cliff when nobody was looking!

My sisters always said I spent too much time in the cinema, and I now had to smile at this cameo melodrama of my own construction, before banishing it from my mind as far as it would go. But it is the melodrama which causes me to date my real involvement with Shangri-La from that magnificent spring afternoon, when my body might so easily have lain broken at the foot of a Californian mountain.

A psychiatrist would probably have told me that at fifty-one I was feeling the regrets of middle age, trying to change fantasy into reality because reality had turned to ashes in my mouth. In fact, I had fought long and hard against Elizabeth's unlikely theories. Shangri-La was to me a figment of James Hilton's imagination: in 1933 he had won the Hawthornden Prize for creating it. I am not even an imaginative man, and certainly not an adventurous one; but I suppose Elizabeth has enough of both qualities to compensate. What she lacked, when it came to the point, was money and moral support. Ever since her father disappeared back in 1975 she had been set on a rescue expedition; but the clues were so vague, and the trail so cold, that everyone who might have been expected to help found reasons for not doing so. Most of them pleaded not only the slim chances of success, but the danger to herself: the high Himalayas, after all, are still among the world's least accessible, and therefore least explored regions. I blamed nobody, for I was myself very sceptical about Elizabeth's hopes, and wished fervently that she would give up the proposal. Nor did Simon Battersby, her half-brother, offer any encouragement to begin with. Indeed, I heard him once tell her that she could go and get herself killed if she wanted to, but not on funds from the family trust. (As it turned out, none could have been made available.) An unattractive young man, Simon, with too obvious an eye for the main chance. Not even young, come to think of it, since he was forty-two last Christmas: but, to use Bernard Shaw's phrase, a man whom age could not wither because he had never bloomed.

As for my joining such a safari, I said no very firmly indeed. Apart from thinking the whole idea fairly absurd, I was far too old for a strenuous caper of that sort, just as I was too old to marry Elizabeth, much as I liked the idea. Friend of the family was my typecasting. Friend of father's, which was worse. I had known the old man pretty well since he became my historical advisor on *Expedition!* back in 1971, and more than once in those days I heard him mention Shangri-La as though it were a real place. Once, when I'd been invited down to Battersby Lodge for Sunday brunch, he took me on a tour of the pictures which covered the walls of his study, and I came across one which seemed hardly worth framing. It was a blown-up black-and-white snapshot of two men standing arm-in-arm on a terrace, against a background of snowy mountains. Only the face on the left was defined with reasonable clarity.

'You?' I asked.

'My late father,' said Sir Arthur. 'With an old school friend of his. The face is in shadow, but it's the only picture I have, and I've a reason for valuing it.' He looked at me quizzically. 'Taken when they met in Afghanistan in 1930, shortly before the fellow disappeared.'

'Disappeared?'

'Got himself caught up in a revolution. He was a consular attaché. Nice man. Taught me to play cricket when I was five, before he got shot up in the First World War. I always had a feeling that if my mother hadn't married my father, he'd have been next in line.'

'And he never turned up again?'

Sir Arthur shrugged. 'He's still missing, so far as the world knows. One of these days I'll mount an expedition to find him.'

'And where will you look?'

Sir Arthur blushed like a schoolboy, but finally said, with a couple of affirmative nods: 'Shangri-La, perhaps.'

I doubtless showed my puzzlement. 'But he looks fortyish in the snap, and that was forty years ago. Do you think he can still be alive?'

Sir Arthur smiled. 'Yes. In certain circumstances, yes, I do. In Shangri-La, you know, they found the secret of longevity.'

Well, although I remember that conversation so clearly, I always thought Sir Arthur was playing a little game with me. He often demonstrated a quirky, donnish sense of humour; and I sometimes thought he should have been pottering about some academic backwater instead of tramping up mountain sides and through muddy jungles. His trouble, I suspect, was that he looked like Sir Aubrey Smith and felt bound to play the part.

His daughter has none of these whimsical characteristics. Elizabeth always means exactly what she says; and tells you frankly what she sees. She certainly spots the flaws in my character, or lack of same, especially when it comes to my reluctance to marry her. She dismisses the age-gap theory as nonsense: in her eyes I'm just afraid to take the chance. Now, that's probably true. I'm simply not a man of action, more a watcher from the sidelines. Somerset Maugham used to influence me a good deal, and I saw something of myself in him, never bored with watching other people's antics as the world flowed past him. Of course, he built them up into stories reflecting the human condition (or his own waspish view of it), and I can make no such claim. But I liked, too, his idea of imposing a pattern on life, with the peak between fifty and sixty, a time when your struggles (with luck) are over and you find yourself on a comfortable high plateau where, assuming you still have your health, life is good and your opinions are respected. You find the flaw when you reach the end of the plateau: Maugham was never too comforting about what might come after; and his own old age, extended by injections of unborn ewe at Dr Neilhans' Swiss clinic, was a desperate and unhappy compound of physical skittishness and mental aberration.

There was a story about his making a speech at the age of eighty, starting with the statement:'Old age, they say, has many blessings.' This was followed by a long pause, after which Maugham added with impeccable timing: 'I'm trying to think what they are.'

You can certainly understand the attraction of a story like Hilton's, about a perfect society where wise men have learned to extend man's natural life span by a careful regime and the use of a rare herb. Normal life is so short. My own friends and acquaintances have already begun to drop off at quite an alarming rate, and a while back my annual medical report began to include such phrases as 'Quite satisfactory for your age.' Only when a new Russian military leader is appointed do you hear any age over fifty described as 'young'.

I suppose I've started to waffle on like this rather frequently, and it only makes Elizabeth click her tongue in that impatient way she has. At least, she said, I could promise to take *Lost Horizon* to California with me, and pay it a little more attention than I'd done through all her years of telling me about it. I could hardly refuse her that, especially since she dropped a copy on my bedside table; and heavens knows I'd *like* the story to be true. An ideal society must make for a saner world, after all. It just didn't appear likely, to say the very least.

Discussion of an ideal society seemed especially ironic in this year's cold English spring, following an even colder winter when our own society had functioned at less than its best. Apart from the inevitable strikes and acts of terrorism, with a couple of aeroplane disasters thrown in, and politicians insulting each other for light relief, our transport systems were taken totally by surprise when in the middle of March the daytime temperature suddenly fell below zero and stayed that way for several days. Still, as a nation we took less than a month to recover from this shock, and my British Airways plane was no more than four hours late when it finally rose from the tarmac. Once it did, I sank back blissfully among the familiar Utopian pleasures of first-class travel: a reclining seat, an adjustable footstool, a few morsels of high-quality food and drink, and eleven hours out of the reach of telephones. By the time we headed across Greenland towards Hudson's Bay I was sound asleep with a damask napkin over my head, and so I remained until the captain announced that we had started our descent into the urban desert of Los Angeles. (My description, not his.)

Now as I negotiated the twists and turns of Wildrose Canyon, scarcely allowing my raging palms to touch the wheel, I reflected on the depression with which I had viewed the city of the angels when our wheels finally touched the tarmac, at what in London was five in the morning but here only ten at night. Being British, we were made to sit in the plane while three American jets unloaded before us, and I could have committed murder when I found myself nineteenth in the shortest immigration queue. My feet were swollen and there was a bilious taste in my mouth, due in my opinion not to overindulgence but to a proper indignation at the thought of so many people hovering over the earth in grossly overcrowded aircraft, drinking themselves silly and feigning interest in glossy magazines full of items to be afforded only on expense accounts. Within a few years the planes would all be on the scrap heap and the passengers would all be dead. How, if at all, could their frantic, scurrying continent-hopping activity be said to have either improved their own lot or affected the history of the world?

A modicum of optimism did return when, ninety minutes after setting foot on Californian soil, I found myself driving north on Sepulveda with no business commitments for three clear days. Joining the freeway at Sunset, I headed for route 14, the twisting thirty-mile pass over the San Gabriels. Then came the flat dark dreariness of Palmdale, where the fifty-five-miles-an-hour speed limit must be carefully observed, making it a two-hour drive to the tawdry truck stop called Mojave. Here I turned gratefully into McDonald's for a quarter-pounder and a hot cherry pie. Even after this sustenance, my eyelids had the weight of anvils, but only twenty weary miles remained to be covered. Follow the signs north for Bishop; then right turn for California City, that most eccentric of all speculative ventures which, despite advertising on a massive scale, California for once seemed reluctant to support. The idea – it had never occurred to me before – was in fact to create a kind of Shangri-La; and if it had worked, California City might have become the biggest retirement area in the world. The desert for miles around it had been mapped out with skeletal gravel streets which will probably never bear the weight of houses. For the site had nothing going for it beyond dry warmth, level ground, and isolation – insufficient attractions for most people with money to invest in in their old age. California City, with neither mountains, rivers nor sea at hand, was dead before it started. The speculators had begun by building three miles of divided road to serve as Main Street. Along each side they had dotted such amenities as a fine new city hall, shopping plaza, airstrip, fire station, cinema, and churches of various denominations. Behind these modern structures, however, stretched the eerie desolation of unclaimed desert, broken just occasionally by a struggling stunted tree or a random clump of wooden bungalows. Such citizens as ventured on to the streets by night had a bland resigned look, like the small-towners whose bodies were taken over by aliens in *Invasion of the Body Snatchers*: men who had come a long way from other milieux and found the promised land a disappointment, not like Shangri-La at all.

Luckily for me, the original development had included a perfectly adequate hundred-room motel called the Lakeshore Inn. The concrete-bottomed lake was stagnant and the golf course was said to want refining, but no matter, the place made a perfect stopover on my annual trek to Death Valley. Even at this time of night the welcome was cheerful, and I knew the breakfast would be good; meanwhile the bed had cool blue sheets, wonderfully inviting to legs which had suddenly refused to fulfil their normal functions. I enjoyed four hours of perfect sleep before waking with the birdsong. Then I made myself a cup of tea, and spent a while on the verandah with *Lost Horizon*. I thought it might match my mood, provide balm for my cynicism, a still centre for the untidy bustle of my life, consolation for the failed Utopia amid which I now sat. Besides, it brought Elizabeth closer, and I was missing her already.

I should explain a little more about Elizabeth. She was at this time approaching her thirty-seventh birthday. She's a trim, no-nonsense sort of person with an Ancient Mariner eye; but everyone knows that now, since her rise to television fame. Before her father's disappearance she shone only with light reflected from Sir Arthur, and seemed to find fulfilment at his side whenever he needed her . . . which was most of the time. In earlier days people would have called her his amanuensis. She fixed his lecture tours, ghosted his books, argued with agents on his behalf. She also went on several of his expeditions, including some pretty uncomfortable ones. But it was Sir Arthur who was called an explorer, his name and his face which sold the books. Alas, all the profits, which were considerable, went into maintaining the family pile at Marlow, a ghastly piece of Strawberry Hill Gothic for which my recommended remedy would have been demolition. It was for the sake of Battersby Lodge that Sir Arthur was still working at full stretch when, at the age of sixty-seven, he disappeared from the face of the map.

Elizabeth passed three desperate months after the last message was received from him. Then some bright spark at BBC 2 had the rather tasteless idea of inviting her to present a programme of hitherto unexposed bits and pieces from Sir Arthur's film library. Despite her melancholy she acquitted herself so well that other assignments rapidly followed, including a round on a frivolous panel game called *Travellers' Trivia*. Even here she put on a show of enjoying herself, and the public enjoyed her enjoyment. Next she was invited to host a series of thirteen television 'expeditions' into various remote places, under the title *Adventure*. Macchu Picchu, the Dolomites, the Canadian Rockies, the Dracula country, Iceland, Yosemite . . . the film material was actually provided by professional cameramen with an eye on the tourist market. A freelance packager in those days, I put the show together as a co-production with Beta Film of Munich, and it was at this point that Elizabeth emerged from the background of my life into the foreground. Hitherto, I had met her only through her father, with whom I had worked frequently; now she became the object of my admiration. Halfway through the series the staff producer resigned, saying that he felt unnecessary. The fact was that Elizabeth had taken over. I watched with amusement as she rewrote the scripts, redesigned the set, improved the lighting; as for her performance, she used Autocue as though it were a normal method of communication. The ratings shot up, way outclassing Cousteau, and she found herself with a flood of fan mail to answer.

Her self-confidence being thus restored, it hardly surprised me when Elizabeth conceived this mad idea of following her father into the remote Himalaya and retracing what most people now consider his final journey. She could not understand why all the possible sponsors demurred. I, however, could understand very well. The Nepalese government was being tricky about permits, and although prices had gone up astronomically, there was a long queue. The territory had become very dangerous: there were stories of rebel tribesmen attacking and murdering strangers. Besides, nobody knew for certain where Sir Arthur had been heading. At Bhaktapur he had abandoned his prearranged route and struck east, apparently in a bid to cloak his real intentions. No trace of him had subsequently been found in that almost unmapped region, where mountains crack and change with the seasons, and where trails have to be trodden afresh for each journey. The Hindu Kush, his original destination for the first leg of the expedition, remained unvisited, so far as anyone could tell.

Elizabeth was forced to give in for the time being. Poor as a church mouse on her own account, she was still paying off the debts which had accrued after Sir Arthur's disastrous 1972 expedition to the Matto Grosso: after the worst weather ever recorded in those inhospitable parts, it had been abandoned without the exposure of any film worth showing. Elizabeth spent next to nothing on herself. Even on television she looked as though her outfits had been rescued from a church jumble sale. She didn't give a damn how she looked; luckily she always looked marvellous. She reminds me of a little Cairn bitch I once had: the same wheaten hair and dark eyes. There are other resemblances. Once she determines that I'm going to follow her, or play with her, or cuddle her, I might as well give in, because she'll get her way eventually. She's always doing *something*: every second of her day has to be meaningfully occupied. A strictly non-business relationship quickly grew up between us. Perhaps we were both oddities: at any rate we liked each other instinctively, held the same values, enjoyed the same entertainments. If I had to explain our empathy, I could only come up with a mutual respect for the lessons of history combined with a distaste for the modern achievements of mankind. It may seem a strange basis for a love affair, and I know people have smiled at us behind our backs; nevertheless, if Elizabeth had had her way I think we would have been married long ago. It was I who preferred not to lock her without deep thought into a contract which she might regret. So we left it. Whenever either of us needed the comfort, we moved in together for a spell; and in any case I phoned her every day at breakfast time, even now when she was in Mexico for production talks. She reluctantly agreed that as arrangements go, it was adequate in the circumstances, the circumstances being that I'm nearly fifteen years the elder. In my book that's too much: I've seen a dozen January–May romances go sour.

I was slightly too young to fight in World War Two, but my elder brother was killed at Arnhem. Like all my school contemporaries, I thought of that conflict as *my* war. The promised land lay just around the corner, Britannia ruled the waves, and those who had given their lives in the cause of freedom would never be forgotten. At university, my friends and I considered ourselves to be the first men of the new generation, men who would build on the foundations so firmly laid by those who had died for all our sakes. As it happened, the new generation never even got a toehold on the post-war world. So many years of austerity followed VJ Day that Britain became too bankrupt, morally as well as economically, even to start the rebuilding process with confidence; meanwhile the Germans, whom we had supposedly beaten into the ground, were cracking along at a rate of knots. The first young Britons with a real chance at a fresh start were the swingers of the Sixties, the ones who weren't inhibited by memories of the war. I remember resenting their lack of gratitude, their bitter mockery of all the standards I held dear; but they certainly got things going.

And now that famous war is virtually forgotten by the populace of our islands. Only the elderly still shed quiet tears for lost sons and husbands. Nobody even pauses to look at the war memorials. Those young airmen shot down in defence of our skies during the baking summer of 1940 thought they were fighting a war to end all wars, and that's an irony if ever I heard one. Who thanks them now? Who in the spring of 1980 even treasured the qualities they died to preserve, qualities like grace and dignity and respect for the past?

I did – but then, I wasn't in a position of influence.

2

Nicholas Brent's Narrative (1980)

'CIGARS HAD BURNED LOW'

After my curious adventure at Agureberry Point, I came to Death Valley itself in the late afternoon. All the mountain ranges near the California coast run north to south. This was a great problem for the covered wagon pioneers who were heading from east to west. In 1849 a few of them turned, by a combination of error and obstinacy, into this lowest and steepest of all the world's natural trenches, and nearly died of heat exhaustion before finding an arduous way out, five weeks later. Geologically, Death Valley is a dried-up lake bed, for most of its length a salt pit covering up 10,000 feet of geological fill. It lay almost unknown to tourists until the mid-twenties of this century, when a couple named Eichbaum set up a crude bungalow resort on a site which became Stovepipe Wells. Then in 1933 Washington made the valley a national monument, and set park rangers in cowboy hats to patrol its shiny new blacktop roads. Since then it has drawn enthusiasts from all over the world, people who like me come back if they can at least once a year for the rest of their lives. If you ask them why, they will probably make some remark on the lines of its being a place where a man could find his soul, if he had one. I think the simple secret is the total lack of trees. There being nothing to wave or rustle in the wind, the valley has about it a unique stillness, and that combined with its massive rocky grandeur enables one to see petty problems in their true perspective. Clarity of vision is part of it too, and purity of air and vividness of colour. People walk out into the empty middle of the landscape and find a salt pinnacle on which to sit and think. Or, quite possibly, only to sit.

Death Valley can't be recommended for the careless. Amid its vastness, human evil seems quite unthinkable, but nature itself can be as cruel as it is beautiful. Sunburn is a major curse; broad-brimmed hats are recommended. Distances between areas of shade are great, and the sun often merciless; the only two places to stay in the 250-mile stretch are twenty-five miles apart. Except at the cultivated date oasis, the primary vegetation is mesquite and tumbleweed. Snakebite is quite possible, and has been known to be fatal. Radiators need very little encouragement to boil over, leaving the driver stranded in the heat with only the car itself for shelter. In such circumstances any exercise, even walking gently along the road, can only increase the risk of dehydration and death. And, as I've indicated, there aren't many people about except at the cooler seasons, which sometimes bring with them a few light showers and possibly an evening or two when sweaters are required. In summer however, the valley can be the hottest place on earth, its air temperature rising frequently to 120 degrees Fahrenheit and sometimes to 130 or more.

Twelve miles at its widest point from mountain top to mountain top, the valley proper runs from Big Pine in the north almost as far as Baker 300 miles south. It's bounded on the western side by the Cottonwood and Panamint Mountains, and on the other by the Grapevines and Funerals. The only crossroad was established more or less centrally, between Towne's Pass and Hell's Gate: here turbulent winds, whistling through these gaps, have formed a constantly shifting landscape of sand dunes. A myriad of additional trails does exist, most of them making for the canyons but only a few emerging on the other side. It is unwise to venture any distance along these routes without notifying a ranger of your intention, so that if you don't return to your hotel, he knows where to look for you next morning. And if you're stranded in a canyon, start to worry when rain clouds break up overhead, for it is the run-off from such accumulations of moisture, called flash floods, which clear the canyons with the effect of a hosepipe, spilling huge alluvial fans of sand and shale out of the canyon mouths on to the valley floor.

Despite all the precautions which sensible travellers must take, the valley is a place of absolute beauty and unceasing wonder. The sensitive visitor must be awed by the yellow, moon-like mudhills of Zabriskie Point; by the multicoloured rock palette of Artist's Drive; by the meagre ghost town ruins of Rhyolite and Skidoo; by the black volcanic crater of Ubehebe, half a mile wide and almost as deep, with its bright orange flare looking as though painted by hand on the bottom of the cup. As I turned right out of Wildrose and began ten miles of coasting gently down to the floor of the open desert, I looked forward to renewing my acquaintance with some of these wonders. But meanwhile, the dry desert air had its usual effect of tiring me out even before I had unpacked. Within fifteen minutes of my arrival among the rudimentary comforts of the motel at Stovepipe Wells, I was stretched out blissfully on a queen-size bed, with nothing to do before supper but nurse my injured hands and read a little more about the adventures fifty years ago of Hugh Conway and company, recovering from their experience on a windswept Tibetan plateau and gazing down from the man-made terraces of Shangri-La into the Valley of Blue Moon.

At six I found I had accumulated sufficient energy to ease myself into a hot tub; then I dressed casually and spent another forty minutes with *Lost Horizon*. Sitting on the verandah with my feet up on the rail, watching the sun go down over the Cottonwoods, I felt like Walter Brennan in some old black-and-white Western movie. Eventually I took myself and my book for a saunter through the gift shop; thence into the hotel lobby, where two park rangers were arranging chairs for the evening lecture, and a lean old man in a Stetson was asking whether someone called Gentry had arrived. And so to eat, in the wood-framed dining room, hung with Indian tapestries and decked out to suggest an old mine. Simple meals only were available, but that suited me fine: hamburger, jello, and strong coffee, with a help-yourself side-salad from bowls temptingly arrayed on a bed of crushed ice. Some time after eight o'clock I strolled into the capacious bar and chose the most comfortable seat, the one next to the wooden Indian, and as far as I could get from the jukebox which I fervently hoped nobody would encourage. With a glass of ice-cold beer beside me, I took one last glance through the window at the deepening purple glow behind the mountain.

Twenty minutes or so later, another chapter through my book, I replenished my glass, noticing as I settled again that the room had filled up. I paid no special attention to the elderly man sitting in a corner close to me, except to note that he was the Stetson owner I had passed in the lobby. I say elderly, because that was my first impression, but I now realized that it was an exaggeration due to his shock of snow-white hair. On closer inspection he probably wasn't much over sixty, and looked pretty lithe and energetic in his beige safari coat and dark brown cravat. Though I tried not to look up, I felt his eyes on me, and was not at all surprised when about five minutes later he chose a lull in the general hubbub to lean forward and speak. What he said was:

'Cigars had burned low.'

That is, of course, the very first line of *Lost Horizon*,

describing the aftermath of the dinner at Tempelhof Airport during which the incredible story of Shangri-La is first brought to the narrator's attention. I looked up from the book. The white-haired man was smoking nothing more than a Panatella, and I an American king-sized cigarette; but both had undeniably burned pretty low, so I could scarcely withhold a nod and a smile. Nor could the exchange end with his returning grin: conversation was inevitable. His frame, I now saw, was rangy: flab could never have gained a foothold on it. With his aquiline nose and healthy tan he looked like a wise old Indian chief: it was a face which belonged on a totem pole.

'You know the book,' I remarked rather obviously.

'Mmmm.' He grabbed a handful of salted nuts from the dish on the table, and talked through them. 'I might say intimately. That's why I had to speak to you. I mean, since you're reading one of my favourite books you must be a halfway decent fellow. Most Britishers are.'

'How did you guess I was British?'

My new acquaintance let out a laugh so resounding that several people looked up from their drinks and stared. 'Only a Britisher would have to ask that question, and even he shouldn't expect an answer.' He edged closer. 'Can we talk? Unless of course you have some pulchritudinous blonde stashed away in your room.'

I chuckled. 'I'm quite alone, and I have no responsibilities except to enjoy myself.'

'Good. I'm Irving Warlock, and let's take the handshaking for granted.'

'Nicholas Brent. Warlock, you said? I like that. It has resonance.'

'A lot of people envy me my name, which I came by quite legitimately. I imagine they think I might *be* a warlock. Never tried: might have liked it. I tell them it's Rumanian. You know, there's a bit in *Dracula* where the good count explains that the Slovak for werewolf or vampire is *vrolok*. I lose plenty of unwanted acquaintances that way.'

'In fact, of course, you were born in Canada.'

Mr Warlock was crestfallen. 'You must be a descendant of Professor 'Enry 'Iggins. Not many people can tell us from New Englanders.'

'New Englanders don't usually wear maple leaves in their lapels.'

'Aha!' Warlock clicked his fingers as though about to start a Spanish dance. 'I forgot I was wearing my patriotic suit. Made in Taiwan, actually. Tell me, are you reading that book for the fiftieth time or only the tenth?'

'Your conversation does dart about, doesn't it?'

Warlock laughed again. 'My friends who are increasingly few, through choice, usually get around to telling me that I have the mind of a magpie, the memory of an elephant, the tenacity of a bulldog – and sometimes the weight of an albatross. But you were about to reveal the extent of your acquaintance with the volume in your hand.'

'This is really my first solid read. I think I skimmed through it, once before.'

'I envy you, sir. I should like to be in that situation, discovering the pleasures and thrills of that book for the very first time. I remember it quite took my breath away. But then, to my generation Shangri-La was such a great symbol that everybody knew about it.'

'It seems very well written.'

'You mean, the man who wrote about Shangri-La gives the impression of having been there?'

I shrugged. 'That's one way of putting it, certainly, though he leaves a lot of details to the imagination. What he *does* tell you seems very thoughtful, very well conceived.'

'You've read some of Hilton's other books, perhaps?'

'I don't think so.'

Warlock shook his head. 'Not the same, not even *Goodbye Mr Chips*. The feeling of essential truth seems to have gone. That suggest anything to you?'

'Only that Conway was probably based on someone Hilton knew well.'

'Or, don't you think, that the book almost wrote itself? Doesn't that sometimes happen when a man's writing directly from experience? The thing springs fully formed to his mind. But I expect you'd say that in this case it could hardly be so.'

I smiled politely. 'I know someone who thinks it might be. But to me a mountain utopia is a fairly absurd concept. In the first place, who wants to live forever?'

Warlock raised a finger. 'Not forever. Only . . . long enough. Certain people would be an even greater adornment to history if we could hang on to them for a while longer. Don't we all wish we had more of Shakespeare in his prime? And Churchill? And your Prince Albert, perhaps, and F.D.R. Just as the public made Conan Doyle extend the span of Sherlock Holmes.'

'Wait a minute, he was fiction.'

'But based on a real person, a great intellect, Dr Joseph Bell of Edinburgh. *He* should have had an extended span. He was a Conway: the whole of *Lost Horizon* is in the Sherlock Holmes stories. A deep-thinking character, somewhat frustrated by everyday life, cleverer than his colleagues, no longer young. Plucked from a cosy existence to meet great adventures, which despite himself he welcomes.'

I shook my head in amusement. 'And where does the High Lama fit in?'

'Oh, he's Moriarty. A reversal, all right? Good for evil. And Chang is Dr Watson, guiding Holmes – Conway – to the truth, but himself avoiding the limelight. You see?'

'I see that your glass is empty.' I said, cheerfully summoning the waiter. 'I see also that you're one of those people who never loses an argument, because any given set of facts can be bent to fit your perverse theories.'

Warlock laughed again: I swear the glasses on the table tinkled. 'I shall take your remarks as a compliment. At least you must agree that with Sherlock Holmes, as with Conway, the story ends with hope for the future of the world.'

'I thought he finished up keeping bees on the Sussex coast?'

'No, no, I mean *His Last Bow*: the fight for right at the beginning of the Great War.' Warlock put one hand, Napoleon-like, inside his coat, and began to declaim. 'There's an east wind coming, Watson, and such a one as never blew on England yet. It will be cold and bitter, and a good many of us will wither before its blast. But it's God's own wind none the less, and a cleaner, better, stronger land will lie in the sunshine when the storm has cleared.' Somewhere nearby there was an outbreak of applause, probably intended with sarcasm. Warlock did not hear: he was prodding my knee in triumph. 'Don't you see? It's the High Lama's vision of the future, after the cataclysm, when Shangri-La could arise from the world's ruins and point the way to better times.'

'Yes, in a way I do see. I see that some optimistic vision of that sort was necessary to our world in the early Thirties. People were surrounded by gloom and unemployment, and nobody would even listen to visionaries like Churchill who told them that war was coming. They wanted the victory without the battle. Hence *Lost Horizon*. It's a dream. A call to arms, perhaps, but only a spiritual one.'

There was a pause while we stared at each other with wry friendly smiles. Then Warlock said thoughtfully,

'Unless, as I said, Hilton was writing from experience. Unless he meant every word. Literally. Are you a literary man by profession?'

'Not at all. I was a film producer of sorts until the whole structure of that business started to crumble. Then I escaped to the comparative sanity of television. That's what brings me to Tinseltown two or three times a year.'

'And why the desert?'

'I found it by accident and come back as often as I can. It's hot and dry and helps me get over my jet lag, and the TV people don't seem to have discovered it yet. I feel at home here.'

'That's wild, for a Britisher.'

'I've always liked to wander in wild and desolate places. Scotland, Iceland, Egypt. I was thinking this afternoon as I drove in that this could be America's lost horizon. Perhaps Shangri-La is just on the other side of Telescope Peak.' I chuckled. 'I told you I was suffering from jet lag.'

Warlock reacted rather elaborately to this, then pointed a bony finger at my chest. 'You know, Mr Brent, it may be rash to say so on such short acquaintance, and desperately old-fashioned in any circumstances, but you seem to be a man after my own heart. I was expecting to be joined here this evening by a close friend. You have more than made up for his unavoidable absence. We have briefly discussed subjects on which, with your permission, I should like to elaborate in the morning. Indeed, it would not surprise me in the least if this meeting were to prove as fruitful in its way as that between John H. Watson MD and S. Holmes Esquire in the Criterion Bar. And now, since we have both finished our drinks, I should like to suggest a short stroll, the reason for which I will explain when we get outside.'

The last sentence had been spoken in a confidential whisper which so impressed me that I was out in the cool dark air before I had time to think. Once through the ranch doors, Warlock put a finger to his lips and led me round the building to a point at which we could look through a window at the area we had just vacated. 'See that little guy in the green suit? He was behind you, but I could see him edging closer to our table, occupying every seat that happened to be left vacant. I don't usually attract that kind of creep, and he doesn't look like a friend of yours. You're not by any chance carrying government secrets about your person?'

It was, of course, my moustachioed acquaintance of the afternoon. Seeing him there, gaudily suited and so out of place in that cowboy saloon, I entertained a sudden thought that the moustaches might be as false as his dank black hair, now visible but in no way convincing as having a life of its own. When we stopped he was pretending to read a magazine, but he kept glancing at the doors, and while we watched he rose and headed for the hotel lobby.

'I've seen him before,' I said. 'Let's go for a walk.' We were close to my room so I stopped by and tossed *Lost Horizon* on to the bed. Then I thoughtfully picked up the heavy cane which I had bought in the gift shop against any ankle strain which might result from the afternoon's adventure. I have always enjoyed walking with a stick, but tonight I had a small premonition of danger, probably from the green man but for all I knew from Warlock, whose loud avuncular presence could, after all, have been a magnificent con job. Nevertheless, as we strolled in the dark – for the moon was obscured by cloud – I told him what had happened at Agureberry Point, speaking as softly as I could in case we were being followed. We had made a complete circuit of the hotel buildings and were back on the deserted main road as I finished.

'I don't like the sound of it,' Warlock muttered. 'Why the devil should he be following you?'

'Who says he is? Assuming he's on vacation like me, and was on top of the mountain this afternoon, where else could he spend the night? There isn't a lot of choice.'

Warlock shrugged. 'I suppose it's just that he doesn't look the tourist type. I can't imagine he even enjoys fresh air.'

At that moment an engine whirred in the darkness, and a vehicle crashed into gear. Headlights flashed on in the parking lot, and seconds later a car shot into view, screeching to a halt at the road before turning in our direction. I stood well aside to let the traveller pass, tugging at Warlock's sleeve to ensure that he followed suit. We were well advised: the car accelerated suddenly and came within three feet of us as it shot like a bat out of hell down the road towards Furnace Creek. As it passed, the moon came out. I couldn't see the driver, but the car looked like a Mustang, and its colour was certainly orange.

'Was that our little green man?' asked Warlock.

'I think it must have been.'

'I trust you are not in the habit of leaving valuables in your room?'

'Everything but a change of linen is locked up in the car.'

'And my briefcase is in the hotel safe. Let's check anyway.'

We walked back rather sharply to the cabins and came first to Warlock's room. The door opened normally to the turn of his key, but inside there was no doubt that he had had an unwarranted visitor. The contents of an open suitcase were strewn across the carpet, and his toilet bag had been tipped out in the bathroom sink. My new friend's lips set in a firm line. 'Nothing he could have taken that would worry me. Come on, let's try yours.'

On the way we checked our cars, which seemed to be

untouched. My room at first sight had not been tampered with either. A toothbrush lay on the bathmat, but I'm an untidy chap and might have knocked it there myself. In bemused silence we glanced in all the corners on our way back to the open door; then a thought struck me and I turned to the bed. 'He did take one thing after all,' I said.

'What was that?'

'You can see the indentation where I dropped it on the bedcover. My copy of *Lost Horizon*.'

First Interlude (1987)

IN ST STEPHEN'S TAVERN

DIP/CON/3/Inf of the Home Office, otherwise known as Pemberton, caught up halfway across Whitehall with his friend Twigley, to whom Foreign Office memos were usually addressed ST/HOPS/5c. Their customary fortnightly lunch resulted not from pressure of urgent business for discussion but from the fact of their having been friends since school days, when for some long-forgotten reason a master who fancied himself as a wit had dubbed them Castor and Pollux, the heavenly twins. The fact that Twigley was now corpulent, and Pemberton on the ascetic side, rendered the jest less apposite than ever; yet their service careers, and marriages, and their subsequent doings in Whitehall, had been parallel and exemplary, resulting already in minor honours, and in more than adequate pensions to come.

Their prandial encounters invariably took place in St Stephen's Tavern, for each had once nourished some ambition to be a parliamentarian; and so both felt comfortable there, surrounded by half-heard House of Commons gossip, even though they had long ago forsaken the excitements of politics for the subtler power of administration. On this Tuesday, however, from the small first-floor alcove table which for years had been theirs whenever they wanted it, there was little time for eavesdropping. For Pemberton had a matter pressing on his mind.

'Now,' he muttered as soon as the first glass of claret had been poured, 'I hope you managed to read that bundle of stuff I sent over? The one marked *Brent: Confidential*? I put urgent stickers all over it.'

'Mm,' replied Twigley, his mouth temporarily occupied

with wholemeal bread. 'Everything seems to be urgent nowadays, doesn't it? I did glance through the first couple of chapters, though. Couldn't make head or tail of it. Why should we have to concern ourselves with a bit of sensational fiction?'

'Because,' said Pemberton quietly through gritted teeth, 'we don't know yet that it *is* that. Did you get to the first bit about Hugh Dearden?'

'Don't recall, old man. Don't think so. Who's he?'

'Well, years ago he was one of our chaps. Oh, I suppose I'll have to wait a few more days, but do get on with it, as a friendly gesture towards me. The boys upstairs are wanting a report, and you know how I value your advice. I don't suppose you even foraged round for a copy of *Lost Horizon* as I asked you to?'

'Now, there you're wrong. It's sitting on my desk at this very moment.'

'But have you *read* it?'

''Fraid not.' Twigley paused long enough to take in Pemberton's shrug of irritation, then went on: 'But I had it read.'

'You *had* it *read*? By whom?'

'Willoughby. Writes a smart memo, that young man, and I should say he's just as good at synopses. Here's what he gave me this morning,' From an inside pocket Twigley unfolded a sheet of closely typed paper and spread it on the table for Pemberton to read.

Lost Horizon by James Hilton. London, MacMillan, 1933.

The novel begins with a story told to a friend in Berlin by a professional traveller named Rutherford. In a Chinese mission hospital in 1931 he has recognized an amnesia case as an old schoolfellow, Hugh Conway, an official in the Consular Service who has been missing since a revolution in Baskul the previous year. Conway was presumed to have escaped after boarding a borrowed plane for India along with Mallinson, his junior; an

English missionary, Miss Roberta Brinklow; and a mysterious American named Barnard. The plane simply disappeared. When Conway, on the way home on an ocean liner, begins to recover his memory he tells an incredible story. The intended pilot of the plane was replaced by an Oriental kidnapper, who flew for twelve hours (with one pre-planned refuelling stop) over the Himalayas to land on a windswept plateau in Tibet. There he promptly expired from a heart attack. The passengers were rescued next morning by men from a nearby lamasery named Shangri-La, which is itself somewhat sheltered from the bitter weather and commands a deep temperate valley of astonishing fertility. On these two levels it transpired that an ideal community had been founded, and Conway learned a little about this from a majordomo named Chang, but much more from the extremely aged High Lama, a Belgian named Perrault who claimed to be more than two hundred years old, having learned the secret of longevity through the use of a local berry named tangatse. It was Perrault who had the idea, or vision, of using Shangri-La to preserve all the best of the world's art, literature and philosophy through the world holocaust which he saw as inevitable, and of bringing to the lamasery occasional strangers, from whom a new High Lama might be selected. Within a matter of weeks it was decided that Conway was the man for the job, and when the High Lama died Conway was on the point of accepting the honour, especially since Barnard and Miss Brinklow also opted to stay. But Mallinson disbelieved the longevity story and had fallen in love with a Manchu princess stranded at Shangri-La many years ago. Conway was persuaded as a matter of duty to escort them into China, but once outside the valley the girl quickly reverted to her true age and died after leading Conway through unspecified hazards to the mission hospital. Mallinson's fate is left unclear. One night Conway simply disappears while the liner is in port, but Rutherford later learns that he set off to find his way back to Shangri-La.

'Yes,' said Pemberton as he passed back the paper, 'that's quite accurate as far as it goes, though I think he'd have done better to stick to the historic present, and he misuses the word 'transpired'. I honestly recommend you to read the book yourself, Bernard. It's remarkably convincing.'

'So is *King Solomon's Mines*, old man, but it wouldn't persuade me to go hunting for diamonds in Central Africa. Anyway, I don't see what this yarn has to do with me, or you for that matter.'

'I agree with you on the latter point, but it's landed on my desk and I really think you chaps are the ones to take it over. It's clearly a Foreign Office matter.'

'Ah, so it wasn't just a friendly recommendation you wanted.' Twigley waved the matter away from him with both hands and a superior smile. 'Don't see how it can be our pigeon. Diplomatic, possibly, since they took over the Consular. But I never heard of a consulate at Baskul, not in my time.'

'I don't suppose you did,' was the dry response. 'Baskul never existed: Hilton invented it for some reason, though from even a cursory reading of the book you can see that he meant Kabul in Afghanistan.'

In the best Foreign Office tradition, Twigley made no acknowledgement of his error. 'Kabul, yes,' he said. 'Just over the hills from Peshawar: my eye caught that phrase in the book. Always was subject to revolutions till the Russkies got their hands on it.' He smiled as he busied himself with a toothpick.

'In the film version they seemed to put it in China. Ever see that? Came out just before the war.' Ronald Colman!

'Believe I did. After the war, though: it was brought out again. Theatre Royal, Oswestry. I may even have proposed to Alice on the way home. She'd be in a good mood after two hours of Ronald Colman. Just the chap to take charge when you're dumped on the far side of an icy mountain on the roof of the world. Sort of challenge I'd once have relished myself.'

'Don't kid me. You'd have been gobbled up by the Abominable Snowman.'

'Who is probably just as fictitious as this story. I met

Sir Arthur Battersby once. Nice chap, but he had a dreamer's eye just as this chap Brent says. I don't know who fed him the stuff about Shangri-La being real, but I do know he never came back to tell the tale, and I'd need more proof than an unsigned typescript.'

'It's signed at the end. And the signature's been checked and confirmed for what that's worth. So will you please do me the favour of finishing it?'

Twigley smiled expansively. 'When have I ever been able to refuse you a favour, old man? Tell you what, Alice is off to her sister's this weekend, so I promise you that after I'm through with *The Times* on Sunday I'll take the phone off the hook and think of nothing else. And if you're prepared to stand me an extra non-rota lunch next Tuesday, I'll tell you what I think.'

3

Nicholas Brent's Narrative (1980)

'ANOTHER GOD-DAMNED GLORIOUS DAY'

From the moment I found the book missing there was no turning back. But I still needed time to think. I was involved in something I didn't yet understand, and you can't turn a watcher on the sidelines into a man of action overnight.

What happened over the next two days in Death Valley may seem to advance my story only marginally, but for me it provided the entire platform on which my subsequent policy was based. I came to Death Valley a sceptic; I left it determined to devote at least part of my life to the search for Shangri-La. My trouble was going to be admitting as much to Elizabeth: after all, just one week earlier I had been pooh-poohing the whole idea. But at that time I hadn't heard the story Warlock had to tell.

After Mr Moustaches decamped, Warlock and I spent a frustrating quarter-hour with the manager, who started by doubting our suspicions and not understanding how anybody could make such a fuss over a book. But when he agreed to have a word with Mr Loewenstein, which was the name our little green man had given, he found that his bird had flown without paying more than a deposit: there wasn't a trace of him left in the hotel. That really got the manager going, but it didn't help us, and there still seemed no rational explanation: professional thieves don't usually expect to hit the jackpot in desert motels, and no other guest reported a disturbed room.

Warlock had not yet heard anything specific from his absent friend, and asked what I planned to do on the following day. I said I might feel sufficiently daring to look for the moving rocks, a mysterious phenomenon of nature which involves a hundred-mile round trip, mostly on dirt roads. We decided to go together; but when I knocked on his door next morning at seven, a glance at his face told me that for him the trip wasn't on. 'Got the runs,' he said. 'The revenge of Montezuma, and I didn't even drink the water. The only hazardous journey I'll make this morning is to the bathroom and back.'

'Sorry about that,' I said, grinning rather. 'I'll bring you back a moving pebble.'

It was a supremely calm and beautiful morning, and the forecasters said it probably wouldn't get hotter than a hundred. As a precaution, I told a ranger where I was going, but he didn't sound all that interested after he checked that I had a four-wheel-drive. I turned north at the sand dunes and made Scotty's Castle in just over half an hour; it's more than forty miles, but there was nothing on the road. After a pit stop, never having been one for guided tours of millionaires' mansions, I headed seven miles northwest to the volcanoes, and stretched my legs around the rim of the main crater until the wind started to swirl the black lava dust around my ankles and into my shoes. And so along a dirt road, beset by warning notices but not too bad if a bit narrow and twisty, nineteen miles south through valleys replete with joshua trees and tall cactus. At Teakettle Junction, where a trail meanders off leftwards in search of the even more remote regions of Hidden Valley, I had my first magnificent view of my destination. The Racetrack is a jocular name for what seemed to me that day an equal for any of the seven wonders of the world, and I was utterly alone to enjoy it. Since leaving the volcanoes I had seen nothing of either four wheels or two legs, though the lines of joshuas on the hilltops sometimes looked like menacing Indians in a movie. But no movie had ever given me a pictorial thrill to equal the sight which lay below me.

I was looking down into the end of a long valley, blocked off four or five miles ahead by range upon range of close-packed hills. In the enormous cup thus formed there lay a flat yellow mud *playa*, which seemed even more brilliantly coloured by contrast with the dark hills which surrounded it. My guidebook told me that its mud is composed of vast quantities of dust which at various prehistoric times blew off the mountains and settled a thousand feet thick in what had once been a melodramatically deep valley. A short range of black granite which originally sat in that valley does break sharply through the mud at the north end, in a finger-like formation known as the Grandstand. That's all there is, but in the sunlight it seemed both sinister and astonishingly beautiful, like a detail from a Salvador Dali painting. If nature could create this, I thought, then surely she could also create Shangri-La and the Valley of Blue Moon. I drove down as slowly as I could and in silent wonder; ten minutes later I had parked the car at the far end and was walking on the dry crusted surface. It was as springy as a ballroom floor; I felt like a man in seven-league boots. I walked, and ran, and pranced on that moon-like surface for an hour, and took pictures of its mosaic-like formations and of the moving rocks, which make curious and, at first sight, inexplicable trails near the south end. They are boulders fallen from the surrounding mountains, and some at least are too big to have moved along the *playa* by mere human power; yet moved they have been, for there in the caked mud I saw tracks four and five hundred feet long, some angular, some tortuously circular, some dead straight. Clearly the tracks had been made after rain; and after enjoying the mystery for its own sake I nodded in agreement with the generally accepted explanation, that on rare winter occasions when ice forms on the *playa* and the rocks are embedded in it, a gale-force wind might be strong enough, as the ice begins to break up, to push the whole arrangement across the slick surface underneath.

I made a mental note to come back in winter sometime; meanwhile I would enjoy for another hour my sense of isolation in this strange place which testified so abundantly to the majesty of God, or of nature. The valley is high enough to avoid the extreme of desert heat, the hills steep enough always to afford shade at one side. So why had it escaped being overrun by man? Presumably because nature had forgotten to provide water. Without that, the Racetrack could never be Shangri-La: and suddenly, as though to prove my point, a shadow passed across the sun and a chill breeze began to blow from the north. Having foolishly omitted to bring even an adequate windcheater, I shivered and ran back to the shelter of the car, in whose lee I ate the apple and sandwich I had brought with me from the snack bar at Scotty's. Then I considered my homeward route. On most maps the trail I was on petered out at the Racetrack, but I knew that in less reliable form it continued to the south end of this high enclosure and began a descent round a western mountain, down into Saline Valley.

Starting the engine, I reached the end of the level bit within fifteen minutes, then paused thoughtfully by a rusty sign which advised that the rest of the road was suitable only for four-wheel-drive vehicles with high clearance. That included me, but the road had clearly deteriorated since the sign was erected many moons ago. Cut roughly into the mountainside, with a steep drop on the left, it was, even at its beginning, little more than a clumsily levelled arrangement of sharp stones on an insecure surface, no more than seven feet wide at best, and it plunged down at an alarming gradient which seemed likely to continue. I locked the car and decided to walk for a while. The trail wasn't even cambered, and at one point tipped over quite dangerously to the left, so it soon occurred to me that discretion might still be the better part of valour; after a mile of so I turned back regretfully, bearing in mind that the return journey would be steeply uphill. But I had ventured far enough to get my first mind-boggling view of the Saline Valley, a good four thousand feet below, with snow-capped mountains rising majestically on its farther side. It was an image which will stay with me for the rest of my life: as I climbed breathlessly up the trail in the hot sun it stimulated me to such unoriginal thoughts as the insignificance of man against nature, the respect which must be paid to such a mighty landscape, and the ease with which a man might fall into one of the rocky chasms and never be found. What struck me most of all, however, was the blazing heat on this side of the mountain compared with the chill at the Racetrack just over the pass. I was, in fact, living out in reverse one of the points about *Lost Horizon* which had seemed the most fantastic – when Conway's party staggered from an inhospitably icy mountainside on to a ledge above a miraculously fertile valley capable of sustaining life in its fullest sense. Above me now was the four-wheel-drive sign, standing in for the stone pillar towards which, at the end of the film, Conway laboriously struggles, to the silent cheers of the audience.

Back on the high level, I had a little difficulty starting the Range Rover: I presumed the high altitude was responsible. Soon, however, it was careering quite happily back towards the Racetrack; and it took me longer than it should to realize that the lurching I now felt was too much to be accounted for by the soft shale surface over which I was travelling. My left rear tyre had gone. I sighed in annoyance, but even I can change a tyre if pressed. I took my time about it, with frequent glances at the scenery, and only looking at my watch when it was time to move off. Then I noted with a slight chill that it was nearly three o'clock: I could not afford another delay if I was to get back to the hotel before dark.

The Range Rover started up very sluggishly, and got me a couple of miles further. Then mystifyingly it gave up the ghost completely, just as I came level with the yellow *playa*. I was suddenly the loneliest man in the world. In the beginnings of panic I tried everything I could think of. After a couple of minutes and several twists of the key, the engine spurted into life again but took me forward only a few feet before coming to a final halt, like a mule which digs its heels in and proposes to go no further. Cursing, I opened the bonnet and studied the engine area with nonchalance. The carburettor leads seemed OK; the petrol pump looked a little twisted, but for all I knew that was how it should be. The gauges, when I switched on again, all registered satisfactorily. I spent fifteen minutes rather frantically reading the manual, without enlightenment of any kind. Ah, well: I had another sandwich, I had water, and the back seat was wide enough for me to curl up in. Tomorrow Warlock would send the rangers for me, or come himself, or both. It seemed unlikely that there would be further visitors before then; I was alone for the night.

I had spent thirty silent minutes looking at the scenery when a distant sound in the sky made me look up. Nothing in sight, yet the humming was all around me and growing in volume. I glanced around the desert in case it was a deceptive echo from a car, but there was no such comfort. I ran out on to the *playa*, turned full circle, and only became more confused. Then suddenly it was upon me, from behind a steep mountainside to my west. A shiny scarlet helicopter, with two people in it. It passed over my head and descended gently on to the yellow surface of the Racetrack, barely a hundred yards from where I stood in astonishment, my hair flapping wildly in the breeze it created. My first thought was that the Park Service must have been telepathically alerted to my problem; but as I waved and ran towards the craft I noted on its door a private crest, and from the great balloon window the cheerful face of Irving Warlock grinned down at me as he waved back, his mop of wiry white hair reflecting like a halo in the afternoon sun.

As the giant red beetle inched its way to rest, I was rather foolishly afraid that it would damage the pristine surface of the *playa*, or sink into it so deeply as to be unable to rise. Neither catastrophe occurred. The three metal feet simply balanced lightly on the mosaic; the rotor blade whirred less certainly, and finally stopped altogether. As Warlock clambered down I began to pour out apologetic explanations, but he waved them aside. 'We only came to look at the scenery and see if we could spot you on your way home,' he said. 'You don't know how good it will make Jim feel to have been part of a rescue mission, especially when he had no such intention.'

The big burly fellow who was the 'copter's pilot and other occupant now descended to ground level, and was introduced to me as Jim Gentry. Of course I recognized him now, and knew why his name should have been familiar. Gentry the multi-millionaire, son of the armaments manufacturer of the Thirties whose one-time friendship with Hitler had caused him some problems during the war. The son had recompensed by distributing much of his fortune among third-world charities, but constantly made more money from the industrial conglomerate of which he was the nominal head. I was reminded of a line from *Citizen Kane*: 'It's no trick to make money, if all you want to do is make money.'

Gentry, however, had the instant look of a man who wanted to do something else. I may be exaggerating, but I thought him closer to seven feet tall than six. His bigness was of the chest rather than of the gut: if his features had been more conventionally handsome he could have played Superman.

'Irving tells me,' he said in a voice that was more of a low growl, 'that you and I should have met last night. Sorry I stood you up. Couldn't get away from a conference in San Diego.'

'With the rich and mighty, always a little patience,' said Warlock. 'Even now the man is only passing through. Anybody else would go to Vegas to gamble. He's going there to make a speech tonight.'

Gentry grinned shyly and looked around him. 'Boy,' he said, 'this is some place. I thought I knew these parts pretty well, but I never came to this valley before.' Rich he clearly was. A huge diamond ring flashed from one finger, and he wore around his neck a bolo medallion that glinted with silver and turquoise. Yet he wasn't overpowering until he reached back into the helicopter and drew out a black Stetson even bigger than Warlock's, and clamped it on to his massive head. Now he reminded me of a mighty tough sheriff, the absolute law in his neck of the woods. 'Come on,' he smiled, 'let's see what's wrong with your wheels.'

It didn't take long. Gentry, who looked at one point as though he was going to pick up the car and shake it, diagnosed the problem as nothing but a poorly ventilated fuel cap, causing a vacuum in the tank as the level grew low. We refilled the tank from the spare can I had brought along, and for good measure left the cap off altogether: the car started perfectly. As usual in such circumstances, and especially because I'm not exactly a novice with car engines, I felt a complete idiot. After several tests Gentry switched off the ignition and handed me the keys. 'I don't think the pair of you will have any further trouble,' he said.

'The pair of us?'

'If you've no objection,' said Warlock. 'Since Jim has to move on anyway, and Montezuma seems to have retired licking his wounds, I thought I'd join you for the rest of the scenery.'

I was happy enough with his company, and suddenly it was all decided: Gentry and I were shaking hands a second time, now for goodbye. He urged us to set off while he absorbed the beauty of the Racetrack; he would follow in twenty minutes and make sure we were progressing satisfactorily. 'The trail's all there,' he said reassuringly, 'we followed it on the way up. Just a little sandy at the bottom, maybe. But don't worry: if I think you're in for trouble, I'll turn round again.'

To my astonishment I realized that Warlock, far from retracing my wheel tracks via Scotty's Castle, intended to brave the precipitous and stony descent which I had tried and decided against. He knew the route well, he said: all you had to do was keep to the right whenever there was a choice.

'And what about the corners where the trail tips us towards the canyon?'

'You just lean the other way, or get out and walk if you'd rather.'

Somehow I trusted the man well enough to let him drive; I never did get out, though I had to close my eyes more than once. While they were open, the landscapes were magnificent, and the lower parts of the mountain track proved less hazardous than the higher slopes which I had tested on foot. Within half an hour we were off the main mountain block, and at its foot a few minutes stuck in sand gave us our only problem. Just as we extricated ourselves the drone of Gentry's rotor sounded above us. We got out and waved: in response he turned a nifty circle before heading off in the direction of Las Vegas. Warlock and I fell gratefully back in the sand against a large tuft of grass, and baked for a few minutes in the now declining sun. 'How do you come to know him?' I asked.

'The mad millionaire? Just an odd coincidence. One of my hobbies is gemstone cutting, and I run some winter classes in Fresno. He simply turned up at one of them. Gave a phoney name, but I had to tell him afterwards that I knew who he really was. I mean I do read the papers. Seems he'd always wanted to learn the craft. He's a simple man, really, but trapped by his own success. Probably had more fun in the last couple of hours than he's managed all year.'

'Isn't he married?'

'Nope. Clumsy with women, or thinks he is. Besides, he'd be afraid every woman was after his money rather than him, and he'd probably be right. He'll stay as he is, a rich lonely man full of dreams. I had a thought that this weekend I might interest him in a dream of my own, but that will have to wait.'

After another hour of rough road we reached the blacktop and turned left for Stovepipe, still a seventy-minute drive. I had taken over the wheel, and for the sake of a break pulled in at the Father Serra Viewpoint, high in the last mountain range before the descent to sea level in the Panamint Desert. Warlock didn't know the spot, and was delighted by the distant view of Death Valley through a wide cleft in the monstrous blocks of stone. 'God,' he said, surveying the coloured hills, made more vivid as the setting sun now cast low shadows, 'it almost convinces one that there's a meaning to life. Everywhere you look is Shangri-La.'

'Not in the heat of the summer,' I said. 'And especially not the place I was stranded in this afternoon, a couple of miles high and without food or water. Without you, I'd still be there.'

He grinned mischievously. 'Did your past sins flash before your eyes?'

'Not exactly. But I did have a moment of panic. And I remember thinking not yet, not yet, I've too much to do.'

'Such as?'

I shrugged. 'Such as finding that meaning you just spoke of.'

'I see, the usual excuse. You been too busy so far, and you need longer. You're obviously ripe for conversion to Father Perrault's theories. The founder of Shangri-La, remember?'

'My copy was stolen before I could double-check on his theories.'

'I'll lend you mine. Incidentally, the only good reason I've thought of for that little fellow to steal your book is in case you made notes in it.'

'Notes? Notes of what?'

Warlock smiled. 'The way to the promised land, obviously.'

I exploded mildly. 'Why the hell is there all this sudden interest in a mythical Utopia on the other side of the world? Damn it, we're in California: I thought this was the promised land for a few million people. You, for one, presumably?'

Warlock shook his head. 'You wouldn't think so if you had to spend a few months in LA instead of a few days. A perfect example of man fouling up his own backyard. A superb climate, so they smog it up with car exhausts. And whoever thought it was a good idea to build a city sixty miles square with no centre? Most of the people who live there are from the east, so they don't know what to do with perpetual sunshine. They hide in little dark bars and restaurants: try finding a place in LA where you can eat in the open air. Then they get guilty because they're living what everybody back home thinks is the life of Riley, and they're not enjoying it. So they go to shrinks or plastic surgeons or group therapy, or try wife-swapping, or get sexual hang-ups, or spend all their time talking about trips abroad, as though home is just a springboard. They hate the place, but most of them can't leave because they're trapped by high salaries. So they sit and wither, and the Indians get the last laugh.'

I had to smile. 'I have a friend out here, ex New Jersey, now of the Encino Hills. He told me that one morning his wife got up before him and went to the window to inspect the view of the mountains over the barbecue pit and the swimming pool. So he yawned without opening his eyes and asked her what the weather was like. And she considered that and she told him, "Another God-damned glorious day."'

'Ah, well,' said Warlock, 'here in the desert we can at least see the stars. So let's not worry too much about the hard-pressed Los Angelenos.'

Almost as we climbed into my still functional Range Rover, the sudden quick twilight changed into darkness, but the moon soon came out from behind a cloud and gave us a series of magical views. Warlock began to talk almost at once, and I sensed from his tone that I was finally going to get what was really on his mind. 'Since I think we may have another thirty-six hours together, and that isn't too much, I suggest I start telling you now what I intended to keep until tomorrow. Incidentally, do you fancy a trip through Titus Canyon, or have you done it too often?'

'Fine by me if we can make it: it'll be my first time.

Whenever I've tried, it's either been closed by flash floods or I haven't had a four-wheel-drive.'

'It's open now, I checked. And it has an application to what I want to tell you. Listen, are you old enough to have seen anything of that big European war? The one that was going to put an end to war once and for all? And no, I'm not changing the subject.'

'All I saw was a few stray incendiaries. I was still at school.'

'Okay. Well, it won't surprise you to know that *I* was old enough, but you may find it difficult to imagine me as a young man in the London blitz in 1940. I *was* there, though, every day of it. Canadian Army Intelligence, you see. Scared hell out of me once or twice, but I came home without a scratch, unless you count a few from a certain colonel's wife when the colonel was away.' Warlock paused, obviously looking for the right words. 'It was during that blitz that I met a man who eventually changed my life, though I have to add that it was a forty-year job. That's how long it took *me* to take *him* seriously.'

For a moment I wondered whether my strange new friend might after all be an evangelist in disguise. I certainly wasn't prepared for his next remark:

'You see, this man said his name was, or had been, Hugh Conway.'

The penny didn't drop at first, but then I felt the back of my neck tingle.

'You mean . . .'

'None other. Though it wasn't his real name . . . He said.'

There was a long pause during which Warlock, at the wheel, kept glancing over to assess my reaction. I hadn't even decided what it was. 'Did you believe him?' I finally asked.

'Believe him? Hah! I didn't even know what he was

talking about. If I'd heard of the book then, I certainly hadn't read it, and I wasn't much for the movies in those days. I tell you, I was a small French Canadian cog in a big Allied intelligence wheel, wearing down my butt translating documents in a Whitehall office that smelled of mouse droppings. Career-wise it was a pretty boring war. Just occasionally, one of us might be landed with interrogating some fellow whose papers weren't in order and who was suspected of illegal entry. Like this particular morning during Battle of Britain summer.

'I'd walked in late, wanting my coffee, only to be told that there was a case on hand and I was the one chap in my branch who hadn't succumbed to some influenza bug that was going the rounds. The mysterious suspect was already in my office, under escort. I groaned at that, and asked what was the mystery, and they said only that he couldn't produce an identity card or a valid passport, and didn't seem even too sure who he was. I didn't like the sound of it, but when I went in the fellow took my attention at once. Middle-aged and weary-looking, as though he'd been through the mill, but clearly an officer and a gentleman, one of the old school that makes us colonials uneasy. Untidy features, but honest, penetrating brown eyes like a spaniel. His suit was brown too, a shabby old thing with pointed lapels, at least ten years out of date. He was polite, but he didn't have much energy: several times I had to ask him to speak up. He made me feel like a fascist heavy putting pressure on a nun. I'd already sensed his despair as he saw my one pip and my beardless chin and realized that we couldn't have any instant rapport. I did my best to be gentle: got him a cup of coffee while I studied the file. There wasn't a lot to go on: you see he hadn't been picked up, simply wandered into the Foreign Office of his own accord and asked to see certain people who weren't available, mostly because they'd been dead for years. The others were on active service, and it seemed there was nobody in the building who knew him, though he'd expected a sort of welcoming committee. He seemed to have been bottled up somewhere, like Rip Van Winkle, totally out of touch.'

'Could he have been in prison?'

'Don't worry, we checked that: no dice.'

'He must have known there was a war on, surely?'

'Oh, indeed. Kept saying that was why he'd come back from abroad, to do his duty. But the fact was, as I say, that he had no papers: no ration book, no identity card. As for a passport, he finally produced one but it had expired in 1934, so somebody must have been careless when he came through Southampton or wherever. When it was drawn to his attention he said he was sorry, but he hadn't been in a position to renew it. And that was about as far as he was willing to go until he was put opposite somebody in authority who was prepared to sit down and listen to his story in confidence. Well, it took a while to convince him that the best he was going to get was me. Finally he gave me a few details I could check: name, age, and to my astonishment a consular career. That all came out right, up to 1930. He was born in 1894, and served honorably in the First World War: mentioned in despatches, even. Through the Twenties he'd held a succession of fairly obscure but not unimportant posts in the Far East. He spoke fluent Chinese: I had to take his word for that. But there was nothing in his file after 1930, when he'd been posted missing after a revolution in Kabul. There was a final note which referred me to the top-secret section, but those files had been removed to Aylesbury for the duration.'

'There must have been a photograph, surely?'

'Oh yes, that corresponded. He was who he said he

was, all right. The question was, where had he been for the last ten years?'

We were crossing the Panamint Desert now, and our headlights fixed a stray *burro* which scuttled off into the darkness. 'Had he no next of kin?' I asked.

'None he could think of except a cousin, and the cousin was away at the war. By his own admission, and by the evidence of his file, the fellow had spent very little of his adult life in the UK. Just the occasional leave, and even then he'd opted most of the time for the Riviera. So there was a mystery to be solved, and I'd been appointed Sherlock Holmes. I remember his wry, cynical smile as he realized what a problem he'd posed me; but I knew that only he could fill in the missing years, and it was just a matter of waiting. I remember he had a trick of raising one eyebrow higher than the other, like John Barrymore. He must have had a sense of humour too, for suddenly as we looked at each other we both burst out laughing; and after that we knew we were on the right footing, so I sent for some more coffee and a bottle of rum to help it along. The sergeants were put outside, and I offered him a cigarette; he accepted, but I rather gathered it was the first he'd had for a long time, the way he rolled it about in his fingers and kept looking at it.

'After we'd enjoyed a couple of drinks we moved over to the armchairs in the corner, and I asked him to tell me his story in his own words. He did, and you'll have some idea how it went. It took the best part of another hour, and I was hooked on every syllable. I kept wanting to ask questions, but I didn't dare stop him in case I broke the spell. His voice was so – what's the word – mellifluous, that I could have listened all day. Every so often he'd have to stop for a deep breath, but I think that was just tiredness. There was a twitch, too, at the corner of one eye. By his own account, you'll remember, he'd been shot up quite a bit in the war. The trench war, I mean.'

I nodded. 'But he was still quite an attractive man, I expect?' I listened to myself asking the question and realized that I had already swallowed the yarn hook, line and sinker. Warlock might well have been quivering with suppressed laughter; but all he said was:

'Not in a regular way, but he had an attractive personality. In a battle, you just knew he'd put the welfare of his men above his own. Glory Conway must have been an apt nickname.'

'So.' I changed gear in order to tackle the steep bends which would bring us up from the desert floor to Townes Pass at six thousand feet. 'Tell me his story.'

'I'll do better; but let me finish the preamble. I had some sandwiches sent in, but after that there was a meeting I couldn't skip, so I asked him whether he'd dictate to my secretary the tale he'd just told me, with any additional corroborative detail he might think of in the meantime. He said he didn't think he could do that, but if I sat him at a typewriter for a few hours he'd have a go at the job himself, at his own speed. It was a skill he'd picked up, he said, you know where. Well, at that time we had a few rooms set aside for important visitors who needed guarding, in an annexe of Westminster School just across the square. The school itself had been evacuated. So we escorted him round there and made him comfortable, and I said I'd be back in the evening. I left him tapping away quite happily with two fingers; if he was tired he had a bed, and even a private bathroom of sorts. The first thing I did was nip into a bookshop and get myself a copy of *Lost Horizon*. I wanted to start on it there and then, but the meeting dragged on and it was five o'clock before I could tear myself away. Then it was back to my office armchair for a quick skip through the book. I tell you, the thought that it might not be fiction quite stunned me: it was like Moses reading the Ten Commandments for the first time, or Joe Smith receiving the Mormon plates.'

'I don't think,' I broke in with a wry smile, 'that either has ever been authenticated.'

'Touché,' said Warlock, 'but we all know in our hearts when we come across something that just has to be true. Anyway, at about nine I wandered across to see how Conway was getting on, and took in a bottle of champagne in case the supper hadn't been up to much. He'd been typing till his fingers ached, but otherwise he was quite happy in the knowledge that someone would at least read his story. On a side table there was a sheaf of what he'd typed, and he said he hoped to finish before bedtime, so I didn't stay long, but with his permission took what he'd done so far and put it in my briefcase. Frankly I couldn't wait to read it. Back home, it was nearly three when I nodded off, but that was partly because Jerry did his worst on that night. From my window in Hampstead I could see three separate blazes in the East End, and a couple that might have been Westminster. I imagined Conway in the deep Foreign Office shelter, handcuffed to a guard and impatient to get back to his typewriter.'

'Or perhaps to the slopes of Karakal.'

Warlock nodded. 'I could guess some of the sights I was going to see next morning. Passing through Bloomsbury was a horrifying ordeal. Whitehall itself hadn't been touched, but as I turned the corner I stopped in sheer horror.'

'Conway wasn't killed?'

'Not that I know, and certainly not then. But the building across the street from the school annexe had taken a direct hit, and the ruins were still smouldering. As I drew nearer I saw that part of its high wall had fallen across the narrow street onto the turret where Conway had been billeted. I learned that it happened almost as soon as the siren sounded: some plane got through unnoticed and dropped its bombs before anybody could be moved to the shelter. One guard in the corridor outside was seriously injured, but half of Conway's room was miraculously untouched, including the table with the typewriter on it, though of course the machine was covered in dust and bits of brick. The south wall of the room was completely down, open to the street one storey below. Since there was no sign of Conway at all, one had to assume that he'd slid down the rubble and done a quick bunk. Maybe not even deliberately, but half-crazy with shock.'

'What about the typescript?'

'Since I'd left him he'd done five more pages plus the one that was in the typewriter. It stopped in mid-sentence. I took the whole thing up to Whitehall right away and had it carefully copied for duplication, down to the last comma. Locked a copy for myself away in a drawer while the top brass considered the original. But that infernal summer wasn't over by a long shot, and with people dying around you left, right and centre it didn't seem quite the time for what was officially thought of as a fairy tale. The war ended with no resolution of the matter, and all I could do was pack the copy among my things when they whipped me back to Canada. It was years before I even took it out and read it again; I'd had other things on my mind, including a marriage that went wrong. When I did get to it, the story really bowled me over, but I'd no money and no influence, and I thought anyone I showed it to would laugh at me. Now I'm old and I don't care if they do. And yes, sir, I do have a copy with me, tucked away in the trunk of the car; and yes I do think that quite possibly it was what our little green friend was after, but don't ask me how or why. You can read it in bed tonight, if you promise to check the room first and then double lock your door.'

I shivered in anticipation. 'Try and stop me. But do you mean to say that nobody in the British Government ever took it seriously, even to the extent of checking it out?'

'There weren't that many details that *could* be checked: our friend was foxy to the last. And since he'd done a bunk anyway, the brass hats were relieved even of the responsibility of taking a view. He was never heard of again, you see, and there were several more important matters for Intelligence to worry about. When you think about it, not too many things in this world are ever done right.'

Warlock shook his head so hard that I feared it might fall off. It had clearly been a strain for him to remain serious for so long; as though to underline the fact, when the lights of Stovepipe came into view he broke into a spirited chorus of 'Ragtime Cowboy Joe'. It seemed to me that 'Somewhere Over the Rainbow' might have been more appropriate.

We coasted downhill for the last ten miles, parked the car in a minor sandstorm, and hurried into the hotel past groups of noisy tourists. A light meal didn't take long, and by nine-thirty, physically exhausted, I was undressing in my room when Warlock arrived with a battered brief-case, from which he took a sheaf of photostatted papers in a yellow plastic cover. He didn't even speak: just nodded and pointed to the door and windows. I checked them all right, then checked them again. Ten minutes later I was comfortably in bed, adjusting the light so that it fell evenly on what was before me. It was a great hour and a half: I savoured each sentence as though Conway's narrative were a newly discovered addition to the Dead Sea Scrolls. For me, what he had to tell turned out to be rather more important.

4

Hugh Conway's Narrative (1940)

'I WAS TRULY MORE AMAZED THAN ALARMED'

I have become known in legend as Conway. Ah, well: at Shangri-La we all take new names when we settle, and it amused me to adopt that of the hero of a novel which rapidly became a bestseller and caused some stir. It even did so, belatedly, within our remote portals. My true name however is Richard Hugh Conway Dearden, and I was born in 1894 to Robert and Frances Dearden of Richmond in Surrey. My father was an accomplished naval engineer who perished in the *Titanic* disaster of 1912. My mother died a year later, I believe of grief, and I was left with adequate financial resources but very little in the way of family, especially since I was an only child. Encouraged by an aunt, who died in the influenza epidemic of 1919, I went on to Oxford and served in what with unconscious humour we used to call the Great War. I think I was always something of a cynic about great causes: but that may be only a different way of saying that I preserved extremely high standards and ideals, even though my early experience of life had taught me that they were unlikely to be fulfilled. When I entered the consular service it was as a temporary measure while I thought of something better, but like so many temporary measures it became permanent. In view of what happened at Shangri-La it seems odd that I once thought of entering the priesthood, and was encouraged to do so by an eminent cleric; but doubts kept creeping in, and I finally decided that in the literal sense I was not good enough. Later I hankered to be a writer. I enjoyed writing. I am enjoying writing this; the choosing of words is to me a great relaxation.

By 1930, although well respected in the service, I considered myself a failure in everything I had attempted, and my doubts had amassed themselves into a formal agnosticism. I know that many old friends thought my years in foreign cities adventurous: they could have no conception of the daily tedium I endured. I was desperate for something which would give meaning to my life, yet deeply suspicious of such events as presented themselves. I could hardly forget having slaughtered seven Germans during the Passchendaele campaign, nor having so narrowly escaped death myself. It disturbed me to be thought of as polite, calm, reliable, and resourceful; for these outward appearances, which I could call upon in a crisis when others were involved, had nothing whatever to do with my real personality.

I might add that intellectually I had become divorced from the main thrust of Western civilization which, however cunningly disguised, was directed at the acquisition of power and wealth. On the other hand I came to realize that no Utopia can exist without adequate funds. Being something of a coward as well as a weakling, I gave up any attempt to rationalize such contradictions. Happiness itself, I decided, is a balance or compromise between optimism and pessimism. Shangri-La itself turned out to be a compromise: its high ideals were securely founded upon the possession of gold. Yet although I discovered it by accident, I felt for it something close to a religious fervour. Something told me that this was what I was born for.

The revolutionary business at Kabul (or, as Hilton rather oddly disguises it, Baskul)! came as a relief – or did until real danger threatened on that nightmarish plane journey which followed our kidnapping. The unexpected revolution at least gave me something to do after two years of upholding the flag and handing round rock cakes. Hilton's book, by the way, is roughly (but in spirit not inaccurately) based on an account given to him by my friend 'Rutherford', actually Jack Molyneux the travel writer: I had treated him rather ungraciously when, in his well-meaning way, he escorted me back to the world I had gladly forsaken. I tried to make it up to him afterwards. I don't know why Hilton thought it necessary to change all the names. It couldn't have mattered less to me providing the exact geography was obscured, and I'd seen to that myself. The book reached me in 1937 and I thought it sympathetic so far as it went, which was about two-thirds of the way to the truth. Not bad considering that it was based on one night of random conversations with a recovering amnesiac. After all, I'd suffered the most harrowing physical and psychological ordeal, putting duty before inclination and being overcome by the ghastliest weather and most difficult terrain. Yes, several times after reading the book I thought how pleasant it would be to have Mr Hilton in Shangri-La for a visit. I think he would have found the ambience extremely congenial.

Since almost all the preliminary details in the book are quite true, I need scarcely explain them again except by the briefest sketch. We were kidnapped, four of us, during the evacuation of Kabul, in a private plane which was supposed to take us over the mountains to Peshawar but instead, by courtesy of a strange gun-brandishing pilot, headed eastward for a thousand miles and more, with pre-arranged refuelling, on the most spectacular journey of my life, past Nanga Parbat and into Tibet. My companions all feared for their lives, but I was truly more amazed than alarmed: too exhausted, perhaps, to care whether I got back alive or not. When after many tense and bewildered hours we finally turned south and crash-landed on a remote icy plateau, the outlaw pilot proved to be a

Tibetan named Talu, who died before explaining his purpose. We learned much later that he had left Shangri-La two years before on a deliberate mission to bring back, by whatever means, a selection of people to supplement his isolated community's declining population. Extremely lucky that we did not share his fate after a night without shelter on the high plateau, we were met next morning by emissaries from Shangri-La led by my dear Chang, a man elderly even then. I later discovered that there was on the mountain of Karakal a crude but effective radio station, well able to pick up signals from the plane as it approached.

Chang, by the way, is still with us, very much so. I could scarcely function without him, and at the ripe old age, by Western standards, of one hundred and six he remains remarkably nimble.

It was an arduous trek to the lamasery, and we found it to be one of the most astonishing places on earth, clinging somewhat precariously to a steep mountainside but connected by a zigzag track to a splendidly fertile valley below. This is basically four miles square, with a long, tapering and well-watered section at the south-western end, beyond which the mountain streams which irrigate the place from the east make an abrupt descent in the direction of a desert floor beyond. The level of the valley is thus far below the snow line, but well above the baking heat of sea level in that part of the world; while the structure of the surrounding ranges provides shelter from wind and forms a natural suntrap. Imagine, if you will, an outstretched, upturned left hand with the fingers pointing up and slightly apart, the thumb highest of all. Turn it to the south and you have roughly the shape of our valley, with the thumb as Karakal and our lamasery halfway up its slope. Here, and to the north, the rock faces are high and totally inaccessible; but to the south the natural barriers tend to spread out into single peaks corresponding with your fingers. These allow the heat of the mid-day sun to percolate every corner of the valley and to linger quite late in the afternoon.

Up at the lamasery the air is naturally a good deal more bracing; but generally speaking, as a piece of pure geography, the thing could hardly have been better designed, with snow and ice surrounding it from the north and barren rock and desert stretching down from it to the south east. The resident could choose his own climate, by either staying with the dry invigorating air of Shangri-La (which is the lamasery itself) or descending to the Valley of Blue Moon (which is the English translation of Karakal). Even the incredible remoteness of the place was considered by the inhabitants to be a blessing. The only available route, Chang told us early on, was via the steep, narrow and quite frightening northern pass whose perils we had experienced for ourselves; from the other side of it, civilization of the kind we know was the best part of a thousand miles away. So callers were rare indeed, and usually more dead than alive after weeks of exposure in the high Himalaya. Those who did survive were persuaded to stay or, to be more realistic, were prevented from leaving, until inevitably they came under the spell of Blue Moon and lost the will to fight their way back to the cities with their railway trains and traffic jams, to which at first they had desired so urgently to return. Meanwhile, the benefits of modern learning and science were gradually being made available to the native community by its benevolent elders, but always with great difficulty and expense; in these days even newspapers seldom reached Shangri-La until they were many months old, and supplies were irregular even though methods of trading had been established after long, unrevealed processes of trial and error.

The monks ruled this earthly paradise with moderate

strictness (in return for which, as Chang told me in his lilting Anglo-Chinese tones, they were satisfied with moderate obedience). They had a vision of the perfect life which, it quickly seemed to me, they were not very far from achieving. It was a life based on two societies. The peasants below tilled the soil and seemed to enjoy their lives as one long working holiday; the monks above were preoccupied by the likely violent end to both Western and Eastern civilizations. In this regrettable eventuality they hoped that Shangri-La's ideals might come into their own, the world being slowly rebuilt from the lamasery's storehouse of accumulated knowledge and philosophy. The high lama, as I discovered when summoned after a fortnight's stay to meet him, was not an Oriental but an extremely ancient Belgian named Perrault; he later claimed to be more than two hundred years old. Although after his death I suffered a brief period of disorientation when I disbelieved all that he told me, and left the valley feeling that I must shoulder my responsibilities towards my junior Mallinson, in my heart of hearts I knew that Perrault's amazing story must be true. I dearly wish I could have known him longer; as it is, I have written his biography and trust that one day it will find an audience wider than the monks of Shangri-La.

What a story! At first given up for dead when, after a fraught missionary journey, he stumbled into the valley in 1719, he was gradually nursed by the natives back to health and activity. Something of a herbalist, he discovered very quickly that the valley produced in abundance all that was necessary for vitality of body and serenity of mind. The recipe for healthy longevity included the imbibing of large quantities of the juice of a unique narcotic plant, the *tangatse*, taken by the rather corrupt native priests of the time as a climax to their yoga-like psycho-spiritual exercises. In his own nineties, fortified by this curious regimen (interrupted by periods of abstinence) and having done much to renovate the physical amenities of what was then a mouldering old lamasery abandoned in the Middle Ages, he was quite pleased when he found himself by common consent the leader of this curious community, most of his elders having indulged themselves to the point of total incapability.

I am given to understand that in recent years there has been evidence of extreme human longevity in places as far apart as Ecuador and Russian Georgia, so perhaps in this respect at least Shangri-La is less unique than I at first thought. I remember, too, from my schooldays the 'not proven' case of Old Parr, who allegedly was nearly a hundred and fifty when he died of a common cold after being taken to London to see King Charles the First.

During the long years of Perrault's leadership, the Valley of Blue Moon went about its business while contriving to preserve its secret from the outside world. The valley people well understood the need for secrecy, and in any case seemed to have no sense of adventure; they did exactly as they were told, though ironically their remarkable herb was less successful in inducing longevity for them than for the occasional European incumbent. Meanwhile, substantial gold deposits found in the mountainside ensured financial stability, and the natives enjoyed most of the comforts money could buy in that particular geographical situation. They were like happy children, though of comparatively low intelligence, a problem compounded perhaps by the high degree of incest which is to be expected in such a closed society. Meanwhile, the slowly growing new society of lamas increased its wit and wisdom by careful study of the books and manuscripts which Perrault caused to be brought in. Newcomers were limited to the occasional lost travellers who stumbled upon the pass instead of freezing to death on the barren plateau. They tended to be mountaineers, merchantmen, explorers and wandering missionaries, which is not a bad cross-section for an ideal society. The average rate of admission never exceeded one per year, and at one time five years passed without a single stranger being greeted; though in compensation there was a remarkable influx when a whole party of mandarins and their attendants, lured into the mountains by an exceptionally benign summer season, were suddenly trapped in the tortuous passes by a wild snowstorm. They found themselves, all twelve of them, marvelling at the sweetness and gentleness of that lost valley, liking it well enough never to return to their homes.

Perhaps after all I would never have made a writer, for I digress where Mr Hilton was succinct. The point in 1931 was that Father Perrault was dying at last, and had long been obsessed by the conviction that he and his associates must atone for their extended idyll by devoting themselves to the urgent reconstruction of a world which was hacking itself to pieces. He clearly foresaw the present cataclysmic war – as I believe did Mr H. G. Wells, whom I remember meeting at my last consular dinner in London in 1929 – and felt that its eventual termination might be the signal for Shangri-La to reveal its presence to the world, and to guide the survivors in the planning of a more perfect lifestyle. To this end the new leader of Shangri-La must be, not a secluded old metaphysician, bound to be claimed by death once he set foot outside the magic valley, but someone who had recently moved in the centres of twentieth-century statesmanship and understood the nuances of world government; someone capable by personality and training of bringing forth from the ashes of Western humanity a new, phoenix-like brotherhood of men who might at last exemplify the original purpose of

God. (Or Gods: Perrault was himself by tradition and training a Catholic, but Shangri-La welcomed all religions to its bosom and showed no official preference for one over the other.) Rather surprisingly, the fifty or so other lamas concurred that they had been out of the world too long to have any real chance of leading it. It was necessary to co-opt someone from the outside and hand him, as it were, Shangri-La on a plate. Hence Talu's strange mission and our random kidnapping. The best Perrault got out of it was me, with bonuses in the technical and commercial skills of Barnard and the incurable optimism of our educationalist missionary Miss Brinklow, who within two months of our arrival was undertaking single-handed a complete revision of Blue Moon's school curriculum.

Our impulsive young Mallinson – I call him still by Hilton's name – was of course a considerable problem. From the moment he set foot in it he hated Shangri-La with youth's fervent intolerance and fear of age. He nearly cost us both our lives with his insane plan to return to the west with Lo Tsen, the lamasery's beautiful Manchu princess who claimed to be still young, though Chang privately informed me that she entered the colony in 1884 at the age of eighteen. Poor misguided lady. A few days on the high plateau showed up all necessary evidence of her real age, but she was of sturdy stock. We were separated by a snowstorm from Mallinson and the porters, and thought they had gone over a cliff. She struggled on until she got me to the nearest mission, where she promptly expired before I could even thank her. After being nursed back to health by Jack Molyneux I returned to Shangri-La a year later, braving on the way weather which was probably even worse than on the outward journey; I was astonished to find Mallinson in residence, seething with discontent and frustration, his hair as white as the snows of Karakal. God knows what fortune redirected him back to the pass, for the lamas said he was half-raving when their scouts spotted him and carried him in. He was a changed man, partly because he seemed filled with remorse at having led me away to what he thought was my death; now that I'd turned up again, he probably found that equally difficult to accept. But never again did he speak of going home, and when I rather diffidently suggested that he might accompany me on this expedition, he refused.

I was intrigued, by the way, to discover that the rather sweetened but not entirely unworthy film version of our story, with which I caught up two weeks ago in Portsmouth, turned Mallinson into my brother. I suppose the writers thought my concern for him too excessive to be explained in any other way (except, perhaps, a homosexual attachment, which of course they couldn't use anyway). The truth is simply that I've always been more inclined to take action on behalf of other people's welfare than my own.

To linger on the film for a moment: I thought it very much captured the right spirit, while falling down to some extent on the details. The settings, for instance, belonged to some rose-coloured Hollywood world, with obviously modernistic architecture and concealed lighting; the real Shangri-La is a rambling old rabbit warren, tucked into a hillside, warm and comfortable enough but rather dark in places, with small rooms, and corridors whose arches are uncomfortably low for most Europeans. I was very flattered to be played by Ronald Colman, an actor I always admired in silent films because he seemed poised between intellectual alertness, physical trimness, and that mild world-weariness which has beset me since my lucky escape from the horrors of the trenches. I fear, however, that I can hardly claim his good looks, which turned the film finally into a fairy-tale with Colman as the handsome prince. The audience was intuitively assured that he couldn't possibly fail, whereas I certainly could – and have, it seems.

The film also turned our elderly Miss Brinklow into a more 'glamorous' character, that of a fallen woman with galloping consumption. Well, to me no young flibbertigibbet could be more fascinating than the real person, an indomitable old dame now slowly dying of a cancer which neither of our doctors can cure. I wanted her to come with me as far as the nearest city and proper medical care; but she refused to leave her dear children, who last year worked so hard to clear and prepare the new playing-fields and pavilion shortly to be opened in her name. The film also felt the need for comic relief – as don't we all? – in the shape of a fussy palaeontologist, so warmly and amusingly presented that he would not have been out of place in the real Shangri-La. In fact, my memory now plays tricks, sometimes assuring me that he *did* exist, along with the man who played 'Barnard' – Robert Mitchell, I think[1] – who is what the true Barnard might call a dead ringer for the real McCoy. That renegade financier and fugitive from the world's police, that former engineer with immense practical skills, is agreed by the brotherhood to be among the most valuable incumbents since the lamasery's historical beginnings. As for my dear Chang, my heart warmed towards Mr H. B. Warner for a splendidly civilized and subtle portrayal; but he is unmistakeably occidental and physically could not begin to suggest the real Chang, who is still on the plump side despite his advanced years, and rather short, with a singsong voice so soft that you sometimes have to strain to hear it. I discovered, by the way, that Chang on his own admission – nay boast – is father to no fewer than

[1] Actually Thomas Mitchell. – Ed.

thirty-one of the valley people, the youngest of them born when he was more than ninety years old; so you may gather that the rule of chastity at Shangri-La is observed with only moderate strictness, as Chang himself might have commented.

So. After a strenuous hiatus I was back again, and the job Father Perrault had offered me was apparently still open to me. The fact may well be that none of the others wanted the responsibility – at least, not more than moderately. I gather that Chang had looked into his crystal ball and assured the conclave that I would eventually return; until I did so, he held the reins himself, in the way of a senior civil servant rather than prime minister, for despite his administrative skills he was still only a postulant. In the end there seemed nothing to do but accept. The duties which fell to me were not onerous, far less so, I imagine, than those of running an Oxford college. No unions to argue with, no tax returns, no boring dinners, no charity funds to raise. It was only a matter of providing a figurehead for the valley people to respect, and of deciding what new facilities were to be brought in. The library and museum were well established and well run, and the religious side looked after itself: I simply let all the different creeds go their own way, providing they caused no friction. One new aspect which I did develop was publication. I felt it was time for the results of two hundred years of contemplation to find their way to the outside world. We evolved our own system of dissemination: you will not need to be told that it was complex, but under various names half a dozen books reflecting the view from our mountain have already been published in Britain alone, and there are more on the way. They range from that book on the Brontës which is mentioned in Hilton's text to an extremely comprehensive work on the eastern religions, and in each case the authorship is well disguised. At such time as Shangri-La feels able to present itself to the world they will be brought together as a definitive series exemplifying what we have to offer.

It occurs to me that the reader may leaf through these notes looking for precise directional pointers to the geographical location of Blue Moon. He may save himself the trouble, for I have been careful not to give them. My reception in London has not been such that I can trust the present powers to preserve Shangri-La's secret, and I think that is essential for the time being. After the end of the present hostilities, if given sufficient assurances, I could certainly be prevailed upon to escort a trusted team of officials on an inspection tour of our achievements, and to allow them to return, providing, of course, that the route were not made known to the press. I would enjoy watching a few Londoners get drunk on the richness of mountain air which has never been polluted except by wood smoke from the valley fires. They might also enjoy the liqueur which the monks evolved with some success (following on the curious practice of other monastic establishments) from the *tangatse* herb. This potion, we believe, is not a quick and easy way to longevity, as the alcohol content cancels out its other effect.

Barnard and I quickly became firm friends. Intellectually he was a rough diamond at best, but eager to learn and immensely grateful for his unexpected escape from the attentions of the police in the society from which he had fled. For my part, I saw in him the practical man I can never be. He vastly improved the rough mining system with which the natives had for centuries extracted our gold, and was constantly tinkering with the primitive generator which kept us reasonably warm and illuminated during the winter months. A great triumph of his was the devising and construction of a series of pulleys by which materials and, later, people could be safely transported from one level to another of the zigzag track which connects us with the valley floor. In 1935 he even shortened the distance and greatly improved the time factor by the construction of a one-hundred-and-ten-foot tunnel complete with rack-and-pinion railway, all the parts for which were laboriously assembled in Chungking and carried to us on the backs of our team of porters. Incidentally, during my very first year we obtained by this method a gramophone together with a hundred classical recordings; and in 1934 Barnard finally located the right spot for a long-distance radio aerial which enabled us to receive, very faintly, transmissions from China, and even on rare occasions programmes in English via the BBC's world links. Meanwhile our library continued to be augmented: I had felt the lack of personal favourites such as *The Prisoner of Zenda* and *The Diary of a Nobody*, while the complete Sherlock Holmes was clearly a must. As time went on we added some Maugham and Galsworthy and Hemingway; we subscribed to the *New York Times Annual Review of Books* and added the *TLS* to Chang's longstanding *Times* order. Sometimes we got a whole year's issues at once, and by then the earliest of them might be two years old, but we were never in a hurry.

It was in 1936 that all our lives took on a new emphasis when Barnard mentioned to me a curious rectangular reflection he had noticed on the mountain wall at the far south-western end of the valley. It was on the higher slopes of a mountain block which we call Salabir: in the valley patois it means pinnacle of the sun. I was sufficiently interested to go with him and explore. From the nearest vantage point the shiny area, contrasting so markedly with the dull brown rock around it, was about four hundred feet above us, and we decided that it must represent the end of a stratum of rare ore. Next day we recruited help and beat a way up the slope through scrub and undergrowth. To our astonishment we found ourselves on an overgrown trail giving way to a series of steps which had been cut, clearly by human agency, in the rock wall. Just as clearly there had been an attempt to destroy them at some later date, although about half the footholds were intact. We'd done all we could that day, so after dinner, in Barnard's presence, I decided to tax Chang with the mystery. Poor Chang made some attempt to be evasive, but I was pretty firm with him, and he soon came clean with an incredible story. Incredible at any rate to the four of us who had entered the valley from the north along a frozen mountain ledge not two feet wide in places. I recalled that when on that first evening Barnard had asked Chang whether the grand piano had come by the same route, Chang had smiled and said: 'There is no other.' Chang was never a liar, but he now admitted that on that particular occasion at least he might have given a fuller answer. In 1931 there was indeed no other exit from the valley. But from the middle of the nineteenth century until 1902 there certainly had been one, and those rediscovered steps had led to it. What Barnard and I took for a reflection, Chang told us, was in fact a recessed area of soft rock. To the right of the recess one could gain entry to a tunnel caused by the gradual collapse of a long powdery stratum, running more or less parallel to the rock face and for most of the way only a few feet from it. 'I never had cause myself to explore the tunnel,' said Chang, 'but Briac was one of those engaged in the excavation in 1897: that was principally a matter of shoring up a previous collapse. He will be pleased to give you more detail, but I believe I recollect that the tunnel is several miles long – probably not more than six miles – and that it descends gently into an open canyon. Both were formed by Salabir's gentle streams, in the prehistoric days when they were raging torrents. After perhaps four more miles in the canyon, the traveller would be disgorged quite abruptly into the northern extremity of an exceedingly barren desert area, facing the mountain ranges of Assam. Those mountains are, of course, hundreds of miles away; but the journey must be practicable, for we believe that our own valley people are descendants of nomads from that area.'

I nodded thoughtfully. 'It always seemed to me that they were too dark to be Tibetan.'

'More to the point,' exclaimed Barnard, 'and not that I'm raring to go this minute, but how far down that desert is the nearest outpost including, say, a bar and a brothel among its amenities?'

Chang raised an eyebrow and considered the question seriously. 'If the tunnel were passable, which of course it has not been since the collapse in 1902, then I believe that a journey of a little over one hundred miles from the canyon entrance would bring you to the nearest village.'

I looked up in perfect astonishment. 'And you let me go north into the frozen wilderness beyond the pass? My dear Chang!'

Chang put a hand on my arm and smiled regretfully. 'You will recall, dear sir, that you did not apprise me of your intention to leave us. Had I possessed any idea that you were committed to so headstrong a course of action, I might well have felt bound as a last resort to suggest examination of the alternative route. Even then, you were certainly too valuable a man to risk losing, whether the loss were to be ours or that of the world outside.'

'Look here,' said Barnard suddenly, 'do you think the tunnel could be reopened?'

Chang pursed his lips and shook his head slowly from side to side. 'I am not competent even to guess whether such a task might be accomplished with the equipment we now have at our disposal. Your own experience in such matters would of course be invaluable. But I recall that in

1902 the seniors decided that nothing whatever could be done, and although the subject remained on their agenda for some years, no further suggestions were forthcoming. Eventually the matter was dropped by mutual consent, and the downward access to our valley from the northern end of the tunnel was deliberately made difficult, just in case any barbaric wanderers from the desert should achieve what we had considered impossible. We were thus saved the trouble of mounting a permanent guard.'

'But now we have dynamite,' said Barnard.

I added: 'Not to mention one of America's foremost engineers.'

Chang raised his hands and opened them towards us. 'But none of us, surely, is anxious to leave this unique and magical place?'

'No,' said Barnard. 'Not ever, not for long. But a man doesn't like to be trapped, and there might be times when a means of retreat would come in right handy. What do you say, Conway?'

I drew a deep breath. 'I can only tell you that I'm a mass of conflicting emotions. Of course none of us wants to leave. But now that we know about the old tunnel I have a nagging feeling that I'd like Barnard to examine it at least.'

'Entirely as you will, my dear Conway, since you attach such importance to the matter,' said Chang dreamily. 'I am only sorry that I did not previously think to bring the subject to your attention. The fact is that I am becoming old and a little forgetful.'

'That's quite all right, Chang, but tell me one other thing. If we ever did force a way through the tunnel, in what country would we find ourselves? A low hot desert doesn't sound much like Tibet.'

'Well, there you raise a most interesting speculation. I should tell you, we have never been absolutely certain that even Shangri-La is within the political borders of Tibet. According to our trigonometrists, the lamasery's height above sea level is approximately five and a half thousand feet. The valley is nearly two thousand feet lower, and the desert of course, much lower again, perhaps even below sea level. The slightest glance at a map will suggest that we must be on the extreme southern slopes of the Tibetan plateau, where the waters run down along roughly parallel glacial and river beds, eventually to lose themselves in the South China Sea. The sheer mountain walls which protect us on all sides are a freak of nature, a last outpost; but exactly where the border lies is impossible to define.'

'And what of Karakal?'

'It is unmarked on any map we possess, though there are several peaks of approximately the same height, some of them on the Burmese side of the border. The desert of which we have been speaking is almost certainly in Burma. It holds traces, I am told, of a dry river bed which must once have been a source for the Irrawaddy. The last visitor who came to us through the tunnel, in 1901, did indeed speak Burmese – I conversed with him myself – but he died of dehydration within a few hours of our finding him on the old steps. Before that, members of our community had on several occasions ventured through the tunnel and returned. They reported finding themselves in an extremely hot, forbidding and infertile area, exploration of which was more than a little difficult: the problem being, you see, to carry sufficient water.'

'But what happens to our own streams? At the far end of the village they tumble over the rapids in the very direction of the desert.'

Chang shrugged. 'Presumably they are blocked by the barrier of the mountain wall which keeps us all isolated. The stream ends in a swampy area, from which we suppose that water is drawn back by underground routes to become part of the great glacier which surrounds us.'

'And the tunnel, you say, simply fell in?'

'It fell in, but not entirely by accident or of its own accord. Our sentinels warned us of a wave of bandits trying to get through from the Burmese side. There was a confrontation in the tunnel and the bandits fired guns. The noise caused sufficient reverberation to bring down from the roof a vast quantity of soft rock. It killed most of the bandits: the others fled. We were never able to retrieve the bodies for burial. We estimate the blockage to be at least fifty feet long.'

Barnard rubbed his chin. 'In those conditions I wouldn't guarantee anything,' he said. 'I used to be a dab hand with dynamite, but without a proper geological survey I could bring down the whole mountain. I suppose Salabir can't be scaled?'

'The peak can be reached quite easily. It is the descent on the far side which is impossible. Or so I am advised: I have not personally made the experiment.'

The idea of Chang as a mountain climber was so absurd that we all lost our train of thought, and the subject was changed. Nothing at all was done about the tunnel for more than two years, and if I thought about it it was only to shake my head and pass on to something else. Then in the late spring of 1938 our porters arrived as usual through the northern passes, and had a particularly rough time of it. Some of our precious supplies were lost in a minor avalanche, and one froze to death during an overnight camp on the plateau, not far from the rusting fuselage of the maharajah's plane which had brought us to Shangri-La so many years before. The porters left early to avoid an even worse spate of weather which had been forecast. It came on cue, and turned out to be among the worst in living memory, which in our case meant the best part of two hundred years. Snow and hail actually fell in the valley, which was unprecedented: we watched the children incredulously playing with snowballs, while on the slopes of Karakal blizzards and avalanches alternated for more than two weeks. Then, almost above our heads, part of the rock wall collasped with a reverberating roar, and when the weather calmed down sufficiently for us to investigate, we found that the debris had completely blocked the pass. The mountain ledge by which I myself had twice found Shangri-La was no more. After an arduous climb over a steep shoulder of mountain I found just one point where it was still possible to look down on what was left of the old trail at the far side of the blockage, but it was a sheer drop of more than a hundred feet, and since the upper vantage point was dangerously smooth and slippery, it would be a major undertaking even to make a connection by rope.

We were caught in a trap. A delightful trap, certainly, and one which amply fulfilled most of our dreams; but the mind rebels at such a situation, and there was also the important question of supplies. Our conclave of seniors decided that by the time the porters were again due we must either have blasted the northern route into working order or be able to notify our contacts that we had found fresh means of occasional communication with the outside world.

Well, we tried the first alternative all through that summer, and it was impossible. Even with Barnard's skilled direction, all we managed to do was blast away even more of the precious ledge; so our thoughts turned perforce towards the tunnel. We authorized Barnard and his team of native apprentices to proceed with blasting, taking every possible care. In fact, the amount of blasting required was minimal, as the men cut their way through the soft rock with surprising ease, and even during the shoring up of the roof there were no accidents. An army of valley people formed a human chain, bringing back thousands of buckets of earth and rock to be tipped down the mountainside. Others repaired the steps, and finally, of course, there were the skeletons to be buried, the remains of the bandits who had died in 1902. Brother Stanley read the Church of England burial service over them. I remember having to suppress a smile: it seemed so wholly inappropriate as to be almost macabre. Finally, the labour was completed, though Barnard was never entirely satisfied with his work on the roof at its most sensitive point: he feared that reverberation might bring it down again. But it has held so far, though we pass under it as quietly as we can.

The problem of transport in the desert naturally had to be thought of: none of us fancied walking over the distances involved. Eventually we constructed some sturdy wagonettes – rickshaws, I suppose they could be called, wide enough to seat two and capable of being drawn by oxen or, if necessary, by teams of men. They proved practical though extremely uncomfortable; we all preferred to walk over the stonier stretches.

Four people volunteered for the first expedition: Barnard, myself, and two youngish Burmese half-lamas who thought they could probably speak any dialect we were likey to encounter. (Barnard and I were to pretend to be under a vow of silence.)

Once out of the canyon we took care to travel only at night when our route could not be followed. On the second night we came close to a small village, little more than a collection of tents, and allowed ourselves, quite casually, to meet a couple of tribesmen who were prospecting in a primitive way for precious metals. Believing that we too came from the south, they gave us to understand that the village was called Ramjigoval and was populated by commercial explorers from two more permanent hamlets some seventy miles south, near the end of the rough trail from Myitkyina. A rumour had spread that gold was to be found in the north end of the valley, formerly thought to be totally unproductive. The next night, having learned all we needed, for the time being, we safely retreated and reached our own canyon at about noon on the following day. Finding it again, incidentally, was a sharp test of our own meticulous observation. When our group had first descended from the tunnel through the winding canyon, I was surprised to find that the exit of the latter faced north: on leaving it we had to turn south, and soon realized that all traces of the accommodating fissure had disappeared. In some panic we retraced our steps for a mile or so, looking for landmarks in the empty desert. Eventually we settled on two useful rocks, or groups of rock, one resembling a lizard and the other a mushroom: having established their relationship with each other, there was no danger of losing our way home. We had thought it might be necessary constantly to obscure our wagon tracks, but it transpired that the shale leading down to the desert floor was so unyielding as to take no imprint.

A month after our return, my two Burmese colleagues were sent with the conclave's blessing on a longer journey as far as Mandalay. It was, of course, a matter for the most subtle judgement, not only for them to select suppliers who would without stirrings of greed accept our freshly mined ore as payment, but also to recruit porters who would not be insatiably curious when Shangri-La's own supply column met them at a point north of Myitkyina, not stirring until the porters were out of sight on their return journey. The process was eventually set up (by a method similar to that of the old Chungking route) through the good offices of a benign religious order; one of its number in this case was later pleased to join us and has become one of our most gratifyingly devoted members.

To come finally to my present predicament. Though absolutely content in my mountain Utopia, with a renewed conviction of my destiny and no sentimental attachments dragging my thoughts back to western Europe, I had long contemplated the possibility of one final visit to London, intending to take my last leave of old friends, to observe developments during my eight-year absence, and to arrange publication of a manuscript at which I have worked over several years. You may smile when I tell you that it is nothing less ambitious than a forecast of the future of mankind: less pessimistic, perhaps, than Mr Wells' celebrated vision (which reached us two years ago[2]) in that it does consider the probability that Shangri-La, spared from otherwise universal holocaust, will be available to speed the processes of regeneration. I have called it *The Other Side of the Mountain*: Mr Hilton's readers will recognize the quotation. Several of the young postulants heard of the manuscript and asked to read it in its incomplete state. Permission was given; later two of them, Luki (our recently acquired Burmese) and a Swede we know as Max, came to Chang and myself with a breathtaking but quite plausible suggestion. It was that the Western continents should be made ready to withstand their terrifying future by the establishment, in suitably protected locations, of foundations able and willing to promulgate the teachings of Shangri-La.

After due debate by our conclave it was agreed that a sufficient sum might be put aside from our not inconsiderable funds for the establishment of two such centres. By my own suggestion, one would be within the boundaries of Great Britain, rather than continental Europe where

[2] *The Shape of Things to Come*, published in 1933. – Ed.

the holocaust, following the advent of Hitler, seemed already to have begun; the other was to be in the United States, clearly a land of unlimited opportunity and potential development. I had also been impressed by Barnard's remark on reaching our local desert floor that he was irresistibly reminded of a place in California called Death Valley, which had extremely similar geology, colouring and climate. He also remembered exploring a canyon whose lower stretches were comparable to our own in its twists and turns. We both reasoned that in the high plateau from which that canyon led, a remote fissure might well reproduce most of the climatic conditions of our Valley of Blue Moon, in sight of the snowline but basking in the tropical warmth of a sheltered cup. With luck we could establish in such a situation a new Shangri-La, remote from the general public yet less than three hundred miles from the burgeoning metropolitan area of Los Angeles.

Our two novices, prepared in pursuit of this great purpose to sacrifice their own hopes of longevity (for it was considered unlikely that the *tangatse* plant could flourish in other climes), were delighted to be offered the prospect of a five-year ministry in the field. Chang had meanwhile persuaded me that as High Lama I must stay where I was, at least until Max and Luki were well established, at which time he seemed to think that a pastoral visit might be feasible. However, just as arrangements for their departure were being finalized, news reached us of the outbreak of the Second World War. Oddly enough, September 3 1939 was a very good day for wireless reception; and we heard faintly, through headphones, a Chinese bulletin embedded in which was a recording of the fateful declaration by Neville Chamberlain. I had never thought of myself as an especially political animal, but as Chamberlain finished I knew that my spirit could not rest serenely in Shangri-La until I had done something to help my native country in its time of crisis. You may suppose with some truth that from my oriental hideaway I saw England through rose-coloured glasses: the yellow stone houses of the Cotswolds with roses round the door, the dreaming spires of Oxford, the green peaks of the Lake District, the church clock at Grantchester, summer teas on the vicarage lawn. Clichés they may well have been, but they were the images among which I had been brought up, and I could not bear to think of them being despoiled by the powers of evil. The distress within me was so obvious that not even my dear Chang, subtle as he usually was, could refrain from mentioning it and trying to console me. In early October of last year, a month after the outbreak of war, I told him that I must reluctantly take leave of absence for at least twelve months, but that I would certainly return as soon as hostilities ceased. I added that if the others agreed I would take the opportunity to travel with Luki and Max and set them upon their chosen paths.

Chang's face was grave. 'Shangri-La,' he said, 'had not thought to lose you again so soon.'

I protested my certainty that the conflict could not last more than a few months, and urged that if Shangri-La was to plan for the postwar world it was only proper to take soundings now of the new Europe. We took our discussion to the conclave. Finally it was agreed that the world was changing so fast as to require occasional examination if we were to have any hope of keeping up with developments.

I packed very quickly and simply: there was little to prepare. On the evening before our departure I walked with Chang up to the ridge and watched the moon rise over the Karakal glacier. It had been a quiet supper, my last for some time with those familiar faces, and Chang in particular was still concerned, though outwardly tranquil.

He asked: 'Might one be permitted, my dear Conway, to enquire as to your mood at this time?'

I chuckled. 'It's a little like leaving the womb again. Or leaving Heaven for the dark Satanic void.'

'Perhaps – and I say this with a tinge of apprenhension – perhaps another Heaven will present itself to you.'

I shook my head. 'I knew when I first stepped into this place that never in my life would I feel myself closer to the fountain of wisdom. And you, Chang, were a picture of an archangel come to life.'

Chang almost purred. 'What a very strange idea of Heaven you must have had! Though perhaps not quite so strange as that of your Mr Sidney Smith, who wrote, I recall, that he expected it to be like eating pâté de fois gras to the sound of trumpets.' Chang's knowledge of minor English literature never ceased to astonish me.

'Not for me. I loathe trumpets and liver pâté with equal fervour. And I assure you that before many moons have passed, you and I will walk here again.'

As though on cue at my mention of it, the moon emerged from a cloud and shone with almost supernatural intensity over the whole unbelievable landscape of ice and rock. 'Could you conceive of such a vision elsewhere?' asked Chang softly.

We descended slowly to the lamasery. I bathed my feet in traditional style, and put on the most sensible clothing I could devise. After the months of doubt and argument, it all seemed very easy. I had already taken my leave of the other lamas, who had returned quietly to their studies so as to avoid an emotional farewell; and it was with no formality at all that my journey began. Chang watched from his balcony until the zigzag hid us from view; then, despite the presence of Luki and Max and the guards, I felt desperately lonely and vulnerable, afraid that from foolish pride and a forlorn sense of duty I was tearing myself away for the second time from what had clearly been selected as my rightful place in the world. Once into the tunnel, however, the sheer excitement of the adventure took over. Our aim was to be well into the desert by dawn, and everything worked like a dream. The three of us passed through Ramjigoval without causing comment, then progressed slowly towards Rangoon and the ship which was to carry us to Portsmouth. We had agents who provided all necessary travel documents, but of course I forgot to have my passport brought up to date. I believe that even master criminals are usually allowed one mistake.

The journey was arduous but successful until, six weeks ago, we reached London and took our leave of each other. I have to admit that I had not anticipated being entirely unknown and unrecognized, nor being treated as a lunatic, though to be sure I tell a strange story. I admit also to disillusion. Clearly I was mistaken in thinking that I have any part to play in the present conflict: that supposition came out of emotional nostalgia for times long gone. Once past their peak, soldiers and diplomats are good only for playing golf and taking long sea voyages. England in 1940 can manage very well without me – as it appears could the England of 1931. My mysterious disappearance must have been quite widely reported at the time, but has now been entirely forgotten. I shall not be sorry when I am put on a boat and shipped off somewhere, preferably back East: the noise here jars my nerves, and aesthetically it seems that beauty has not marched hand in hand with progress. Of course, if one makes such a remark one is brusquely reminded that 'there's a war on', which seems to be both the reason and the excuse for everything.

At least my companions appear to have kept their enthusiasm and their optimism. Max writes from

California that he has found a likely site and three recruits. Luki is at the English location, not two hundred and fifty miles from London. It was chosen by a most curious coincidence. I had been turning over in my mind the relative advantages of Glastonbury, of Anglesey, and of the Nant Gwynant Valley in North Wales. Then on the ship as we came into Southampton I got into conversation with two monks, and when they told me their home base it reminded me of my childhood and a sea

(Here the typescript ends.)

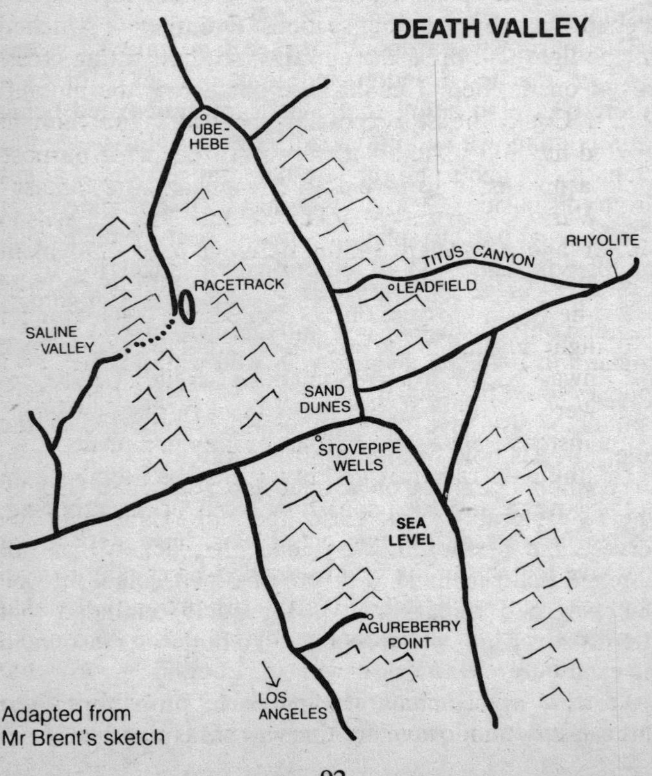

Adapted from
Mr Brent's sketch

5

Nicholas Brent's Narrative (1980)

'IT WAS AWESOME IN THE CANYON'

What I held in my hand was a bad photocopy from a faint carbon, and some of it wasn't easy to read. By the time I reached the abrupt end, my eyes were aching for sleep, but the rest of me was as alert as though I had heard a call to arms. I tossed and turned for a while, then sat up to read the last page again. I read it twice, then turned back through several other sections. Eventually I switched off the light and drew the curtains, so that, sitting cross-legged on the bed, I could gaze out across the moonlit desert. Could the story possibly be true? The thought dazzled my mind. And if it were not true, what purpose could a man have to invent so circumstantial a fantasy? Was Warlock a practical joker on the lines of Wilson Mizner and H. Allen Smith, deriving pure enjoyment from leading the world up the garden path? If so, why would he waste his time on hoodwinking a total stranger who might be gone in the morning? Could the man known as Conway be the joker? Somehow I couldn't think so: there were in the typescript many turns of phrase which I found instantly endearing but not exactly humorous.

The thoughts raced around in my head as I fell back on to the covers; and then somehow I was up and shaving, though in between the two acts I must have slept for at least five hours. On the way to breakfast I caught up with Warlock, and as I handed back his property I could manage at first no conversation beyond a deep sigh and a shrug. Finally I said: 'I was in London myself that summer, as a small child. My first visit. I probably walked past the very window where Conway sat typing.'

Warlock put on his wide comical smile and shook my hand heartily. But all he said was 'Let's eat.' We were out in his battered Bronco – he thought it would manoeuvre better in the narrow places – before he would speak of Conway again, winding our way up to Hell's Gate, where in 1859 the already exhausted pioneers from the East took their first dismaying glimpse of the valley of death. As we eventually began to descend through a canyon to the Nevada side, we took our bearings. We were to return through Titus Canyon, a parallel cleft some way to the north: its rocky trail was one way in the reverse direction, and could be approached only by a jeep track cutting back from the road we were now on. From my last visit I remembered the signs, and my frustration as I read them: ONE WAY ROAD. JEEPS ONLY. TWENTY-FIVE MILES TO DEATH VALLEY. TAKE WATER. And finally: CLOSED TO ALL VEHICLES DUE TO WASHOUT. 'Damn,' I said, 'we forgot to bring water.'

'There are two containers in the back,' said Warlock. 'We'll fill them up at Rhyolite, that's the ghost town just past the Titus turnoff.'

'Last time I went there it poured with rain.'

'Not today. Look.' Sure enough, as we continued to descend we clearly saw the scattered township remains glistening in bright sunlight, just a mile or so to the left of the black ribbon of road which unwound before us across the dim desolation of the Amargosa Desert. Technically we had left Death Valley behind; but we would return, by the most arduous of routes.

Five minutes later we turned left to face an irregular range of mountains showing evidence of mining disfigurements. Between them and a sizeable single outcrop lying close to the road lay an area which in 1907 had held a township of ten thousand inhabitants, all hoping to get rich quick. It must have been a dusty, windswept place to live, with no protection from the gusts which undoubtedly blew through a large gap to the east; through this, two railways once ran to the town of Beatty three miles on. What was left of Rhyolite now was an uphill main street, roughly tarred for the benefit of tourists; the stone façade of a general merchant's bearing the date 1906; three walls and an arch or two of a bank which had cost sixty thousand dollars to build; the railway station buildings, virtually intact but uncared for; most of the school, well set back from the road; and a little house constructed entirely of green bottles instead of bricks. Cross streets could still be distinguished; but when we parked and explored them the only evidence of previous inhabitants was the occasional rusted fragment of a cooking stove, a variety of tin cans, a few bicycle wheels, and hundreds of thousands of long nails drawn out from wood-frame dwellings which had been dismantled for subsequent erection on some other site. Little grey lizards ran furtively across the remains. The bottle house was kept going as a depressingly amateur museum; we filled our water containers and bought a souvenir book.

'Amazing,' said Warlock as we stood outside in the already baking sunshine. 'Before the ore ran out this place had two newspapers, three hotels and its own red light district. And here are the pictures to prove it.'

'Where are the snows of yesteryear?' I asked rhetorically.

Warlock held up a hand. 'Please. The snows of yesteryear are getting to be a pretty sore point with me. In 1906 I hadn't even been thought about, and now I'm not feeling so good myself.' He projected his jaw and stroked his scrawny neck upwards from collar to chin. 'There again, if we are to believe Mr Hilton and Mr Conway, in 1906 Shangri-La had a one-hundred-and-eighty-year history and at least one inhabitant who saw the whole thing through from the beginning and still had twenty-five years to go.'

I kicked a stone vaguely in the direction of the bank. 'Show me the ruins of Shangri-La, or better still Shangri-La as a going concern, and I promise to believe it. But not till then – not quite. These ruins I see because I can touch them. People were here. In my mind's eye I can see them eating, working, washing, shopping, writing letters, getting drunk, whoring around. I can almost smell the cooking, and the horse manure. Here I'm really in the presence of history.'

We walked up the main street, thinking of all the families who had congregated there after trekking across the desert to scrape a living and hope for gold. After a couple of years they had all been forced to uproot and move on in pursuit of some other rainbow. At the top of the hill we neared the railway station, which bore crude signs: MUSEUM DRINKS FREE ENTRY.

'Come in here, if you want to be really depressed,' said Warlock.

We pulled back a screen door and entered a room which had much the same ambience as small local railway stations all over the world, except that it was a long time since a window had been opened. The air was stale and sickly sweet. Behind the long mahogany bar there rose into view an extremely ancient female person. She seemed to be dressed in trailing ribbons of pink georgette, small festoons of which were tied into her hair as though she were to be crowned Queen of the May. Despite her fragile appearence she proved eager for conversation, and sold us two beers with alacrity. She owned, she said, quite a bit of local acreage and was ever hopeful that it would shortly prove to be goldbearing. 'Not in her lifetime,' murmured Warlock as he led the way down a dark corridor to the museum room, where mouldering jumbles of silk and lace hung on dressmaker's figures. The walls were hung with undusted framed photographs of Rhyolite in its heyday, and on the tables were piled unattractive chunks of the local ore which had proved not worth getting out of the reluctant earth. One photograph, never very sharp and now brown with years, showed the post-master, his wife and their baby outside the brand-new post office, built in 1909 by a government department which must have heard the bad news but could not move quickly enough to cancel the building order. 'Recognize anybody?' asked Warlock; I shook my head. 'The young mother, about sixteen years old I'd say: she just sold you a beer.'

Suddenly the air in those unhealthy rooms seemed twice as stifling as before. I headed for the exit, gladly dropping a dollar into the old lady's prominently displayed collecting bowl. With the door half open I could not resist pausing to ask her, with what I meant for a friendly smile: 'Do you like it here?'

'Oh,' she said, chuckling queerly, 'must be, I guess. Always did like the earth, and my own company. Soon be part of the earth myself: not much sense getting used to town folks again.' She swung a filmy scarf round the lower part of her face and for a second was recognizable by her eyes as a grotesque caricature of the girl in the picture.

'I imagine she had a pretty good life in a way,' mused Warlock as we ambled down the wide empty street. 'Seems a smart old bird, probably worth a mint of money.'

'A good candidate for Shangri-La?'

'Maybe. Yes, given an extended span, she could have had things to contribute.' He waved me into the Bronco and we regained the blacktop, shortly turning right at the Titus trail, where I took a photograph of my new friend against the forest of warning signs, which seemed especially apposite if this was to be Conway's canyon of secrets, as Warlock obviously took it to be.

As we bumped and lurched along the rutted trail, there was little to see at first. To the south, the flat desert, looking an acrid green from the tumbleweed, receded endlessly into the horizon. To the north it rose gently before ending in a mountain range perhaps ten miles away. The sun on our heads was warm, but seemed to be biding its time. It was ten-thirty. Warlock said it was best to take this part of the route at forty, so that you sailed over most of the bumps, but after a while I decided that this must have been a malicious rumour and asked him to slow down and spare my spine. Before we reached the mountains his hands were swollen by the vibration, so I took over and proceeded at a careful twenty miles an hour. After half an hour of this we entered a low pass, but the road surface got worse instead of better as we veered first right, then left, circumventing innumerable groups of rock. We caught our first sight of high peaks ahead, and five minutes later were surrounded by them. Our route descended sharply into a thinly wooded valley, then rose up an apparently sheer mountain wall in a series of hairpin bends to a level where most of the trail had fallen away. Suddenly we rounded a high shoulder, and ahead of us a massive mountain seemed by an optical illussion to move into view from the right; a patch of copper red on the road surface looked to be evidence of recent work by a bulldozer. 'That's Bloody Gap,' cried Warlock above the roar of the engine. 'We come to the difficult bits pretty soon.' It struck me that this attempt at humour was singularly ill-timed, as my half of the Bronco was hanging over a sheer precipice.

At the top we paused for ten minutes to photograph as best we could the massive panorama of jagged peaks which filled the northern horizon. The air struck chill under the influence of snow not too far above our heads.

The route ahead was blessedly downhill, but it was perhaps the worst road along which I have ever travelled, all the soft red soil having been washed away to leave a surface so jagged that I doubted whether our tyres could survive even if the vehicle found room to proceed in the very limited space available on the mountain ledge. Somehow it did, and we crawled down to a softer but much more crumbly section where the danger was that we might stick in mud caused by the flash floods which had recently washed across the trail. When we stopped again I reached for my map, but Warlock put his hand on my wrist. 'Don't worry about getting lost,' he said. 'There's only one way through, and we're on it. The trail just follows the lie of the land. Here, I stopped to show you something interesting.'

We parked the car safely and I took stock of our position, in a barren but protected plain about a mile wide, surrounded on all sides by hills which strained for the sky and ended in jagged pinnacles all of which seemed to have faces on them. We had braked beside what at first I had taken to be a huge heap of stones fallen from the mountain; but on the north side it turned out to be a low building of which boulders formed the back wall, while at the front a corrugated iron roof was held in place by timbers which had once shaped a doorway and a primitive window. 'What they called a Cousin Jack, don't ask me why,' said Warlock. 'Miner's hut from the Twenties.'

'So people did live in this God-forsaken spot? As recently as that?'

'My dear sir, you are now standing on the townsite of Leadfield, which in 1926 had its own post office and general store.'

I looked around at a scene of natural desolation, though I could now make out a few pockmarks in the grey hillside, where mining shafts had been sunk. 'Wasn't it all a hoax?'

'One of the most famous in the west. A speculator bought title to hundreds of acres and issued handbills showing the Amargosa River running through the canyon. It's actually bone dry and twenty-five miles away. He sank a few blank shafts himself and issued photographs of the "work in progress". Get-rich-quickers poured across the desert eager to buy, and even when they found they'd been stung – the land around here is absolutely valueless – two hundred of them stayed for six months.'

'Didn't they lynch the speculator?'

'If they could have found him, they probably would have. You know what's amazing, there's even a shot in one of my books of a string of Model Ts lining this trail.'

'The road we came on must have been better maintained then.'

'Maybe a whole lot less. Those poor folk thought they had a reason for getting here, that's all.'

'How depressed they must have been to see what they'd bought. It's all so ugly. Like slate and cinders.'

'Yep. Another Utopia that failed. But this area changes every five minutes. I mean, did you ever smell purer air? And come over here, I want to show you something. Bring your cane, it's a ten-minute walk. Bring the box lunches too.'

'What a good idea. A nice quiet lunch on a mountain top before we head back to civilization.'

Warlock turned and grinned. 'Are you so *very* sure that you are away from it?'

I remembered Chang's line of welcome to Mallinson, and began to get an inkling of what Warlock had to show me. We strode across a stream bed full of caked mud, then joined what had clearly at one time been quite a well-trodden footpath. It led quickly to a point where we could turn for a comprehensive view of the town site, with our Bronco pointing down towards the natural defile which was the beginning of Titus Canyon proper, winding down through a fault in the impermeable mountain to the desert still ten miles away. Climbing again, we found the clay trail fainter from this point, and steeper too, but there was a refreshing breeze which prevented us from sweating. We surmounted a crest, walked on the flat for a few yards, then found ahead of us a great slit in the rock leading into a sunnier and warmer area, obviously so because it faced south and was supremely well protected by nature. Holding a hand over my eyes, I could dimly see below us the expanse of Death Valley, though everything within twenty-five miles was blocked out by projections of rock which gave the area where we stood the shape of a saucer. It was about a quarter of a mile square, with just a few stunted trees at one end. The other vegetation was limited to tiny desert flowers and some relation of mesquite.

'Let's sit for a minute,' said Warlock.

We found a flat rock and did so, savouring the balmy air and watching the flight of a few birds which seemed to have nests somewhere in the mountain. I began to eat an apple, and followed it with a cold hamburger. Warlock followed suit. We tried to preserve the sanctity of the place by not even rustling paper.

'You think this is it, don't you?' I said eventually. 'Max's branch office of Shangri-La.'

'Well, I think it may be. After all, we know Barnard must have surveyed the whole area.'

'Barnard,' I said thoughtfully. 'Imagine him existing after all.'

'Call him Chalmers Bryant if you insist, but that isn't a real name either. I checked. What my researches did throw up was a so-called swindler who fled from Wall

Street in 1930 *and* was chased by the police of five countries *and* was neither found nor ever heard of again. His name was Ben Pegley. Now, nobody says he ended up in Afghanistan, but nobody says he didn't. He had to go somewhere. And here's the real funny thing. In 1924 Pegley was a mining engineer associated with the copper project at New Ryan, just the other side of Furnace Creek. So there's every possibility that he was still around this area when Leadfield had its six months of life, and came to see what all the fuss was about. In which case this natural curiosity could have led him up here. And ten years later he might well have told Conway that this was a perfect site, because no prospector would come near it after the hoax, and here you've got the ideal climatic balance between snow up there and desert below. Of course, I don't know what he proposed for water, but he must have had ideas about that, other than climbing down the hill with buckets. Perhaps a pipeline down from the snow: they did that at Shidoo. What's the matter, am I going too fast?'

I sipped at my prepackaged milk through a straw thoughtfully provided. 'You really want to be taken seriously?'

'Oh, sure. Don't we all? Even that funny little thief in the green suit was playing for keeps. He stole that book for a purpose. He couldn't find the typescript and he thought you might have made notes in the margin.'

'But what in hell did he want?'

Warlock shrugged. 'There's the mystery. Before the sealed-room solution, we shall have to await the clues. As Sherlock Holmes once remarked, it is a capital mistake to theorize without data.' Minutes later I shared Warlock's certainty. Wandering on, we came to an area at the southern end of the saucer; here the air smelled natural because there was moisture about. The hard surface gave way to mud, the weed to a fine grass. The ground was fertile! I have come across similar spots at highish altitudes on Helvellyn in the Lake District, where the ground rocks are sufficiently impervious to hold rain; here the amounts would be small but clearly enough to support life.

'You see,' said Warlock from a high ledge, 'even the most desolate places can have secrets.'

I scrambled up and thought at first he wanted to point out far below in the desert a vehicle moving along a ribbon of road which turned round the sand dunes and led to a brown pinprick which must clearly be our hotel. But Warlock redirected my gaze behind us into the saucer. There was no doubt about it: a faint crossword arrangement of tracks, a grid system which couldn't possibly be natural. And scattered on the rocks were several odd pieces of shaped wood and rusted metal, items which had been made by man and had no natural place on the high shoulder of a desolate mountain.

'Magic,' I said, shaking my head.

'Karakal,' murmured Warlock. 'In sight of the snowline but basking in the tropical warmth in a sheltered cup.'

I remembered Conway's description. 'But you see,' said Warlock between exertions as we clambered over rocks to examine the view in all directions, 'what Barnard couldn't have foreseen was that in 1933 the State Department would make Death Valley a National Monument, vastly improving the roads and bringing tourists here in their thousands. And even though only a few of them in the early days would have taken a chance on Titus, and even fewer would stop at Leadfield and find their way up here, sooner or later the rangers would be bound to spot anybody who tried to set up house. For a start, the settlers would have had to have transport, and once Leadfield was demolished there'd be nowhere to hide the vehicles.'

'Couldn't they have walked?'

Warlock gave me a withering glance. 'Yes, they could have, but for half the year the valley below us rates as the hottest place on earth, and they'd have a choice for shopping between Beatty maybe twenty miles back and Stovepipe about twenty-five in the other direction. No, my guess is that Max finished up on the fringes of Los Angeles, feeding ersatz religion to wealthy widows. How do you feel about that?'

'I feel like an astronaut trying to make sense of a new planet.' I gazed across the prehistoric landscape and pointed to a thick grey mist which had settled on top of the northern mountains. 'Isn't that unusual at this time of year?'

'It sure is, and it's coming this way. The wind must have changed.'

'It makes the canyon look like something out of Dante's *Inferno*. And you're Charlton Heston playing Moses.'

'No,' said Warlock, drawing out his camera, 'I'm a tourist taking a picture.' He clicked away and sighed. 'You wouldn't think that Las Vegas is only a hundred miles down the road. Every time I get dragged to that dump I imagine God must be telling Noah to build another ark.'

The sky was still darkening twenty minutes later as we climbed into the Bronco. We were tired now, and sticky from the increased humidity. At least the way seemed easier. No more hairpin bends or narrow ledges, just a graceful curving descent through ten miles of gradually sloping canyon which had originally been cut through the mountain by the pressure of water trying to find the least problematic way to spill itself into the valley on the far side of this massive range. As we entered the upper reaches of the canyon, the surface beneath our wheels turned into loose shale resting on the bedrock, shale washed down over the centuries from the rock walls which rose gradually on either side until they were ten, then twenty feet above our heads, the distance between them becoming narrower as we progressed. Soon there was only a glimpse of dark sky above, almost indistinguishable from the treacle-coloured walls. It was awesome in the canyon, every minute of it, even before the danger threatened. I remember thinking I must tell Elizabeth that in Titus she had a ready-made one-hour television special, waiting only to be photographed. But she'd need to know who the original Titus was, and that was something I couldn't find in my guide book.

From time to time, heavily contorted strata were exposed, making us realize what monstrous upheavals had taken place even before the canyon itself had been formed. At one point all this primitive geology was explained on one of the familiar dark red historical markers, which came as something of a shock. In this remote place we had forgotten that we were still watched over, albeit irregularly, by ever thoughtful Authority, anxious that we should be instructed as well as enthralled. Further on, Indian stone pictures were pointed out, though more recent graffiti had almost effaced them: even in Titus Canyon hooligans sometimes lurk. Not far away we were directed to the site of a dry spring around which colourful cacti still thrust themselves from the cracks in the rock. Everywhere the walls bore fascinating veined patterns as we descended ever deeper between them, following the dry, dusty, gravel-filled watercourse. Having journeyed through this fantastic canyon one could disbelieve nothing – not even the possibility of Shangri-La. Our dream-like progress was interrupted suddenly by a muffled explosion. The radiator had boiled dry and the top hose had split: luckily we had adhesive tape. Clearly our temperature gauge wasn't working, but in these conditions we should have checked at frequent intervals. The vehicle skidded to a halt at a point just wide enough to allow any following car to pass, though none offered to do so during the hour it took us to fix things. As I finally tightened the cap a drop of rain fell on my back like an icy dagger. I looked up and saw another awaken Warlock, who had fallen asleep on a slab of rock, with his mouth open. I had just time to take in the pattern of spots making its presence felt on his shirt when there fell upon us such a deluge as one reads about in books on desert travel, but never expects to experience. There were cracks of accompanying thunder, and lightning which struck the high cliffs well above our heads but might well have showered fragments of rock upon us. The direction of the rain being diagonal, the canyon walls would have afforded a fair amount of shelter, but instinctively we shut ourselves in the Bronco and turned on the air conditioning.

'The clouds have chosen these bloody mountains on which to break up,' spluttered Warlock.

'We're dry and in no hurry.'

'I don't know about that. Remember that this canyon was formed by rain. And there's lots of the stuff falling now.'

I saw his point. 'Hadn't we better turn back to Leadfield? It's more open there.'

'No time, we're past the point of no return. Besides, the trail may wash out altogether. In half an hour this canyon could be filled with boulders, in which case we'd be smashed to bits. Better get on with it: it can't be more than six miles to the open valley.'

I needed no further urging. The wheels gripped well enough in the narrows but in the wider sections the wet shale was already turning to slush, and it was as much as we could do to hold a middle course and not dash ourselves on to the projecting edges. On corners particularly, puddles lay deep in the ruts, and in places the whole canyon was awash. All this time the canyon walls were getting higher, one winding bend following another until I was dizzy. When the strain of holding on to the wheel brought my nerves to the surface and threatened to reduce my hands to a pulp, Warlock hurriedly took over; but even his weathered face soon bore the wild gritted look of a man who knows he is slowly losing control and can do nothing about it. It was not the kind of situation on which I thrive, but I steeled myself not to panic. Just as in a plane I leave all the worrying to the pilot, so now I was content that Warlock should hold both our fates in his hands. All the same, my eyes kept scanning the immense walls for ledges or caves to which we might leap for safety if we had to abandon the car to the slowly swelling waters. Warlock's eyes were fixed on the constantly changing width ahead. Often it seemed too narrow to accommodate us, but we always got through. Once from the shadows ahead a pair of darkly luminous eyes stared at us; they proved to belong to a stray *burro* which turned and bounded ahead to the safety of the open desert.

'Didn't even wait to have his picture taken,' yelled Warlock. His voice echoed around the canyon and died away, to be replaced by a sound I had not heard before, a loud persistent roar, almost like organ notes. Ahead, we were caught in a maze with no apparent solution; behind, waters from a wide area of the mountain range had collected in the dip below Leadfield and now began to gush and gurgle after us through the narrows, eager to carve out another inch of depth to the ancient passage. In other parts of Death Valley I had seen tarmac roads torn up and hurled asunder in this way: Golden Canyon, down which I had once driven, was now closed except to hikers who at one point had to climb from the old roadway to a level nearly three feet higher. However shallow the waters behind us might be where they collected, they must get deeper as the canyon grew lower and narrower, and at the other end they would gush out into the desert like a fountain: stories were told of torrents fifty feet high. I imagined bits and pieces of us and our vehicle being spewed out with the spray, and shook my head to lose the image. We skidded furiously down an unusually straight length, and as we rounded the next turn I glanced back and actually saw a bubbling tide of water, like a river bore, surge into the section we had just left. Warlock saw it too, in his mirror, and let out a yelp. 'Christ! Where in hell does this canyon end?'

He swung the wheel ever more frantically, but I had no confidence that we would make it now. Then my eye fell on an upward slope to the left, where soft strata had been washed out of the rock and had formed a ledge which might almost have been designed as a car port, sloping up out over the canyon floor at a height of five or six feet. It was barely wide enough to take our wheels, but it looked like our only chance. I pulled at Warlock's arm and gestured. He understood at once and swerved towards the slope, bumping over rubble which in other circumstances he would have taken great care to avoid. The Bronco humped itself up the smooth rock, shuddering to a halt less than a foot from the far edge. Within seconds, before we even had time to look round, a great wall of water thudded against our back windows and hurtled through our wheels, shaking the whole vehicle and slurping in through the doors to soak my ankles. I had a momentary vision of our canyon transformed into one of the more spectacular and terrifying sections of the Colorado rapids.

Five minutes later the rain stopped just as unexpectedly as it had begun. What had become a roaring river diminished with astonishing speed into an unhurried stream. Then, as we watched, it dried out altogether, sinking through the shale with a fizzing noise and leaving in its wake no more than a few puddles. When a fringe of blue sky appeared above our heads, and the sun once more cast a shadow on the high walls, we judged it safe to inspect the damage (which was slight) and continue on our too dramatic journey. The engine spluttered at first, but we managed to back our way off the ledge without incurring more than a scratch on the nearside rear wing.

The canyon even now still descended, the sheer walls still grew in height: the guide book said they reached five hundred feet. Warlock drove slowly but surely, stopping occasionally while I moved a boulder which had been washed down with the flood. The mountain smelled overpoweringly damp and earthy, vibrant with the scents of the mosses which clung to it. Our vehicle always got through, but sometimes with no more than six inches to spare on either side. This part of our journey seemed afterwards like a kind of daydream, accentuated by the fact that we were driving over a bed of soft white pebbles which absorbed any bumps. The effect was that of a cushioned Disneyland ride through mechanical dangers which would all be avoided, though only at the very last moment.

'We've made it,' said Warlock suddenly above the engine noise. 'We really have. I remember that jutting rock up there: it looks like Queen Victoria, crouching.' I barely had time to smile at the unlikely image. We swerved to the right, to the left, to the right again, and then the high vermilion walls parted like a stage curtain to reveal a widening vertical shaft of blue. This expanse of sky and sun, as we approached it, was blinding after the darkness of the canyon, but it was a relief to get away from the smell of waterlogged rock. We emerged at the high point of a rough but graded road which connected the canyon exit with the main north–south blacktop. A couple of No Entry signs were bolted to the mountain wall; to the left was a small parking space. And before us was spread out the entire northern half of Death Valley, clean and vivid after the rain. Evidence of the latter still clung to the Cottonwoods, facing us, in the shape of dark grey clouds, but on our side of the valley the water had now sunk deep into the alluvial fan over which we drove in triumph. This massive accumulation of rock particles had once filled the space of the canyon through which for the last hour we had been driving with such apprehension; and today's flood would have added only a minute fraction.

We had travelled no more than a quarter of a mile down the fan when Warlock pulled to a halt and told me to look back at the canyon exit. I was amazed to find that it had completely vanished. My gaze fell on an implacable rock wall, as apparently impossible of access as Conan Doyle's Lost World; even the car park signs had merged into the desert landscape. 'You see,' said Warlock, 'it's like Conway's exit from Shangri-La. The exit from Titus points north, and we're now driving south. But even from the north you wouldn't see the opening, because it's three miles from the road and at that distance the narrow gap is camouflaged by the rock pattern. To all intents and purposes it's as though the mountain blocks had moved together and sealed.'

'After this weekend I feel that the forces of nature are conspiring to tell me that anything is possible.'

Warlock stretched his arms yawningly into the air, as though trying to pull down the sun. 'In places like this – and the Himalayas – you learn to expect the unexpected. You also have to be wary of the tricks of nature and of little green men. But with a little optimism and a lot of luck you can make it. Conway did.'

'But Max didn't,' I reminded him.

Second Interlude: 1987

IN ST STEPHEN'S TAVERN

'Don't look so impatient, old man,' chuckled Twigley as he tucked into his steak and oyster pie. 'I wouldn't want you to have a fit when I tell you that I haven't finished it yet.'

'What? Then you're getting this lunch under false pretences.'

'I know, and I'm enjoying it. Sorry, truly sorry, but in Alice's absence my neighbour took pity on me and carted me off to Sunday golf. You know what that leads to.'

'All too well. Drunken hours at the nineteenth hole, and the rest of the day sleeping them off. So how much did you read?'

'Oh, at least another couple of chapters. Well, exactly another couple of chapters. But I did read them very carefully. You know, Pemberton, that account of Conway's, whoever wrote it, is very persuasive, but the whole idea of a tropical paradise in the Himalayas just isn't on. I mean, not at that altitude.'

'It's precisely the unlikelihood of it which makes it remarkable,' said Pemberton as he refilled his glass with Niersteiner. 'Geographically, I gather it's perfectly feasible, providing that several rather freakish conditions coalesce. It would be quite possible, climatically, above Death Valley: I checked. But what the story doesn't take into account is that any soil up there probably wouldn't be very fertile: after all, it's just rock dust.'

'Perhaps whoever wrote it wasn't up to snuff on geology.'

Pemberton speared a small onion and swallowed it at a

gulp. 'If you're suggesting an elaborate joke on the lines of Hitler's diaries, don't forget how very elaborate it would have to be. And Conway did exist: there's no doubt of that. And Brent and his friends did disappear.'

In a rare moment of seriousness Twigley looked steadily at his old friend. 'You're really suggesting, aren't you, that the apparent fantasy contained in those papers is in fact the absolute truth?'

Pemberton shrugged, and licked his lower lip. 'The absolute truth,' he said. 'Yes, that's what I believe.'

Twigley returned his gaze to his plate, but seemed suddenly to have lost his appetite. 'I don't get it. You've always been a level-headed sort of chap, even to the point of some people thinking you were dull. If I'm really to take you seriously on this matter, I shall want a lot more detail. For instance, you never told me how the papers came into the hands of the Home Office.'

'Incredibly simply. Our man in Assam sent them in the diplomatic pouch. Seems there was a tea planter minding his own business one afternoon, a very remote tea planter up and away in the hills, when a party of men arrived on foot from the east, pretty dishevelled but apparently meaning no harm at all. Their leader was a bronzed Englishman of fifty-odd, who behaved almost as casually as he might when visiting an old friend in Worcestershire. Now, the planter's nearest neighbour is fifteen miles west, and in the direction from which these strangers came there's not known to be anything much at all, not for at least five hundred miles. Just steep downward slopes until you hit an immense desert floor of supposedly unbearable heat and aridity. Further on still, and slightly north, are the southern foothills of the eastern Himalayas, mostly uncharted ranges with peaks ranging to twenty thousand feet and more.'

'So where had these people walked from?'

'That's the sixty-four-thousand-dollar question. Of course they didn't say, not directly or precisely. But the natives among them weren't Assamese – or so the planter says – and all of them showed signs of having endured a very rough journey. It was getting dark when they arrived, and all the Englishman volunteered was that he and his men were from a distant lamasery and that their purpose was to make maps of the areas which surrounded theirs. This they had accomplished with some success, and meanwhile the planter had been recommended to them – don't ask me by whom – as a man of perfect integrity who on his next visit to Shillong would surely not mind handing over a sealed package to the appropriate British official. The planter, of course, did not mind: hence the speedy delivery.'

'How long ago did this happen?'

'The package was in my hands within a month of the encounter. For his trouble the planter was offered, and accepted, a gold nugget of astonishing size and purity. For his part, and on behalf of his tired men, the mysterious Englishman welcomed the offer of overnight hospitality. After a mainly silent meal – for they were all quite exhausted, especially after a dip in the planter's pool – the strangers were bedded down in an outhouse. But when the planter went to look for them shortly after dawn, the whole party had moved on.'

'Moved on? Moved on where?'

'Who knows? Presumably back whence they came.'

'And was it Nicholas Brent? We must have pictures of him, surely?'

'The planter was shown one last week. He says yes, it's quite possible, but his man was heavily bearded.'

'I see. The plot thickens.' Twigley beckoned a waiter, and selected a crème caramel from the dessert trolley. 'Oh well, since you're standing this extra lunch, I suppose

I'm morally obliged to finish reading the thing.'

'You certainly are.'

'Weekend it shall be, then; but don't forget next Tuesday's lunch is your regular turn. By the way, who was the package addressed to?'

'It consisted of two copies of the papers you have. One for to whom it may concern at the Home Office, the other for Sir Bruce Thomson at the *Clarion*. He helped to finance Brent's expedition, you know.'

'Surely there was a cover note?'

'For Sir Bruce, yes.' Pemberton unfolded a single sheet of paper and began to read quietly from it. 'Dear Bruce: I hope you'll say, better late than never. What's enclosed may or may not be the kind of report you expected seven years ago. I suppose we should have taken a journalist with us. Actually we always intended to tell you our story in person, but you'll see that for six years events conspired to prevent us. Now that a way has been found, a duty is a duty. Besides, there are violent deaths to report: the record needs to be set straight on that. We do hope to see you again one day; meanwhile we send our best wishes to all who remember us, and hope that in the judgement of history we shall be found to have performed some small service for mankind. Nicholas Brent, December 1986.'

'So who was killed?'

Pemberton smiled. 'You'll know by next Tuesday, won't you!'

6

Nicholas Brent's Narrative (1980):

'SO YOU REALLY BELIEVE IT ALL NOW?'

I rolled away from Elizabeth's sweet-scented body and lay on my back under the single sheet, gazing at a label which read: 'one hundred per cent American percale'. The sexual encounter had been rewarding for both of us, and I had needed it; but I am never completely relaxed in hotels, even in the Beverly Wilshire where mine host sends up half a bottle of complimentary champagne to all incoming guests. Ours sat on the sideboard in its bucket of melting ice, awaiting our attention whenever we chose to disentangle ourselves and stray with a bubbling glassful as far as the balcony. There for a while we might assume the guise of the idle rich, looking down to the second-floor roof with its shell-like swimming pool. Here within Mexican-tiled surrounds international starlets disported themselves, more for the public pleasure than for their own. The scene was deliberately reminiscent not of the business-suited Hollywood of today but of the golden age which can never come back. It was a pleasant delusion; but I know better than most that the old Hollywood was irretrievably eroded by the collapse of the studio system and the emergence of young business school executives whose sole concern is to make money by the fastest possible means. I knew that a few elderly stars still lived within a ten-minute limousine ride of the hotel, rattling about in the mock-Tudor mansions of North Canon Drive or the shaded canyons of Bel Air; but they had no place in the public Hollywood of 1980, and they knew it. Just occasionally they might accept an offer to play a cameo role in a TV movie, or evoke instant nostalgia and applause by a brief appearance at an Academy Awards ceremony. But most of the time their chief pleasure and distress was to see their old movies mutilated on television, or to give frugal dinners to each other at glass-topped tables in candlelit rooms, while their even more aged butlers tiptoed sepulchrally down fusty passageways.

For fifty years, more or less, I had accepted the briefness of life as inevitable, old age as something we must all make the best of. Now I was suddenly obsessed with the possibility of Shangri-La – the possibility not only of extending the span but of benefiting mankind at the same time. I could not tell whether my thought processes were irrational, but in any case I was helpless to change them. Everything that happened to me now seemed to have a bearing on the matter. On my way to Los Angeles I had stayed the night with a bachelor friend in Calabasas. Sharing the American desire to cling together with as many neighbours as possible, he occupied a small but elegant house in a condominium by a man-made lake. This means that all the homes in the estate were built by a speculator and are individually owned, but ownership involves service fees and participation in various committee activities which proliferate strict rules for the general benefit. The result slightly suggested the presence of secret police: it was too perfect. Discreet signs laid out the correct behaviour for most eventualities. Around the irregular sheet of water, with its light craft and its water birds and its air of calculated naturalness, were set more than two hundred individually designed homes, the last word in comfort and gadgetry. Kites soared above the common; a flight of geese was visible against the sun; trees planted in careful patterns gave the opportunity for shade. The sky was blue, the air aggressively pure, the temperature a comfortable eighty. Yet the people who lived in this Californian Shangri-La did not look happy.

They looked rich, all right. But they were old, and their usefulness was at an end, and they were afraid of death.

Charles was a voluntary worker at the Motion Picture Country Home and Hospital not a mile away, and next morning before I set off for Wilshire Boulevard he invited me to an early lunch there. Here in Calabasas, by courtesy of massive charitable grants from the giants of the industry, actors and technicians gathered to spend their final years among distant friends, usually preferring them to impatient relatives. Those who could count themselves ambulatory enjoyed a busy life in pleasant surroundings, the walks being agreeably tree-lined and the interiors smelling only slightly of disinfectant. I helped a ninety-year-old Scottish carpenter to get through a verse of 'I Belong to Glasgow', and chatted in a corridor to an animated lady vaudevillian who would shortly celebrate her hundredth birthday. The hospital section was less cheerful: Charles warned me that it was a rough atmosphere for the stranger, but I elected to go anyway. I found myself surrounded by emaciated caricatures of a dozen once-familiar faces, overtaken by racking disease, by senility or by sheer contrariness. An actress who throughout my childhood had played the perfect aunt in innumerable movies lay silent and helpless in bed, turning her doe-like eyes on me in some unspoken plea. A round-faced man who until recently had been playing cynical journalists and country lawyers grinned vacantly at me and began to talk sloppy-mouthed nonsense which I could not understand. A warning card by an open doorway signified the lonely presence inside of a person who was once a household word, a manic singer of nonsense songs. I was never more pleased to reach the open air; as I did so I was wondering whether the 200-year-olds at Shangri-La had found better ways of facing the inevitable than these one-time celluloid giants who had already lived too long. This part of Calabasas had nothing in common with the Valley of Blue Moon.

It made a pleasing contrast for me to find Elizabeth awaiting my arrival; and if she thought my declarations of affection rather more physical than usual, she made no complaint. After the sex, the shower and the champagne I lolled across the bed in a fleecy white towel and began to tell her in detail the odd, coincidental story of my weekend's adventures. By the time I had finished it was nearly dark, and we watched the flat dreariness of Los Angeles turned by millions of lights into the semblance of a magic kingdom.

'So the unexpected Mr Warlock did more to convince you than I ever could?' asked Elizabeth at length. 'You really believe it all now?' Smiling that little crooked smile of hers, she lit a Sobranie and pushed it into one of those plastic holders which absorb tar but are likely to kill you from collapsed lungs.

'I don't see that I'm left any alternative,' I said, almost grumbling to myself. 'You know I've read every Agatha Christie mystery there is. It's not in my nature to back away from one that comes up to me in real life and proves its case at almost every point.'

We dined that evening at Chasen's with Manny Fox, the soon to retire president of Target Television. Both of us counted him an old friend, and he knew all about Elizabeth's theories. When we brought him up to date on what was now my project as much as hers, he was immensely sceptical. 'You're both crazy,' he announced in a voice loud enough to bring a nervous waiter scurrying. 'There's no audience for that kind of stuff.'

'We're not looking for an audience,' I said. 'We're looking for the truth.'

His eyes twinkled. 'You mean you *don't* want to sell me the idea for a series?'

'If we hit the headlines – and we may – you'll be first in the queue to buy it. The fact is, we may not be in a position to make it public. But if we can, what's to stop it becoming a new trend? You know, people having their noses pointed upward for once, instead of down into the gutter.'

'Inspirational pictures went out with high-button shoes.'

'I remember you said something like that to Lew Grade when he was making *Jesus of Nazareth*, and look at the ratings *that* got.'

'A fluke. The other channels were playing re-runs.'

I bit my lip to suppress a smile. 'You'd really take the responsibility for preventing this sensational story from reaching the American public?'

'Listen, you know the advertisers' image of the typical American viewer? A fat little guy in Milwaukee, slouched in an armchair with a can of beer in his hand. It would take him less than five seconds to zap over to the *The Incredible Hulk*.'

I never expected to win with Manny. I had only brought the matter up in order to hear myself telling the story to a hostile audience and standing firm against the inevitable scepticism. At least with Manny you got a lively evening, and he was smart enough to know that his wisecracks had only strengthened our enthusiasm. He might even have wished he could join us; but Manny was first and last and always a commercial animal who never allowed himself to be swayed by emotion. When they carry him out for the last time, he'll be doing a deal with the undertaker.

After he paid his way out of the restaurant, handing greenbacks to every attendant in sight, we shook his hand warmly but refused the offer of a lift, electing to walk back to our hotel through the now deserted shopping streets of Beverly Hills. Manny could not understand anybody who would walk rather than ride in a limousine.

'Don't blame me if you get mugged,' he cried as he was driven away to his Trousdale estate. 'And if you do find your Shangri-La, make a reservation for me. Pretty soon I'm gonna need it.'

We dawdled by the absurdly expensive shops in Rodeo Drive, seeing nothing we would have bought at even a quarter of the price. 'So,' I said as we waited for the Wilshire Boulevard traffic lights, 'you really expect to be in Shangri-La by the end of the year?'

'More than ever now, by hook or by crook. *And*, you'll be surprised to hear, so does Simon.'

I cocked an eyebrow. 'Simon? That's a twist.'

'It is, rather. Dad's papers have been available to him all these years, and this is the first time he's shown the slightest interest. He turned up out of the blue, the night before I left for Mexico, and wanted to know how I was doing for finance.'

'You mean he wants to be on our team?' I grimaced at the thought: Elizabeth's half-brother was not my favourite acquaintance.

'I think he'll be hard to stop. Besides, a united family front must impress any potential angels. Son of the house and all that, seeking his lost father.'

'If you say so, but I wouldn't have thought that mountain trekking was much in Simon's line. I could have understood it if we'd been setting off in a millionaire's yacht from Monte Carlo.'

'So he'll add a touch of glamour. Besides, he knows more about the inner workings of a Land Rover than you do.'

'He could scarcely know less. I just don't fancy him at close quarters for what could be quite a long trip. I'd put him on a par with the resistible Mallinson, who nearly buggered up Conway's first trip.'

'You're casting Simon as the villain already?'

'Not the villain, not quite yet. Not till there's a plot to put him in. I have a distinct feeling that the villain of this piece is going to be the terrain. Since until this weekend I never intended to be a part of your expedition, I didn't think to ask, but have you made any accurate surveys of the possible danger to life and limb?'

Elizabeth laughed. 'You forget that fifty years of high technology have passed since Conway's kidnapping. If we were approaching from the west, Nepal is now wide open to tourists from high income groups. They're talking about opening a modern hotel at the very foot of Everest, so by the time we got there they'd be selling Coca-Cola along the route. In the north, the Chinese have even opened up Lhasa, which in Conway's day had just got its first telephone: nearly 2,000 tourists have been there this year, along the new highway from Peking, which passes not much more than fifty miles north of the Valley of Blue Moon. It's just Shangri-La's good luck – assuming the luck still holds – that nobody has thought of developing the very high mountain region which surrounds Karakal.'

'But if the place is so close to Burmese towns . . .'

'It's close, but nobody knows it's there. The Burmese are put off by the hundred miles of desert which separate the range from Myitkyina, and as a country they don't encourage tourists: I'm having to pull quite a few strings. By backing away from western contamination they've kept themselves just about where they were before the war, which is helpful to us if not to them. I propose to take full advantage, and not to notice the drug smuggling and the lousy food. If we keep our health it'll be a doddle.'

When we reached the hotel lobby I was about to collect the key, but Elizabeth took my arm. 'Not quite yet. I promised to have a drink with somebody, and I'd like you to say hello.'

I was tired enough to see no special significance in her remark, and allowed myself to be led into the dark recesses of El Padrino. She stopped before a banquette and stood back to let me see the solitary figure already seated at the table. 'I don't think,' she said, 'that you really need to be introduced.'

It was, of course, Irving Warlock. I sensed it a split second before I actually looked into his beaming face. Somewhere in the background a trio played a dramatic chord which chimed perfectly with the appearance in my line of vision of his creased and craggy features.

'I promised you your own copy of the Conway story,' he said, thrusting an envelope at me, 'and I decided to bring it in person.'

I turned to Elizabeth, who was smiling at me as she would smile at a child opening a birthday surprise.

'Sit down,' she said, 'order the drinks, and I'll explain everything.'

There wasn't a lot to tell. It was a very simple put-up job. Warlock had been on holiday in London at the end of the previous year, and happened to read an article about Elizabeth and her father's disappearance. He thought Conway's narrative might interest her, so he rang and made a date. Of course she was overwhelmed; even after the briefest skim through it, she could barely contain her excitement. Her first thought had been to show it to me, but a couple of nights earlier I had been at my most scathing about the entire project, and she feared that if she merely pleaded the new evidence I would remain unconvinced. When I mentioned my planned weekend in Death Valley, she had the idea of a more dramatic revelation by Warlock himself. The concept had worked like a charm: without being in any way misled, I had accepted from a total stranger information which I might have doubted from my most intimate friend. Now, as I had to admit, I believed the story both instinctively and intellectually.

'And if you're wondering,' said Warlock, 'which is the best month to visit the Burmese desert, I've already researched that. It's October.'

Hearing myself forced into action, I felt bound to retreat, to need persuading. 'Hold on,' I said, 'there's a lot to be settled first, such as who's in charge of this expedition. When it comes to action, I'm over the hill: I've got used to travelling first class. Anyway, there's no great rush, considering you sat on the typescript for thirty-odd years before doing anything about it.'

'But I didn't have the right kind of stimulus. Some of the most fantastic exploits in history haven't required a great deal of imagination, only a certain kind. I'd probably have gone to my grave with the story if it hadn't been for the mere chance of reading about your good lady here. And my guess is that she won't move without your strong right arm. So you see, you're the key to the whole enterprise. And the timing feels right: it'll soon be fifty years since Conway first arrived in Shangri-La.'

There was no answer to that – as a television producer I'd often preached the appeal of anniversaries – so I changed the subject and asked Elizabeth who else had read the story.

'Nobody. Irving swore me to secrecy until he'd met you.'

'Simon?'

'No. He knew Irving brought some new evidence, but he doesn't know what it was. I took my copy straight to the bank vault. Oh, I told Bruce Thomson something about it – I met him at a party – and he promised to see me when we get back.'

'Newspaper tycoons, now?' Warlock was impressed. 'Sounds as though we're getting somewhere already.'

Warlock's car was in the hotel garage; and he had a two-hour drive ahead of him. Still chatting, however, we took a final constitutional round the block. Past the still lighted windows of Brentano's bookshop; past the façade of a Chinese restaurant which had once been Romanoff's, where Bogart and Sinatra used to snarl at each other; past the august portals of William Morris, the most powerful talent agency in the business; past the sharp little corner windows of Tiffany's, with souvenirs starting at twenty-five dollars.

'You know,' said Warlock, 'here on this block you have a collection of the most and least attractive aspects of western American civilization. I mean, they're all attractive if you're rich, but most of us aren't. And I just thought of something. This was the best James Hilton could do for a Shangri-La. He settled here and worked here, at MGM as a screenwriter.'

'I wonder,' said Elizabeth, 'whether he thought of Wilshire Boulevard as another Valley of Blue Moon.'

'I rather doubt it,' said Warlock. 'He died of liver cancer when he was fifty-four.'

7

Nicholas Brent's Narrative (1980):

'THE PROBLEM IS GOING TO BE SECRECY'

So Shangri-La was real: it was decided. We were going to find it. In a sense I had always believed in it, but as a state of mind rather than a geographical location. I could find it in a friend's back garden, drinking sweet milky tea out of china cups under a summer sun. It could even be in my own study, with my books around me and my typewriter rattling away almost of its own volition. The Shangri-Las I've actually visited have, on close inspection, proved to be disappointing. When I first flew the 'kangaroo route' to Western Australia, via the unsettling strangeness of Bahrain and Kuala Lumpur, I thought I had found Shangri-La in Perth, that clean, tidy little city on the idyllic reaches of the Swan River, its Victorian false-fronted buildings suggesting the pioneer spirit of the Wild West after it had been slightly tamed. But the citizens I met recited as though by rote statistics about underemployment, and the sticky summer flies, and the fact that Sydney was further away than London is from Moscow. Honolulu, which I visited on the way back, may well have been a Shangri-La once, but soon after touchdown all my visions of grass skirts swaying in a tropical paradise vanished. The place has become a concrete megalopolis full of badly designed high-rises. Its freeways look exactly like the ones I so hate in Los Angeles and, since Hawaii is an American state, even have signs in the same style; the climate is humid, and it rains a lot.

The real Shangri-La must, of course, have its drawbacks. My only hope is that the forward spirit of the inhabitants will transcend them.

On the morning of my solitary departure for London – Elizabeth had a call to make in Oregon – Warlock rang to say that he thought, but wasn't sure, that his little villa on Pine Mountain had been entered in his absence and carefully searched. 'Bastards must have got my address from the hotel register,' he mused. Once again nothing of value was taken, and the Conway papers remained well hidden, but it was more than a little worrying.

'The problem all along,' said Warlock, 'is going to be secrecy. You can't even divulge everything you find to the people who are going to subsidize you. It won't be fair to Conway, if you find him; not without his consent. And he won't give it because he knows that as soon as word gets out he'll be trampled underfoot.'

It wasn't the only problem. We had to decide on the composition of our party. Warlock himself had decided, he said, to give it a miss, on the grounds that he wouldn't sound like a good risk in our prospectus. He was coy about his exact age, but I deduced he was nearer seventy than sixty. I said I'd argue the point later, once we'd got the finance; but he insisted he'd wait for the second time round, when we'd organized holiday packages in Shangri-La for senior citizens.

As soon as I got back to London I sprang into action. Well, comparatively speaking. I decided that it would be useless at this stage to consult army intelligence, who even if they now had information in their files were not likely to release it to anybody below cabinet level. When jet-lag had faded I did make an attempt with what was left of the consular service, representing myself as acting on behalf of an aged and distant cousin of Hugh Dearden whom I had met in California. The civil servant who received me in a dingy Whitehall office asked rather sharply why the distant relative had not made his enquiry in person. I replied mildly that I had only volunteered to find out whether there was anything in the files to warrant a six-thousand-mile journey by an infirm old man. At this the official softened and went to investigate, returning after ten minutes with the news that the file had been marked non-active long before the war. The last thing on it was a mysterious note that in 1941 army intelligence had interviewed a man claiming to be Dearden, but for reasons unspecified the meeting had proved abortive.

At least Warlock had not invented the entire story. I turned my attention to Conway's book, *The Other Side of the Mountain*. Had it ever been published? I had endured the bored reactions of three possible publishers of philosophical works before I remembered a supposedly infallible short cut: the British Museum, which keeps a copy of every hardback published. Within twenty minutes of my arrival in Bloomsbury I was poring through the 1941 acquisitions. Nothing there; but with 1942 I was luckier. Dearden, Hugh: *The Mind of Future Man*. A different but quite possible title, and the author surely clinched it. 192pp, 8s6d, Cook and Cary; no other works by this author. It was the business of a few moments to fill in a card requesting the book, and within ten minutes it was before me. I touched it gingerly. Clearly a wartime economy edition, very slim, and printed on paper which had yellowed long ago. Plain buff jacket, slightly torn; no picture of the author (or of anything else). Not a likely bestseller, I thought. I turned first to the blurb:

The author of this book prefers to remain elusive as to biographical details, but the initial narrative makes it clear that he is well travelled in some of the less accessible parts of the pre-war world. However, this is not a travel book. Mr Dearden has a thesis to propound, and he does so both succinctly and persuasively. As he sees things, the civilization we know is fatally unstable, doomed to extinction within a generation or two. He recommends that those in authority should make urgent plans to collect together all that has been thought first-class in literature, in music, in philosophy and in art; to preserve it in safe places, under wise guidance; and thus to ensure its availability to generations yet unborn who may need to be completely re-educated in these matters once the present holocaust has passed. Mr Derden's analysis of the treasures of our world's culture – some of which, alas, have already fallen to the Nazis – is a fascinating catalogue, a miracle of compression and a joy in itself; whether or not the reader can entirely agree with Dearden's pessimistic analysis of contemporary history, he cannot fail to realize that here we have a thinker of freshness and daring. We confidently submit that here is one of the key theses by which, after victory, the rulers of our democracies must regulate the future for all of us.

My perusal of the volume fully occupied the next two hours, and I was not entirely surprised to find it quite as boring as most learned arguments. Though elegantly written, it rather sadly lacked illustrative examples, presumably because Dearden was bending over backwards not to divulge the astonishing secrets he had discovered but was unable to share. At least the final paragraph, though too overfilled with rhetoric for my taste, incorporated Conway's original title and so clinched the identity of the author:

Man will be reluctant to accept that he has nothing more to learn, that his task for the future is only the more perfect assimilation of knowledge which has already been offered to him; knowledge with which he must reconstruct man's unique heritage. History has given him every opportunity for advancement, every comfort save that of a sure and unassailable religion. Indeed, man stands now in the unfortunate position of knowing too much, and believing too little. He says with Frederick the Great: 'Oh God, if there is a God, save my soul, if I have one.' The path to faith lies through understanding of his own destiny and of what Bernard Shaw has called the life force. Others have had different names for it. Truth lies on the other side of the mountain; and the mountain waits to be climbed.

So strong a call to moral armament could have had great appeal to a country immersed in total war, but there was nothing on file to indicate that the book had reached a wide audience. The only review which my research threw up was from the *New Statesman*, written by a Labour politician whose name I vaguely remembered. He had been killed during a V1 rocket raid in 1944.

Of the many jaunty assumptions which Mr Dearden tosses at us in this rather academic treatise, which is short but not short enough, his favourite appears to be that the best of us will always require a sheltered environment and firm regulation of our daily lives so that our minds may be set free for contemplation of our souls. From his final peroration one might think that he had already discovered a personal Utopia to suit this purpose, but if so he gives no directions for reaching it. The difficulty throughout history, as he sees it, has been to reverse man's basically aggressive nature by devising controls gentle enough not to cause resentment, yet strong enough to resist overthrow by those elements of evil which must always exist, as they did in Dr Henry Jekyll, alongside the good. For the sake of the guardians, however, these bonds must be silken; for history shows that all power corrupts, and absolute power corrupts absolutely. Alas for us all, true wisdom comes only with age, and with age comes physical frailty and frequent unreliability. What mankind seeks is some method of staving off the latter stages of life long enough for the accumulated wisdom of our active years to be properly exercised. Whether with this end in view he has consulted doctors or devils, Mr Dearden does not say. The logic of an ideal society ruled by rich, healthy, altruistic old gentlefolk is hard to fault. The possibility of such a society being founded, however, is so remote that long before the last chapter Mr Dearden has begun to seem more than a little naïve. Has he forgotten original sin? And who is to elect the wise men from our ranks? No, Mr Dearden's somewhat chilly vision must in the end be regarded with as much scepticism as all the other Utopias of history and literature. With the best will in the world, none has proved practical.

It seemed clear that in 1942 Conway's book had dropped among war-conscious Britons with all the sensational effect of a raindrop falling into the ocean. Few in those dark days were thinking in terms more prophetic than the urgent protection and future reconstruction of the pleasant if rather befuddled society in which they had all grown up. At least a few years must be allowed to elapse before they could be expected to worry about what might eventually replace it. Even such a popular prophet as H. G. Wells was in those days finding himself ignored, and a year or so later was derided when he brought out a pessimistic vision called *Mind at the End of its Tether*.

The address given for Cook and Cary was 99 Baskerville Street, only a short walk from the British Museum. I might have saved myself the journey: the firm had long been defunct, and the original proprietors defunct even in 1942. The ancient long-serving janitor of the building just remembered them from his boyhood, and helped me to discover that in the fifties the struggling little company had become part of a larger entity specializing in library formats of genteel classics. This itself had succumbed in the sixties to a takeover bid by, of all industrial monoliths, one of the independent television companies. Through an old colleague here, I was able a few days later to get an unofficial glimpse, in a dusty cellar in Wandsworth, of a score of bundles which were all that remained of the Cook and Cary files for the war years. After two grubby hours I found just one mention of the author of *The Mind of Future Man*: a note reminding all concerned of the new address, actually a PO Box number in Rangoon, to which all communications were to be sent. A scribbled note indicated that the advance due on publication had been sent there, though not until after the end of hostilities; and that was the end of business between Messrs Cook and Cary and Hugh Dearden Esquire.

With the mounting excitement which befits a disciple of Sherlock Holmes, I retired to my club-like Edwardian apartment in Chiswick and got out my box of maps. First I underlined in the typescript what clues I could find in Conway's last interrupted paragraph to the location of Shangri-La's British branch. *Sea. Monks. Suitably isolated. Not two hundred and fifty miles from London.* Seaside and isolated must surely mean an island. Not two hundred and fifty miles probably meant more than two hundred. I got out a compass and began making pencil circles, coming rapidly to a conclusion which had already settled tentatively in my mind as the result of a Welsh driving holiday some five years previously. There was only one stretch of coast which brought me, just short of two hundred and fifty miles from London, to a small private island which might well suit Shangri-La's purpose. That island was Caldy, a mile off the coast opposite the quiet old watering place of Tenby. What was more, it was already inhabited by a colony of Cistercian monks who lived in the most stylish monastery of my experience (which was admittedly limited so far as such establishments were concerned).

I contrived to leave the office for a long weekend, and on the following Friday morning took an extremely early train from Paddington. Tenby was still out of season, but occasional flat-bottomed motor boats could be persuaded to make the ten-minute trip to the island, where I was left on the beach soon after lunch with the strict warning that I must be on the jetty by five-thirty for the return journey. 'Otherwise,' grinned the boatman, 'you'll have to bed down with the reverend fathers.'

Caldy is a flat little island, about a mile by half a mile, and all the soft ground on it is cultivated by the Cistercians who live in the attractive nineteenth-century buildings at the south end. From almost any point on the footpaths the Pembrokeshire coast is visible, and as I paced my way to the monastery I could see Tenby draping itself along the cliffs, retaining most of the charm it must have had in Jane Austen's day. Caldy seemed an exhilarating place to be, but this was spring: I could well imagine it in the wilds of winter, bleak and windswept and chill to the feet. Ringing the monastery bell, I sought and surprisingly quickly obtained an interview with the abbot, a remarkably well-nourished cleric of nearer sixty than fifty. In his brown cassock, with a shiny leather belt encircling his ample meridian, he reminded me of Friar Tuck, though I soon sensed a shrewdness which belied his open features.

I came straight to the point, describing my researches into a mysterious typescript which had come into my possession and which hinted at the possibility of an independent religious community on Caldy during World War Two. Could the abbot confirm any establishment of that kind?

He smiled. 'You are going back through the guardianship of at least three of my predecessors, all of them buried on the island. On the other hand, from 1945 I was a novice here myself.'

'That's possibly too late for my purpose.'

'Possibly but not necessarily. You see, although I was in the navy during the war I made several visits here during my leaves. To make sure, so to speak, that my place was being kept warm.' He rubbed his double chin. 'So I think I do know the people you mean. It was probably in the spring of 1941 – a very cold spring, I remember, for one just back from the Mediterranean – that I met a young Chinaman here. At least, I think that's what he was. The then abbot had given him permission to do as he wished with some ruinous buildings at the north end of the island. They originally constituted a kind of farm, but they had long fallen into disuse.'

'Are they still there?'

'Oh yes, but they have suffered several partial renovations. We sell ice cream from them in the summer, not to mention our famous pottery and herbal perfume. I wonder why so many monasteries seem to spend their spare time in the manufacture of items which cater to the sophisticated tastes we're supposed to abhor? I expect it's to show that we're human after all. At least we haven't got around to a liqueur yet, though a proposal has been made.'

'How many people did the Chinaman have with him?'

'Oh, nine or ten at most, at that time. Two or three of the men shaved their heads: I think of them sometimes when I come across today's Hare Krishna followers. They had a similar wish to share the blessings of nature with others, though one blessing I think they hadn't counted on was the English winter. I remember the abbot said he'd offered them shelter within the monastery walls, but they'd refused. They looked fairly depressed when I met them, but they didn't seem to be poor. That was a miserable time, though – the low point of the entire war – and stuck on this tiny island they seemed to lack purpose and direction, even if they just about managed to keep warm. The whole nation was fired with enthusiasm to beat Hitler, and didn't need any new religions, because the old ones had come back into their own. Whatever message the Chinaman and his chaps wanted to bring, simply got lost in the shuffle. You can imagine how absurd they looked, preaching on Sunday evenings under the Tenby market arch. Not really understanding the English, they seemed at a loss to get on the right track.'

'Were they all oriental?'

'Pretty well. I remember an Englishman with them just once; he can't have stayed long. An elegant, rather saintly-looking man with a slight twitch in one eye. Might have been shell-shocked. I can see his face now.'

'You wouldn't remember the leader's name?'

'Oh, indeed I do. We all called him Luke. It wasn't

quite his name, but something like it.' I must have sighed rather obviously, for he went on: 'I should like to know more about this rather belated investigation of yours. Perhaps you would care to enlighten me over tea.'

I was glad to: at least I had the chance of an appreciative audience. The tea was peppermint, the cakes unexpectedly toothsome and home-made. It took me half an hour to tell the whole story, and I don't think he interrupted me once. At the end he nodded slowly to himself and said, 'I wish I had found more time to question Luke about his beliefs. You see, several of us here have read about Shangri-La and been inspired by the concept. However, our land here is infertile, the weather very chancy, and we haven't so far discovered a miracle herb.'

We talked on about Luke and his crew, and the man with them who might have been Conway, but there wasn't very much more detail to be had. Clearly the abbot, for all his benevolence, had found them in some way unsympathetic, probably because as the little band increased it took on what we would call dropouts. The abbot was a little ashamed of his own attitude towards the vagrants. 'I was a young man then and very keen on the more spectacular rituals of the Church: brass and gilt and stained glass and all that. This lot frankly seemed to let the side down. They gave our island a look of Cold Comfort Farm. Of course, they may well have tried to redecorate their premises and not been able to get the stuff because of the war. It was a cheerless time all round.'

'And what became of this singular foundation?'

The abbot threw up both hands in the air and clapped them on his knees. 'When I came back to stay, in 1945, they'd all gone. I never knew how or why.'

'Didn't you ask?'

'It seemed less important than you might think. You see, the old abbot was dying. It was hand-over time.

There was a lot of uncertainty among us: even I had come back minus a leg, and I was preoccupied with getting used to the false one which serves me so well now. To be quite honest, I never gave a thought to the fate of Luke and his friends until somebody brought it up in casual conversation. Even then it was the beginning of another bad winter, so it wasn't until the weather eased many weeks later that I took my sticks and hobbled round to inspect the old farm buildings. They were in a terrible state by then: the roof had fallen in at one point. No clues are left there now, I assure you.'

'And no records remain at all?'

'The only mention I've seen is in Father Tiplady's journal. He was my distant predecessor, the one who died in 1945.' The abbot went to a cupboard, selected and drew out a heavy ledger, blew the dust off it, and sat down. His long index finger riffled the pages. 'He wrote very little about Luke and his crowd, perhaps because he thought his successor might disapprove. But here, I think, is a relevant passage – ah, yes – for May 1945, three months before I was demobbed.'

It was a paragraph of spidery handwriting. I read:

May 21 The Tregony buildings have begun to look very much the worse for wear, and I fear may have to be pulled down. I feel guilty that during the recent extended period of privation I allowed our guests to remain even in such conditions, but we have all done unusual things since 1939. We trust that Luke and his friends will prosper in Spain, where at least they will have one less enemy to fight. The climate here has worked against them, and I am sure it took them by surprise. Their funding is still a puzzle to me. I wonder why I have always felt further means were always at their disposal, but were not flaunted because that might have caused enquiry.

I looked up. 'And that's all?'

'All that I know, though you are welcome to look

through the four other volumes which remain. Regrettably, those for 1942 and 1943 were either mislaid or destroyed. Probably the latter. A stray bomb sliced off a corner of this building, you know. The corner in which I am sitting.' He chuckled.

I rose to leave. 'I don't think I need to miss the last boat on that account. I'm sure you've read them all thoroughly. You've established that Luke and his friends were here: that's all I wanted to know.'

'I see that you intend to pursue your strange enquiry to the bitter end.'

'Do you really think I could stop now?'

'No. No more could I, if I had two legs and were in your position. And some day I hope to hear the outcome. But I am a little puzzled about your motives. You do not seem to me a religious man, and you have no personal axe to grind. Is it mere curiosity which drives you on?'

'I hope not. Rather a consciousness of something lacking in myself, something that Conway may have found. I hope to persuade him to share it with me.'

The abbot nodded and smiled. 'There are more things in heaven and earth, I'm sure, than we have dreamed of here on Caldy. They simply await discovery. What Shangri-La may have achieved, if it exists, is only an extension of man's other achievements, a superstructure built on the foundations of its predecessors.'

'Would you counsel me not to go?'

'By no means. Only to prepare yourself for the possibility of disappointment. After all, your strange story may yet prove to be an elaborate hoax. Or the Valley of Blue Moon may have been buried under an avalanche. Worse still, it may have been corrupted and spoiled. But hope is the best kind of religion there is.' His eyes twinkled a little. 'Meanwhile, one certain boon and blessing to mankind in my view is our home-made dandelion coffee. Let me offer you a cup before you leave. Don't you worry, you have twenty minutes, and if I ring the bell once, the boat will wait.'

8

Nicholas Brent's Narrative (1980):

'THIS IS NOT ENTIRELY A WELCOMING COUNTRY'

Entries from my travel journal:

October 15. I don't know what I expected of Rangoon, but certainly none of my fantasies were satisfied by our first day here. After all the strings that had to be pulled to get us into Burma at all, my impression as we drove from the airport was of a bedraggled and humid Manchester, the inner city being heavy with boring-looking Victorian buildings. The difference is that dark and emaciated orientals jam the streets, and you don't see many cars. The hotel has an international three-star rating which it doesn't seem to deserve. We had been firmly told that all payments must be made in foreign currency, which it seems is the only condition on which visitors are allowed into Burma at all these days. Even so you have to get special pink passes that are not always given. Luckily, great newspapers sometimes have influence in these matters, though the final arrangements had to be made not at the Burmese Diplomatic Mission in London but by the *Clarion*'s man on the spot in Rangoon, a 'stringer' who is allowed to live here by virtue of a Burmese wife, who they say he never sees. 'It's five or six years since I met Ralph Abel,' said the foreign editor in Fleet Street, 'but I can't imagine he's changed. Trust him about as far as you can throw him. Not an inch further. Value him only for knowing how to wangle the permits and fix the transport.'

My room is on the sixth floor, which is high for Burma, and I can see how the city is laid out in geometric patterns. In the dim moist atmosphere it's like a ghost city, the ghosts being those of British colonialists. It was they who designed the pattern of the streets and erected so many buildings that look like Victorian railway stations or citadels of insurance. Unlike callous modern planners, however, they took care to leave room for the elegant religious effects which already existed, ensuring in particular that the business section was kept clear of a cluster of sacred spires called the Shwedagon, which is the central point of Rangoon's spiritual life but a good four miles from the city centre. The million and a half inhabitants are mostly poor and can't possibly be healthy in this god-awful climate. I understand it won't dry out much until we're well north of the cities. It's raining now: Abel says it will clear tomorrow, though even then it will stay sticky. He met us at the airport, and certainly knows how things work. I never expected to get myself or my baggage into a communist country with so few formalities. He apologized for not bringing the Land Rovers, but it seems there's a government prohibition against foreigners driving in the stretch of country north of Rangoon, so we have to go through Mandalay by train and pick up the vehicles as far north as Myitkyina. I hope we can trust him; he assures us that his arrangements are immaculate.

At dinner one couldn't easily escape curry, so I ate very abstemiously. Abel joined us. On his card it says he's an independent agent. God knows for what commodity: white slaves perhaps, he looks the part. Shifty and seedy and somehow out of date, like a character in a Somerset Maugham story, left behind when the British evacuated. Perhaps he's a remittance man who can't go home and spends his time running brothels in Asian bazaars – the sort of chap who ruined the Empire. He claims to have been born in Gloucester and sports an Old Etonian tie to his threadbare white Airey and Wheeler tropical suit. Why he wears a tie at all in this muggy heat I can't imagine: the hotel isn't properly air-conditioned even in the public rooms, and Abel was constantly passing a finger round the inside of his collar, an unedifying sight. His main characteristic is clearly an eye for the main chance. I'd put him at about fifty, but with thin wiry people it's difficult to tell.

Abel spent the last part of dinner trying to divine our real motives. He clearly doesn't believe the official announcement, which rather vaguely suggested a reconnaissance for a future television series. Luckily he seems to know even less about northern Burma than we do from our crash course; until a couple of years ago he was based in Hong Kong, which presumably grew too hot for him. Lord knows what stories he provides for the *Clarion*, as he seems even less interested than I am in international politics, and there can't be much else to report on from here.

I am amazed, as we sit here on the brink of what we hope will be a great adventure, how easily everything finally came together after more than a month of depression and discouragement. The fact is that Elizabeth's urge to find her father had been too well publicized for too long, so that everyone thought that we'd have got our backing much earlier if our proposal had been sound. The BBC's very firm turndown was leaked to the press, and I can't deny it came as a shock, but the management was smarting from the fiasco of an expensive attempt two years back to track down the Yeti: not even a footprint had been found. As for the ITV companies, they're always a problem because they won't finance expeditions as a group, and individual programme controllers have whims which are more political than creative. Even Bruce Thomson, who seemed the likeliest prospect in Fleet Street, had a lot of trouble persuading his Board; when we finally got their verdict it was that they would provide only half the finance, and that conditionally on our raising the other half from non-competitive sources. The weeks passed agonizingly quickly as we all tried, and failed, partly because of the *Clarion*'s insistence on controlling all the publicity after our return. Then one day I walked into my office and found in the foyer, seeming to absorb all the available air, a huge man in a red woolly shirt and a Stetson hat. It was, of course, Jim Gentry, and I need hardly say more than that; having heard through Warlock of our problem, he'd come to offer an open chequebook. We refused his total commitment, because we didn't want our job to be that easy, and because we thought we might value the outlet which the *Clarion* would provide. But we left Gentry in no doubt of our gratitude.

Big Jim was even willing, it turned out, to attend the *Clarion*'s official launching party and be photographed shaking hands with Bruce as the rest of us clustered round looking (in my case at least) rather sheepish. When the press had left, the exploring party joined its two financiers for dinner in a little private room at the Chesterfield, and over coffee we briefly discussed our real intentions. In fact, it seemed that there was little left unresolved; but during a silence which might have been awkward, Elizabeth found something to say:

'I want to tell you a story which I never even confided to Nick because it isn't conclusive and could mean nothing at all. But now that we've come so far, it does seem to slot in, rather like a keystone. When I was a tiny tot I remember sitting on Daddy's knee one evening while he was trying to clear his desk. Not surprisingly several batches of paper fell on to the carpet, and when I picked some of them up I came across a photograph which didn't seem to be attached to anything else. You couldn't make anything out very distinctly, because it was a black-and-white snapshot and rather blurred, but what it showed was some peculiar-looking white buildings backed by a mountainside. On the terrace in front was a man wearing a strange kind of flat sun-hat. His face was in shadow, but he was wearing . . . well, what looked like a long silken dressing gown. I suppose it was the hat, and the fact that the eaves of the buildings finished in long points, that made me ask whether the picture came from a fairy story. Daddy laughed and said he didn't know for sure, but it might be. Then he took pity on my bewilderment and said the man was a college friend of his father's, a man who'd been to some pretty strange places in his life. This man had paid a call on my father shortly before I was born, and then set off on more travels, never to be heard of again. No more was said, but I always remembered the picture, even though I never saw it again for more than thirty-five years. Last month it fell out of a book I was dusting. The book was Heinrich Harrer's *Seven Years in Tibet*, which incidentally has a picture of a man in just the same kind of hat. Here it is – and here's the photograph.'

With instinctive drama Elizabeth produced her evidence, and we all craned our necks forward. I have to admit that the snap, now very faded indeed, could have been taken almost anywhere: the first impression the buildings gave me was of the Austrian Tyrol. But as soon as we had been allowed enough time to doubt, Elizabeth smiled and turned the snap over. On the reverse, in neat old-fashioned handwriting, were the words: *Dreams sometimes can come true. H.D.*

'And I've checked,' said Elizabeth. 'Hugh Dearden and my grandfather were at college together.'

After that we all got quite excited on our after-dinner drinks.

The agreement was that discreet but comprehensive photographs were to be taken of Shangri-La, if we found it; that the more adventurous parts of the journey were to be covered by cine-film; and that on our return Elizabeth and I would lend our reputations by affidavit to the published account of the journey. It was fully established, however, that no public mention of Shangri-La was to be made without the consent of its inhabitants and that its exact location was always to be kept secret. (In this connection I should mention that in giving earlier an apparently verbatim version of Conway's typescript I did, in fact, omit a single sentence containing an exact directional bearing from Ramjigoval to Myitkyina, and an indication of the route back to Shangri-La by which one particular dry valley may be singled out from the scores in that particular slope of the mountain plateau.) The team which was to fill our Land Rovers would be completed by a volunteer from the National Mountaineering Society who had been selected, briefed, and sworn to secrecy by the *Clarion*. His name was Chris Cole, and during our single meeting I recognized in him a healthy though friendly scepticism which would no doubt act as a useful corrective to our excitement.

Before packing I had another consultation with my Wimpole Street man. He conceded that I had been behaving myself and that the latest X-rays showed some improvement over the previous ones. He still felt that my best bet was an immediate operation for the removal of part of my pancreas. I promised to think about it, but two days later I rang him to say I'd take a rain-check. The new direction in which my life had moved was in itself a violent spur to the vital juices, and apart from the occasional twinge I felt better than I had for years. Even if the operation was entirely successful I didn't fancy the recovery period: I know how lousy you can feel for a year or more after an operation of that kind. Meanwhile this trip was a now or never enterprise; once we let the pressure drop, we might talk ourselves out of it.

On the evening before we left London I put through a telephone call to Warlock, and we had a long, jokey chat. It was with very mixed feelings that I eventually hung up. I knew that I might never speak again to an unexpected friend whose wry humour and even wryer view of life I truly welcomed. It was true that although a tough old bird he was past the normal age of explorers in strange lands. But then, so was I. So I had found time before packing my bags for ten days at a health clinic. I came out feeling, as they say, like gang busters, nearly a stone lighter and bursting with energy. I could only hope that the golden glow might see me through the next two months.

Simon's here, of course, and I have to say I wish he weren't. I never feel at ease with him around. He almost blackmailed us into allowing him to come, by saying that if we didn't he'd write a piece for another paper throwing cold water on the whole enterprise. We couldn't let Bruce in for that, and in any case Simon had some sort of claim.

Quite unpredictably, during that last rushed week, Simon had come round to see me. He rang first, one evening at about ten, from the phone box round the corner. He said he was in the neighbourhood and had checked first that my lights were on. I could hardly refuse to invite him up, but in the few minutes before he arrived I had time to wonder why I found the prospect of his visit so unattractive. It wasn't only that he persisted in calling me Uncle Nick, even though I was only eight or nine years the elder; he would have found some equally childish way of expressing his resentment of *any* prospective brother-in-law. I think most of my problem with him was that he never found it easy to smile. It seemed to me, indeed, that his pale blue eyes showed no feeling for me except thinly veiled contempt; and his straight flaxen hair always put me in mind of the Hitler Youth. No single career had ever attracted him. When young he tried his hand at this and that, but showed no scruple in his frequent applications to his father for the odd hundred pounds, which of course never came back. Luckily the river house was in trust, or he would have sold his share in it as soon as he came of age. Simon lived in a world where fact and fiction got themselves inextricably mixed up. If you happened to ask him where he was going for the weekend, he was quite likely to say with conviction that he'd been invited to join a party flying down to Cairo in a Lear jet; or that he was having dinner with Elizabeth Taylor to discuss a script he'd written for her; or that he would be incommunicado, right up against a publisher's deadline for a novel which had brought him a huge advance. No further evidence of these enterprises ever came to hand, and one gradually came to assume that everything he said was invented on the spur of the moment to give his life an importance it would not otherwise possess.

It soon became clear that his desire that evening was to ingratiate himself. 'Look here, Uncle Nick,' he said, as he lounged in the fireside chair swilling a balloon-glassful of my Hine Antique, 'I think we ought to call a truce, don't you?'

'I didn't know we were at war.'

'Oh, come on, everybody knows you don't want me along on this safari. I'm sorry if I cramp your style, but you must admit it's a bit hard to deny me a chance of joining an expedition to look for my own father.'

'That's perfectly reasonable, if it's your only motive.'

'Well, I'd like to think that Elizabeth was being taken care of properly. After all, she is my sister. Blood counts for something.'

'Even at half strength? You did have different mothers.'

He stood up and drained his glass. Hine Antique should be sipped: I winced, but after all I'm no longer allowed to drink it myself. 'I think that makes my altruism all the more commendable,' he grinned. Let's face it, I'm not demanding a share of the spoils.'

'What spoils?'

For a moment I thought I had provoked him into some sort of admission, but Simon was not easily caught out. 'Jade, I suppose,' he said. 'Isn't the north end of Burma just the place for it? We may stub our toes against a great boulder of the stuff. I've been reading up so that I'll recognize it.'

There was nothing else I could say. Simon is an equal member of our merry band, and here he is in Rangoon tonight, though not with us: he went out to see the night life, whatever that means, and Abel volunteered to show him. It's bed for me, in the hope that I can sleep below the very noisy fan. We have to be up at five and away before six.

October 16. It's just as well after all that Simon did come, though when he joined us at breakfast Elizabeth was clearly dismayed by his jaundiced appearance. By his own admission he got to bed at two after drinking several glasses of the local liqueur out of an unlabelled bottle. The food at breakfast was not such as to pick anybody up, but at least the coffee was strong. Then Ralph Abel turned up – incredibly he was wearing the same collar and tie as last night – to announce, with what seemed to me more like malice than regret, that Chris Cole wouldn't be joining us. Coming off the 747 during the stopover in Delhi, he had fallen down the aircraft steps and smashed his ankle. He would be in the hospital for several days and unable to put any weight on his right foot for as many weeks. Waiting for a replacement seemed unthinkable as our pink passes would run out and might not be renewed; but it was perhaps a little foolhardy of Elizabeth to announce so promptly that the three of us would go on alone.

For a moment I was afraid that Abel was going to offer himself as fourth member, but instead he murmured that one of the native drivers who would be meeting us in Myitkyina with the Land Rovers was a mountaineer of some experience and would be of general all-round usefulness. Though I had my reservations, it seemed on the whole sensible to accept this offer, as the boy evidently had no family responsibilities and could be with us for however long it took. The drawback is that it means letting a stranger in on any secrets we may find. Still, when we get to Myitkyina I can always give back word, and fob the boy off with a handsome tip. After all, we're not expecting anything but an easy route, once we find it. No jungle, no arduous climbing that we know of, no dangerous animals, and with luck four wheels will take us to within twenty miles of our goal. If we don't find what we're looking for, we simply come back, and that's it.

I was more than a little surprised to hear that the train journey to Mandalay would occupy eleven hours. Elizabeth, on the other hand, was happy that we would learn something of Burmese geography. The tracks more or less followed the Irrawaddy, and I must admit that the journey was interesting if not very comfortable. The rolling-stock must once upon a time have been rather grand, but now it lurched and jolted so unpredictably that we were often astonished to find ourselves still on the track. Our first-class compartment, though much cleaner than one now expects from British Rail, had the very worn look of faded plush, and the guard seemed to take no notice when it filled up at the first stop with natives who didn't look as if they could possibly have afforded the fare. The only air conditioning came from leaving the window open. The great plus was reclining seats: they weren't contoured, but at least they gave me the chance to nod off occasionally.

The journey had begun promptly at seven-thirty, and in the already steaming terminal there was much excitement as friends and relations were waved off. For a supposed express the train stopped rather frequently, sometimes at tiny halts with no sign of civilization. No refreshments were available on the train itself, but at every station a hundred or more passengers leaped out to avail themselves of whatever the primitive platform cafeterias had to offer. Others simply leaned out of the windows to buy from pedlars with trays. We scarcely needed Abel's advice to stick to our digestive biscuits and cans of warm cola: one look at the slimy cakes was enough.

At Pyinmana there was a formal lunch stop, but by then it was far too hot to think of eating.

Elizabeth was busy all day making notes for a series of articles commissioned by *National Geographic*. I made a few entries in my own log, but the truth is that there was little to report. Everywhere we looked, whether or not we could see the Irrawaddy itself, there seemed to be swampy water with buffalo and elephant working in it under the command of teenage boys who all looked like Sabu. After lunch the air got a bit drier, and the condition of the line seemed to improve, probably because the further we got from Rangoon, the less use it got. We were surprised at the number of intersections: the British again, I suppose.

A few minutes after six-thirty, not very late, we arrived in Mandalay.

Certainly it's a city that deserves to have a song written about it, though possibly not that one, which gives a heroic sense to a community which is essentially gentle and abstracted. Though Mandalay basically dates back no further than the nineteenth century, and its central plain is as boring as that suggests, it is decorated by hundreds, possibly even thousands, of quite elegant buildings, mostly shrines and palaces. All its traditions, not surprisingly, are alien to western eyes, but they're perfectly friendly. As with Rangoon, the people make it untidy – so many of them lolling about the streets with little or nothing to do; but administratively the city is kept clean, and has not so far been contaminated by supermarkets or any form of advertising. We drove to the hotel in a very ramshackle taxi, and asked to see something of the centre on the way. There were a lot of open shop-fronts and impromptu markets, with instances of skills long dormant or forgotten in England: iron work, woodcarving, and so on. Though a bit too dazed and sticky to take it all in, we could not be unaware that we were participating in one of the world's oldest religious cultures. Buddhas loomed everywhere, in all shapes and sizes, though the new ones in the little shops have a disappointing air of Woolworth about them and are probably all made in Taiwan, trade knowing no political barriers. Very little outward sign, by the way, of the expected communist influence.

After a blessed bath and an unexpectedly tolerable dinner in an hotel half-heartedly fashioned after the American style, Abel surprised us by saying that a friend of his would join us for a drink, a friend who lived in Mandalay. On the stroke of ten a curious apparition minced its way across the foyer to the couches where we were reclining over coffee and brandy – in Simon's case rather too much brandy. Mincing is perhaps the wrong description for a person so short and floppily plump. Like Abel, he wore a white tropical suit, but his was freshly laundered, and to set it off he carried a silver-topped cane. He gleamed in the dim light, not only because of the suit but because there wasn't a single hair on his glistening head, not even behind the ears: he looked rather like an overgrown baby. Even more remarkable, I saw on closer inspection, were his eyes, for one was green and the other blue, a deep blue that had a hypnotic quality to it.

The newcomer was introduced as Dr Pavel Lorenz. In his native Czechoslovakia, Abel said, he had been a surgeon of eminence, but a chronic illness had driven him to Mandalay, which provided the humid climate he needed to survive. Dr Lorenz nodded agreement to all this, with the help of smiles and shrugs: he did speak English after a fashion, it seemed, but preferred to listen. A queer couple he and Abel made, like refugees from a Hollywood melodrama, and sinister ones at that: only mischief, one felt, could have brought such disparate characters together. Though Lorenz may have been badly affected by his illness, I can't say that even in his prime would he have been welcome near me with a scalpel, nor yet with a hot towel. His weird eyes and generally shifty demeanour inspired in me none of the confidence a surgeon should, and the worst thing about him was that he was drenched in cheap scent. I put him at about forty-five, but he may have been older: overweight people seldom look their age.

Simon called for a good many drinks, and I yawned my way through a bad hour of the kind of small talk typical of Europeans who don't know each other but are thrown together in faraway places. Then suddenly, after an extended Ralph Abel discourse on world events, Lorenz fixed me with one eye – I couldn't be sure which – and enunciated a sentence in remarkably clear, if halting, English:

'I understand from my good friend that you set out upon a mysterious expedition.'

I smiled at Abel in the friendliest way I could muster. 'Not mysterious to us, though it's true we've had to make it clear that we are sworn to secrecy, on some points at least. Our main aims have been published, but there are secondary possibilities which . . . well, if they were prematurely revealed the story would be spoiled. If there is a story.'

'Which there probably isn't,' added Elizabeth.

'I understand,' said Lorenz. 'You leave me with the most interesting . . . speculations.' He leaned back into his creaking basket chair and lit a brown cigarette. Then, since nobody else spoke, he puffed smoke into the air and thrust his round smooth head forward at me. 'I do hope that your adventure does not prove unwise. This is not entirely a welcoming country. In the desert wilds there are a thousand dangers which the unwary may not suspect until the worst has happened. All the caution you can imagine may not be too much.'

All this, delivered in a light lisping tone which seemed suddenly very sinister, struck me as quite unnecessarily ominous. I replied: 'I assure you that we shall take every care.'

Lorenz laughed, and I thought at once of Conway's description of Chang giving a laugh with no mirth in it, the kind orientals use as a face-saver when further response might be embarrassing. 'I shall ask no more questions. But I shall think them, and perhaps one day I shall be able to read all the answers.'

As soon as seemed polite, or perhaps even sooner than that, I broke up the uneasy party and went to my airless room. Trying to get a double one in Burma is useless without some proof of marriage, and it was too hot for physical closeness in any case. I showered again, and stretched out in bed with a sigh of relief. Then I discovered the absence of my gun, the Biretta in whose use I had reluctantly taken so many tedious lessons. Before going down to dinner I had placed it carefully under my pillow. Now it was nowhere to be found.

I went along to tell Elizabeth, who was no more than slightly upset: she said it was the kind of thievery one must expect in these parts, and I was lucky to be out of the room when the burglar found his way in. Luckily we had taken the precaution of bringing with us no copies of the Conway typescript, the essence of which we knew by heart; Elizabeth had taken down a few significant details in shorthand. Simon, of course, had to be given a copy but we drummed into him the importance of keeping it to himself, and with Elizabeth's unwilling agreement I arranged for it to be doctored, to the extent of lacking a few important geographical directions. I didn't think he had it with him, though short of searching his room I couldn't be sure.

I stood thoughtfully by Elizabeth's bed, fingering the mosquito net. 'Do you want to stay the night?' she asked.

I smiled. 'Yes, but we both need all the sleep we can get. I was just wondering . . . why Lorenz wasn't invited to dinner?'

'You think that while we were eating, he was up here searching our rooms?'

'I can't think he had many pressing engagements elsewhere. Any sign that your stuff's been disturbed?'

A grimace was her reply. 'I can't be sure. I just shoved them all into the briefcase, higgledy piggledy. And I didn't bring my fingerprint outfit.' Her expression became suddenly serious. 'If you're right, Abel must be involved too.'

I shrugged. 'They seem to fit together well. A couple of first-class international parasites. They must have pricked up their ears at the thought of well-heeled strangers trekking into what looks like desolate and uninteresting country. In their eyes there could only be one motive.'

'Gold?'

'Who knows? Even if they don't know about the deposits at Shangri-La there could have been other rich mineral strikes not far from here. And of course they wouldn't believe in any more altruistic motive. Not everybody has the betterment of mankind as his chief aim in life.'

Elizabeth lay back on her pillows. 'I didn't give a thought to this kind of trouble. Let's hope you're jumping to conclusions.'

'I hope so too. The gun was probably taken by a sneak thief, Abel and Lorenz may be holier than Moses, and Simon will finish up the hero of the hour. In any case, the only thing we can usefully do now is get some sleep.'

9

Nicholas Brent's Narrative (1980)

'I WAS NEVER SO ASTONISHED IN MY LIFE'

October 17. I don't think I was jumping to conclusions.

The morning began well enough. Abel reported at breakfast that the Land Rovers were already on their way to Myitkyina, so that they would be well tested by the time we picked them up. We had a couple of hours for more sightseeing, but we cut that short because the air here takes some getting used to: just a shade drier than Rangoon, but damned hot and sticky. It will be a relief to go north into the wide desert plains which connect Burma with Assam and Tibet.

Precious few of Mandalay's half million people were on the streets. We concluded that they must all be home on their prayer mats, for never in any city in the world did I see more religious symbols, and that despite the communist takeover. Elizabeth and I had a quick tour of the famous palace, superbly ornate with all the elegance of an Egyptian tomb. Simon didn't even bother to come with us. When we got back, in urgent need of a shower, he was lounging on the hotel verandah with Abel and Lorenz, holding a tall glass of some pale green drink. We were astonished to learn that Lorenz proposed to join our flight, being in need of a change and never having seen this part of Burma from the air; he and Abel will return by train tomorrow.

At two-thirty a taxi took us out to the tiny airport, where we piled into a De Havilland six-seater which had seen better days. The pilot was an inscrutable type, and for a moment I thought of the air kidnap which fifty years ago set Conway off on his adventure. However, once the engines whirred into life, the fellow made short work of two hundred miles, and set us down soon after four on the desolate airstrip of Myitkyina, the most northerly Burmese outpost in which modern facilities can be obtained. We had passed over various kinds of wooded and mountainous terrain, watching the Irrawaddy virtually dry up before our eyes; but what really excited us was our first glimpse of those northern deserts, stretching emptily away from us for more than a hundred miles before the rippled Himalayan foothills began to close in.

By the time we had finished unloading ourselves and our gear into a little fleet of vehicles, even more battered than the ones available in Mandalay, I felt more than a shade depressed. This sandy wasteland scarcely seemed a favourable launching point for a great adventure. The outskirts of Myitkyina, as we rattled towards them, consisted of a dismal collection of beige-coloured mud huts; the smell was appalling; and we could not believe that the centre contained the modern hotel we had been promised. In fact, we later decided that the description could be thought fair: it rather depended on one's definition of the word modern. The community's chief claim to historical significance is as the starting-point in 1942 of a tragic trek westward. Burmese peasants were fleeing into India from the Japanese advance. The distance they aimed to travel was no more than two thousand miles, which should have been feasible. Yet twenty thousand of them died. The reason for this castastrophe was so simple as to be terrifying. It rained for ten days, and ten days is the incubation period for malaria. By the time the rain stopped, almost all the refugees were gibbering with fever. Those few who finally staggered across the Indian border had seen incidents which turned their stomachs and their minds. If the tragic caravan had headed north-north-west, the refugees might well have found Shangri-La instead of a gibbering death.

Myitkyina did not improve on closer inspection. It was a busy enough place, but somehow insubstantial and dusty, like one of the wood-and-canvas communities of the American west. One straggling main street holds all the business and shopping amenities, including two quite respectable cafés and a corrugated iron cinema which on the evening we arrived was showing some incomprehensibly titled Burmese musical. There are also several churches, but on nothing like the scale of Mandalay or Rangoon. Almost every structure looked just as likely as not to fall down in the next high wind. When twilight approached the scene became even more garish, with bright neon lights picking out the flowing white gowns of the passers-by and also attracting myriads of mosquitoes which clustered round the lamps in dense clouds. Luckily we had all had the right jabs.

'The end of the world,' whispered Abel as we looked back from the hotel doorway. 'Or perhaps you know better?'

It was a comfort to see one of our shiny white Land Rovers in the hotel car park. The beaming driver was the young Burmese who, Abel now said, was perfectly willing to replace our injured mountaineer. His name was Pegu, and he reported that the vehicle had behaved itself perfectly on the way from Mandalay apart from requiring a small adjustment to the carburettor. In case we doubted his skill he carried with him a diploma from the technical college of Rangoon: he displayed it twice and had to be persuaded not to do so again. We invited him to join us at dinner, which so far as we were concerned was a sorry meal: the cooking in this part of the world apparently takes quite a bit of getting used to, so since we had no desire to spend the next few days in physical distress we stuck to fruit and some cold meat with boiled potatoes.

It was during dinner that we heard of the latest development in our chapter of accidents. Abel took a phone call, and came back with a grave face to announce that the second Land Rover, now three hours overdue, would not be arriving for several days, as a hundred miles south it had driven into a ditch and broken a front axle. A spare had been urgently sent for, but it was not even sure that there was one in Mandalay. Most of our equipment was coming along in a relief car, but no other reliable four-wheel-drive was available in Myitkyina, and anything less rugged was useless for our purpose.

Elizabeth, Simon and I retired to the bar to consider the problem. Now that we were on the spot, Elizabeth thought, the terrain seemed much less formidable than she had expected, and the distance we had to cover was not great. She was for ditching part of the equipment, going ahead in one vehicle, and turning back if things got tough. Simon agreed with her; I was more doubtful, but certainly didn't fancy hanging about in Myitkyina for the best part of a week. Eventually it was decided to accept the majority vote, especially since we were due, fifty miles to the north-west, to pass through a mining belt where help would be on hand if we found ourselves *in extremis*.

When the others retired I found myself left with Abel, and decided to test him by telling him about the theft of the gun. He was at his suavest, seemed genuinely astonished, and said we should have registered a complaint with the hotel management. Unfortunately the law in Burma was such that there was no possibility of buying a replacement weapon without considerable formality in Rangoon. But it was unthinkable, said Abel, that we should proceed into the unknown with even one gun less than our very modest roster – Simon had a pistol and there were two rifles among the equipment – and so he insisted on loaning me his own silvery little Birmingham, together with four packets of bullets which he ran upstairs to fetch. There seemed nothing for it but to thank him profusely.

Abel left me at ten-thirty, and as I made for the stairs I was surprised to find Elizabeth on the way down. Her room was too hot for sleep, she said. We sauntered outside, wearing the absurd-looking mosquito helmets which the hotel provides for the night protection of western visitors: they are light but stiff affairs which cover the whole head and clip on over the shoulders, a vital precaution at night in rainy seasons, when throngs of insects hover round the lights of the town. In fact most of the cheap neons had been turned off: nobody in Myitkyina stays up late. It would have been dark in our part of the street but for naked torches attached to each corner of the hotel for the purpose of frizzling up any insects which got too inquisitive. These, together with a dim moonlight, were enough for us to take a short circular constitutional, just as we had at the Beverly Wilshire. As we came to the end of the second circuit, gazing into the northern darkness and feeling on our arms the warm wind from the plains, we spoke of the mysterious things which had happened so far and the dangers we might face during the next few days. The thoughts of both of us were clearly on Ralph Abel. 'Are you sure,' asked Elizabeth, 'that you don't want to change your mind and invite him to tag along?'

'Absolutely not. That's what he's waiting for. We might find ourselves desperate for an extra pair of hands, but I wouldn't be happy if they were Abel's. Instinctively I don't trust him, and that's that.'

'Quite right,' boomed a familiar but unexpected voice. 'The question is, do you trust me?'

Probably I was never so astonished in my life. Into the light, from the other side of the hotel doorway, strode an absurd figure which could have stepped out of a space fiction film. A hand came up to remove the helmet, and there before us was Irving Warlock, as large as life and twice as welcome. 'I was so good at it last time,' he announced, 'that I've turned professional and gone into the surprise business.'

Elizabeth was speechless. I could only say 'Good God.'

'Perhaps he is, but I wouldn't bank on it. And if I were us, I wouldn't talk so loud. In this stillness, sound could carry even to Mr Abel's room at the back.'

He was right, of course. We retired to a very dingy café across the street and sat with cans of beer in front of us while we heard his explanation. He really had had no intention of following us; but a couple of weeks ago Jim Gentry came back into his life and asked if he'd like to come along on an expedition to Burma to suss out a TV mini-series which he was thinking of financing on the real River Kwai story.

'He gave me forty-eight hours to make up my mind, and if things had gone right we'd have been back in the States by now. But Gentry got delayed and we didn't get to our Rangoon stopover till the day before you. So I couldn't resist parting company with him there and finding out how you were getting on. I intended to wish you well from there, but I thought there might be some advantage in watching you from a distance on the way north. When you'd taken the train I flew ahead of you to Mandalay. Last night I sat in the balcony and watched you have dinner. Today I was up at dawn to get the train, but as I left the hotel I saw your Land Rover set off. I thought you planned to have two.'

'We did. It seems the second was wrecked on the way here.'

Warlock rubbed his chin. 'Maybe,' he said, 'but there only ever was one on the road. The train followed behind it all the way here. Came into town an hour before dark.'

That was something else to think about, but what could we do? At present Warlock had something else on his mind. 'I take it the young Englishman with you is Simon?' We nodded. 'And Ralph Abel I heard quite a bit about in Rangoon; seems he sails pretty close to the wind there. The one I'd most like to know about is the fellow who joined you for coffee last night.'

'Friend of Abel's. Dr Pavel Lorenz. That's about as much as we know except that he's Czech.'

'Didn't you think you recognized him from somewhere?'

'Well, for a minute, yes, but it couldn't be. I mean, how could anybody forget meeting a man like that?'

'Odd eyes, no hair, white suit?' I nodded, and Warlock nodded back. 'Did you never hear of the old FBI trick? If they had a fellow they wanted to disguise, and he was pretty recognizable by his shape – as Lorenz is – then they'd make all the details of his appearance as outlandish as possible. I mean, a contact lens could account for the odd eyes. Hair can be shaved.'

I was still dazed. 'But who is he?'

'I'm not absolutely sure, but you try in your mind's eye taking that guy and adding instead of taking away. Add an obvious wig, and a big moustache, and maybe even a corset. Then try adding a green suit, the kind that isn't just something you wear but an item so striking that it takes over your personality . . .'

I bit my lip in rapid thought. 'You're right. At least, you may be. That little fellow in Stovepipe Wells.'

'The one who may or may not have tried to push you over a cliff. And came close to running you down. And stole your book.'

'But why?'

'Oh, I can't be sure of all the details, but it's clear to me that our pretty pair think they're on to something –

something important enough for one of them to chase half way round the world last April to find out more about it, and probably to stop you from being part of it. Want to turn back?'

'Not likely.'

Elizabeth said: 'We'd never get another chance.'

I demurred. 'What about the risk to Shangri-La as well as to ourselves?'

'Surely there must be ways of shaking off anybody who tries to follow us? It's pretty open country.'

I looked at Warlock. 'Us includes you?'

'Oh boy, now I've come so far, give me just half a chance.'

'All right then. What we need is a plan of campaign.'

So we worked one out. Let's hope it holds.

October 18. So as to take our rest during the hottest part of the day, we started out early, soon after six. It was a slightly jaundiced farewell; Simon as usual was hung over, Abel was tending to let his mask of amiability drop, and Elizabeth and I were saying as little as possible. Only Pegu had the right air of cheerful excitement. Preserving as much bonhomie as we could, we handed to Abel some stamped postcards which he promised to mail from Rangoon; then we climbed in beside and behind Pegu, who followed our instructions precisely and soon left the graded roads behind. I was carefully watching the milometer, and exactly one mile from the hotel, when an intervening rise had virtually hidden Myitkyina from our view, I told Pegu to pull in and stop. 'What I do wrong?' he asked. I reassured him; it was difficult to believe that those cheerful features held any guile, but it was best to take no chances. We chatted for a few minutes, checking route details on my map. It seems he has a brother working in the jade mines we shall pass en route, so I shan't feel so bad about ditching him there.

Suddenly, over the bump in the road behind us, there soared one of Myitkyina's few taxis from which Warlock promptly dismounted with his familiar grin and a theatrical gesture. Pegu was astonished, as well he might be, whatever his real motives. I explained to him that we must take on another passenger. He said there was no room; I said we must make it. In fact Warlock had brought no more than could be stowed in one carpet bag, and there was quite enough room for three of us along the front seat, though the pressure of our bodies against each other made us all sweat. Pegu clearly suspected some lack of trust in himself, but there was nothing he could do but drive on as commanded. Simon, incidentally, was just as bewildered, as we had had no opportunity to explain to him our overnight change of plan (and probably would not have done so anyway).

From now on, I shall be as sparing as I can with geographical details: suffice to say that we shortly came to a fork. One road would have led towards India; we took the other. Our trail wound its way through some low treeless hills before finding a level valley with a base of brown sand which was almost as firm as the road. We veered on to it experimentally a couple of times. At one point we stopped on a rise and looked back, seeing to our surprise puffs of steam away to the south: the daily train was chugging its way back to Mandalay. The landscape ahead was what the Australians call scrub, a low growth of pale green bushes scraping what existence they could from the barren soil. At one point the road had been washed away by a flood, so for the best part of five miles we had to pick a tortuous way across dunes and around boulders, just occasionally finding our wheels on a patch of dry grass. The bumping was so bad that we took an unscheduled ten-minute stop in order to exercise our joints, and I had the opportunity to acquaint Warlock with our view of the geography. Conway had assumed that the new route from Shangri-La ran directly into Burma, but we had decided that it might first run through a corner of Assam. The boundaries of these two countries and Tibet, or China as it now is, are not too clear even on the most detailed maps; but of all the desert valleys which might fit the bill the most likely was one of half a dozen which began to the east of the Himalayas and crossed in and out of Assam before running south to the barren plateau across which we were now struggling. Of these, my best bet was one which at its north end seemed to have a steep eastern ascent to an unnamed mountain peak which could be Karakal. The oasis of Ramjigoval, we had established, appears on no map whatever, so it must have been abandoned before it had any chance to become official.

We regained the main trail shortly before lunchtime, just as it passed to the east of the last of the villages on the map, clusters of wayside, half-abandoned mud dwellings with nothing to distinguish one from the other, nor any apparent reason why men and women should ever have wished to live in them. The trail was clearly kept open only by the traffic from the jade mines: during the entire morning the only vehicles we met were two jeeps racing each other back to Myitkyina.

It was slow going, and when just before noon we came in sight of what amounted to an oasis, or rather a group of dwarfish trees growing out of boggy ground, we decided to rest in the shade until the heat of the day was over. During this rest period, an unexpected solution presented itself to the problem of Pegu. As Warlock said with some exasperation: 'There are five of us here in this steaming hot and fly-ridden country, four of us westerners who aren't used to the climate. So why does the native get the bloody fever?' It was a rhetorical question to which there was no answer. But fever it was. Almost since the beginning of the journey I had watched with growing alarm as the back of Pegu's neck glistened until the perspiration turned the collar of his khaki shirt a deep and uniform brown. When I asked him how he felt, he replied only with his gleaming white smile and a nod, but his eyes were glazed, and at last I ordered a halt so that we could force him to take what medicine we had to offer. When we finally came to the trees he almost fell to the ground from his seat, and was unconscious in the shade almost as soon as he reached it. He was certainly breathing badly, and straining from side to side, but so far as I could tell his condition was not dangerous. Once when he became conscious for a minute or two he murmured something about malaria: I gathered that he had not been expecting another bout so soon after the last one, so he had taken no precautions.

'How far to the mines?' I asked.

'First one is . . . two, three mile,' he gasped.

I felt sorry for the boy, but it could have been a happy chance for us. The only thing was, we couldn't now dump him in the desert as I had planned: we had to hand him over to another human being, despite the risk of subsequent identification. So the moment we saw the first man-made tunnel burrowing into the hillside, Warlock and Elizabeth cocked their guns, and Simon primed a rifle at the rear. The precautions proved unnecessary. A group of temporary-looking buildings came into view, spread between a collection of mud hills, and from what appeared to be a portable office stepped three surprised Burmese. With the help of a phrase book our plight was quickly explained. Enquiry about Pegu's brother was met with bewilderment, though it could be that we failed to make ourselves undestood. The important thing was that the mine officials agreed to take charge of the invalid and get him back to the hospital at Myitkyina by a van due to leave within the hour. The men wanted to know where the rest of us were going, but we only pointed north and smiled. We lifted Pegu out from his temporary bed atop cans and boxes, and said goodbye. It was difficult to tell whether his eyes reflected fear, discomfort, regret, or anger; at least we did not have to resolve by violence the question of his loyalty, or lack of it.

From now on the chief consideration was to cover our tracks. We decided to avoid the rest of the mines just in case we were expected, so once away from the trail we had to work by compass. The main route, if one might so dignify it, had seemed to work clockwise round a block of hills. We took a chance in working anti-clockwise, which may have added four or five miles to our total but otherwise presented no insuperable problem. Indeed, after a few sticky moments, when we were confronted by a head-high wall of rock and thought we would have to turn back, we found a narrow aperture which just accepted the width of the Land Rover once the wing mirrors were bent back; and after that it was fairly plain sailing across a sandy but rock-hard surface which took us around a projecting peak and through a basin of mudhills. Finally we came to a track on the left of which had to be the remains of our original route. According to the maps it petered out entirely at this point, so from here on in we were absolutely on our own.

October 19. Sixty-eight miles yesterday. Not much of an accomplishment: it works out at an average of ten miles an hour over seven hours of actual driving. Actually we did twenty along some stretches, but of course there were plenty of others when we were reduced to five, and the heat and the flies made us seek the protection of shade more often than we intended. We finally camped in a short dead-end canyon which, facing north, had taken comparatively little heat. It was early, and we should have taken advantage of the cooler evening, but we were dead beat, and there was no real hurry. Best to be fresh enough to tackle any fresh obstacles the morrow might bring. And so we woke with the dawn, a wonderful sight as a massive red globe of fiery red came slowly into view through the mist above the distant eastern hills. At this time of day in these remote uplands the air was wonderfully pure. At last there were signs that we had moved out of the humid zone, something we hadn't even noticed last night; there were no flying insects now and the morning heat was no more than balmy. After a light breakfast we strolled in the crest of a nearby sandhill and took pictures of ourselves against a background of unbelievable emptiness in three directions out of four. Even Simon seemed excited, and I thought for the first time that he was going to buckle to and become a useful member of the expedition. We put our hands over our eyes so as to see the high Himalayas dancing in the northern haze.

The extensive northern flatness soon proved to be something of a mirage, as we shortly found ourselves careering down a long slope into a lower area, and sank almost to our axles in some kind of bog. We cursed ourselves for having failed to take due notice of the subtly changed ground colour. Luckily there was hard rock only inches below the mud, and as our wheels now rested on it we found it comparatively easy to reverse up the hill and take an alternative route; but we kept a sharp vigil from then on. The Burmese-Assamese border presumably stretched along the mountain tops to our left, but we were not surprised to see no sign of customs posts.

'That gap,' said Elizabeth, pointing, 'must be the Chaukan Pass. And if it is, the low range ahead must be the Kumons. We have to find a way through. It may mean a twenty-mile detour, but according to the map there are breaks somewhere east of us.'

We found the gap, but it was a very rough ride: I preferred Titus Canyon. After a short spell at the wheel, Simon sought oblivion by resorting to the bottle. Warlock was feeling the heat and Elizabeth preferred navigating, so I took over the wheel and congratulated myself on the result. The ground was still stony all the way, so it was impossible to say whether other vehicles had preceded us, even years before. The pass itself proved so steep that I thought even the Land Rover would protest at further punishment. Finally we emerged to a spectacular view from a wide ledge commanding not only the northern snow cap, but, seventy or so miles behind us, the dim outline of Myitkyina.

Our obvious route forward was down an uninterrupted slope of alluvial fan, beyond which we could see a rippled landscape, probably the choice of valleys we had been looking for. But which one to choose? What faced us was in fact a prehistoric river delta, formed as water from the Himalayas came rushing south to the sea; the ground below us, when we reached level country again, was nothing but hardened silt. In more recent eons, landslides had probably caused the onrush of water to dry to a trickle, and this had dissipated itself in the hot and humid areas around Myitkyina; further south the old channel was now what we called the Irrawaddy, fed by water flowing from the east.

The valleys of this inland delta were seldom more than a mile wide, but we could now see that there were many more than we thought, perhaps as many as fifteen or twenty, separated from each other by silt ridges up to a hundred feet high. Some of these ridges continued into the northern distance, diminishing into the sand so as to link two valleys. Others did not begin until some five or ten miles from where we stood, tending to run more steeply back into the distant mountain mass. Another handicap was that between the valleys and the mountains we were skirting was an immense well of sand about a quarter of a mile wide. This had apparently blown down from the north and settled into the pit at the base of the fan. Careful testing by foot made us reluctant to take the Land Rover on to this dry, sifty surface: once stuck, we might never get out.

All through the heat of the day we sat depressed, contemplating our sizeable problem, which only a helicopter seemed likely to solve. We cursed ourselves for not bringing one; but we hadn't wanted it to be too easy, and had been obsessed by following Conway's overground trail. Warlock was feeling the heat quite badly, so we made him rest in the shadow of a great rock while Simon and I ventured forth to examine the five or six central valleys. As we plodded on, an alteration in the shade of sand suddenly caught our eye: we found ourselves on a firmer ridge which, we realized with delight, might be long and wide enough to carry the Land Rover across the sand pit. We took it very gently indeed, with Warlock walking in front to test for any possibility of sinking wheels; once across, I steered the vehicle between two rock piles of similar size, so similar that they could have been man-made markers.

'Are you sure we're in the right valley?' asked Elizabeth anxiously.

I could see her point. Here on the wide desert floor we were much more exposed to danger than we had imagined from looking at maps, while the unending landscape seemed not merely bland and anonymous but positively menacing. We needed a sign; and suddenly Warlock found one, on a low stone with a flat surface about two feet long. In its dead centre was a marking, a design, which had nothing to do with veining. There was no way of deciding whether it was intended as an arrow, or some other symbol; it was very faint but one thing was sure – it had been made, at some time, by man. Taken together with the rock piles it could have been enough to confirm a direction for somebody who knew what he was looking for.

'Well,' I said finally, 'let's listen to any objections, but it seems to me that since the ground surface is now as hard as granite, we should go on and hope for the best. If we don't find any lizards or mushrooms, we can always come back and try again.'

I must have sounded more confident than I felt.

10

Nicholas Brent's Narrative (1980):

'THE DANGERS WHICH MAY LURK IN THE DARKNESS'

October 20. We realize how foolhardy were our plans. Our expedition should have been much better equipped and manned. Yesterday we were four; now we are three, and as I write these notes by the light of a long-life torch, my imagination stirs at the thought of the dangers which may still lurk in the darkness. The balmy warmth of the night air is misleading. At first it comforts tired bodies, but later one worries and wonders about the strange scents and breezes it carries. The others are still more or less in shock. Let us hope that by morning we shall be in fit condition to face another day of adventure, for I am sure that adventure there will be before we find our destination; still, to turn back would be something we'd regret to the end of our lives.

The rock-hard sand and grit of the lower valley gave way to a caked surface of yellow mud, in places crazed over and as springy as a ballroom floor. In these areas our tyres left faint traces, but we thought we were far enough away from the turn-off point north of the sand pit for this not to matter. No birds sang now, no burrows showed in the earth, and in the occasional sand dune to our left not even insect traces were to be seen. To all intents and purposes it was dead land through which we travelled, reminiscent of pictures of the surface of the moon – one of the most primeval places I had ever seen. Very gradually I became aware that the valley was narrowing, and its direction veering slightly from north-west towards the north. I steered as central a course as I could, fearing all the while that some prehistoric iguanadon might come stamping at us from one of the canyons.

We drove on last night until ten, then camped and enjoyed a simple meal. We meant to be off again before dawn, but to our surprise we all overslept, and something in the air made our morning preparations very sluggish, so it was almost nine before we set off. In fact, the morning was virtually wasted, because what we all thought at first was a revolver shot turned out to be a burst tyre. By the time we had fixed it – and we can afford only one more of those – it was too hot to carry on and there seemed little to do but order a siesta until four. The only shade was a narrow ribbon by the side of the Land Rover, but it sufficed. We stretched out as well as we could and surveyed the scene.

'No wonder Barnard was reminded of Death Valley,' grunted Warlock. 'Except that this seems even longer and more barren. Boy, how I miss the oasis at Furnace Creek! Cold drinks in the bar, and raspberry Jello for supper.'

'According to the thermometer in the back of the vehicle,' said Simon, 'the air temperature is a hundred and three, and humid. You can understand why the communists haven't felt inclined to put roads through this and call it a national monument. Rather a long tourist trek from Rangoon. And since everybody's supposed to be equal around here, there wouldn't be much point in laying an airstrip, would there, Uncle Nick?'

Elizabeth of course thought the whole vista supremely beautiful. All being well, she said, she'd be back in the spring with a team of photographers. She had lain awake in the night planning a picture book called *Mountains of the Sun*.

Soon after we started, heading north-north-west into an infinite horizon, Warlock yelled above the engine roar that his keen old eyes had spotted lines on the desert floor away to the east. The lines were less easy to make out when we reached the spot: clearly only the low angle had made them visible, with the help of a tea-time sun. But enough evidence remained to convince us that at some time there had been a community on this site, chosen it seemed because an angle of rock from the eastern massif probably deflected the north wind and the sand which would be carried with it. For half an hour we paced around looking for further evidence, and came up with a half-rotted piece of bamboo with a nail in it, also a couple of short lengths of post and some kind of corroded metal clip. Was this all that was left of Ramjigoval? It seemed more than possible, in which case we had no more than fifty miles to go before looking for our exit. Tomorrow, we had some justification for hoping, we would see Shangri-La.

Petrol-wise we were doing well: just over half in the tank, and thirty gallons in reserve. But the loneliness was getting to Simon, whose alcoholic consumption was now severely rationed by common consent; and even to Warlock, who soon after we started up again had a distinct feeling that we were being followed. We stopped and looked behind us, but there was nothing at all to see, even through binoculars. Twilight was beginning to encroach, and the night had to be faced. In fact, we drove another five miles before spotting a high area to the left where the fan levelled off in the lee of a rocky outcrop, providing an accessible and half-protected parking space; behind it there was even the suggestion of a cave.

Warlock was still scratching his head under the solar topee which he had brought along with him. 'Hell,' he said, gazing back into the southern darkness, 'I could swear I heard something. A hum in the distance, like a light plane.'

I considered the possibility. 'They may use planes at

the jade mines,' I said. 'But more than likely it's just the atmosphere getting to you. We're all a bit twitchy.'

Warlock took as much offence as was possible for his basically cheerful nature. 'I've never been twitchy in my God-dammed life,' he muttered. 'But I *have* had intuitions, and they've always been on the beam, and I tell you there's somebody on our trail. And I don't know why you should look so damned surprised, because after all we've been half-expecting it. Maybe we just haven't been so clever as we thought at obscuring our intentions.'

We all listened to this outburst, and had nothing to say in answer. Silently we made camp. An hour later, as well nourished as it is possible to be out of cans and bottles and dehydrated packs, we sat in camp chairs close to the Land Rover, all the men smoking small cigars and Elizabeth using our limited illumination to make notes. Eventually she paused and looked around her in a kind of dazed wonder. It was dark, but there was enough moonlight to illuminate range upon range of mountain peaks.

'A penny for 'em,' I said.

'I was thinking of that Agatha Christie novel I read on the plane. The one set in Petra.'

'The rose-red city carved out of the mountain?'

'Mm. The tourists lived in caves – I don't know what they did about mod cons – and this awful old lady sat all day in the mouth of one and when they went to bring her to dinner she was dead.'

I patted her on the hand. 'I don't think we have quite enough suspects for a murder mystery.'

'I wasn't planning one. I was only thinking that here, in one of the few untouched corners of the world, surrounded by this pure yellow sand and rock and even a glimpse or two of snow on the peaks, it seems quite a reasonable thing to die, become absorbed again in the giant processes of nature. I mean, I wonder whether

Shangri-La has got it all wrong? Isn't it somehow immoral to fight a natural process?'

Warlock chipped in. 'Me, too. Sitting here, I can't think of one thing in favour of living for two hundred years. Mind you, I could change my mind tomorrow, but right now it seems to me the end is the same, no matter how you get there. And then it doesn't really matter whether you have a state funeral, or get thrown to the vultures like Indian parsees, or die in the snow on the slopes of Karakal. If you can find Karakal.'

Simon stood up abruptly and walked a few feet away to flick the ash off his cigar. 'I'll hang on just as long as I can, thank you,' he said. 'But not, I hope, in this God-forsaken place.'

'That's funny,' I mused. 'If there is a God, I never felt as close to him as I do here.'

'Wait till your water runs out,' said Simon with a slight sneer. 'You'll trade in your religion for a drink and a bath.'

'That could be. Meanwhile I'll cherish my hope for Shangri-La a while longer. I think of people like Winston Churchill. Even though he lived to be ninety-one, for the last ten years he was more or less gaga. Don't you think the world might have benefited from having him around at full strength for a while longer?'

'I don't see what was so great about Churchill,' said Simon. 'Mind you, I scarcely remember that old war.'

'In which case,' said Warlock, 'kindly allow a few loyalties to those who do. Churchill was a man and a half, even maybe a man and three-quarters. Politics hasn't bred his equal since, and I don't care which country or which party you belong to. I'm for Shangri-La if it can show us a Churchill or two still going strong at a hundred and seventy-five. Or even a Shakespeare. You never know.'

I stood up abruptly. 'I may be crazy,' I said, 'but I

could swear I just saw a light up ahead. Over there on the eastern ridge.'

Warlock steadied his gaze in the direction I was pointing. 'Something blinked in my eye too, unless I'm coming down with migraine.'

Simon fetched the binoculars and we all stared north-east into the dark sky, for the moon was momentarily behind a cloud. Just before it emerged, we all exclaimed as the effect was repeated: a pinpoint of light, somewhere near the crest of the mountain range. A white light moving once, twice, three times from side to side. 'But it wasn't in the same place,' I cried. 'I swear it wasn't. The other was more to the left; this was an answering signal.'

'More like shooting stars,' said Simon.

'Hah!' exclaimed Warlock. 'To begin with, stars don't move from side to side. For another thing no other stars are visible in this hazy sky.'

'It's just possible,' said Elizabeth, 'that we were fooled by fireflies hovering near our light.'

'Yes, it's just possible, except that I can't imagine two fireflies exploring this vast desert on their own. I'll stake my life – and don't forget I live on a mountain – that that light was eight or ten miles away. And on the other side of where it was, that's where we're all expecting Shangri-La to be. Boy, I can see Conway at this minute, finishing his chop suey.'

We were almost too excited to sleep, but we discounted the idea of edging forward on headlights, just in case whoever controlled the lights proved unfriendly; in that case we would be at his mercy. We turned in, Elizabeth in the Rover and the rest of us in sleeping-bags on the warm gravel. It took me about half an hour to drop off, but drop off I did, intoxicated by that wonderful air. What woke me two hours later I don't know, but I saw from my watch that it was nearly one o'clock and noted almost simultaneously that the clouds had cleared and the stars were now fully visible. In fact, the moon was lighting the valley in so dramatic a fashion that I wanted to waken the others in case they should miss the spectacle. There was no need. As I stirred, a hand fell on my shoulder.

'I've wakened Simon,' said Warlock, 'and we've got the rifles. Elizabeth will stay where she is. Edge over quietly till you're covered by that rock: whoever it is is just below us.'

I did as I was told and strained my eyes to see signs of movement in the direction he was indicating. Almost at once I did see something, a man or an animal, dodge from the shadow of a low cliff to that of a nearby boulder. My heart pounded: danger was only a stone's throw away.

'There's at least three of them,' said Warlock. 'I had my eyes peeled for twenty minutes before I woke anybody. I don't know whether they're wandering tribesmen or some of your dear old friends. Either way I don't fancy being stabbed in my sleep. I'm for letting 'em know we're armed.'

Before I could stop him he raised his rifle, and I heard the crack of his shot reverberate from side to side of the valley. It had barely died away when two answering shots were heard, one of them too close to my ear for comfort. I fell flat on the ground in something very close to panic, scraping the side of my face on the gravel. Elizabeth was scrambling out of the Rover on the far side, and I hissed at her to lie flat. Warlock was swearing to himself, but he didn't fire again, and nor did the others. Simon was silent: I called out to ask whether he was in order. The reply was unintelligible. I crawled over to where I thought he was, and found him flat on his back, groaning. I touched his sleeve. It was wet: from what I could gather in the semi-darkness, one of the shots had grazed his shoulder.

These moments are already jumbled in my memory.

Eventually, leaving Warlock on guard, I dragged Simon back to the north side of the Rover, away from our attackers. Elizabeth, as our first aid expert, diagnosed a not too serious flesh wound, and dressed it as well as she could, but Simon's temperature was naturally up and he was already jabbering away incoherently. Presently he seemed to have fainted, so we put a cushion under his head and covered him with a blanket.

The remainder of the night was long. Simon still slept; the rest of us tensed ourselves for further action which never came. Assuming our attackers had retreated, I wondered what we would do when it was light. A mercy dash back to Myitkyina seemed unthinkable, but it might be necessary, meaning a second, anti-climactic attempt in a few days. In fact, that was almost certainly what we were in for unless Simon made a miraculous recovery.

As the first faint flush of dawn broke in the east, I edged my way across the site to see how Simon was. He wasn't there.

Our confusion and distress can be imagined. Apart from the mystery and shock of losing him, if Simon had been abducted it meant that the mysterious strangers had surrounded our position and attacked from the rear, and could easily have killed the rest of us had they chosen to do so. It seemed more likely, however, that Simon had awakened and wandered off in unexpected delirium, in which case it surely could not be difficult to find him in this open terrain.

October 21. It was, though. In fact, there was no sign of him at all. We began the search just as soon as light permitted and we had inspected the damage to our Rover. It was slight, but one of the bullets had struck and penetrated a petrol container, another disaster, though one of less concern at the moment. Very gingerly, and with rifles cocked, Warlock and I explored the immediate vicinity, including every rock which could have given cover; then we packed the Rover and set off to patrol the desert floor in ever-increasing circles. In a sense we took more care than was necessary, because short of a totally unexpected and unlikely ditch there was absolutely nowhere that Simon could have hidden or fallen. A quarter of a mile to the south we did locate the faint tracks of tyres which were clearly not our own; and that was that. Simon had vanished off the face of the earth, off this particular part of it at least.

Eventually we ate a grim, silent breakfast. We weren't in the least hungry, but we had to have strength. There appeared to be no solution to the puzzle, except our first conclusion, that Simon had been kidnapped. In that case, would we be followed all day, or would a man with a white flag come along and demand ransom?

By ten-thirty there seemed nothing we could do but move on. We didn't say so, but I think each of us would have preferred Simon to be the first casualty, if there had to be one. By eleven we were parallel with the peaks from which the mysterious lights had shone, but this morning there was nothing to be seen but barren rock. At least from this point on we had the advantage of a distinctly cooler breeze from the Himalayas. And a little later, by common consent, we began to look for the strange rocks which according to Conway would point us in the direction we sought. I pulled to a halt in the middle of the valley, and we all got out to stretch our legs, breathe the increasingly fresh air, and survey the landscape. We were all conscious of our three tiny figures, and the single vehicle, as unbidden intruders on that vast silent plain. Apart from some white mineral deposits edging the probable banks of the dry river bed, the ground below our feet was everywhere of the same brown, muddy colour. Not far ahead loomed the first suggestion of an upward slope, indicating that at some point the foothills would close in completely and mark the valley's end. The Himalayas, perhaps a hundred miles, were now clearly visible ahead. One's first impression was of a uniform mass; then the haze seemed to clear and one saw purple hills with white crests, behind which were sheer white peaks piling up like clouds to form that incredible plateau known as the roof of the world. Lhasa itself, once the most remote township on earth, was probably not more than a hundred and fifty miles north of us, though not accessible by any form of ground transport from where we were. As for the narrowing valley in which we stood, its mountains remained comparatively featureless, more than two-thirds of their height consisting of alluvial fan before the final rock peak banked steeply to form short sharp pinnacles which made access for the climber somewhat improbable.

Suddenly, unexpectedly, I heard a cry from Elizabeth. 'Over there! The lizard!'

11
Nicholas Brent's Narrative (1980):
'THE CAVE ARCH WAS TWENTY FEET HIGH'

And there indeed it was, perhaps a mile and a half ahead. Occasional sharp ridges of rock stretched across the middle of the valley, no doubt visible stretches of subterranean strata reaching out from the mountains to our right. One of them, even from that distance, was quite clearly construable as a large spiny-backed reptile, squatting slightly and facing towards Assam. Excitedly we clambered back into the Rover and drove forward, watching the dark shape first increase in vividness and then change, as rocks will change according to the angle, until it became a mere shapeless mass on a slope to our right. I reversed slowly until we again struck what seemed to be the best vantage point for lizard fanciers, and we all critically surveyed the dark treacly colours, the low sharp pinnacles on the crest, the stooped head, even a blemish which suggested a half-closed eye, beadily glinting at us in the blazing sun. The whole formation was perhaps two hundred yards long. The head even seemed to be cocked slightly towards us, as though the huge creature, aware of our approach, was poised to slither away. At this moment we would scarcely have been surprised had it done so.

There really wasn't much doubt any more that the Conway typescript had been vindicated. But where was the mushroom? That was as vital as the lizard, to show the way we should follow. I had vaguely imagined that the lizard might be pointing the way with its nose, but now the reverse seemed true, since the rocky beast pointed north-west, and our route had to be somewhere to the east. We all found ourselves looking in that direction: without further guidance we faced an implacable mountain wall which it might take us many days to explore. And there was nothing in sight which looked anything like a mushroom.

'The hell with it,' growled Warlock eventually. 'We have the lizard, and there's a porpoise treading on our rear end. We have to get out of sight as fast as we can, so I'm for high-tailing it to the mountain wall and hiding in the first canyon we find. Anything's better than another night under fire.'

'Agreed,' I said, 'but let's not make a panic decision. It's possible that this isn't even the right lizard: there may be another further north.'

'I doubt if there's another as recognizable as this,' said Elizabeth. 'And perhaps we'll spot the mushroom better as we climb the fan. I vote for the time being we follow the direction of the lizard's tail.'

So it was agreed. The alluvial fan proved unexpectedly rocky, with furrows cutting across our route, but we made fair progress. It was hot work though, and the sun had a long way to go before there was any hope of a cooler breeze, even though the temperature at noon had been the most tolerable so far. It was Warlock who spotted something away to our left. 'What do you suppose that is?'

I braked, and we clambered out. It was easier. After a few seconds of deliberation I led the way about a hundred yards over the scree to an outcrop of broken rock. In the centre was a jagged rock pillar about five feet high, very dark in colour, probably basalt. Other pieces of the same colour were lying about the formation, but the base was grey granite. 'I think I see a possibility here,' I said. The dark pillar might originally have had a kind of mushroom cap. It would have seemed very striking on the grey base. If it split apart, by a natural process, or perhaps was split by lightning, these bits and pieces could be its debris. Who's good at jigsaw puzzles?'

Elizabeth was already tugging one great section towards another. 'These fit pretty well, and it looks as though one side has the right kind of curve.' Five minutes of exertion were enough to convince us that we had found our inedible mushroom: a smallish centre piece even proved to fit perfectly on to the stalk. We returned, overheated but jubilant, to the shade of the Rover. 'All we have to decide now,' said Elizabeth, 'is how exactly these two rocks lead us to the canyon.' She glanced back to the lizard a mile away, looking from this point more like a Christmas tree, and produced a small shorthand pad. 'Conway's exact words were : "Having established their relationship with each other, there was no danger of losing our way home." He leaves it pretty vague.'

'Maybe,' said Warlock, 'as soon as we recognize them, we're supposed to head between them.'

'That's pretty imprecise geometrically,' I said. 'By the time you hit the mountain wall you could be several miles out in either direction.'

Elizabeth was impelled to a spurt of imagination. 'Think of it from their point of view. Although on the way home they needed to recognize the rocks from the south, in order to understand their usefulness in the first place they would have had to recognize them from the canyon mouth. So that surely means that one must have been behind the other. Ergo, our route must lie from the lizard directly over the top of the mushroom.'

It seemed unarguable. We drove back to the lizard and clambered on top of it. Then through our telescope we took a fix on what remained of the mushroom and looked directly above it to the top of the fan. We could see no sign whatever of a canyon, but at least we could fix the location of the cliff because there was a sharp peak directly above it, the right-hand one of a group of three. So now our Rover laboured back up the slope, past the remains of the mushroom, skidding occasionally on the shale. As we got closer to the mountain wall our marker disappeared behind the lower crags, but we all kept our eyes instead on a reddish scar near the ground. Still no canyon was visible. No wonder a whole community could tuck itself away behind these primitive giant castles of rock, and never be found unless it wanted to be. We looked back one last time. On the western hills, ridge after undulating rock ridge ran north-east to south-west, the scene suggesting a tribe of giant serpents in a hurry to reach the Indian Ocean.

The twisting line of our mountains basically faced west, but at one point the cliff jutted out sufficiently to make, as we saw to our delight, a northern face about ten yards wide. Conway's typescript was being borne out at every new development. As we approached the rectangular patch of shadow I suggested a final check that we were leaving no tyre tracks. I also cast a careful glance down the valley to the south, and scoured the entire landscape with my telescope to ensure that nobody could follow us. The desert was completely empty as we moved out of sight.

It took us a few moments to get used to the comparative darkness of the shaded area, and at first we seemed doomed to disappointment, for no canyon opening was visible. It did not become apparent until we wandered almost into the far corner, for its opening faced not merely north but almost north-east, a unique piece of geology: the substance of which the jutting cliff was formed must be so hard that through the ages it had resisted all attempts at weathering, forcing the water from the inner canyon to flow around it. Anybody working his way *south* along the rock face might possibly have spotted the gap, but not otherwise: it was a fine piece of natural camouflage. Even when, wonderingly, we entered, it appeared no more than a small recess; only a second bend revealed it as a true canyon, floored with shale and just wide enough for a four-wheeled vehicle to pass. There was no doubt that it would lead through the mountain, for like Titus Canyon it had been formed by water. Its disguise was made complete by the fact that the water from it, instead of spilling straight down the fan and so possibly forming it a telltale crest of residue, had run north along the rock wall until it merged with the spill from a gully a quarter of a mile north.

We drove in bottom gear into this gigantic split between rocks at least four hundred feet high, feeling like Alice having finally found the key to the enchanted garden. But no flowers bloomed here. Instead, the rich golden walls of the lower canyon, rough as sugar candy, gave way to long stretches of a more translucent off-white rock which none of us were able to name. Very soon the canyon narrowed to such an extent that we had to park and lock the Land Rover. Taking with us just as much as we could backpack comfortably, we left the vehicle in a natural alcove, not knowing when we would see it again. Now, the narrowing canyon led us temptingly ahead, a twisting avenue of mystery and possible danger. Except for occasional stretches we were sheltered from the sun, but excitement was making us perspire still. To our surprise, after six or seven bends we stepped out into a scrub-covered valley whose high walls must have resisted the prehistoric flood waters except at this one weak point, where they found their way through to the desert. A fairly well-defined path lay along the foot of the mountain to our right, and we were not slow to take it, though our sudden shortness of breath made us realize that the trail was steeper than it seemed. Shortly our view up the valley was obscured by a projecting elbow of mountain, into the depth of which we found ourselves led by way of an enormous cave mouth which yawned at us unexpectedly as we turned a corner. The cave arch was twenty feet high, and just below it the path crossed the old water course, becoming muddy enough for us to discern what appeared to be wheeltracks, not much broader than those a bicycle might make, but in double file. There were also what looked like the prints of flat shoes.

It was dark in the cave, and the incline continued steeply upward. I wondered how long our torches might last: we had brought extra batteries with us. But as we turned the first corner the way ahead was brilliantly illuminated in a way we couldn't at first understand. Then we realized that the tunnel was very closely following the outer wall of the mountain, and the light came from natural windows which had been formed in soft rock. I remember a similar effect in Utah, in Zion Canyon, I think. The windows were, of course, on our left, and we hurried to the first one to find ourselves overlooking a carpet of the prickly green scrub which we had been so pleased to leave behind us. Obviously the valley had once been the lower end of a lake, the contents of which had been diverted through the canyon mouth. The valley itself was no wider than when we last saw it, and was now hemmed in by mountains of ever-increasing size which considerably reduced the view in all directions. All we could surmise was that our tunnel must shortly bear to the right, which indeed it did, still climbing all the way.

I seem to remember that it was three-thirty when we stopped at the first window, and realized that we had less than three hours of useful daylight left. As I write this I know that we were in the tunnel for between two and three hours, yet apprehension made it seem to pass in minutes, and I have no clear recollection of any conversation. I remember that according to Hilton four previous traveller was equally vague: 'Conway never exactly remembered how he and the others arrived at the lamasery, or with what formalities they were received, unroped, and ushered into the precincts.'

Our own elation was still mixed with concern and perplexity over Simon's disappearance; perhaps we were too emotional to talk. Whatever the reason, we didn't; if we had tried, I think we might have burst into tears. Even when we saw a strip of torn yellow fabric hanging from a sharp rock on which it had presumably been caught, we only looked at each other and smiled happily. We must have been affected by the altitude: our drive up the fan had added two thousand feet to our elevation, and the tunnel probably two thousand more. We began to cross little rivulets, springs from the right-hand mountain mass which found their way across the tunnel floor to an exit in the outer wall. They made the atmosphere mustily humid, and the floor soft and yielding from the soil and grit they brought with them. Sometimes for whole stretches the tunnel lacked windows, and here we swung our torches around us, making crazy shadows and occasionally dislodging a stray bat from its cranny.

Without warning Elizabeth collapsed, crying out. Warlock's light showed that she had stumbled into a fissure: her right foot was caught in the rock. Between us we extracted her and established that the injury was not too serious, but she had twisted a muscle and from then on could only limp along, supported between us, so our progress became much slower. It was some consolation that the tunnel had now levelled out; there was in fact one length where we were decidedly going downhill. For a while it was also very dark, but at last we rounded a bend and saw ahead of us a long stretch illuminated by two more natural windows on the left. And in the pool of light thus cast were the figures of men.

Two of them were tall and burly, dressed alike in soft hats and long fur-trimmed coats, at sight of which I realized how the temperature had reduced since we entered the canyon. They stood on guard in the background. The two other men appeared slighter and older, and were more simply dressed in ankle-length woollen robes. At sight of the group we had momentarily stopped, but they made no reciprocal movement. We looked at each other, shrugged, and moved slowly ahead until we were within ten or so yards of the strangers. Then the leading pair closed their eyes and bowed formally; the gesture spoke of courtesy and not of menace. As the light caught their faces, one seemed obviously oriental, but the other might have been German or Scandinavian. I decided to ignore the unlikely possibility that they had weapons concealed. Shivering a little after our long trek through the cool tunnel in tropical gear, I left Warlock to support Elizabeth, and moved forward, imitating their bow as well as I could without feeling ridiculous.

'Your friend is hurt?' asked one of them in the softest of English accents.

'It's nothing really,' called Elizabeth with a firm tone. 'I foolishly slipped and sprained my ankle.'

'It is well to take the greatest care,' came the answer. 'There are no doctors here.' He turned to me. 'You are the leader?'

'We have no leader. We are friends who come in peace to seek the lamasery of Shangri-La. This is Mr Warlock from Canada. Miss Elizabeth Battersby and I are English. My name is Brent.'

'You are indeed far from your homelands,' said the spokesman, 'and ill protected against the temperature at this elevation.'

'We have warmer clothing back in our vehicle, which is concealed in your canyon.'

He nodded approval. 'It can be retrieved in due course. Meanwhile I suggest that you drape these blankets around your shoulders, for we shall emerge at the side of the mountain which has received no sun all day.' He motioned to a guard who produced blankets as though by magic; actually he had stepped for them into a natural alcove which was invisible from where we stood.

Before we all moved forward, one of the guards stepped into another alcove and from it trundled out a most extraordinary vehicle. It was a little single-seat wagonette or rickshaw which seemed to be made entirely of wood, mostly bamboo. The wheels were roughly banded with some rubbery substance, and at the back was something suspiciously like a luggage rack, mounted between two long handles or shafts. The guard bowed to Elizabeth and waited obediently for her to enter.

'Go ahead,' I murmured, 'or they'll be insulted.' When she was secure, the strangely assorted party moved on in procession, and as the tunnel narrowed again, my nostrils were assaulted by air which was dry and sweet. Clearly we were not far from the end of the tunnel. Momentarily we went through darkness again, then a single high window revealed a forbidding distant view of darkening hills, snow and barren trees. We had been walking perhaps for ten minutes when the rickshaw stopped and Elizabeth was courteously invited to disembark. The carriage was neatly stowed in yet another handy recess, and now Elizabeth limped forward with the support of both guards. As she did so, Warlock grabbed my arm and pointed. What I had taken for the continuing darkness of the tunnel wall was in fact a patch of twilight sky framed in the tunnel exit. A few low-intensity stars were scattered around a clouded moon, and below this group an unmistakeable collection of earth lights suggested houses on a distant hill. With virtually no further warning at all, our party emerged on to a terrace about six feet wide, cut out of the mountain which soared above us to the right. At our feet, steps cut out of the sloping rock led down into what had to be the verdant, scented, overwhelmingly inviting Valley of Blue Moon.

So I'm really here, I thought, and Karakal really exists, for there it is, rising out of the twilight mist. My eyes, once accustomed to the gloaming, seemed to take in everything at once. The long, slightly fan-shaped valley below, the snow-tipped mountains all round; the little points of light dotted high in the distance. And above them, crowning the picture, the solid majesty of that white, cone-shaped high peak, which according to the only available figures ran Everest a close second in height. As we gazed, entranced, the moon crept out from behind a thin cloud and seemed to make luminous the zigzag track which three or miles ahead left the valley, climbed up the mountainside, and led the eye to what I could perceive as a lonely group of buildings on a terrace. They must constitute the lamasery. I understood now the phrase which I had savoured so very often in Hilton: 'clinging to the mountainside with all the chance delicacy of flower petals impaled upon a crag'. As a view it was beyond magnificence; every inch of it cried out to be explored and recorded. I even thought I could make out, above and beyond the lamasery buildings, a deep cleft which very likely contained the old northern pass, now snow-blocked, through which Conway first came to he magic valley. Conway! I scarcely dared think about him. With supreme bathos I recalled my terror when as a boy of nine I was first carpeted in my headmaster's study. Would meeting Conway be like that? Might he resent our seeking him out in this way? Could he still be alive?

Our escorts were already politely directing us to the steps, and another guard at a signal appeared with an awkward bundle of rope, which unrolled into a hammock for Elizabeth. Unprotestingly she allowed herself to be carefully carried down the staircase, swinging from side to side with an apparent nonchalance which I was sure she could not be feeling. Warlock followed, and I came last, dropping from step to step with a blitheness I had not felt for years. It was as though, in my mind, a choir was singing Hallelujah; indeed, I felt capable at that moment of persuading the mountains which surrounded us to stand up and sing. I couldn't have said whether there were sixty steps, or eighty, or a hundred; but at the foot, within what seemed to be a village clearing, was a semi-circular space formed by an assembled group of brown-skinned natives, variously dressed, but all with sufficient clothing to remind one that this was no South Sea island. Indeed it was far less cold than on the mountain, but that may have been because several of the onlookers held aloft long, wooden, tar-burning torches, which cast a dramatic light on the scene. Some of the faces offered welcome, some bewilderment, none suspicion. I noticed an oriental slant to the eyes, and on closer inspection one or two looked prematurely wizened, as is usually the way with Eastern peoples; but my first distant impression, the one I shall remember most vividly, is of a race easy-going and willingly led, rather as one imagines the Polynesians in Gauguin's paintings.

When the priests – for such I assumed our welcomers to be – reached ground level they stood back until the party was complete. Then, with the slightest tilt of the head, the one who had spoken to us indicated that we should make our way after him through the obviously excited but benevolent crowd, some of whom reached out to touch our unfamiliar clothes as we passed. I realized that Warlock and I were still idiotically draped in blankets; we left them over the arm of the nearest guard as we came again to open space and to an area of slightly raised ground. Here, on a wide path, stood a single carriage drawn by two ponies. In it a man sat quietly, watching our approach, a man whose very posture suggested infinite wisdom and patience, though his actual features were half-obscured by the shadow of a palm frond. Behind us I felt the valley people silently massing, cutting off any possible retreat. To my right Warlock moved like a man in a dream; to my left and slightly behind were the two men bearing Elizabeth. My own steps grew slower and shorter, and finally stopped altogether when I was five yards from the carriage. I saw that its occupant proposed to get out. Two men moved forward to assist him, and after an easy descent there stood before me a person dressed in priestly robes and leaning on a malacca cane.

I observed a slightly smiling, delicate-looking, apparently middle-aged man with an English look. His hair was short, with the conventional parting of the old school. He wore the kind of thin grey moustache which used to be called military. He bowed gracefully, but I found myself momentarily transfixed, unable to respond. When I did find my voice, it sounded unfamiliar.

'Conway?' I asked rather tremulously, thinking how idiotic I would feel if he replied in Burmese.

The man took two steps forward; his robe swished expansively around his ankles. He bowed to Elizabeth, then to Warlock. The crowd began to murmur. He opened his palms towards us, and his smile became a little more open, as he enunciated in a voice that only just carried the distance, 'You are all most welcome in Shangri-La.'

12

Nicholas Brent's Narrative (1980):

'WOULD YOU SAY THAT WE HAD MET BEFORE?'

October 21 (continued). In fact it is now 4 am on the 22nd, but a day can't be counted over until one goes to sleep, and that is something I haven't yet been able to accomplish. If I lie down, my heart races with excitement. If I stand up, I am faint from emotion. Several times after our arrival I found myself reduced to the brink of stammering idiocy by the mere realization that I am here, here in Shangri-La, that the Valley of Blue Moon really exists. I remember, when I first found myself in Los Angeles after a 6,000-mile trip, flinging the window open to take deep breaths of the unfamiliar air and then to bathe in the traffic noise so far below. It isn't practical to try that here. There isn't any noise at all; and the mountain air is too cold to be beneficial other than as a momentary shock. Oddly enough, during dinner I had the greatest difficulty in staying alert, and couldn't even feel my legs. It was as though I had been drugged: I remember Conway reported something of the same trouble on his first evening here in 1931. He thought something had been put into the food to relieve the difficulties of respiration.

We *were* drugged! Of course we were. How can I have forgotten that strange little ceremony down in the clearing? Conway – for Conway of course it was – had barely issued his welcome when my attention was taken by a native who stood silently facing me with a tray in his hand; on it stood a porcelain jug and some small delicate cups. Conway waved the three of us together and began to pour. 'It will be helpful,' he said with some diffidence, 'if you will kindly drink. The potion is a harmless compound of herbs and fruit juices, but the valley people believe that it keeps us all what you and I would call immune from germs. Or, as I think you now say, viruses. We have few illnesses here, and anybody who did not drink a little *pavla* on arrival would be looked upon with great disfavour if an epidemic were to strike. To demonstrate its palatability, please select a cup for me.'

Warlock took two cups, considered them, and gave one to Conway. 'Cheers,' he said. 'If this contains the juice of the *tangatse* berry, I came a long way to sample it. Mm: like sweet redcurrant.'

Conway downed his beverage at a gulp, but I saw his eye flicker at Warlock's mention of *tangatse*. Elizabeth and I sipped appreciatively, and smiled as we placed our empty cups back on the tray. Then instinctively we bowed, to Conway and to each other; it seemed the proper thing to do. After a pause Conway said: 'We have much to explain to each other, but our conversations will find a more comfortable setting inside the lamasery.' He gestured towards the twinkling lights on the hill. 'Our transportation is not swift, but we find it efficient enough.'

The pony-drawn vehicle from which he had alighted was not unlike a Victorian dogcart. Now a second drew up behind us in the clearing; both were driven by boys who sat on a little jump-seat, legs dangling between the two ponies. Elizabeth and Warlock were helped up into the rear vehicle. Because of her strained ankle Elizabeth overbalanced at the first attempt, and two women came forward enquiringly to assist. When I turned back, Conway was already seated, and I was virtually lifted into the place beside him. His fine silk robe nestled around his ankles. His feet, I noticed, were enclosed by soft moccasins covered with the same material. It seemed clear that he did little walking: they were scarcely more substantial than travelling slippers.

We did not make an easy way through the friendly but excited crowds who surged around us, now apparently wanting to touch Conway's gown. He allowed some to do so, smiling and waving the while. The way was stony and the carriage poorly sprung, but these were the least of my concerns. Behind us I could hear the muffled clip-clop of the second pony as we followed a cutting through a thick wood which surrounded us with marvellous natural scents and scenes. Sometimes there was a stone bridge over a stream, and nearby a single house, with another in a cultivated area up a side road. The houses, basically log cabins, were made welcoming by soft yellow light streaming from the interior. Each was roughly central to its plot, simply designed but given grace by wide eaves and surrounding raised platforms which in this evening light made the houses seem like boats on a silent sea. In many cases the occupants sat on their front steps and waved at us – or rather, I suppose, at Conway. Racially they looked to me now as close to the American Indian as to any other strain, though their skin was darker and there were instances of the flattened nose which suggests a Mongol influence. To be truthful, my attention was fully focused on the man beside me, his profile nobly etched in the light of the moon which now pierced the mist. I looked at his hands as they lay folded on his lap, and wondered whether they could really be nearly ninety years old. As I stared, one hand was lifted to pat my wrist briefly, as though Conway were aware of my deep emotion; but when I looked up his eyes were closed, as though he were engrossed in silent prayer. He looked rather younger than I felt; and just now I was feeling pretty good.

Although as we headed up the valley we soon left the thick woods behind for a dark featureless region, we did occasionally pass more verdant land. The closer mountains to our right were in shadow; those a few miles to our left had their snowcaps brilliantly lit by the moon. The track rose gradually to a crest from which, breathtakingly, there was suddenly revealed the most astonishing view of Karakal in almost its total height, the lamasery lights twinkling on its lower slopes. I must have sighed audibly, for Conway, who had been politely taking little notice of me until I acclimatized myself, now turned and murmured the mountain's name. I nodded perhaps too readily, for I sensed his puzzlement that I had not needed to be told. This slightly uneasy situation had the effect of restoring my ability to converse.

'Wonderful,' I said. 'Simply wonderful. And the air. You could sell it in little green bottles.'

Conway smiled. 'Moonlit evenings in the valley are almost my favourite time of day, though as we climb more steeply it will become quite chilly. Indeed, the weather at the lamasery can be quite piercingly cold. By a fluke of nature the valley escapes all that, which is lucky for the townspeople.'

'I didn't see anything that could be called a town.'

'There are three – call them villages if you like – away behind us in the woods. The valley people, of whom by the way there are just over a thousand, call the largest Pojema, which in their patois means meeting-place. Even Pojema cannot be seen from a distance, for the reed in that part grows to a height of nearly twenty feet. Some of the houses are built from twisted coils of it.'

His voice, unforced yet pleasing, had subtle timbres which in certain circumstances, I suspected, might have a hypnotic effect. There would be no need for such a man to make a claim to leadership: it would be his by common unspoken assent: he would be a natural foreman of any jury. I lapsed into silence again, for there was so much to ask that I did not know where to begin – just as one is tongue-tied in the presence of the old and valued friend who greets one at the airport after a long parting.

The mountain ranges now pressed in from each side, revealing crowded low peaks of a twisted kind which reminded me of the Troll range in central Norway. Unexpectedly, out of the purple shadows ahead there loomed an enormous archway of carved wood, a highly decorative affair in the Japanese style, with flying gables, gilded dragons and intricately designed gates. The latter stood open to allow our passage, and as we rattled under the arch, I discerned a colour scheme of black, red and gold.

Conway spoke again. 'The Arch of Happiness is almost entirely the work of one man, our only brother from Korea. Unfortunately he died before he could quite complete it, though the deficiencies are noticeable from the north side only. They serve to remind us of our loss.'

'Was he . . . very old?' My lips trembled slightly on the question.

Conway seemed to smile a little as he replied: 'By local standards, no. Not really old. He was nearly ninety. His intention was that the arch should mark the boundary between the Valley of Blue Moon, of which you have gained the briefest introductory impression, and Shangri-La proper, which awaits you. The one is fabulously fertile, a natural paradise; the other can claim to sustain only spiritual growth. You will find no decorated arches on our mountain, but our friend was an artist who needed that kind of outlet. Since the valley people like their symbols, there was no possible objection.'

The terrain was becoming rocky indeed, and whoever engineered the road without bulldozers must have had a tough time. Soon we rounded the foot of a projecting mountain block, keeping as close as possible to its cliff face. Abruptly the trail plunged into the heart of the mountain itself; the ponies snorted as they tackled a short but steep canyon ascent before being allowed to rest on a natural platform from which we could view not only the valley we had left but, by craning our necks, the low pointed towers of the lamasery high above, apparently suspended in mist. I realized that we were at the first of several hairpin bends which would inexorably bring us up to the exposed plateau on which the lamasery stood. Some stretches cut straight through the mountain, one of them by way of a short tunnel; others climbed its outer wall, like the Belach na Bo in Wester Ross. As we laboured upwards, Conway contributed the occasional explanation: 'This route was constructed between 1944 and 1946. For heavy goods there is also a rack and pinion railway system. You may have noticed the lower station on the last bend. It eliminates the only really arduous section and takes wider loads than this mountain track can accommodate. The old pedestrian route was so vertiginous that even our native porters would, I'm sure, find it impossible now. Indeed, I sometimes wonder how we dared use it. But we did, for centuries, until a visitor from America, through his professional skills, showed us this much more comfortable possibility.'

Since we entered the canyon, only the occasional distant clip-clop of hoofbeats had told me that Elizabeth and Warlock were still following. I would have given much to see their faces, to read in their eyes whether their reactions were the same as mine, to watch their fantasy come true. There was no fantasy, however, about the weather, which by now had turned briskly autumnal. Conway began to wind a scarf round the lower part of his face, and as he caught my eye he smiled. 'Even in Shangri-La, it is wise at my age to protect oneself against the night air. On this particular mountainside there is always a tendency to dankness, as it takes no sun even during the day. At the top, however, we are normally left exhilarated by the effects of a dry east wind, from whose worst excesses we are protected by the wall of the Karakal glacier.'

'I'm feeling a little dizzy. I suppose that's the altitude.'

'Very likely. But we have very nearly reached our destination: this is the last bend.'

The fascinating journey from the top of the old steps had occupied less than forty minutes. Flecks of soft snow blew around my head as we emerged from between two massive boulders on to a wide, level stone platform. The first thing I noticed was crazy paving, which seemed hilariously out of place; but I rapidly became more concerned by the apparently icy wind, which took my breath away. I was grateful for a travelling rug which an approaching guard placed round my shoulders. Elizabeth's carriage followed close behind us; a third vehicle contained the two men who had met us in the tunnel. Elizabeth scrambled out as best she could with her bad ankle, and clutched my hand constantly. Warlock seemed able only to shake his head in bewilderment at the sights which confronted him. Before us, half-sheltered by the mountain, stood a long, low, white building reminding me only of an English country house: there was even a wall of half-timbering. Behind it, crowding up the slopes, I could discern other buildings in a miscellany of styles. I took a few steps to a nearby parapet, but thick mist now covered the valley below, and in any case Conway lost no time in ushering us towards a welcoming double door. We found ourselves in an old-fashioned staircase hall, comfortably furnished, with softly candlelit corners; but it had a chilly effect because its walls were whitewashed and the ceiling went all the way up to the second-floor roof. Dark contrasting beams made me fancy the room suitable as a set for Frankenstein's castle or, with the addition of a few chintz cushions and curtains, for a performance of *Rookery Nook*.

Silk-clad servants were now offering us glasses of a warm liquid which tasted like punch: it certainly had a lot of cinnamon in it. Conway stood silently but with a touch of impatience, as he shared this ceremonial welcoming drink. As soon as our glasses were empty he waved us towards a carved oak staircase, at the top of which we found an L-shaped corridor of bedrooms. Everywhere the effect was the same: plain white walls, heavily impressive furniture, plenty of space and a general absence of fuss. Pictures dotted the walls, pictures in both oriental and occidental traditions, though I recognized nothing as having outstanding merit or originality. The air was well warmed, and there was a faint but delicious aroma of Chinese cooking. Rust was the colour of the floor tiles, which here and there seemed warm to the feet: I suspected a hypocaust system similar to that of the Romans. Laid out on each bed was a silky-warm, high-collared, intricately embroidered house-gown with a maker's label in Chinese. Less predictably, each room had a private bath, which in my case may well have been more than fifty years old because, as Hilton noted of the baths in *Lost Horizon*, it was of green porcelain and made in Akron, Ohio. It did not seem to have been very much used.

Conway, I suddenly realized, had contrived to absent himself, but a smiling servant assured us in halting English that his master would look forward to joining us in one hour, downstairs at supper. After a little further information about laundry baskets, the three of us were left at our doors, staring uncertainly but happily at each other along the landing. With shrugs and grins we briefly explored each other's rooms, finding them quite similar; then we retired with such remarks as 'see you at supper', for all the world as though we had just motored down from London to a seaside hotel in Dorset. A few moments later I heard a polite tapping on Elizabeth's door and looked out to see two women with buckets and bottles, indicating to her that they had been sent to give further attention to her leg. She seemed pleased enough to see them.

Disappointingly unostentatious, even ordinary, as the building may have appeared at first, its details eloquently testified to the good taste and wisdom of its designers. Bookshelves were filled with modern and classical works in a variety of languages. For twenty minutes or more I relaxed languorously in warm foamy water, and afterwards attar of roses lingered round me like an invisible shawl. I sprawled out on my four-poster and felt I would never move again. Yet five minutes before the appointed hour I was dressed, alert and expectant, even willing to be constructively critical. My mother used to say that when I went to heaven I would not only tell St Peter his floors were dirty but seize a mop and clean them myself.

In the plain slippers which had been provided, I padded down the wide silent stairway. At the foot a servant was waiting with a silent bow to direct me into a sparsely furnished dining room, with an elliptical table which would have accommodated a dozen. Four places only were laid, and at one of them Conway sat, smoking a brown cigarette in a long white holder. He waved me to a place and pushed a box towards me, while an attendant poured sherry for both of us. 'Habits die hard,' he remarked. 'My rule is to limit myself to one glass of Dry Sack and one cigarette a day, fifteen minutes before dinner. But tonight we are late, and so I indulged at my usual time, and now again.' He smiled like a sheepish schoolboy caught in the act.

I lit up gratefully. 'I don't need this to calm my nerves,

but I'm all for new experiences. Is the tobacco a local blend?'

As I asked the question I glanced at the cigarette and saw the name Lambert and Butler. Conway laughed aloud at my crestfallen face. 'I can imagine it must seem odd to you, but we never claim here to be good at everything; only to recognize quality whatever its source.'

I nodded. 'At least I can commend you for your moderation, both in the rule you set for yourself and the tolerance with which you vary it.'

Conway looked up at me quizzically. My deliberate use of the word moderation was another pointer to my knowledge of at least some of Shangri-La's traditions. But before he could decide how our conversation should proceed, Elizabeth and Warlock arrived almost simultaneously, and the business of eating occupied us for a while. The food was presented in steaming bowls from which we helped ourselves liberally, appetites having become almost painfully acute without our even realizing the fact. We ate chicken, bamboo shoots, mushrooms, water chestnuts and dumplings, to the accompaniment of tasty brown rice, with a sweetish white wine to wash it down. The wine, Conway assured me, was indeed local. Afterwards there were chapatties smeared with a fragrant berry jam, followed by a dish of peaches and a cheese which to me suggested goat. Tea came in the usual delicate bowls, and while we sipped it as a *digestif* Conway judged it right to break the silence which had prevailed during the meal, if one discounts the murmurs involved in passing dishes and expressing appreciation.

'Let me assure you all that I know very well how oddly the air of Shangri-La can affect the newcomer, and I suggest that we look forward to longer conversations tomorrow, when you are more fully rested. As you are clearly aware – and your awareness is a puzzle which I look forward to solving – I am generally known as Conway. I welcome you most humbly and sincerely to this unique resting place, which has received many a weary traveller, though it is not as yet listed in the pages of Michelin. Tomorrow I shall take pride and pleasure in giving you as comprehensive a tour as religious rules permit; but perhaps before we retire, and over a glass of this rather good Tibetan brandy' – a servant was already pouring – 'you would like to tell me, in as few words as may be, what fortune or misfortune brought you here.'

I glanced at Warlock, but it was Elizabeth who spoke. 'It was neither fortune nor misfortune, Mr Conway. We were actually *looking* for Shangri-La.'

Conway's slightly raised eyebrow was the only visible reaction. 'And how could that be? We have never advertised our existence.'

'I'm sure you haven't.' Elizabeth smiled mischievously. 'And yet in a sense you led us here yourself.'

'Ah,' said Conway, putting his fingers together and sinking back in his chair to await the now inevitable explanation. It was given by Warlock.

'Mr Conway, if you could imagine me a much younger man – forty years younger – would you say that we had met before?'

Such a clue made it too easy: Conway clearly suspected the truth at once. To verify it he produced from a pocket a pair of gold-rimmed pince-nez and balanced them on the end of his nose, looking for a moment rather like Will Hay beset by idiot schoolboys. He gazed steadily at Warlock who, delighted by his own ability to mystify, offered first one profile and then the other. After a very few moments Conway sighed, removed the glasses, and looked up at the ceiling. 'As it is forty years since I was away from this valley,' he said, 'the possibilities are quite limited. I think you must be – you have to be – the young intelligence officer who was so courteous to me in London during the air raids. In 1940, I mean.'

'Hit it on the nail,' said Warlock, nodding vigorously. 'Full marks. After all, you could be forgiven for not remembering. You've worn so much better than I have.'

Conway shook his head with a half-smile. 'So that's why you all seemed to know so much about Shangri-La. At least you will be spared the boredom of my opening remarks.'

I thought it was time I said something. 'We all read your typescript. A little belatedly, but thoroughly. It brought us more than ten thousand miles.'

Conway nodded. 'For years, for decades even, I expected somebody to follow the clues I left. And I reproached myself bitterly for giving away even a few of our secrets, in case the wrong people should be tempted to come. I can only claim, sir, that when we met my morale was at its lowest ebb. It took fifteen years for me to decide that nobody was coming at all, that in all probability nobody cared. I never thought anybody would arrive forty years later. It's a lifetime in your terms.'

'But in yours, surely, only a pause for reflection.' Warlock took the old man's hand and held it firmly for a moment.

There was a half-smile now on Conway's face, and he waved a hand in self-deprecation. 'Only you can judge whether our extra span, when it is granted, gives us extra value. You who are of the great busy world lead short and crowded lives, that's sure, but at the end you have much to remember and often much to be proud of. Here, in this isolated Utopia, we have perhaps too much time to reflect over too few actual happenings. One week, one month, with us, is very like the last, or the next. Very little happens to reflect upon: very litle happens at all, except what we are pleased to call the increase of wisdom but what may in fact be merely the accumulation of useless knowledge. You see, I have lately come to doubt whether there *can* be real wisdom without experience. All the saints, all the martyrs and prophets had that; whereas our little actions and reflections in Shangri-La may prove in the end to be merely incestuous.'

Warlock gave a muted version of one of his piercing laughs. 'Now look here, sir, we can't have this, not on our first evening. Let's at least have the good news first.'

'That's all right,' said Elizabeth. 'Mr Conway doesn't want us to be carried away by our own enthusiasms. I promise we won't. In any case, I'd always understood Shangri-La's role to be a passive one, to provide an extension of time in which mankind can learn to rise above its petty frictions and wars. Time for the race to find itself, without having lost its art and history and philosophy in the process.'

'Oh, that we do,' said Conway. 'We store, we guard. But so could a robot. We are men and women. In the end some of us need to feel useful in ourselves – not merely as protectors of other men's creations.'

Warlock struggled visibly to stifle a yawn. 'Well I'm sure you have plenty to teach me for one. And I'm looking forward to learning it.'

Conway waved a gracious arm. 'Perhaps you're right. I was seizing the rare chance to be devil's advocate, and quite possibly making too good a job of it. One thing we certainly can teach, and that is how to relax, to take life at a slower and more sensible pace.'

'In that case,' said Warlock, 'you have one satisfied customer already. Guaranteed.'

Conway rose, sensing our need for sleep, and offered a hand to each of us in turn. 'It is good to have you here, and I would not like to shock you on your first evening. I am not at all contemptuous of the accomplishments of

Shangri-La. Perhaps, however, after fifty years of guardianship one may be pardoned for wondering whether the job is being done as well as it might be. Besides, to use an old phrase, you have caught me on one foot. I have never before greeted a guest who knew our history. The revelation has always been a gradual process, spread over many weeks.' He smiled. 'Though come to think of it, we did once receive a Scandinavian who had actually read *Lost Horizon*, and thought he was living through a delirium, that in his brain fact and fiction had become inextricably entwined. I am pleased to tell you that he recovered, to the extent at least that he now regards the world outside as fiction.' Conway's eyes twinkled briefly then became serious again. 'But to think that you travelled that great desert without guides!'

I smiled. 'But with a very modern motor vehicle.'

'Still, it is something which has not previously been accomplished. When our sentinel spotted you from the crest of Zarnak, he could scarcely believe the evidence of his own eyes. Since my own indiscretion we have always half-expected an attempt from the Burmese side, which is why we keep a moderate watch. But a party of only three . . . !'

'We were four,' said Elizabeth quietly. 'My half-brother Simon was with us. Last night he was shot and wounded by bandits, and this morning we could find no trace of him despite a thorough search. We have to presume he wandered off in delirium and was kidnapped.'

'My dear lady . . .' Conway was all concern.

Elizabeth shook her head. 'Simon was more a relation than a friend. Nick here suspected his motives all along. What happened was terrible, but I can't assume grief I don't feel.'

Conway nodded. 'And this attack was by night, you say?' I realized his concern was not entirely for Elizabeth.

'I wonder what bandits can have been doing in that empty valley? I presume your last supply stop was in Myitkyina. Can they have followed you from there?'

We all looked a little embarrassed. I said: 'We did have some suspicions of the fellow who'd arranged our facilities, and our prime concern was to avoid bringing you unwelcome visitors. We certainly weren't followed on the last thirty miles. We drove deliberately over rocky ground so that our tyres wouldn't make tracks. And earlier on we took wide detours to make sure we were alone. How the bandits found us is a mystery, except that if they spotted us further back our general direction must have been obvious.'

Conway nodded. 'You are obviously careful as well as adventurous.'

'I don't know about the others, but for me it's hard to think about it as an adventure, except for that final trek through the tunnel. Strange perhaps, but planes and four-wheel-drives make travel very easy these days, if you have an idea where you're going and what you're looking for. The trick was to work out from your very slender clues which was the right valley and how to find the canyon. We were lucky to get it right on both counts, more or less first time. If we hadn't, if we'd exhausted our supplies or our petrol, we'd simply have gone back to Mandalay, rested, and tried again. I don't suppose any of us thought about danger.'

'Oh, I did,' said Warlock. 'I welcomed it. My life needed a little salt and pepper.'

'But you've none of you tackled this kind of journey before?'

'Well, perhaps not exactly. Though you'll be surprised to hear that – of the three of us, Elizabeth is the only one qualified. She's Elizabeth Battersby: the name means something back in the UK. You see, she's an explorer by profession, though not of quite the kind you'll remember, unless you're equipped to receive television here.'

Conway smiled and began to shake his head, but almost immediately started in surprise. 'Battersby, did you say? Elizabeth Battersby?'

Without quite meaning to, we had arrived at Elizabeth's moment of truth. Despite the accumulation of evidence that this quiet ageing Englishman really was the Conway her father had sought, despite our triumph in arriving safely at a destination most people would have thought imaginary, she asked her next question timorously, as though afraid of the possible response. 'My father . . . came looking for you. It was several years ago. He never came back. Have you any idea . . . what happened to him?'

For a moment or two Conway looked close to his real age. His jaw sagged helplessly; then composure returned. 'My dear lady,' he murmured again. 'This building is my home. It has a very few rooms, used for our occasional guests during their period of acclimatization. At an English university you might have called it the Master's Lodge. Behind and above us, straggling up the mountainside' – he waved a hand – ' is the lamasery proper. You will see it, or perhaps I should say much of it, in the morning. Miss Elizabeth, your father is there. But I am sorry to tell you that he is in our hospital wing.'

13

Nicholas Brent's Narrative (1980):

'OUR TESTING TIME IS CLOSER THAN I THOUGHT'

October 23, ten pm. We have been residents in Shangri-La for little more than a day, yet I am astonished to find how unquestioningly we have accepted as normal all the previously unfamiliar details of life here. Perhaps that is only because life here seems just a shade less immediately exhilarating than we had hoped. No strain, no timetables, and no callers. The compensation, presuming that the longevity business really works, is that one needn't be afraid of wasting time.

Today we all experienced something akin to jet-lag, and for me at least eating in the evening was impossible, which is why I came to bed early, only to find that I can't sleep. Even at lunch I could manage only a few spoonfuls of the vegetable biryani which was placed before me. Conway came in a little while ago with a small glass jugful of a drink he calls *calpis*, which is apparently processed from milk mixed with non-acid fruit juices. I remember drinking something like it years ago in Yokohama. It's refreshing and soothing, and I imagine quite nourishing; all in all the perfect drink for Shangri-La. Lying here since eight, my limbs strangely heavy and swollen, I was afraid at first of missing something, but I hadn't the energy to go back downstairs. At least I'm keeping my log up to date while things are fresh in my mind.

I woke this morning to a resplendent view of the high snow slopes of Karakal, perfectly framed through my window. A picture postcard couldn't do better. The mountain was drenched in sunshine as it rose majestically above the lamasery buildings, which I now see are rather more interesting architecturally than my first impression suggested, being an attractive mixture of many styles and no style. Oriental domes and turrets are there all right, but they don't predominate. It was a scene that should have been set to music, like the heralding of a new life. Before breakfast the three of us met on the stone terrace and surveyed the view in the other direction, across the deep valley with its still rising mist, already being burned away by a sun which blazed proudly from a deep blue sky. Elizabeth was busy with the cine camera, and I took some snaps which I hope will give a better impression than my descriptions. (Talking of snaps, there's no doubt at all that those monastic buildings are the ones seen in the background of that old photograph found by Elizabeth in her father's library.) The problem is to get a vantage point from which the whole spread of the buildings can be included. As Conway told us when he came to usher us in to breakfast, the main concern of the various architects was not achieving beauty but building as close to the rock as possible, so as to avoid the winds of near hurricane strength which occasionally whistle down from the glacier. The many different levels which result are connected sometimes by interior staircases, but whenever practicable (in view of the extreme age of some of the inhabitants) by long winding ramps. Similarly the outside doors are reached by looping pink paths which wind their unhurried way through rockeries and small flower gardens. It's all fascinating, though a mite muddling to the eye. The sun helps when it's out: difficult to believe that as much as forty degrees can separate noon and evening temperatures.

Breakfast was taken in a calm plain room where white curtains moved gently in an almost imperceptible breeze. Despite the sudden revelations of last evening, Conway was clearly still concerned to lead us as gently as possible into serious discussion, and not until the meal was over did he give us a description of Sir Arthur's precarious state of health. From his diary, which had been preserved, it seemed that the old explorer had found his way quite unerringly to his destination, though the journey had taken far longer than he thought and cost the lives of some members of his expedition. By disregarding everybody's advice he had eventually come to the now fragmentary wreckage of the plane which had brought Conway and his companions to the high northern plateau in 1931. (It occurred to me to wonder, though I refrained from asking, whether the lamas ever found a way of honourably recompensing the Maharajah of Chandrapore for his very considerable loss.)

The excitement of the find had been too much for Sir Arthur in his already weakened condition. He collapsed on the icy ground with what appeared to be a stroke of medium severity. His remaining bearers thereupon strapped him to a makeshift stretcher and were about to attempt the return journey when emissaries from Shangri-La prevailed upon them instead to make the short climb south-eastward to the lamasery. After that Sir Arthur, though much fêted on his arrival and for a while apparently recovered, varied between good health accompanied by keen intellect and relapses into an almost comatose state. On some days, Conway said, it was possible to have long talks with him about his career and about the future of Shangri-La, while on others he merely gazed listlessly out of his window, refusing food and disinclined to do anything except hum the popular songs of his youth.

'Is it a form of senility?' asked Warlock.

'If it is, it's premature,' I answered. 'He's only fifteen years older than me. Has he been told of our arrival?'

'Not yet,' said Conway. 'I would like your advice on

that point. I have a suspicion that the sudden shock of seeing his daughter again may have the restorative effect for which we all hope. On the other hand it could kill him. We have only lay doctors here, and it seems that our guess is as good as theirs.'

In the end it was agreed to leave a decision until the afternoon, when Sir Arthur was generally at his strongest. The servants came in to clear away the breakfast things: I asked our host about the aromatic marmalade I had enjoyed, but he would tell me only that its name was Conway's Reform Club. He used the pleasantry as an excuse to stand up and take his leave, on the grounds that he had matters of administration to attend to. He looked forward to further conversation at lunch, and meanwhile suggested that we should spend an hour or two exploring the terraces and gardens; though he warned us to take care before venturing on to the mountainside itself, and not under any circumstances to walk on the glacier. Should we so wish, we would be allowed to enter the lamasery unattended, providing we turned back at any sets of blue doors we might find. These led to the private quarters of the lamas, who had all been apprised of our arrival and would not be surprised to find us in the library, the music room or the art gallery. As he completed these instructions, he bowed and was gone.

'If I hadn't heard of English reserve,' cried Warlock, 'dang me if I wouldn't call that man's reluctance to discuss things downright inhospitable. There are a hundred questions I want to ask.'

I felt bound to demur. 'It seems to me we've done a fair amount of talking since yesterday afternoon.'

'Yes, but we haven't learned a lot. I feel as though I'm playing a part in a mystery movie, and a supporting part at that.'

Though naturally preoccupied, Elizabeth managed to

raise a smile. 'He's adapted very thoroughly to oriental manners. Never rush into an encounter which promises to be rewarding or enjoyable: make the early stages last as long as you can.'

'You'll notice,' I added, 'that he avoided asking us how long we intend to stay. But then, *he* wasn't asked that either. He was allowed to discover for himself Shangri-La's most curious custom, of making its guests thoroughly at home and then preventing them from leaving. A custom, by the way, which we all knew of when we came.'

Warlock nodded. 'I sure did. Though frankly, unless they intend to immobilize the Land Rover – or already have – I don't see how they could stop us. I mean, there's an easy way out now, and force just isn't in their line.'

With plenty to think about, we moved through French doors into the warmly welcoming morning, and spent half an hour by a fountain, simply sunning ourselves and breathing in great lungfuls of intoxicating air. I shall refrain from further detailed descriptions of our physical surroundings, as my account will eventually be accompanied by annotated illustrations, each as revealing as my Zeiss and I can make it. I must, however, make it clear that although lodge and lamasery are separated by no more than sixty yards, into this space a finger of mountain obtrudes itself, and the area has been developed into formal gardens and rockeries connected by paved promenades. We climbed gradually through these to a point above the lamasery buildings and found that we could look over a low wall into a paved area where twenty or more lamas were variously occupied in walking conversations or in group discussions while seated on low stone benches. Some of their heads were tonsured, some completely shaven; their gowns were all of bright brown, with tasselled white belts. Since we were probably being watched, it seemed unwise to stare, and so we climbed still further. On the crest of the hill was a small green pavilion which had been neatly fitted into a more or less circular saucer in the granite; having gained this we discovered ourselves to be in command of yet another magnificent view, perhaps the most striking we had seen so far, away across an extensive glacier which filled the entire area between Karakal to the north-east and Zarnak to the south of us. In every direction the view was closed off by snow-tipped mountains, one range behind another. Surrounded by such magnificence, we sat contented for an hour or more; the library and the music room could plainly wait. Our reveries were disturbed only once, by a servant who climbed up to us with lemon tea in tall glasses, and little cakes which tasted like hot cross buns.

We were careful about putting thoughts into conversation, as it had been decided that our first impressions should go straight into my log. (I was the only one with even rudimentary shorthand.) Eventually Elizabeth expressed her opinion:

'It may seem silly to say so, but the whole place reminds me of Monaco more than anywhere else. I mean, have you ever been to the gardens at the top of Eze village? And in Monaco itself there's Rainier imposing a benevolent despotism on his handful of subjects, from his fairy-tale palace which doesn't have too obvious a relation with what goes on below. Of course, you couldn't call modern Monte Carlo a Valley of Blue Moon, not with all those concrete high-rises. To get that impression these days you have to trek all the way up the mountain to La Turbie and see the Roman ruins of the Trophy of Augustus, which is about the same height above the Hotel de Paris as we are above the valley people here. From that height you can just about ignore the commercialization and concentrate on the geography.

'People here obviously lead much more useful lives

than the rich parasites on the Cote d'Azur. And there has to be a bit of magic about, because you never even asked about my leg this morning, and the answer is I never thought about it myself since those women anointed me last night with God knows what. All kinds of goo, and what looked like pine leaves but probably weren't. Probably from that *tangatse* plant that keeps all the lamas young. The women looked pretty much as you'd expect, no sign at all of retardation, but then the legend says that the valley people themselves can't benefit. Racially almost indistinguishable from what I found four or five years ago in the Hindu Kush and Afghanistan, though perhaps there was a touch of Chinese about the oldest one. No English spoken, of course.

'Vegetation in the valley seems ample but unexciting. But did you notice the birds this morning? The valley must be a natural sanctuary. I saw an odd little grey lizard too, and something that looked like a hairy dormouse, and from one of the houses I distinctly heard a dog barking. Most of the houses were in a simple tent style, with a stout pole up the middle supporting a thatched or rope roof. It looked as though every room is built separately in this way, then joined together according to the size of the family. I'm dying to explore the communal life.

'Well, plenty of time for research. I suppose I'd better go easy on this ankle for a few days. Conway said he'd lend me a cane, which will help a lot. Obviously one's breath is constantly going to be taken away here, not only emotionally but physically. That's hardly surprising. Within a few hours we climbed out of that sun-bleached desert with its equatorial climate to the Valley of Blue Moon, which is tropical and humid and can never be anything else because it's so protected on all sides. Then the drag up here brings us to temperate and more so, depending I suppose on the season and the wind direction. Even on the lower slopes of Karakal, just above the lamasery, there are snow slopes that look permanent. By the way, I noticed this morning that at one spot in the snow there's an odd rectangular formation that doesn't look natural. With the sun high you can't see it, but it's as though a giant had been making patterns with the tip of his walking-stick.

'I notice there are no locks on any of the doors. People trust each other; indeed, what point would there be in stealing? I hope we don't contaminate them. There was a play I always liked called *Our Town*, by Thornton Wilder, about a New Hampshire community at the turn of the century. In the first act they didn't have locks on their doors either. Then in the second act they did: civilization had caught up with them. The narrator said there hadn't been any burglaries yet, but everybody had heard about them. Heaven preserve Shangri-La from the need to defend itself.'

Warlock seemed so embarrassed as to be out of character:

'I don't know why you should want my opinions at all. I'm not even supposed to *be* here, I just came along for the ride. What most impressed me so far was the way we were dosed on arrival. Like California for keeping out everybody else's mouldy fruit. I wonder what would have happened if we'd refused to drink the stuff? Not that I even thought of doing so: it was important to show Conway that we trusted him. And it *was* trust, even though he drank himself. After all, he could have switched the glasses some way, or taken an antidote beforehand.

'Well, I suppose I'm just tickled pink that we made it. I can't wait to tell that son of a bitch Gentry that one of his investments paid off at last. Whether Shangri-La is everything I expected, that's too soon to say. All I can tell you is I feel like gangbusters, just rarin' to go. Mind you, that's this morning. Last night I wasn't half so sure. Do you know I couldn't sleep? Kept missing the news and the late night movie. Conway must be telepathic because about midnight he knocked on my door and chatted for a while. Brought me some guides to the region: seems to think I'm the navigator among us. Needless to say, Shangri-La didn't figure in any of the indexes. I finally nodded off reading *Robinson Crusoe*, which seemed appropriate enough. Did you see the moon over the mountain? Nearly full it was, and everything as bright as a freeway intersection.

'Frankly, I'm terrified by the way I just accepted it all, but once you're here there isn't much else you can do. It's as though we'd caught the wild goose without even chasing it. Do you know, on the back of my bedroom door is a carved panel that's already so familiar to me I could swear I'd known it for years. Talk about familiarity breeding contempt. But then, as the man said, you need a little familiarity to breed anything.

'The only drawback so far is the absolute lack of mystery. We've still to be shown the lamasery, but I guess even the full tour of that can't occupy more than a day or so. Do you suppose the lamas really know we've arrived. Are they peering at us now, through telescopes? Do they care? Are they just pretending they don't, like the English in railroad carriages? Oh, I suppose the place can't help getting anglicized, after fifty years under Conway's rule. Fifty years! *There's* a creepy thought. Conway's hardly changed at all, not from across the table at any rate, yet when he first came here I was still at school. Maybe he knows a good plastic surgeon, somewhere on the road to Mandalay.

'The food won't be a problem: San Francisco Chinese,

I'd say, Cantonese cuisine, as near as dammit. Somehow I don't think there'll be any red meat, which is just fine by me.

'Well, that's about it. For a while there last night I felt like Jonathan Harker at the Borgo Pass on his way to Castle Dracula, but now I've seen the place in daylight everything's fine: nobody's going to boil us up in a pot. I'm going to like it here, no doubt of that, especially if the library's all that it's cracked up to be. Not that I can get anything out of my visit except a pleasant old age: I don't think you can sign on for the extension once you're past sixty. What was that crack in *Citizen Kane* about old age? It's the only disease you don't look forward to being cured of.'

I began dictating into my pocket memo:

'I want to know more about the valley people. We saw them only briefly, but they gave me the impression of knowing instinctively what life is all about. You simply can't imagine discontent here, but if there is any, I expect it's looked after very effectively by the principle of moderation. Unless any of them get ambitious – and why would they? – Those people down there have it made: an idyllic place to live, and up on the hill a group of benevolent despots making sure that equilibrium is preserved.

'I wonder whether Conway's writing another book about Shangri-La. The life of Perrault is fine and admirable, but there must be a lot of incidents worth recording in the daily life. By the way, did you notice that slight limp of his? I have a feeling it gives him some pain, though he covers it up very well . . .'

I was interrupted by an already familiar voice. 'It is most kind of you to be concerned, but I think it is your own problems that must first require attention.' By emerging from the lodge at a level some way up the slope

Conway had contrived to approach us unseen, and now stood at our side, amused at our discomfiture. 'Over the next few days I look forward to hearing all your impressions, and I am delighted that you are recording them. But now I come as the bearer of two items of news. First, Sir Arthur is reported to be on the better side today; not perhaps at his brightest, but serene. So you may look forward to meeting him this afternoon. He has been given a slight sedative so that any shock will hopefully be absorbed. Second, the midday meal, which in Shangri-La we do eat at midday, awaits you.'

It was the lightest of repasts, but Conway informed us that he had long ago introduced the English habit of a substantial tea at four, and that if we were hungry at any other time we had only to say so to any of the servants.

'I don't think any of us,' I said, 'are as hungry for food as for information. For instance, I understood you last night to say that Sir Arthur came here by the old northern route. Yet according to your own 1940 account that was blocked in the mid-thirties.'

'So it was, and so but for a tragic accident it might have remained. In 1947 a solitary traveller was observed to stumble alone through the high passes in that area and to fall prostrate in the snow. At great risk to themselves our hardiest mountaineers went out to investigate, but by the time they reached him he was frozen stiff. On their way back the mountaineers observed not far from the previous landslip a series of ledges from which they felt sure that pulleys could be let down to raise and lower items at least as heavy as a man. A path was easily made from the lamasery to the top of the ledges, and the new system was put into practice just as soon as we could obtain the necessary apparatus. Apart from the humanitarian viewpoint, there are not so many of us here that we can afford to waste the lives of possible incumbents, especially since our few women lamas are well past childbearing age. There was also the consideration that providing secrecy can be maintained the northern route gives a useful alternative access for porterage, especially since the mid-fifties when the Chinese completed their long-planned road from Chengtu to Lhasa. It runs, in fact, not much more than fifty miles to the north of this spot, though direct access to it is quite impossible: one has to circumnavigate a range of unscaleable peaks. By trial and error our porters learned to pick it up at a trading post some twenty miles further east.'

At this point we all heard a discreet tap on the door. Conway sprang to his feet. 'You will find that there are very few secrets in Shangri-La,' he said. 'But now, since it is high time you met other residents, here is someone of whom you have certainly heard.' He opened the door. 'My very dear Chang.'

There was a chorus of exclamation as we rose to our feet at the sight of these two legendary figures in the same room. Indeed, I found myself almost gasping for breath as I beheld in the doorway an extremely aged yet sturdy-seeming Chinaman of short and rounded stature, leaning on a finely-carved chest-high walking stick which I instantly coveted. Conway bowed affectionately to him; we followed suit, and the gesture was graciously returned. We all sat down, Chang with obvious care but perfect balance, and more tea was brought in. What was on all our minds was a calculation of Chang's age, but Conway saved us the trouble.

'I did, of course, invite this precious person to join us for breakfast, but he never did eat much, and these days he lives primarily on honey and milk, with one light meal in the evening. However, I am happy to confirm that his wits and his hearing are as sharp as ever. Two nights ago he demolished me at chess, even though he celebrated last month his one-hundred-and-forty-seventh birthday, thus quite belying the stories he passed on to me years ago about orientals not benefiting from the regime at Shangri-La.'

'There are exceptions to every rule, my dear Conway,' said the old man, extending to each of us in turn a cool and feathery hand. 'Indeed, I believe I may still claim to look younger than my real age.'

I smiled at the joke. As none of us had previously seen a one-hundred-and-forty-seven-year-old man, it would have been difficult to make the comparison. Chang sipped his tea and began to recomend several varieties of leaf grown in the valley. I found his accent disorientating, perhaps because it did not have the suave quality suggested by his remarks as quoted in *Lost Horizon* and by the performance of H. B. Warner in the film. Here instead were sounds more comparable with the pidgin English expected of Charlie Chan, uttered in a voice so light and delicate that one sometimes had to strain to hear it. But if the manner of his conversation was slightly unexpected, the matter was shrewd and positive. He joined with Conway in eliciting our story, and his comments were never less than pertinent. Warlock described his renewed post-retirement interest in Conway's typescript, his approach to Elizabeth and their need to involve me. She talked of her father's stories, his plans for his last expedition, and of Simon. I came in with the Death Valley aspect and my London researches. Conway's frequent nods and litle exclamations indicated that he was following our adventures with almost boyish enthusiasm. But as we came more up to date, and a temple bell announced the time as two o'clock, his tone became more serious, and he interrupted the narrative.

'I think we should postpone discussion of what happened in the desert until later, for you will be more concerned now to prepare yourselves for the meeting with Sir Arthur. In due course, I trust you will not mind repeating your entire story to our Council of Seniors, who will have many questions to ask about the outside world. Perhaps, however, I should ask now about your ultimate plans. You came here knowing something of our rules. Is it your intention to obey them?'

Warlock laughed. 'You forget, my dear sir, that none of us was certain that Shangri-La even existed. We had only your word for it.'

'I must confess,' I said, 'that my chief feeling, assuming the truth of your story, was that you should be persuaded to share it in some way with the hundreds of millions outside. I have no idea how that might best be accomplished, but they have never needed encouragement more than they do now. The world stands perhaps at the most dangerous corner of its history, with enormously powerful national groups capable of blowing each other up at the touch of a button, and taking the rest of us with them. Sooner or later, that may include Shangri-La. Our own remarkable success in finding you only demonstrates that you are less remote than you were. Or perhaps that, if one does not have faith, curiosity is the next best thing.'

Chang and Conway both sat silent and motionless at this, until a servant came in to clear away. Then Conway nodded to himself and stood up, smiling reassuringly at me as he did so. We all moved into the open air, Chang availing himself of a wheelchair which was waiting. Conway guided him along the parapet and pointed to the northern snows. 'Over there, below the twin peaks, is where we found your father, Miss Elizabeth,' he said.

'What happened to his party?' I asked. 'Those who survived, I mean.'

'One European died after a week. The Nepalese were restored to full health and lead contented lives as lamasery servants. One of them waited on you at lunch.'

'And what medical treatment has my father received?' asked Elizabeth.

'Our brother Franz was a qualified doctor, from the University of Berlin.'

'Was?'

'I am sorry to say that he died two years ago. We would dearly like to recruit another medical man, but that is in the lap of fate. Perhaps we should go out and kidnap somebody.' He smiled at his own irony.

'And Brother Franz diagnosed a stroke?'

Conway was pensive. 'As I recall, there was no doubt in his mind that a light stroke was a matter of medical record, but it seemed that that was not the crux of the matter. The direct effects passed, and yet your father was not well. It was more than disorientation, more like amnesia. One day he made me look into a mirror with him, and I knew he was troubled by his knowledge that I was his senior yet appeared so much younger. He had forgotten all he knew about Shangri-La. He had trouble, too, in articulating his thoughts. He began to have trouble buttoning his clothes, and had to be helped. At meals I would notice him in perplexity as to which spoon or fork to use. Franz at last came to the conclusion that Sir Arthur had indeed recovered from the stroke itself, but was now suffering from the distressing malady which used to be called premature senility. I believe you have a more dignified name for it.'

'Alzheimer's disease,' said Warlock. 'My brother-in-law has it. But shouldn't the life here help that? I'm given to understand that the chief cause is hardening of the arteries caused by stress.'

'We have tried everything we know.'

'If I may interpose,' said Chang, 'there is nothing unfamiliar about this disease to the inhabitants of Shangri-

La. There was a singular case of it in 1912. The sufferer had been with us for a number of years but was of course still a novice. I think he was seventy-eight at the time. He had not yet, at any rate, been admitted to the full lamasery ritual which involves increasing doses of *tangatse*. His consumption was increased immediately, and within the year he had so far recovered his wits as to be allowed to return to all his projects. He was subsequently admitted to the senior brotherhood, and I am pleased to say that he is still with us, and very active for his venerable years.'

Conway nodded, with a faint smile. 'Chang will not mind my revealing that he is speaking of himself. Your father has not yet responded so favourably, but of course he has been with us for a very short time whereas Chang had had twenty years or more of the modified regime. We can only wait and see whether time and *tangatse* will reverse Sir Arthur's chemical balance; though a professional doctor, if we could import one, might call us foolish for entertaining any such hope. Meanwhile, though it may be an exaggeration to say that Sir Arthur is enjoying life, I can assure you that he feels no pain.'

There was a pause. 'And Franz died?' I said. 'Even after many years at Shangri-La?'

Conway shrugged. 'It happens sometimes. He was more than fifty when he came, and in some cases that is too late for the expected benefits to accrue. He died at a normal old age, in his eighty-eighth year.'

On a northern-facing balcony of the lamasery I watched a brown-robed figure take the sun as we now padded in our house slippers towards the rambling main buildings. At our approach the impressive main doors were opened as though by magic; once inside, Chang was wheeled away by servants through a curtained alcove, while we took stock of an octagonal entrance hall with gilded fan vaulting. There was a smell of incense which I liked, though I saw from his expression that it was not to Warlock's taste.

'The ornate door on the left leads to the library,' said Conway. 'Follow me, please.'

He led us through a darkened ante-room, up a rising ramp from which we had a view through pointed windows of interior gardens, and along a landing through a blue double door. On the other side, in fresh air which made our cheeks glow, six steps led down into an ornamental garden which had been excavated into the shape of a shallow cup, its length stretching away from us. At the central low point was an irregular tiled pool about twenty feet by seven, fed at the far end by a sparkling stream which must have come straight from the glacier. Carp and other exotic fish lurked beneath the water lilies. Surrounding this pool was a narrow crazy-paved path, and from this base alternating small lawns and flower-beds ran up to the next level, which was accomplished either by steps or by a spiral ramp. Here there was less sense of a sun-trap; above the path the landscaping became more natural, losing itself in long grass and a small wood, clearly the one from whose upper reaches we had this morning peered briefly at the lamas. At the far end there was access to a narrow terrace, where those who could stand a wind which was to say the least invigorating, might enjoy the most breathtaking view across the icefield. Between us and the ice, on the other side of a low wall, was a gap about nine feet wide revealing what may have been a hundred-foot drop to an irregular row of broken subterranean peaks as jagged as sharks' teeth. Despite these unwelcoming if magnificent sights, the prevailing impression in the garden itself was of brilliant warm sunshine under an azure sky.

Conway had once again contrived to absent himself

without my noticing. For a brief moment I suspected some sort of trap, but then I observed that there was another human being in the garden, someone from whom the immense view had distracted us. At the high level there were two sun shelters, and under one of them a wheelchair with a man in it, a man whose white hair gleamed in the sun but whose face was half turned away from us as though entranced by the majesty of Karakal. In Agatha Christie's *And Then There Were None* there is an elderly character named General MacArthur who sits on a cliff top waiting for the end which he knows must come and which he is incapable of diverting. Just that impression was given by this our first view of Sir Arthur, for of course it was he, ten years older than when I last saw him and looking at least twenty. His gaunt profile was still intact but his eyes had lost their lustre and peered vaguely at us as we approached to stand about ten feet from him in a little row, Elizabeth gripping my hand in nervousness lest we made too sudden a movement.

'Good afternoon,' I said. 'We are newcomers to Shangri-La. I believe you are Sir Arthur Battersby.'

There ensued ten seconds, perhaps, of total silence while the old man's gaze wandered from one to the other of us and finally fixed on Elizabeth. He opened his mouth to speak. It seemed at first that he was going to stammer, but he conquered the impediment. 'Daughter,' he said.

The emotion of the halting conversation which followed, with Elizabeth crouching at Sir Arthur's knees, was too great for me to convey it in words. Indeed, Warlock and I took a turn round the paths for ten minutes so that father and daughter could be alone. Then a servant arrived with tea and some curious little sweetmeats like petits fours; we all perched on teak stools as though we had been invited to a party, and chatted about the weather and how we had found our way to Shangri-La, giving the story of our adventures in little pieces so that the old man would not get too excited. It was not at all clear how much he took in. There was no doubt that he knew Elizabeth, and he seemed to remember me too, but could not call either of us by name. We avoided mentioning Simon. We spoke of London, and Marlow, at both of which he nodded vaguely but showed no interest. We told him what a great success his own expedition had been, and congratulated him on finding his goal. He sighed at that, but his meaning was hard to determine. When he spoke, it was in half-sentences which were empty of emphasis and usually trailed away incoherently, leaving his mouth sagging open in pursuit of some expression which simply would not come to him and the search for which he eventually abandoned. This was no more than the shell of Sir Arthur Battersby.

After half an hour it was a relief to see a curious little procession making its way up the path to join us. Conway and Chang were reaching the second level in bamboo wheelchairs pushed by smiling servants. As he caught my eye, Conway made a gesture of mock shame, but I guessed he needed to conserve his energy. The pair of them reminded me irresistibly of valetudinarian ex-army men at Worthing or Bexhill, working up an appetite for their boarding-house mulligatawny soup and roast saddle of mutton.

'I trust that you approve of our little garden,' whispered Chang to me when they were settled on the terrace. 'We were lucky enough to acquire some years ago a novice who had been a topiarist and landscaper. It was he who devised this arrangement and supervised the excavation. I think we may award him high marks, for although we have several gardens this is the only one which is pleasant at all seasons when the sun shines – which, you know, it often does.'

'It seems to me that pleasant is too modest a word. This must be one of the most perfect spots in the entire world. The view across the glacier reminds me very much of Yosemite, but I imagine that here you are not much troubled by bears.'

'Not here, certainly,' replied Chang in his sing-song undertone, 'though we have been told that they can be encountered in the mountains across the desert to our west. We have not been sufficiently concerned to authorize an expedition. We were however successful in founding our own cattle herd in the valley, so that fresh milk is always available. You see, we do constantly strive to improve our situation. And here comes our brother who has been most responsible for our scientific development. Brother Franklin, who was once Mr Barnard.'

Once again I failed to resist the impression that I was living in the pages of a story book. If Chang had announced the Wizard of Oz, I could scarcely have been more impressed. The American, who like the rest of us wore a richly-decorated ankle-length gown, was as gnarled and contorted as the popular picture of an aged leprechaun; but he seemed full of energy and almost excessively cheerful for a man who must be just about reaching his century. I liked him at once, and it was clear that he and Warlock would have much to say to each other. His accent was still definitely American, his slang stuck in the early thirties: he sounded like a character out of Damon Runyon. 'I don't know what in hell's happened to American get-up-and-go,' he grumbled. 'Do you know I've been waiting fifty years to be joined by a compatriot? And now I'll have to make do with a Canadian.' As I sipped my tea a little later I noticed that Warlock was learning from Barnard how the rack-and-pinion railway was installed; Elizabeth was showing her father some of the English varieties in the flower beds; and Conway was discussing with Chang the advisability of another coat of paint for the pavilions. Chang then signalled his desire to be taken indoors, and with gracious gestures left us. 'He's sometimes quite frail now,' said Conway to me as he departed, 'though in argument as subtle as ever. I use my chair occasionally in order to keep him company; he doesn't like to be the odd one out.'

We strolled up into the wood, which had its own path in the shape of a figure of eight. 'There are no words to express any of this,' I said. 'Barnard even looks like the actor who played him in the film, though Chang, of course, does not.'

Conway smiled. 'I'm sure you expect to wake up shortly. But by tomorrow, perhaps, you may be convinced that Shangri-La is no more remarkable than, say, an Oxford college. It's just that here there are no double-decker buses rumbling down the High. We do everything we can to remove the stresses from which your world suffers.'

'You can have no idea how those stresses have intensified since your last visit.'

'It's true that I have no actual experience, but we read things even in *The Times* which make us shudder. Newspapers reach us now within three months, you know, and we all take the greatest interest in practically every item. Of course your explanations will be even more vivid, and we look forward to hearing them. But there will be time enough: we shall not press you and you must not feel impelled to hurry. Opportunities for discussion will arise quite naturally, as intervals in your exploration of our amenities. And it will take you at least a week to become physically acclimatized.'

'I must admit I'm still a bit jet-lagged.'

'Jet-lagged. That is a phrase I have seen here and there in *The Times*, but never fully understood.'

'Travel was more gracious in your day. You've obviously heard of jet aeroplanes.'

'Yes, indeed. The invention of Mr Whittle, I believe.'

'That's right. They get you from one place to another at seven hundred miles an hour, the Concorde now at double that. But businessmen who circle the world in two days have developed an ailment called jet-lag. Their metabolism gets thrown out of gear. Imagine going from London to Los Angeles, that's six thousand miles, in less than eleven hours. But Los Angeles is eight hours behind Greenwich time. So if you have breakfast and lunch at home, then climb on a plane and eat lunch and supper, not to mention a few drinks to pass the time, you arrive in LA perfectly bloated at a time which to you is midnight but to them is still afternoon. By the time you get to bed, thoroughly jaded, you've probably eaten yet another meal at a time when your body expects to be sleeping; and when you do want to sleep, it's breakfast time in London, which means that your body wants to wake up. You toss and turn all night, and next day at lunch your eyes seal up on you and you're good for nothing all afternoon.'

Conway made a clicking noise with his tongue. 'It does not sound attractive. I used to enjoy my travel. The ocean liners took their time, but one arrived completely refreshed. I read that your aeroplanes these days can hold up to five hundred people. The safe sustaining of such weight in the air to me is inconceivable.'

I grinned. 'To me too, but I'm no scientist. As I recall, it's something to do with engine thrust over wing span.'

'And the cost of a flight such as you just mentioned?'

'You'll be petrified. More than two thousand pounds return in first class, and constantly increasing. And for that you can't even stretch out in a berth. In fact, there's no way in which the quality of life can be said to have improved since your days in England. Except in the home, that is. Every man has in his own kitchen the appliances which forty years ago only plutocrats could afford: central heating, refrigerators, washing machines. And television, of course – a constant supply of virtually free entertainment. Step outside the house, though, and you'll see how social life has suffered, because people simply can't afford to congregate very often, with cinema seats in London at four pounds a head, and fifty pence – that's ten shillings to you – for an ice cream.'

Conway smiled in bewilderment. 'But what has caused this tremendous inflation? The cost of materials?'

'It isn't the materials, it's labour, and that's unreliable as well as expensive. It sometimes seems that today's average British workman would rather strike than get on with the job. The Germans call it the British sickness. Ever since the war, when Labour got in, the unions have called the shots, and most of them have no wider horizon than the size of the wage packet. Their members have more money than they know what to do with: they take a forty-hour week and continental holidays for granted, but they don't contribute. It's all take and no give. They don't understand, or perhaps don't care, that they've reduced Britain to a second-rate power.'

'So you have a new class system based on money?'

'Partly on money, but race comes into it too. No white Briton these days will take on a menial job. The bus conductors and street sweepers and lavatory cleaners are all Pakistani or West Indian immigrants. They've assimilated very well, and in fact they're the only people who still have an old-fashioned idea of service: the white Briton has forgotten how to say thank you.'

'And is this grim picture you paint equally true of other countries?'

'Some. Perhaps most. Big cities are soul-destroying places now: concrete high-rises and hamburger bars make them all look the same; even in Reykjavik last year I saw signs for Kentucky Fried Chicken.'

'I beg your pardon?'

'An American fast food chain. In some cities it's dangerous to be out on the streets at night. Even the holiday spots have lost their character, since they all started to cater for package tours. And the model they follow seems to be Las Vegas, with endless banks of slot machines taking money away from dimwitted tourists.'

'You make it sound as though the cataclysm which Father Perrault feared may be closer than I thought.'

'We've stood on the brink of it many times. For the last forty years the world has consisted of shifting areas of unrest, rubbing up against each other and trying to provoke a fight. The fact that several groups have a stockpile of devastating bombs is all that prevents any one of them from pressing the button: the fear of retaliation.

'I presume you are thinking principally of Russia and the United States, but what other groups seem to you to endanger the world?'

'The Arabs and the Israelis are constantly at each other's throats. The Irish always did like a fight, but now they've become terrorists fighting for a cause which doesn't make sense. Iran got rid of a tyrant and replaced him with a maniac. Uganda spawned a monster called Amin who ruled the country like a buffoon and kept his enemies' heads in a refrigerator. The president of the United States was forced to resign after denying that he was a crook. Planes are at the mercy of hi-jackers; old ladies get battered to death by burglars; young children are sexually assaulted; homosexuals have become not merely respectable but admirable. When you catch a criminal there's always some intellectual prepared to stand up and defend him as a socially deprived person, or even as a freedom fighter. I don't think you'd like our world at all, Conway.'

'That's quite a speech.'

'It's the reason I so wanted to find Shangri-La. Perhaps I really wanted to tell you what had happened to your world, and to persuade you to do something about it.'

'Oh, but no world can be perfect. Mine certainly wasn't. I lost fifteen close friends, quite senselessly, in the Battle of the Somme alone. Even here in Shangri-La, though we still cherish our ideals, we are concerned at one physical aspect of our lives which seems to be not what it was.'

'And what is that?'

He smiled. 'The weather. We sometimes think that we are in for a new Ice Age. The average noon temperature on this terrace has gone down every year except three since 1960. There are more avalanches too; only last year two of our valley people were killed in one.'

'I have to say I was surprised by the chill winds.'

'You wish Father Perrault had built Shangri-La in the valley?'

'Not exactly. Up here, it makes some sort of point for the valley people – a symbol of perfection to which they aspire, not knowing of our occasional discomforts. Perhaps Perrault thought of our icy winds as a kind of hair shirt; but I sometimes think that if I were creating an idyll, I might choose a South Sea island. I see you smile. Would I be wrong?'

'I'm afraid you would, now. The South Sea islands you remember have all been contaminated, taken over. The cities look like anywhere else. I was in Honolulu last year and it might have been Blackpool.'

He shook his head sadly. 'And when I went there in the Twenties, it was like a Gauguin painting come to life. Do you ever think there are too many people in the world?'

'Indeed I do, all bent on doing their own thing and

intellectually out of control. Most people *need* controlling: they can't think for themselves. That reminds me, I read your book.'

'My book?'

'*The Mind of Future Man*.'

'But surely you were scarcely old enough – '

'No, I mean I read it this year. In the British Museum.'

'Ah, yes? I suppose control became its theme, though I began by thinking on quite different lines. I'm sure that my views will be changed again after I have heard all you have to say. One is bound to be out of touch when one lives in a society where there has been no crime for a hundred years.'

'Unless you count your own kidnapping. In some American states that would have incurred the gravest penalties.'

'It's all a matter of viewpoint. As for the book, I stopped being pleased with it after I heard that it had been praised by Oswald Mosley.'

I smiled. 'And have you written no more?'

'Oh, indeed I have. But a man has only so many books in him, especially when he is no longer able to draw on his experience of the world. So I have made no further attempts at prophecy. My mind turns increasingly to the remote past – which is, of course, a very large country indeed.'

We took a final turn round the twisting paths. As we approached the others Conway put a hand on my shoulder and said: 'We must talk long and deeply. You have come at a fortunate time. For years we have badly lacked a realistic sense of the world whose future we presume to influence. Meanwhile, relax and enjoy the amenities of a place where, for the time being, fear is unknown. A place, as the prayer book says, of light, of refreshment and peace.'

'I'm afraid that's been changed too. They brought in a

new version in colloquial English. All the poetry of the seventeenth-century version has been dismissed as outdated.'

'And have they filled the churches by such an action?'

'Oh, no, they are emptier than ever. Though seventy per cent of Englishmen call themselves Christians, only one in a hundred goes to church regularly.'

As we rejoined Elizabeth and her father, Sir Arthur seeming brighter, Conway was stopped by a group of monks who took him aside. He returned to us with a grave face.

'It may be,' he said, 'that our testing time is closer than I thought. Apparently you were followed after all. Our scouts on Zarnak have just changed shifts, and the retiring ones report that yesterday evening a motorized vehicle not dissimilar to your own was driven all the way up to the north end of the valley. Having discovered no exit, it came back slowly, as though the occupants were trying to establish how else you could have disappeared. Probably they failed to do so, and have now gone south. But there is the possibility that they may return. I have ordered extra sentinels.'

Warlock groaned. 'I'd be damn sorry to think that we'd brought bad luck with us.'

'It may not be so. Our policy has always been to welcome strangers. It is only a little perplexing to find so many on our doorstep within two days. Incidentally, our scouts also reported some kind of aeroplane far to the south, but it was too far away for a detailed description.'

'What can we do?' asked Elizabeth.

Conway shrugged. 'At least we shall have ample warning. Meanwhile, I recommend an hour or two's rest before dinner. And if either of the gentlemen should fancy a game of billiards or snooker afterwards, we have an excellent table.' He smiled. 'Yes, made by Messrs. Riley of Burnley.'

14

Nicholas Brent's Narrative (1980):

'HERE I SHALL LIVE FOREVER'

The events which followed our first exploration of Shangri-La were so crowded together that they allowed no time for journal-keeping; and these notes are written some little while after our adventure's melodramatic climax, which so unexpectedly reshaped our intentions and our lives. First things first, however: I shall continue to relate events in chronological sequence, including all I can remember of my conversations with Conway. Elizabeth and Warlock had conversations too, of course, but I shall have to leave them to set down any necessary additions after they have read my own account.

Our second full day at the lamasery broke blue and bright, and whether or not the beginning of a warmer spell it seemed to encourage optimism even about the strangers in the outer valley. No further news of them came that morning, and as the day passed we relaxed into a receptive and inquisitive mood. Elizabeth spent as much time with her father as seemed sensible, and at lunch told me that he had called her by name. Meanwhile Warlock and I had had a fascinating morning with Conway, wandering through the more accessible portions of the lamasery, including the music room which boasted a fairly modern record player and one of those clumsy, heavy old tape-recorders whose existence I had almost forgotten, although I once owned one. The Shangri-La's relic had been rigged up by Barnard to fit into an electrical system all his own. There were discs or tapes of most major classics, though in the field of popular music Shangri-La seemed to have stopped at Glenn Miller and Benny

Goodman, which was fine by me. The library was as described by Hilton, an enchanting place full of silent bays and reading corners. Hemingway, Maugham, Scott Fitzgerald and other twentieth-century writers had now taken their places beside Swift and Balzac and Dostoevsky. I asked Conway, who had a habit of turning up at my side when I least expected him, whether he did not fear that when Shangri-La eventually came into its own the art of reading might have been succeeded by the easy availability of video versions of all the classics. (I had to explain what I meant.) He said no, that such methods could only lock into the mind someone else's interpretation; whereas reading was a process enabling the student to unleash his own imagination.

I took back to my room before lunch a copy of *The Diary of a Nobody*, not because I needed to read it again – I practically know it by heart – but because its Victorian propriety seemed so deliciously inappropriate on the slopes of Karakal. After the meal I decided to continue reading in the garden where yesterday we had met Sir Arthur; they call it Jethro's Pool after the man who designed it. The others went off to a piano recital, and as I sat on my secluded terrace I could faintly hear the distant notes of Schumann. I closed the book and, glancing up to the azure sky, thought for a moment of shock that I saw an aeroplane; but it was only a silent bird. As I lowered my eyes, I realized that Chang was watching me from a window seat in a sheltered balcony on the next level up.

He bowed almost imperceptibly. 'I trust that by now you are feeling at home with us.'

I put the book down and wandered over to him, leaning back on the terrace rail below his lofty perch. 'I don't know when I've felt so – so satisfied with things. Even though I'm still worried about what news your scouts may bring.'

'I urge you not to concern yourself about that matter. We are content that you took all possible precautions; and after all, I understand you lost a member of your own party in the process of getting here. Occasionally it is necessary to take chances. As Conway may have told you, since his return in 1941 we have welcomed less than a score of new residents, yet our numbers have been reduced by death to a considerably greater extent. It is indeed a game which death is winning. But let us be optimistic. At least our wild life is flourishing. The bird you were studying just now was a Bantu eagle, a very rare species.'

'And I took it for a plane. Incidentally, I suppose you must see planes now and then, which raises the question, don't they see you?'

Chang smiled. 'We are fortunate to be far from the normal commercial routes, and even today very few small craft could attempt a crossing of these mountains. They could of course fly along the valleys, but since they appear to lead nowhere there could be little point to such a proceeding. We do take certain precautions. You may observe that the roofs of these buildings are now brown, whereas your studies of Mr Hilton may have told you that they were originally blue. I believe the word for the scheme is camouflage. As for the Valley of Blue Moon, it is so very verdant that few signs of its inhabitation can be discerned even from this altitude, and at night a mist usually obliterates the lights. No, I am assured that from the air we are virtually invisible, unless a craft were to fly very low.'

A servant brought out a little tea table for Chang, and two minutes later performed the same service for me. Alone with a man three times my age, amid terrain ten thousand years older, I succumbed blissfully to a unique atmosphere, enjoying not only the civilizing beverage but the delicately coloured porcelain in which it was presented.

'Do any of your servants speak English?' I asked.

Chang shook his head. 'It is not an easy language. I remember the great difficulty I had with it myself, back in the Eighties. It was Perrault, you know, who insisted that I should become fluent. As it is hoped that our mission will eventually have much to say to the world at large, he thought it best to do so in the language which that world best understands. Your airlines, I am told, have come to a similar conclusion. However, those of us in full lama-hood make an effort to converse readily in all three valley dialects. We also have to cope occasionally with Tibetan or Burmese porters. Chinese, of course, gives me little trouble.'

'I don't look forward to following your example. Languages are a young man's game.'

'Ah, but in our terms, Mr Brent, you are young indeed. And your friend Miss Battersby – she seems even younger.'

'Much younger.'

Chang pursed his lips. 'Not enough to matter here, I think. She is, I take it, your particular friend?'

'I don't think we have said so, but you are very astute.'

'And has her injury fully healed?'

'Not yet fully. She was walking with a stick this morning.'

'It will come. These small tricks we can accomplish, like a conjuror. But we cannot work miracles. I doubt that her father will ever again be the man you remembered.'

'That may be. Still, I think Shangri-La itself is a kind of miracle. And you yourself are a living legend. Apart from your scene-stealing appearances in *Lost Horizon*, surely your age must make you unique in the world.'

'I regret to contradict you. You will shortly meet several of my seniors. Three have passed two hundred, and one of those is in absolute possession of all his faculties. As for me, I fear there are days when I am made to appreciate every year of my age. Yet in conversation with you, sir, I still feel myself to be your equal in all respects save that of physical exertion. Which reminds me that it is time for my rest.'

We both stood, Chang a little unsteadily. He smiled apologetically. 'I spend too much of my time attempting to preserve the equilibrium.'

'Before you go, one question. Who is now the High Lama: you or Conway?'

Chang's answer was wistful. 'When my dear friend returned from his European wanderings he insisted that he no longer felt worthy of the supreme responsibility, although it had been bestowed upon him by Perrault. After much discussion, it was agreed to leave the matter in permanent abeyance. I had, I trust, been an able deputy, and continued in charge of administration until my poor sight made book-keeping impossible. To the valley people, however, who instinctively recognize the qualities of leadership, Conway is the only ruler of this place. I believe also that not a single lama would reject any suggestion he might make.'

'Despite his disaffection in 1931?'

'Oh, but we all understood his motives at that time to be of the highest.'

'You knew of his intentions, then?'

'Some things do not need to be spoken. I certainly knew that he would do his duty by Mallinson. I stood in a high window that night and watched them leave. But I knew also that he would return if he could. What I did not realize was that Lo Tsen was to be of the party, by her own insistence. That was foolish, but Conway was not to know. She was a free agent, in his view. It was she who had bribed the porters and was waiting with them beyond the pass. Conway has never spoken of what happened out there, but after a few days it must have been fearful, with Lo Tsen quickly resuming every appearance of her real age. Apart from that horror, neither Conway nor Mallinson can fully have appreciated the arduousness of the journey, even at the mildest season. As it was, he lost his memory, his health, his vigour, but his life was spared. So soon as recollection returned, he came back to Shangri-La by the swiftest possible route, and was accepted by all of us as though he had never been away, for he has unique qualities that cannot fail to be recognized. How often in your country have you sought a leader, and how seldom have you found one?'

Even while he spoke, Chang was being led away, but as a door was about to close on him he turned and held up a finger. 'All I have said about Conway is the truth, but there is something else. He is a lonely man, as all rulers must be. Your coming here, three people who know so much about him, may prove unsettling. I ask you only to take care that you do not in any way seem to diminish his achievements. Encourage him, reassure him. And Shangri-La will be grateful.'

I found Elizabeth in the library just as four o'clock was striking. Her father was sleeping and she was about to look for me, for Conway had invited us to take tea with the lamas on the northern balcony.

'Where's Warlock?'

'Digging for gold.' She squeezed my hand. 'Barnard took him down to look at the mines.'

'So let's go.' We set off along the parapet, but suddenly I stopped and looked down at her leg. 'I knew there was something. You're not limping.'

'It's a miracle cure all right. I came from the final session half an hour ago. Rubbing with some strange dry leaves that tickled, then immersion in warm wax for ten minutes, and bob's your uncle. Come on, I'm dying to see the lamas.'

'You make Shangri-La sound like Regent's Park Zoo.'

The northern balcony, a projecting extension of the first floor, gave a first impression of a sun-roof at a genteel English spa; but the way it overhung the main terrace, to give a vertiginous view of the valley below, was alarming indeed. Three doors opened on to it, and when we arrived, more than thirty robed brothers, and three or four female counterparts, had already emerged to congregate in the waning sun. There was a big enough strolling area for them not to seem like a crowd, and refreshments were being served from a corner table. (I had begun to calculate that the regime at Shangri-La was based on no fewer, than five pints of tea per day.) The sense of the lamas' combined years was overwhelming; when Warlock came in a few minutes later he looked like a boy in comparison. Some gazed quietly at the ever-changing vistas across the valley; others studied the growth of half a dozen giant potted palms; almost all made it their business in turn to approach us, shake hands and introduce themselves. I was left with an impression of white halos of hair and a few names: Julian, Hans, Gosta, Jean-Pierre, Sumi, Matthias. There were women too, Gunilla and an oriental name which sounded like Miyoshi. One was from Klagenfurt on the Wortesee; another from a small town in Norway called Molde, near the Arctic Circle. One asked me whether croquet was still played in English country houses, another whether I had visited the new cathedral in Liverpool. A very skeletal old fellow asked what I knew of recent books on the Brontës, and I naturally wondered whether this could be the chap who on Conway's first visit had claimed to have visited the Parsonage at Haworth while the sisters were still in residence. Conway confirmed later that he was.

'It's rather refreshing to see,' Elizabeth remarked, during a pause in the various conversations, 'that over there sits one fellow who doesn't seem to want to meet us at all.' She pointed out an old man with leonine features, who sat as though posing for a sculptor, gazing out across the valley in the manner of one who waits for a message but has an idea it won't come. He reminded me very much of a picture I once saw of Sir Henry Irving, playing some mad king about to be deposed. Yet with this man, the only hint of madness lay in his eyes, which were slightly too open for comfort; the rest of his face was as composed as a death mask. Half silhouetted against the roof of the world, a wooden crutch by his side, he seemed with his bushy white eyebrows and hair impossibly larger than life. At first sight he was to be taken for an energetic seventy, but in Shangri-La first sight, as we already knew, could be misleading. We walked over to introduce ourselves.

'Good afternoon,' said Elizabeth. 'Do you speak English?'

The monk turned his face to us with an expression of controlled fanaticism. There was something frightening, unsettling about him: his lips were loose and pendulous, giving the impression of a body incapable of carrying out the wishes of its supposedly controlling mind. He nodded silently, rather sadly. 'You are the visitors,' he said in a low voice. 'Conway told us. You came from the south.'

'That's right. We hope to make friends with you all. Can we tell you any particular news of the outside world?'

He shook his head fiercely. 'I don't want to hear any.'

This was a conversation-stopper, but I persevered. 'What do they call you?'

'They call me Saul. But it isn't my name. Oh, no. I won't let them use my name.'

'Are you . . . still a postulant?'

He flashed a rather wicked smile. 'Oh, yes. For years yet. I have to atone, you see. But I work. I'm working on a book about the eastern religions. Would you like to see the manuscript?'

Elizabeth was slightly taken aback. 'If you think I'd understand it.'

The old monk rubbed the end of his nose and changed the subject. 'You're trapped, you know,' he said, his eyes roving from one to the other of us. 'You'll never get away. Not unless you're much cleverer than I was. Mind you, I like it here now. I've forgotten the old life. Out there, over the mountains, I'd probably be dead. There was a history of weak hearts in the family. But here I shall live forever, like the Green Man of Sinai. I pray in the morning, and I write for the rest of the day. I can't walk much now; my leg never healed, you know. Do you think that was God's will? But I help in the gardens. I help everybody. Do you want any help?'

'It's very kind of you,' said Elizabeth, 'but I really don't think we need any.'

'You come from England, I know.' The transition was abrupt. 'I was from Gloucestershire. Bishop's Cleeve. I was going to marry a Gloucestershire girl. In 1928, we met, at a ball. I can still see her, standing on a little bridge, her dress white with a yellow belt, her hair flowing gold against the Cotswold stone. I see her every night, when I close my eyes to go to sleep.'

'Memories don't fade, then.'

'Some do. Others still hurt. But it doesn't matter. The world to come is what matters. That's right, isn't it?'

Agreeing, we contrived to take our leave. Warlock had wandered off, but now rejoined us, making a face. 'Not too great a commercial for the old place, is he?'

I shrugged. 'They can't all be Conways. I suppose to the wrong sort even Shangri-La can seem a prison. His bit about the Green Man of Sinai made me shudder, though.'

'I don't know the story. Will it make me laugh?'

'The man who got his wish and couldn't die. He wandered over the earth for all eternity, with nothing to live for.'

'Nice. Compared with that, your friend over there has had his sentence commuted. He'll die all right, in fifty or seventy or a hundred years' time, barring accidents. But by then he'll be one of the seniors, happy with his own importance. I don't blame them for making him wait, after the problems he gave them years ago.'

'What problems were they?'

'I *thought* you didn't know who you were talking to. That's Mallinson, Conway's junior from the consular service, who persuaded Conway to leave in the first place. I'm told he was the first one back, his hair white from fear. By the time Conway returned a year later, Mallinson was in a blue funk of self-reproach, which isn't surprising if he really did once threaten to send a squadron back from India and bomb this place to merry Hell. I'd say that's a detail he conveniently forgets to remember.'

15

Nicholas Brent's Narrative (1980):

'I THINK NEXT WEEK WILL DO'

That night it was Warlock who tired early, which wasn't altogether surprising. After our tea with the monks, Barnard had him scrambling up and down the mountain-side for a second excursion, learning to tell one ore-bearing rock from another, and finishing up with a short but breathtaking walk to overlook the northern pass. Dinner was heavier than usual, with fowl in a sauce and a vegetable that tasted like parsnip but apparently had some unpronounceable local name. After the cold rice pudding Warlock pushed back his chair and announced that if he didn't go to bed immediately somebody would have to carry him. Elizabeth too said she had no energy to do anything but lie on her bed and read, so Conway and I were left alone to converse. I think we both looked forward to that. We retired to his private study, a heavily oak-panelled chamber with comfortable hide chairs like those in a London club. Here brandy glasses were replenished and I availed myself of one of the local cigars, long thin green affairs filled with non-narcotic tobacco substitute. It wasn't an unattractive taste, but I found that unless I puffed at it every few seconds it needed frequent relighting.

'And so, today's report,' said Conway with his shy smile.

I shook my head. 'I don't think I'll offer one. Ask me in three weeks. Or maybe three months. I'm in no hurry to make my mind up about anything. I came to look for Shangri-La for the same reason that Hunt climbed Everest, because it was there. Or I should say, because I thought it *might* be there. I wasn't principally lured by the longevity thing.'

'Nevertheless, that process will be offered to you in due course.'

'But I would only want it if I could be assured that the extra years would be useful.'

'Ha!' exclaimed Conway with a smile. 'If you refer back to Mr Hilton I believe you will find me represented as saying much the same thing to old Perrault. I remember that on the day of my first interview with him I had been sitting high on the mountainside reading *Gulliver's Travels*, the part about the Struldbrugs.'

'Weren't they the allegedly superior beings who grew very grotesque but could never die?'

'That's right. I think I can put my finger on the passage.' He rose and brought from a shelf a small blue volume which I recognized as belonging to the Oxford World's Classics. 'Here we are:

'They had not only all the the follies and infirmities of other old men, but many more which arose from the dreadful prospect of never dying. They were not only peevish, opinionative, covetous, morose, vain, talkative, but incapable of friendship and dead to all natural affection . . . Envy and impotent desires are their prevailing passions . . . At ninety they lose their teeth and hair; they have at that age no distinction of taste, but eat and drink whatever they can get without relish or appetite, the diseases they were subject to still continuing without increasing or diminishing. In talking they forgot the common appellation of things and the names of persons, even of those who are their nearest friends and relations. For the same reason they can never amuse themselves with reading, because their memory will never serve to carry them from the beginning of a sentence to the end.

'Then Swift describes how they looked:

'They were the most mortifying sight I ever beheld, and the women were more horrible than the men. Besides the usual deformities in extreme old age, they acquired an additional ghastliness in proportion to their number of years . . . The reader will easily believe that my keen appetite for the perpetuity of life was much abated. I grew heartily ashamed of the pleasing visions I had formed, and thought no tyrant could invent a death into which I would not run with pleasure from such a life.'

Conway closed the book with a snap. 'Pretty strong stuff,' I said. 'I wonder it isn't banned from your library.'

'How could it be? Censorship is against our principles.'

'Even in moderation?'

'Oh, I think all my colleagues are well able to tolerate Swiftian satire, even when it seems to be turned against themselves. You see, we are all more than *moderately* certain of the value of our own discoveries. You will remember that I came here myself as a thorough-going sceptic. Although I was indeed far more receptive than Mallinson, it did take many weeks for me to be absolutely convinced that Shangri-La has both a point and a function, just as old Perrault envisaged more than two hundred years ago.'

'To shelter wise men through the holocaust, and to help mankind reshape an all but destroyed world.'

'You quote precisely. A pretty tough job, and you may well decide that we're not up to it. As I've told you, I've had doubts myself, especially when the news bulletins so often convince us that our time of testing is near. It's then that I realize that in normal terms I should be long dead, and I wonder whether the mere trick of longevity entitles me to control the future of the world, or whether each generation shouldn't be left to its own devices?'

I smiled wryly. 'The Sixties must have worried you. The Cuban missile crisis and the Arab-Israeli war.'

'Yes, and especially since in those days our main news had to be translated from Chinese broadcasts, which seldom gave the western view. Lately we have been able to put more trust in what we hear. Would you care to walk across and hear the latest bulletin?'

I shook my head. 'I think next week will do. Or even the week after. You see, I'm already falling perfectly willingly under your influence.'

Conway changed the subject. 'Have you been a religious man?'

'Only technically, I'm afraid. And you? Is Shangri-La's creed still catholic, in the lower-case sense?'

'Exactly. We believe in God, but to us – to me at any rate – he probably isn't an old man with a long white beard. After my experiences in the trenches I could scarcely tolerate so benevolent an image. Shangri-La is optimistic about an after-life, but addresses itself mainly to this world, where we believe that true godliness is best expressed in deeds. In love, in friendship, in mutual understanding and tolerance. I'm sorry, you have a cynical look.'

'Oh, I was only thinking that we need some new words in the language. It seems to me that whenever we talk about the things that really matter, all we come up with is platitudes. Somerset Maugham wrote a book about a man searching for eternal truth – '

'*The Razor's Edge*. We have it. The hero even has a spell in a Tibetan lamasery which sounds suspiciously as though it were modelled on this one.'

'That's right. Yet all Maugham could come up with at the end, after his hero had renounced wealth and wandered the world for year after year, was that goodness is the greatest force of all. To me that isn't enough. And I'm not sure that moderation is enough either. It just isn't positive.'

'You have contempt for our admitted uncertainty?'

'Not contempt. Fear, perhaps. Fear for me because

there is no comfort in it, and fear for you too. Suppose bandits attacked the valley for the sake of your gold. Suppose the strangers you now have under scrutiny find their way here and want just that? Wouldn't moderation oblige you to sit back and let them have it?'

'Oh, I think not, not any more than the British allowed their country to be invaded in 1940 by the Nazis. Good must be defended against evil. But we would hope to fight with strategy rather than weapons. Indeed, a major part of our strategy has been to prevent such a situation from arising by keeping our existence a secret. Nature has of course been helpful in that respect.' Conway poured himself another small brandy.

'I have sometimes thought that the greatest danger to us arises from discontent within our own ranks. For this reason our religious services vary from week to week. Some years ago we fortunately acquired an enthusiastic Seventh-day Adventist. I can't honestly say that I follow his creed at all clearly, for it seems to me that the naming of the seventh day depends entirely on the part of the week in which you start. But next week it will be his turn to direct the order of service. If you came to the chapel tomorrow, on the other hand, you might feel that you were standing in Westminster Abbey. Or perhaps not, since you tell me that the old prayers have been rewritten in a presumably vain attempt to curry favour with the masses. They must have left the Lord's Prayer alone, surely?'

'I'm afraid not. "Bring us not into temptation" has become "do not bring us to the time of trial," which is not even easier to understand.'

Conway shook his head gently as he stared into his glass. 'There are so many improvements which the world could be making. Instead its leaders seem intent on undoing what has already been achieved.'

'Speaking of religion, do your lamas marry?'

'Should they be so inclined, we have no rule against it. Several of the younger ones have done so, though naturally there is a shortage of suitable partners; and since our female lamas are by their own choice celibate, I doubt whether the birth rate can ever keep up with the death rate, which of course was one of our hopes.'

'That reminds me, I haven't seen a cemetery.'

'I am sure you have, though you may not have recognized it. If you will stand at your bedroom window and scan the slopes of Karakal, you will see a formation of dots in the snow.'

'Elizabeth did wonder what they were.'

'That is a place where the snow maintains a constant depth and firmness, summer and winter. Though almost as firm as a rock, it can be dug with a spade, it never melts, and the cold acts as a preservative. It seems a fitting place to inter our honoured dead.'

I shook my head. 'In America they call that crionics. Wealthy people can be buried in ice-filled capsules, in the hope that one day the disease which killed them may be curable and they may then be restored to life by the new science.'

'How very remarkable. We have no such ambitions, being content to pass on our wisdom at last to succeeding generations.'

The last tea of the evening was brought in. 'Tell me,' said Conway, 'as we imbibe this mild narcotic, some of the good things about the western way of life as it happens in the nineteen-eighties. You were scathing yesterday: be more generous this evening.'

'The good things?' I sought an honest answer. 'Certainly I have to count better health, generally longer life. Nobody dies from TB or pneumonia any more, and even cancer gives way sometimes. People have more leisure and a longer old age, but not many of them know what to do with either. Domestic comforts I think we covered. Money is made and spent in great amounts, and never holds its value for more than a month or two, so it has no real meaning. Inflation is sometimes up to ten per cent a year. Common items cost twenty times what they did in my childhood. The seller charges what he likes, and the buyer has to pay what he's asked. Of course, he then goes on strike for a higher salary to compensate. What they call a vicious spiral. People take what they get as their right and constantly look for more, if possible without working for it.'

'But without work there can be no satisfaction.'

'But people today have never had to work. Everything's given to them on a plate. One sensation has to follow right on the heels of the last, and what you enjoyed yesterday is already written off because it's dated. If you came back to London now, I'll swear the noise and bustle and sheer lack of style would drive a man of your generation mad within a week.'

'But is all the world the same? What of my beloved Paris? There was a city with tremendous style.'

'No longer, I fear, unless you go on a Sunday in August, when everybody's on holiday. Of course, the tourists take over then. For most of the year Paris is the most congested city on earth, with cars bumper to bumper whether they're parked or moving. They say it has five million motor cars, and whenever I go there they seem to be all on the streets at once.'

'All this frantic activity must surely have an effect on people's minds.'

'Of course. The British and French have never taken to psychiatrists like the Americans, but everywhere the incidence of mental illness is way up.

'Despite the socialist state, with free medicine even for the poor? We were most impressed by the Beveridge Plan.'

'That was forty-odd years ago. There are no really poor people now. Nobody wants to be unemployed, but idle people find it quite comfortable to live on the dole and the social services, which are generous even to the undeserving. Those who go to work demand wage increases every year. If the slightest disciplinary action is taken against a lazy or incompetent worker, the whole factory comes out on strike. You simply can't fire anybody these days, unionized or not, unless you have absolute proof of misbehaviour.'

'I know something of your industrial relations,' said Conway. 'We have a small library of talking films, and one which was recommended some years ago is *I'm All Right Jack*. But surely that is a comedy, an exaggeration?'

'A true statement disguised as a farce. I'm sorry, but I need a minute to take that in. Movies at Shangri-La!'

'But why not? We have been very selective. What we need is an accurate picture of the life we no longer know at first hand, so naturally factual films outnumber the fiction.'

A clock somewhere struck ten. 'There goes my normal call to bed,' said Conway, 'but I am fascinated by our conversation. If people have acquired so many material comforts without working for them, then surely they must have become extremely aimless and discontented?'

'Of course. Especially since the decline of organized religion has robbed them of optimism, discipline, any sense of fitting into the scheme of things, even the society of the friends they used to meet at church every Sunday. Sunday has become a day when most people prefer to glue themselves to their television sets. The streets are empty all day. And because the Church has permitted its own decline, so false prophets have sprung up all over the world to make easy money out of unhappiness. I'm thinking of the moonies, and scientology, and EST, all imposing on the gullible and defenceless members of society who haven't the guts to carve their own swathe through life.'

Conway leaned forward. 'And you, you who have told me so much about what is wrong with your world, what do you think is best for the future? What do you believe in?'

'Perhaps I *will* believe in Shangri-La. I certainly believe in courage, and inspiration, and imagination, and altruism. And fun too, lots of fun. And excitement. But as for praying, I think I could only use that form of Frederick the Great's.'

'Oh, God, if there is a God, save my soul, if I have one.'

'That's right. I can accept no assertion but I deny no possibility. If Shangri-La, the perfect creation, can exist, then so can God, the perfect creator. But the way things have gone this century, he must be a pretty ruthless God, it seems to me.'

Conway rose, walked to the window, and looked up at the snowy mountains under twinkling stars. 'The masses must return to religion before long,' he said, 'if only because these things are cyclical. But surely nobody can believe for long in the evil cults of which we hear: they sound more horrifying than inspirational. For instance, we could scarcely credit the accounts we received of the appalling mass suicides in Guyana two years ago.'

'That was quite impossible to explain except in terms of mass hypnotism. Even so, the whole thing was an aberration, though the chain of events seemed clear at the time. As I recall, the American guru objected to the investigations of a visiting senator, and thought he could get away with having him murdered. When he found the finger pointing at him because the job had been bungled, he persuaded all nine hundred of his followers to join him in drinking poison. The world seemed suddenly to have gone mad. And wasn't it during the same month that the press had a field day with the unedifying spectacle of a leading British politician accused of conspiracy to murder?'

'That, of course, would have seemed unthinkable in my day.'

'Unthinkable in any day since Richard the Third's. But it happened. The way things are going, you may have to start from scratch when you open your ark. Even Sodom and Gomorrah may have utterly destroyed themselves.'

'And our ark is not entirely sound. At various times I have observed among my brothers the sins of covetousness, or pride, and even worse, of despair. Mallinson is of course an extreme example: I watch him very carefully in case he should infect the others.' He rose. 'But come, it is late. Your jet-lag seems to have passed, but mine has not, even though I have travelled nowhere.'

'May we enjoy one last stroll on the terrace?'

Conway gladly consented, and we were both surprised to find the evening still fairly warm even though moonlight glinted on the ice of the glacier. 'What is it you wanted to ask?' he said.

I looked at him appreciatively. 'You are perceptive. I only hoped that you would tell me – how can I put it – whether your age retardation process is entirely natural, or whether it depends on self-hypnosis, or on some sort of magic formula.'

Conway laughed aloud. 'You still suspect hocus pocus? I can assure you there is none. No sinister concept, just an accidental discovery, as natural as any other. I have always been convinced that the real secret lies in the purity of our climate. We assist it, of course, by living carefully, without pressure, by taking exercise and by indulging in what one might call local herbal remedies. I remember being brought up on a bronchial elixir called Liqufruta, compounded among other things from honey and garlic and liquorice. My grandmother thought it would cure anything, and sometimes it almost seemed to.'

'It is still sold.'

'Amazing. And I am sure that despite all your progress it is still effective. To tell the truth, our local *tangatse* blend is not dissimilar, and smells just as vile. You would doubtless be correct in assuming that at least half its effect is psychological. But after a certain stage we all take it – religiously is the word, I think – every morning, and the manufacture of it gives almost constant employment to Brother Pietro. *Tangatse* is also taken neat by senior members of the brotherhood, primarily to put them into a suitable state for what used to be called transcendental meditation.'

'You make it all sound very simple. What about disease?'

'Our air is so pure that we have little to fear from bacteria, and our careful regime forestalls the ailments brought on by overindulgence and stress. There are no migraines here, and very few stomach disorders. But the human body is subject to many unpredictable attacks, and even we are not immune from cancer, from heart disease or from any kind of organ failure. We import adequate supplies of drugs, but having no skilled medical advice we are now unsure how to use them. And of course our case of surgical instruments lies useless.'

I felt confused. 'I hadn't thought of your needing surgery.'

'But why not? Indeed, I may be in need of it myself.'

I stopped walking. 'I'm very sorry to hear that.'

'You noticed that I limp slightly. For several months

there has been insistent pain in my left knee. Brother Prosper, who had limited medical training when Victoria was on the throne of England, thinks it may be only a form of arthritis, and had prescribed a regime of drugs, ointments and wax baths. But they haven't helped, and I see doubt in his eyes. We both know that I should consult a properly qualified doctor in case it is something more . . . progressive. And there the devil gets his own back, for the nearest doctor is in Myitkyina, and he would ask questions which I would not wish to answer. Besides, if I were to venture so far I would very likely die of exposure to the impurities in that malaria-ridden air, or simply from being deprived of this unique valley.'

I stared at him unblinkingly. 'Suppose someone were to bring a doctor to you?'

'By another kidnap? I really don't think so. I never entirely reconciled myself to the manner in which we were first brought here. The intention was admirable, but I was always taught that means do not justify ends. After all, apart from the four of us every member of the brotherhood came to Shangri-La either by accident or of his own free will.'

'Did you never have a second Mallinson? Someone who hated it and was determined to leave?'

'Once. He was a fur millionaire called Horowitz. It was in 1967, I think, and he had subsidized an expedition to catch a yeti.'

'The Abominable Snowman?'

'Yes. There seemed to be worldwide interest in the creature at about that time. Almost the entire party perished in an avalanche. Horowitz was the sole survivor, so far as we know, and when our scouts picked him up he was more dead than alive, but he did recover, and demanded to leave. Like most millionaires, I suppose, he simply couldn't understand not getting his own way. We told him the usual excuse about porters, but he saw through it. He simply couldn't live without the fast pace of New York; he wouldn't give Shangri-La a chance. We tried to calm him with *tangatse*, but we could hardly keep him perpetually under sedation, and one morning we discovered that he had set off alone. It was a simple matter to follow his tracks to the edge of the glacier, but it would have been foolish to follow. From the western end of this terrace there is an easy way on, and it looks as though one might get back that way to the desert route, but in fact the surface is honeycombed with crevasses. I myself hastened with a telescope to the highest vantage point, but there was no sign of him.'

I shivered. 'Does it ever occur to you that this is not such a friendly place after all?'

'Oh, yes. Our cosseted existence is a mere whim of nature. At any time the lamasery could be sent tumbling into the valley by a major avalanche on Karakal. Or the great glacier, which our scientists claim is moving inexorably in this direction, could simply split the mount-Barnard once assured me, with a jocularity which seemed a little misplaced, that the main fault runs right under the refectory. Am I dissuading you from staying?'

'Not by the threat of a natural disaster.'

'You would like to leave your options open then?'

'It's far too early to be sure. We have responsibilities to the people who financed us. Left to ourselves, well, I'm sure that Warlock's here for life. As for Elizabeth and me . . . perhaps we shall have to make separate decisions.'

'But I had assumed that you were committed to each other.'

'We've been more than good friends, but I wouldn't presume to think for her.'

'I have a feeling she would like you to do just that.'

'It wouldn't be fair. She's fifteen years younger.'

'In Shangri-La that can hardly matter.'

'Be that as it may' – I changed the subject clumsily – 'I do think that the time may have come, with your consent, to announce your existence to the world. The world thinks of Shangri-La as an idealistic concept, a fantasy, a bubble in the mind. If people started thinking about it as an achievable object, it could change the course of history. Of course nobody would want you to be invaded. We'd have to find ways of proving your existence while getting guarantees of secrecy as to your precise whereabouts. I don't doubt there'd be a flood of volunteers to replenish your numbers, which is one good result for you. And I'd put a doctor right at the top of my shopping list.'

'Well, that's a suggestion we shall have to consider. I have to remind you however that our elders will remember what happened last time we tried to evangelize.'

'What did happen? What happened to Luki? I tracked him down to Caldy Island, you know.'

Conway smiled. 'You were standing next to him this afternoon, on the balcony. I saw him pointing out something to you, something in the valley.'

I chuckled. 'And I thought I was talking to a young man of thirty-five.'

'He recovered rapidly from his disappointment. He had a good team for a while, including a cheerful Englishman who became his deputy. And in 1946 the Englishman disappeared with all the group's funds. Luki was too upset to ask for more. He disbanded the community and came home via Africa. I suppose I should have taken on the job myself. For Luki the British climate was a shock. He stuck out the war, but then found it difficult to cope with the beginnings of post-war austerity. It was a sad time, he told me: people were so desperate for physical comfort that they had no urge for spiritual fulfilment. They had won the war, and simply couldn't understand why they seemed to have lost everything else.'

'I remember that feeling well. What about Max, who went to America?'

'We never heard from him again. I expect he succumbed to the pleasures of California, which I am told are many and various.'

I briefly described the Leadfield site and Warlock's view of what might have happened; but Conway, despite his interest, was now plainly tiring, and led me back to the door as I was speaking. We parted at the foot of the lodge stairs, and as I undressed in my silent room his last words echoed in my ears:

'It does appear, as Perrault told me, that there is only one Shangri-La. Those who seek others are expecting too much of nature.'

16

Nicholas Brent's Narrative (1980):

'IT SEEMED THAT SOMETHING MOVED . . .'

I had not relayed to Warlock all my conversations with Conway, and on the following evening at dinner I was amused at the Canadian's reaction when he asked Chang whether it was only on Saturday nights that Shangri-La threw wild parties.

The ancient Oriental kept a straight face as he said: 'As a matter of fact I was about to ask whether a cinema performance would amuse you? We hold one every two weeks in the library, and my brothers would make you most welcome. Good. Then I will advise them to expect you in about thirty minutes.'

Warlock was too astonished to reply with more than nods. We had spent the day in separate pursuits. Elizabeth had asked to be left with a postulant called Wilhelm, who was a specialist in geology and kept a small museum classifying the various rocks found in the area. Warlock, who really seemed to have palled up with Barnard, again went down with him into the valley, this time to see the more intricate workings of his gold mine. I fancied a spot of mountain walking, and took sandwiches with me. My camera was kept busy as I made my way back along the ridges, and being unused to the thin mountain air I had to take frequent rests. Now at eight-thirty we were all pleasantly tired, and it did not seem especially odd that we should find ourselves taking pride of place, seated on an enormous lumpy settee at the back of a room in which twenty lamas sat cross-legged on rugs, enjoying a Laurel and Hardy comedy projected on to an improvised screen draped over a bookcase. Elizabeth, next to me, snuggled into my arm and put her feet up. I think she was asleep before *The Grapes of Wrath* came on, heralded by its Twentieth Century Fox searchlights, which can seldom have seemed so out of place. The film itself was as magnificent as ever, though it must have given to some of its watchers a very curious and dated view of America. Personally, I kept imagining myself back in a high street cinema in some English provincial city in the Forties, about to catch the last bus home from the stop on the corner.

Elizabeth woke up for the last hour or so, and might have applauded at the end had not the monks risen promptly and silently to their feet, nodding to each other in silent dispersal. Every one of the lamas took care to bow and smile to us on his way out.

'I gather from Barnard,' said Warlock when we were alone, 'that they have forty-seven movies in stock. At twice a month they must start repeating after two years.'

'You don't have to *come* twice a month,' said Elizabeth rather severely.

We strolled out on to the terrace and Warlock lit his pipe. 'What are you going to do,' I asked, 'when your supply of shag runs out?'

'Oh, Barnard tells me that'll be no problem. They get pretty reliable supplies these days, from Rangoon or Mandalay. I haven't yet figured out how it works.'

'The point,' said Elizabeth, 'surely is that it does work, and damn well. The whole community works. All the essential balances are immaculately kept by nature, and man has only to assist when he needs luxuries. Timber, stone, crops, minerals, there's even a small oilfield that they haven't bothered to develop yet. It's like one of those isolated Bavarian valleys I used to see illustrated in Grimm's fairy tales, the castle up on the hill and smoke curling from the cottages of the peasants below, everybody happy doing what he does best.'

'But the sad thing about those fairy-tale valleys,' I said, 'is that sooner or later a fellow on a black horse used to ride in like a bat out of hell and upset the equilibrium.'

'If he hadn't,' said Warlock, 'there'd have been no story. No story, no happy ending.'

'I should have thought Shangri-La was a happy ending in itself.'

'I'll drink to that. And if you were thinking of leading up to any delicate questions, I can tell you for sure that I'm happy to stay here for the rest of my days. With my gem-cutting know-how, it seems I shall be an honoured resident.'

We both looked at Elizabeth. 'I have to decide what's best for my father,' she said. 'He ought to have better medical attention, but maybe it would cause more trouble to move him. I just can't come to any conclusion just yet; give me a few more days.'

'And of course we have to think of Gentry, and the *Clarion*,' I added. 'OK, let's go to bed and I'll have another chat with Conway tomorrow.'

There, as it happened, I was wrong. I had another chat with him that evening. We all went to our separate rooms, but after half an hour of *Three Men in a Boat*, I felt restless and decided on a little more air. The night was cold and still, and from the terrace the moon, poised over the glacier, looked incandescent. It must have been midnight, or very near it, when I sensed Conway's presence beside me as I leaned on the low wall, listening to faint animal cries from the other side of the valley. 'A penny for your thoughts,' he said.

'Oh, they're hardly worth it. I was remembering some wonderful holidays I've had, in places which might in a way seem comparable to this. In Iceland, in Oregon, in

Norway. I adored them all. But I was remembering too that there came a day when the holiday was clearly nearing its proper end, and I was aching to get back to work.'

He shrugged as he wrapped a heavy scarf more closely round his neck. 'Shangri-La has no shortage of work.'

'I'm sure there are always things to do here. But it must be a hell of an adjustment to realize that never again will you earn a salary, never again flex your muscles against the opposition, never feel the little stimulations and petty jealousies and triumphs of that terrible civilization that we've created for ourselves back home. Can a rest cure work when you've nothing to rest from? I remember when I first went to Perth in Western Australia, thinking that it was like Shangri-La, with a wonderful climate and unpolluted air and a nice friendly little city that reminded me of the American West after it had been tamed. But nobody there was contented. They actually complained that geographically Perth was the most isolated city on earth, and how much it cost to fly to Sydney, and how shopping was easiest in Singapore, and how every summer they were invaded by nasty black flies.'

The air was heavy with our thoughts as our slippered feet led us back through the lamasery and up the ramp leading to the enclosed garden. 'I don't suppose you will find absolute perfection anywhere on earth,' said Conway. 'It could only breed discontent if you did. As I used to say myself, man always needs to know what's on the other side of the mountain. But Shangri-La works at a great cause, a cause which requires many great skills. Have you sensed here no task which aches for you to complete it?'

'Oh, with the help of your library there are about ten books I could write straight off. And you need somebody to index your archives up to date. They seem to stop in

1964 with the Beatles getting their honours from the Queen.'

'Yes? I do seem to remember Brother Albert giving up in some perplexity at that point, and his sight will not allow him to continue. You must admit now that it would be hard to understand from the top of a mountain on the borders of Burma and Tibet.'

'I found it pretty hard to understand from where I was in Piccadilly. You did know who the Beatles were?'

'Oh, yes. We even imported one of their gramophone records, but it was not well received.'

As we passed again from the musky corridor into the open air, we took blanket cloaks from a hook to wrap around us, for we were now ascending from Jethro's Pool to the glacier level, and a night breeze blew in our direction along the gleaming surface. Moonlight illuminated the whole vast icy landscape, framed by black mountains with snowy peaks. 'Fill your lungs,' said Conway, 'and you will surely sleep well.'

'Indeed I will. Incidentally, by what name do you like to be called?'

'Conway will do very well.'

'But it isn't your real name. Why do you like to be known by the name a novelist gave you?'

'Well, it is not quite a lie, for it is indeed my middle name. When one has been resident here for five years, it is traditional to rechristen oneself, as a kind of pledge that one will put the past behind and dedicate the future to Shangri-La. What could be more natural than that we should adopt the names which Mr Hilton had thoughtfully given to us? Thus Jeremy Clifford became Mallinson, and Ben Pegley – for there never was a Chalmers Bryant – became Barnard. At the same time, I think as a token of our strong friendship, Ho Chen decided to become

Chang. By the way, if you decide to stay here, what name will you call yourself?'

'I hadn't given it a thought. Austen, perhaps, after Jane. A very civilized and cultured person.'

'It will be most appropriate. And will you marry your Elizabeth?'

I gave him an appreciative glance at the shrewd thrust. 'You said yourself that there is no guarantee of any physical benefit for those who come to Shangri-La in middle age. I don't want to think of her as an active and vigorous sixty-five, looking forty and having to tend to the whims of an eighty-year-old invalid hanging on by the skin of his teeth.'

'Do you fear death?'

'Not in itself. In a way we die every night when we sleep. But I would hate to abandon life altogether while I still find it exciting. And I do. One way or another I suppose I shan't give death much of a welcome when it comes, if I know it's coming.'

'And what of the after-life? Do you believe that the soul lives on?'

'I can't see the sense. I remember when I was about fourteen spending a lot of nights thinking about it. It gave me the shudders. Oblivion seemed far preferable to an existence with no end and no clear beginning except as a kind of leftover from a previous life. All that interminable perfection would surely appal a civilized mind.'

'So you don't believe in any heaven except the kind you make for yourself.'

'In practical terms I can't see how it would work. Both it and the other place must be damned overcrowded after all these centuries. Besides, suppose someone you love dies – your wife perhaps – and then thirty years later you join her. She wouldn't recognize you!'

Conway nodded. 'It is a familiar argument with which I

have to agree. In spite of what Perrault used to call the pleasant optimism of most religions few of us here expect to meet again in some everlasting fairyland in the sky. Our hope, as I said yesterday, is simply to enrich mankind by extending our most productive years.'

A wisp of cloud had been passing across the moon, and as it cleared, the glacier seemed to shine even more brightly, like some incredibly dazzling stage set. Conway reached into a cupboard and produced a small telescope, which he handed to me. I raised it to my eyes and scanned the silky surface of the ice with its sharp-edged black cracks, then up the right-hand snow slopes to the moon itself, presently framed by a high, smoothly contoured mountain pass which set it off perfectly.

Suddenly I felt Conway's tight grip on my arm. 'It seemed that something moved,' he said. 'Up there in the pass, where you were looking.'

'I saw nothing. Could it have been your sentinel?'

'No, no. He stays on the western side of Zarnak.'

'An animal?'

'Not at that height. Look, it moved again! Like a man, but I don't see how – '

My telescope panned slowly over the snow, and this time it was my turn to jump. 'Good God, you're right! And more than one!'

What had seemed at first to be only a natural excrescence in the rock of the pass (which appeared in the glass so close as to be touchable, though in fact it was at least five miles away) now suddenly grew like a tiny fungus and separated itself into a group of minute figures which could scarcely be other than human. Only the moon full behind them made them visible at all. I handed Conway the telescope. 'Surely they'll freeze to death out there,' I said.

His face was grim as he surveyed the startling image. 'That depends on whether they're professionally equipped. And I'd say that to have got up there from the desert they must be. None of which makes them any less foolhardy. If they step on to the glacier they'll find it honeycombed with almost bottomless pits, and very slippery.'

'Do you think they've seen us?'

'From that point they must certainly have seen these buildings. They are – they must be – the people who were spotted in the valley the other day. They sent back for reinforcements, I imagine, and then began their search for a canyon. Unfortunately for them, they've found the wrong one.'

'I feel terrible about this. We've obviously led them to you.'

'Don't worry. Among our beliefs at Shangri-La is a belief in fate. Kismet.'

'Aren't you worried?'

'Only a little, until I know their numbers and their motives.'

'And supposing they do seek your gold?'

'Then, since we do not believe in force, we must hope to conquer them with wisdom.'

'With some men it takes both.'

'Then we shall fail, unless we can add a little trickery to the mixture. What we need first is all the rest we can get. I will raise the guards. Unless our mysterious visitors try to make it across the glacier by night, which would be suicidal, there is plenty of time for sleep. I suggest we meet here at first light to reconsider the situation.'

I don't doubt that Conway got some sleep, but I didn't. At the first gleam of dawn I alerted Elizabeth and Warlock, and they looked pretty haggard too when I told them what we had seen. Without thinking of breakfast we made our way to Jethro's pool, noting throughout the lamasery buildings an unaccustomed air of urgency. We met Conway in one of the upper corridors, and Warlock mumbled his own apology, but Conway waved it away. 'It had to happen sooner or later,' he said. 'It is well for our resources to be put to the test.'

He turned with us and we moved into the grey cold morning. Several lamas as well as guards stood by the glacier wall, the older men looking clumsy in the thick blankets which protected them against the morning frost. One of the telescopes, trained on the tiny figures across the glacier, showed me that they had already broken camp, and were inching towards us down the eastern slopes of Zarnak. Within forty minutes the figures were down to the level of the icefield, where they paused in obvious indecision as to the route they should take. By now I was able to count fourteen of them, some heavily laden.

Elizabeth drained the steaming coffee mug which had been brought to her, and took over my telescope. 'They're roping themselves together, in two groups, I think. It looks from their gestures as though they're intending to come straight at us, as the crow flies.'

Conway shook his head. 'That would be the worst possible way. I would warn them if I could. I really fear for their safety.'

Warlock could not resist a snort at such altruism. 'I think you'd better start fearing for your own,' he growled. 'I don't see how their intentions can possibly be honourable.'

It seemed that we all stood there for hours, trying not to shiver in our thick protective wrappings, and stamping our feet to keep the circulation going. Presently we could see movement, even without the telescopes: the figures were picking their way across the ice with what looked like improvised ski sticks. There was a group of eight in the front, followed by a group of six. 'Isn't there any way of warning them of the danger?' I said to nobody in particular.

'Only something they may misunderstand,' said Warlock, drawing a revolver. 'Mr Conway, do I have your permission? In that case, will you please ask your colleagues to cover their ears?'

When this was done, Warlock pointed the gun into the sky and fired. The crack of the shot seemed likely for a moment to start a small avalanche on Zarnak, and certainly stopped the distant figures dead in their tracks; but after a few moments the echoes died away. Having gained the attention of the strangers, we began some vigorous waving, with cries of 'Go back.' There was a pause, then one of the figures in the first group raised two fists in the air and shook them. It could mean only one thing, defiance; and almost immediately they came on again, one slow step following another. Conway half raised his arms in despair, and I saw him shiver despite his warm covering. A servant noticed also, and wrapped an additional blanket round his shoulders.

Suddenly the worst happened, without warning, and in horrid silence. The small black figure on the left of the forward group stumbled and fell to the ground. The man roped next to him stooped to help, and both found themselves slipping. The third and fourth travellers pulled for their lives at the rope, but evidently found no soft snow in which to dig their heels. The first man by now was slipping below ground level, down some hidden gap, and his weight was clearly sufficient to pull all the others inexorably forward. There was absolutely nothing we could do except gaze in horror as all seven of his comrades were dragged to the sloping ground, clawing uselessly at the smooth ice before disappearing one by one down some chasm invisible to us. It was as though the glacier had opened to swallow them up.

A little distance behind, the second group of six stood rooted to the spot in unbelieving terror. Time stood still: I can't say how long they took to inch forward as close as they could to the scene of their companions' disappearance, or how long it took them to be convinced that there was nothing to be done. Eventually they separated carefully into two groups of three, and shuffled back with slow pace in the direction from which they had come, occasionally testing possible side routes but finding none. By ten they were back on the mountain slopes and appeared to be making a temporary camp, though by now clouds had so obscured the sun that it was difficult to make out even through the telescope exactly what was going on. Still the lamas watched in silence. Only when the gong sounded for a meal did Conway stir himself to make a little speech to those assembled, first making a gesture of helplessness towards Chang, who had been sitting motionless and half-invisible behind his upper window.

'Miss Elizabeth, gentlemen, brothers: if those benighted people did not set out in search of Shangri-La, they have seen it now, and the survivors will almost certainly try to find the only route to us. We do not know who they are, but we know that they are persistent. It can take them only a day or two to regain the valley and make their way north along the mountain wall until they find the canyon which will lead them to us. They are well equipped, and will arrive, despite their shock, in a much less exhausted state than most of our visitors. We must therefore be ready for them. I will send word to our scouts, and ask them to increase the frequency of their reports. By this time tomorrow our plan of action must be prepared. Meanwhile, at six this evening we will all meet in the chapel to pray for those who fell to their deaths on the glacier.'

A trio of guards remained on watch; the rest of us dispersed, I to the terrace where I stood gazing down into the valley, my head afire with the frustration of helplessness. Eventually Conway came out to persuade me to take some lunch. It was not a happy meal; but it had an unexpected climax. We were sipping our tea in silence when from outside there came the strangest of sounds, a loud metallic whirring, too loud by far to be issuing from the only piece of mechanism nearby, Barnard's rack-and-pinion railway. The sound rapidly increased in intensity, and after glancing at each other in puzzlement we all hurried out on to the terrace, where we found monks also hastening from the lamasery to crowd the wall and gaze at something quite unbelievable. The sound was coming from the Valley of Blue Moon; and as we gazed down into the light mist, there came through it from the east a sight we could not possibly have expected. A helicopter was making its way towards us.

I had begun to think that the new arrival must in some way be connected with the figures we had seen on the ice, when Warlock yelled in my ear: 'Jumping Jehosaphat! Look who's here!' And some surprise it was.

Gentry, the big Kansan, was visible at the open window of the blue-and-white four-seater as it hovered before us, veering from side to side while its solo pilot looked for the best place to land. He must have made out at least one of us, for he waved cheerfully, like a friend who was just popping in for a drink. Then the machine made straight for us, and we all scattered like buckshot to the safety of various doorways. There was, in fact, plenty of flat space on the terrace, but I don't think Gentry took enough notice of the rockeries, fingers of which spread out in all directions. It seemed to me that one of the machine's three landing feet touched and skidded off a rock before settling on the crazy paving; but we were all too excited to pay very much attention. As the rotor blade was switched off I found myself shouting into Conway's ear that this was a friend who was thoroughly reliable, one whom we would have liked to be part of our expedition. Conway nodded readily enough, but I saw in his eye a thoughtful look, and I realized his fear that such a machine might turn out to provide too quick and easy a connection between Shangri-La and the outside world.

The door of the helicopter was opened and Gentry was among us, shaking every hand in sight and beaming in schoolboy triumph. Explanations were hastily made: he had paid very much more attention to the Conway typescript than any of us thought, but had not offered to participate because of the complexities of his business situation. These had suddenly cleared up, and he could no longer resist. By now we had the support we needed, and he did not want to spoil our adventure, but decided that a little back-up might be prudent. Since Warlock seemed likely to demur at a direct suggestion of Gentry's involvement, the millionaire had merely offered the carrot of a free ride to Burma, being himself supposedly on the way to another destination. That accomplished, Gentry simply covered our rear, letting us get well ahead but following our tracks. 'You thought they didn't show, I imagine. Well, the flying eye sees everything: from up there it was a faint broken line in the sand. You had me fooled when the tracks suddenly stopped and left me gazing dead north at the roof of the world, but I soon realized that that was where you headed east over the gravel. The first two canyons I tried were dead ends, but the third one had your Land Rover in it, so I just curved along with the valley, over what looks like a swamp. Then the mist covered everything, and I was just a bit worried when I saw this place ahead of me up on the hill. Well, it was just like the music welling up at the end of a movie.

My only complaint is that the landing space is a bit limited.'

A bewildered Conway – he had brought from the lamasery a small and excited retinue of young postulants – was introduced, and we all retired to a table by the terrace wall where mulled wine was served. 'Boy, this sure is some place!' muttered Gentry appreciatively as he gazed down through the now clearing mist at the Valley of Blue Moon.

'Did you notice that we were followed?' asked Elizabeth at last.

'Notice? What do you think I've been doing for the best part of a week? I based myself at what passes for a hotel at the Myitkyina airport, and made a sortie every day in this direction. I gave you a day and a half before I started. You weaved around a bit, and I lost you altogether for a while, but as soon as I found the desert valleys there you were again. I just hoped you'd chosen the right one.'

'So did we,' muttered Warlock.

'Thought you'd spotted me once,' the big man grinned.

'No, but we heard you,' said Elizabeth.

'Yeah, I did a few quick whirlies. The funny thing was that on my way back the second time I spotted another bus heading after you into the same godforsaken territory. That didn't seem to make too much sense unless it was on your trail. So a day later I made a second sweep. The valley was hazy, and I never saw you at all, but there was the other bus on its way *back*! When they got to Myitkyina I was waiting with eyes and ears open. It was just an overnight stop, but they took on supplies, and hired an extra two buses, and recruited some local hands. I just lay low and let them get on with it. They turned back north the very next morning. I gave 'em a day and a half and then followed along. Then this morning I spotted half a dozen of them making their way in this direction along the mountain wall. I reckon unless they're very careless they'll find your canyon tomorrow morning.'

'That is also our assumption,' said Conway.

'You know about them, then?'

We related the tragic events of the morning. The big man shook his head. 'Seems I miscalculated. I should have been here sooner.'

I was impatient for information. 'Those men out there,' I said, 'did you find out what they want or who's leading them?'

'Not really, I thought it more discreet not to show my interest. But there are three Europeans among 'em.'

'Three?'

'Yeah, two in white safari suits, one fat and one thin.'

'Sounds like our lovely boys,' said Warlock. 'Lorenz and Abel, the Laurel and Hardy of Burma. I'll bet you.'

'The other . . . well, I didn't get much of a fix on him, but he had one arm in a sling.'

Gentry was made welcome. He locked up his machine, amused by the crowd of natives which had already gathered inquisitively around it, and announced his intention of spending the afternoon stretched out in the sun.

'I think I'm going to like it here,' he said. 'By the way, the back of the chopper is packed with firearms, just in case. Of course,' he added on sight of Conway's pained expression, 'I won't even bring 'em out if you don't want me to.'

The afternoon passed uneasily for all of us, but we could only wait for the confrontation. I found myself chatting in the tea pavilion to the lama who had written the book on the Brontës, having himself been a caller at Haworth Parsonage on a summer day in 1838. It was difficult to imagine him now as a young and enthusiastic curate. He was still jovial if very thin, but his hands trembled and his mind had begun to wander; he put me in mind of Mr Dick in *David Copperfield*. Propped up on the desk before him was a book of Victorian sermons; but his notebooks seemed to be mainly filled by irrelevant doodles in the form of Gothic lettering an inch high. He claimed to be heavily occupied in an investigation into the influence of the Church on Victorian literature, his prime examples being Carroll and Kingsley, but I doubted whether he would ever complete it.

Chang was wheeled through at one point and stopped for conversation. In answer to my question he described Conway as 'rather worried', which has to be the understatement of the year. Chang himself was clearly well past showing any mental upset at the possibility of imminent invasion by an unsympathetic force. But he sensed, and said so, that over some of his brothers there had settled a distinct sense of unease.

'Comfort them as best you can, my son,' murmured the ancient Chinese as he was wheeled away; but when I was left to my own devices in the silent library I felt the atmosphere suddenly so oppressive that I had to have comfort myself, or at least escape. Of course I remembered Mallinson's description in *Lost Horizon* of the community of Shangri-La as a conspiracy of sinister, spider-like old men. Today they looked the part, especially since Mallinson himself sat in a corner, ostensibly occupied with some fat volume of German philosophy but spending his time darting malicious glances at his fellows as he fidgeted with the tassel of his gown. It had grown quite dark – there was never much natural light in the library – and huge beeswax candles were being lit in the heavy chandeliers.

Twilight has always been my unfavourite part of the day, and this twilight seemed more ominous than any I could remember. Waiting for the end of the world could scarcely be worse. I had to walk, it didn't matter where.

I left the library. I moved slowly and aimlessly down apparently endless corridors, inhaling scented air and pausing from time to time to look at the sumptuous wooden carvings in the wall panels. Across courtyards, under small arches, my Japanese sandals clattered on tessellated marble floors. I met only a few lamas, mostly in couples, but I spoke to none of them and they seemed too absorbed in thought even to give me their usual polite greeting. Everywhere I wandered, there flashed before my eyes, as in myth to a drowning man, scenes from the life I was forsaking. They dangled before me like a chimera of Dickensian cameos.

At the age of four, lying on my mother's newly completed peg rug as I listened to some comedian singing 'You Can't Do That There 'Ere' on the radio. At nine, basking in the applause which followed the end of my recitation in the school concert. At nineteen, enjoying tea and crumpets before the gas fire in my college rooms. Sometime in my twenties, reading Sartre as I sprawled across a pile of cushions in my two-room Islington flat, fortified the while by mugs of dandelion coffee. I tried to banish these stabs of nostalgia from my mind, but I was still haunted by the minor pleasures which were available to me only a week ago. The cheerful, reliable tones of Radio Four, keeping me abreast of the times every morning as I soaked in my bath. My bedside bookshelf towards which on any night I could stretch out a hand and encounter a hundred old friends. The possibility, if bored with routine, of cancelling all engagements at a day's notice and hurriedly booking a weekend in Tunisia or Copenhagen. The endless spring and autumn days when I casually motored on half-empty roads over tracts of fen and mountain, feeling like a John Buchan hero ready and willing to take on whatever adventure might present itself. (None, alas, ever did.)

It hadn't been dull, even when events conspired to thwart me. I remembered with strange appreciation days in the Shetland Isles when the fog never lifted and I was reduced to endless games of chess with a pompous fellow Englishman in the assembly of angular white boxes known as the Lerwick Hotel. Then there was a winter weekend in the Scillies when they were the only part of Britain not covered by snowdrifts (which miraculously cleared for my return). Even more wistfully, I recalled weekend explorations during business trips to California and Mexico. North to Bodega Bay, south to Cabot St Lucas, the whole thousand-mile coastline was now familiar territory which had provided me with gloriously idle days in La Jolla, Santa Barbara and Carmel. The crowded Saturday night bazaars of Tijuana, the isolated tourist village of Yosemite, the old-fashioned boardwalk at Avalon – all told stories which my memory now released. So, closer to home, did the priest holes of Havington Hall, and the ceremonial haggis once served to me in the Outer Hebrides, and the failure of ghosts to materialize at my command during a youthful visit to the ruins of Borley Rectory. There were, of course, more sophisticated pleasures too. Broadway audiences applauding a score of impeccably staged musicals. The Albert Hall and the Milan Opera House. The Salle Empire in Monte Carlo's Hotel de Paris. Even a Buckingham Palace garden-party: I was not likely to attend another of those.

Dizzy with sensation, I emerged into the open darkness of the terrace. The air had again turned chill, and I was ill protected against it. Still, with a feeling of possession I lingered by the low stone wall and gazed down towards the twinkling lights of the wondrous Valley of Blue Moon. If I elected to stay here, if indeed my life was spared in whatever hostile action tomorrow might bring, I could close the book on such experiences as had just filled my brain. And much as I admired the theory of Shangri-La, would I not find the practice just a little dull, as all forms of perfection tend to be? Would a decision to stay result merely, as E. M. Forster said of T. E. Lawrence, from a desire to efface myself, to crash from the heights of command to the depths of obedience?

My thoughtful steps brought me eventually to Elizabeth's room. She sat by her window, gazing at the snowy slopes of Karakal, and no doubt preoccupied by much the same thoughts as mine. 'I don't know how it seems to you,' I said, 'but I think it's decision time. Assuming that after tomorrow's confrontation we're still in a position to make up our minds, are you for staying or going?'

She came over, smiling, kissed me on the forehead and took my hand. 'Does your staying depend on my staying?'

'I thought that was the idea.'

'No. You're under no compulsion. We can always beg to differ.' She began to walk around the room: as on television, movement helped her to express herself. 'I don't want to behave here as I'd behave in the Thames Valley. This is a chance we'll never get again. We've shed our responsibilities towards each other, simply in bringing each other here. Now we have to think of ourselves: it's the only way.'

'All right.' I knew better than to argue. 'So what do you want? To become a lady lama?'

'I think I want us to be close, but not to own each other. There's no point in that here. Part of us, if we stay, has to belong to Shangri-La.'

'And to Conway.' It was said before I intended it, but it was said. And she took it without even raising her eyes.

'Perhaps he needs me more than you do, in a way. And without him, this whole enterprise fails. Oh, I don't mean he needs me in a physical way, but he needs the encouragement and the time I can give him, until his inspiration comes back. Everyone here uses him. He's been alone. He can't go on like that. Why are you smiling?'

I changed the smile into a chuckle, and I meant it. 'I was only remembering: I thought it wasn't fair to ask you to marry me, because I was fifteen years your elder. And he's more than twice your age.'

'Are you very upset?'

'It's the wrong word. I've been thinking since we saw those men on the mountain that I owed Conway something, because his crisis is partly of my making. But I never imagined that I'd have to give him you.'

And that was all we said on the subject.

17

Nicholas Brent's Narrative (1980):

'DON'T ANYBODY EXPECT TO BE HOME FOR CHRISTMAS'

If *sangfroid* is still an acceptable term, Conway received us with it at breakfast next morning. The strangers, he said, were still being carefully tracked, and there was nothing to be done until at least after lunch. He turned to Gentry. 'It is seldom indeed that I have to repeat my speeches of welcome within so short a time. I hope you are finding out everything you need to know.'

'Absolutely. You have an able deputy in Warlock here. And if we're not going to meet those creeps till after lunch, I'd just love to spend the morning getting better acquainted with this valley of yours I flew over.'

At first hearing it seemed a preposterous suggestion, but I realized that there was no more useful action to be done; besides, if there was going to be a fight, we might as well be reminded of what we were fighting for. Knowing that neither I nor Elizabeth had spent much time on the valley floor since our arrival, Conway elected himself our guide. Warlock decided to stay at the high level, so it was a party of four, and Gentry and I shared a wagonette. He was as excited as a small boy at his first party.

'I think you always intended to follow us,' I said.

'Oh, sure I did. I just didn't want to promise anything until I was positive I could manage it. You see, all that money's one hell of a responsibility. If you're going to disappear from the face of the earth for a while, it's only fair to make sure other folks don't suffer by your absence. I might have caused another Wall Street crash. But I fixed things. If I reappear within a month, fine. If not, well, it's just a different sequence of events.'

The valley was all that he or anybody else could have expected: wondrously fertile, and filled with contented people. We watched some engineering work at a point where flooding of the principal stream had caused part of the bank to crumble. A new bridge was being protected by stone shoulders of a kind I remember seeing below the glacier streams of South Iceland, and the toughest of the local men were getting the job done with the aid of enormous mallets. Nearby, an animal shelter was being built, with men, women and children all lending a hand. In the distance I once saw Barnard supervising some other activity: he waved cheerfully but did not pause for conversation. He had met his millionaire compatriot only briefly on the previous afternoon, but fifty years at Shangri-La had clearly worn down his American impatience. Now, although he would probably be most interested to begin further talks, he could wait until the occasion arose.

The strangest thing happened on our way back for lunch. I spotted in the trees an enclosure with a large barred wooden shelter in it. The structure had protective netting, topped at a height of twelve feet by barbed wire, and I wondered what kind of animal was contained within: it was so dark below the branches that I could see only a few bobbing shapes of a nondescript colour. It was with a half-smile that Conway let the way closer. Muffled grunts and squawks became audible, and as we neared the fence there leaped towards us several examples of a most unusual species of large furry animal. It was like a large long-armed monkey, well able to stand on two feet and more than five feet high when it did so. Its fur was piebald, brown mixed with grey, and pretty unattractive; it had a pot-belly like an orang-utan; its eyes were defiant but intelligent, its face a dark surrounding mask; its shrill chatter sounded like actual conversation in some language I couldn't understand. When it had inspected us and found us boring, it gathered its dignity and returned to its shelter.

'What kind of monkey is that?' I asked in astonishment.

'That is what I asked,' said Conway, 'when I found one tapping on my window two winters ago. It was a particularly severe season, and more than a dozen of these creatures seem to have been forced down from their normal habitat above the snowline. When we fed the first group, several others appeared, some of them apparently at a very low ebb. We fixed up this shelter so that they could be out of the wind. They responded to kindness, and it turned out that in return for their keep they were intelligent enough to be put to work of a simple kind. Brother Leonard volunteered to teach them elementary words of command, and the odd thing was that if you taught one, all the others seemed to understand and obey too, as though they told each other. We got them house-trained too, which is a blessing, when we let them out to work for the villagers. We still keep them in this compound because one proved temperamental and bit a villager, but we hope that in due course they will adapt sufficiently to our ways to be allowed unguarded dwellings of their own, like willing but backward members of the community.'

I listened hard. 'But they're *talking* to each other,' I said. 'Do you think they could possibly be – ?'

'Oh, yes,' said Conway. 'I think we have examples here of what European travellers and newspaper reporters have called the yeti. Your Abominable Snowman. As you see, there is nothing at all abominable about them. Before very long, with luck, they will be able to communicate with us. I am most anxious to learn what they have to say.'

The sight of these strange creatures, which the world thinks as mythical as Shangri-La, quite possessed me over lunch. When my attention came back to the general conversation, I found Gentry trying to explain to Conway some of the electronic advances of the last few years. Everything around me suddenly seemed quite unreal, and I was relieved when a guard came in with the latest news. After reading the message Conway ordered a bell to be rung, with the result that what looked like the entire population of the lamasery assembled shortly afterwards on the terrace. I was reminded of the finale of an Ivor Novello musical comedy. Apparently it had been decided during the morning, in conclave, that the intruders should be met by Conway, four guards, Warlock, myself and two young lamas. Conway now announced that the unknown visitors had discovered the other end of the tunnel, and that it was time for our party to set out. Elizabeth was fairly happy to be left behind with her father, but Gentry now pleaded to come along. 'After all,' he said, 'you have to admit that in this situation a man of action is likely to be handier than a man of religion.'

After a glance passed between Conway and Chang, it was agreed. But I was surprised when the final volunteer proved to be Mallinson. Conway hesitated slightly before agreeing, and I realized that after all these years he still had no real understanding of the impetuous youth who had been in his charge, was still perhaps somewhat in awe of him because of his own quite unnecessary feelings of guilt.

Chang stood to wave us farewell, his fragile figure supported by two of his crutch-like ornamental canes. We set off down the hill in a series of carriages, and at the foot picked up Barnard, who Conway agreed, after a hurried colloquy, should also join us. Warlock and I made room with us; he was cheerfully loquacious as ever and seemed to have no worries about the future. We travelled by a subsidiary path on the west side of the valley floor, and passed two hamlets I had not previously seen, before arriving in the clearing which had been the scene of our first welcome. Above, the steps climbed up the mountain wall to the ledge and the tunnel opening. As we alighted, news was coming through by a species of semaphore that the strangers, having made temporary camp at the tunnel entrance, seemed now about to proceed. Conway himself translated this, his eyes fixed through binoculars on the lone figure of a scout on a shoulder of the mountain. He turned to address the crowd which had gathered.

'I am afraid our worst fears have been confirmed. Tien Sing, our forward sentinel, must have allowed himself to be seen; he has been shot by one of the intruders. He was seen to fall into a deep gorge – I am afraid there is little hope for him.'

The news was received in stunned silence; our ascent of the steps was made in deep gloom. Conway insisted on going first, but he needed frequent pauses and made it slow going. I must have shown my apprehension, for Barnard at one point tugged at my sleeve and chuckled, 'I wouldn't worry too much. There's one trump card we haven't played yet. Wait and see.'

In solemn procession we set forth into the semi-darkness of the tunnel. It seemed danker than I remembered, and suddenly I felt immensely tired, as though the entire trip should have been undertaken by a younger man. Warlock marched along like a soldier, Gentry was clearly impatient for action, Mallinson was sunk in some private anguish. Conway was being propelled along the bumpy surface in one of the bassinette-style wheelchairs which had accommodated Elizabeth on our arrival, and the guards surrounded him at every turn. Eventually we reached the long straight stretch where we had been met, and Conway appeared to be searching for a particular point before he signalled for our little procession to stop.

Barnard elbowed me, not too gently. 'You still haven't spotted my defence strategy. And you're standing right under it.'

Warlock and Gentry joined me in gazing upwards, and I had a momentary impression of our three faces with the mouths open, as though catching flies. An enormous slit had been scooped in the softish rock of the ceiling, and suspended in it was a massive contraption of wood and metal, with chains attached at the sides. 'Watch this,' said Barnard, shuffling off into one of the side tunnels. Conway motioned us to step back. A series of creaks and grindings ensued, and slowly there inched down into view a formidable studded portcullis which not only stretched from side to side of the tunnel but had screwed into it sharpened bolts. It must surely prevent an enemy from rushing us. When the apparatus was in place, Barnard's face appeared at one of the little windows in it. 'What do you think?' he asked. 'It's a little brainwave I had some ten years back. Works on a big ratchet.'

'Very comforting,' said Warlock. 'But suppose it sticks?'

'We can still get round it.' The small figure of Barnard, more than ever like a leprechaun, disappeared from view, and almost instantly reappeared at our side. 'I cut a side tunnel in the rock,' he said. 'Very narrow, so that anybody squeezing through with a gun would find it not much use against one of us with a long pointed pole. Everything was worked out on the best engineering and strategic principles. And today's the first chance we've had to use it. I'm quite excited.'

Conway smiled grimly. 'It is what the western world calls a deterrent,' he said. 'But first we must give our strangers, despite what happened on the mountain, every opportunity to demonstrate their peaceful intentions if they have any. And so I shall go forward to meet them, and the rest of you will remain behind the portcullis.'

There was a chorus of disapproval at this suggestion. Eventually it was agreed that Gentry and Barnard should remain with the guards, demonstrating our power by poking rifles through the portcullis. The rest of us would go through the side tunnel, standing to the wall side of the portcullis so as not to be in the line of fire. Conway remained in two minds about this arrangement. 'We don't want to alarm them by a show of force,' he said.

Mallinson spoke up unexpectedly, his voice booming along the tunnel like a schoolmaster contemptuous of his class of backward children. 'There are six of them. We'll still be four unarmed people, even though covered from behind. That isn't a show of force.'

'All right,' said Conway. 'Three of us in view, with Mr Warlock in reserve. If our visitors keep us waiting, I shall need two stout shoulders to lean on.' But they did not keep us waiting long. After no more than fifteen minutes, the wall of the distant bend in the tunnel showed elongated shadows, followed by the related substance of six human figures. With a sinking feeling I clearly recognized the rounded form of Dr Lorenz and the slimmer, stick-like figure of Ralph Abel. It was however with horror and disbelief, as another figure came into view and was illuminated by a shaft of sudden sunlight, that my eyes fell on Simon Battersby. The three supporting men were clearly local Burmese, but bigger and tougher than the average. I thought it unlikely that Abel would have trusted them with guns. I whispered my conclusions to Conway, who nodded and stepped forward to receive his unbidden guests.

As he stood in half-profile before me, while in the far

background the newcomers approached in silence, I seemed to see several Conways at the same time. It was as though the man had been magically divided into paper layers, each now peeling away from the others to reveal different facets of his total experience. There was the charmingly urbane and ageing host of Shangri-La, guardian of an ideal if rarefied society. But there was also the eager young officer of the 1914–18 war, leading his men across the Flanders mud in a spurt of action which must result in some disagreeable mixture of death and glory. There was an even younger Conway, packing away his tennis racquet and changing for dinner in the panelled bedroom of some stately home. There was Conway among the dreaming spires of Oxford; did he ever try to hang a chamber-pot from the Martyrs' Memorial? And, of course, Conway the smooth diplomat, shaking the hands of eastern potentates and in the cause of duty eating countless dinners he didn't want, with only the vestige of a smile on his lips to suggest that most of his attention was really elsewhere. Finally, Conway in London during the blitz, lost and bewildered and ten years out of his time in a country which had changed beyond the possibility of his understanding. The privations of the 1926 general strike and the subsequent muscle-flexing of the new Labour Party had given way to a classless solidarity in the face of the Nazi threat, the platitudes of party politicians to the commanding internationalism of Churchill. However miraculously Conway's little grey cells had been preserved by *tangatse* and peace of mind, it would be impossible to convey to him the flavour of an England thriving on Arab finance, Monty Python, and the Sex Pistols. But he would always know right from wrong, and good from evil.

'Good afternoon,' he said when the visitors were sufficiently close and had paused for consideration of their next move. 'My name is Conway.' He added the expected welcome, with some words of commiseration for the eight men lost on the glacier. Abel, who stood slightly ahead of the others, seemed taken aback by the civilized reception, but rallied sufficiently to shake Conway's proffered hand. His words however were cold.

'I hope we shall have no misunderstandings. This is my colleague Dr Lorenz. And Simon Battersby.'

Conway glanced at Simon's awkwardly held arm. 'But we had heard with sorrow of this gentleman's unfortunate death in the desert.'

Simon grinned wolfishly. 'My obituary was a bit premature, though I'm sure Uncle Nick there was glad to recite it. I just thought it was time to get back to my real friends.'

I could not prevent myself from standing forward in accusation. 'It was you who passed on all our information!'

'As much as I could get. You see, I thought I'd toss in my chips with someone more commercially minded than you two. I used to know Abel in Singapore. You didn't even want the gold, and I knew you'd make it difficult for me to take any; but he'd do anything to get it.'

'And it was worth sending Lorenz halfway round the world on a murder mission?'

Abel took charge again. 'That was an improvisation. Apart from the fact that the good doctor has a penchant for killing people, it would have been easier to persuade Miss Battersby with you out of the way; but all we really wanted was any notes you might have made. Look upon us as businessmen. Like all businessmen we try not to make mistakes, but we did make one. Or rather Simon did, in coming over to us too soon, before we knew exactly where the right canyon was. That cost us time, and eight lives. But we shall make no more mistakes. We hope to spill no more blood.'

'I am happy to hear that,' said Conway. 'You will be made welcome here if your intentions are honourable.'

'Our intentions are to take your gold, as much of it as we can carry,' said Abel curtly. 'I've been hearing rumours about this place, but I never thought they were true. It just goes to show that an agent should know his territory.'

'The gold does not belong to you,' said Conway, 'but to the people of this valley, who have lived here for thousands of years.'

'Can they produce a deed of ownership?' cooed Abel. 'If not, I really think . . .'

'Why do you waste time talking?' cried Lorenz with sudden petulance. 'Let's move on. They can't stop us.'

Abel waved him back. 'My friend is impetuous, but I sympathize with his sense of urgency. We are armed, you know. Yes, I'm sure you know. So will you please raise that contraption?'

'Abel,' I said, 'have you no conscience? This is a religious community which seeks only peace and independence.'

'Which it achieves by trading in gold. No, Mr Brent, I'm afraid that puts it in the straight commercial class. And I am nothing if not commercial. However, I daresay that after we have taken charge we may be persuaded to allow your religious community right of tenure and a modest allowance.'

Lorenz's nerves were clearly on edge. 'Stop talking!' he almost screamed. Then he saw me take the Biretta from my pocket. 'No, Mr Brent, we were careful to equip you with blank bullets. You have no effective weapon.'

'But the man who joined them in Myitkyina probably did,' said Abel, 'and I don't see him.'

'Now you do,' said Warlock, stepping out from the side

tunnel with a gun aimed straight at Abel's head. Abel reached instinctively for his own weapon, but it was too late. He shrugged instead and spread his hands wide.

'I know you religious fanatics,' he said. 'You won't be the first to shoot. And you can't stop us leaving, either. If we do, we'll be back, with a regiment if necessary. One way or another we can blast your stupid lamasery to kingdom come.'

'I regret, my dear sir,' said Conway evenly, 'that such an eventuality could not be permitted.'

'And who would stop us? Your bunch of she-men?'

As he spoke he made a kind of jabbing gesture with his left hand, and I was too slow to recognize it as a signal. As Abel threw himself to the ground, one of his Burmese aides raised an arm, and a knife flashed through the air at Warlock. It failed to connect, but my friend had to duck, and as he did so the Burmese lunged forward at him. Warlock went down on his back, and though Gentry ran through the side tunnel to his aid, and deflected the Burmese with a swift kick, it was clear that the scuffle had put the ball back in Abel's court. Or rather, in Simon's; I should have guessed that Abel didn't like handling guns himself. He stepped back now to reveal Simon standing there, rather nervously but in control, his legs apart and the gun in his two hands, pointing at Conway, who I now decided was incapable of dealing with the situation in any realistic way.

'Simon,' I said, 'listen to me. I don't want you to get hurt, for Elizabeth's sake – '

'You can stop being sentimental, Uncle Nick. The only person I care about is me.'

'Then in that case you'd better not fire that gun. And I'd better not fire mine, even if it is loaded with blanks. Because you are standing right under a weak spot in the tunnel, a spot where years ago the roof fell in and killed several people. The slightest sound could bring it down again. So you see, neither of us can really use our guns. I can't because I don't want your deaths on my conscience, and you can't because you'd be the ones to die.'

Simon's hands trembled on the gun as he tried to glance upward without losing his aim. Abel sensed his uncertainty. 'Take no notice,' he hissed. 'He's fooling you!'

'Fire one shot,' I said, 'and you'll be the first to find out who's fooling.'

There was a desperate pause. I felt the situation had gone badly awry, with Warlock groaning on the floor behind me, and Conway no longer in effective command.

Suddenly Abel muttered thickly: 'Take him.'

Some kind of click came from Simon's gun as he raised it. At the same moment there emerged from behind me what I can only describe as a manic bellow. It was Mallinson, enraged and breathing like a stampeding bull, I half-turned, and caught an indelible impression of madness in his eyes as he seized his unexpected chance to rush forward and defend the community which he had once been so reluctant to make his own. He made straight for Simon, seeming to knock Abel flying en route, and made a grab at his right arm. Instantaneously the gun went off. The bullet ricocheted from the side of the tunnel, and everybody leaped back to avoid getting it on the rebound. Simon and Mallinson were rolling on the floor, the latter's shock of white hair gleaming in the dim light. Then, with a rustling, sliding, cracking sound, the roof fell in. As thunder follows lightning, so the physical effect of the single shot, delayed for a few seconds, was a thick cloud of yellow dust, followed by a cascade of pebbles, followed by boulder after boulder falling in apparent slow motion, deafening and blinding the watchers behind the portcullis until the tunnel was almost completely blocked by an amalgam of solid rock and dust.

Only the narrowest of gaps was apparent, near the top of the inside wall.

My first instinct was to see that Conway was safe. He was: Barnard was already winding up the portcullis and guards were creeping below it to retrieve their leader. Gentry had dragged Warlock to safety, and none of us three still on our feet seemed to be hurt beyond being temporarily choked by the fine dust which filled the tunnel. Coughing, we masked our noses and mouths as best we could until it settled, then turned to see what could be done for our unwelcome guests.

It proved to be little enough. Shoes projecting from beneath the pile of rubble told us what had happened to Simon and Mallinson. Abel was nowhere to be glimpsed, but Lorenz, who had somehow or other finished up unharmed on our side of the rockfall, was hysterically clawing at the boulders in a vain attempt at rescue. We pulled him away at once in case he should start another slide, and he sat cowering silently on the floor, alone in what he no doubt took to be a totally hostile environment. I peered cautiously out of the nearest natural window, and found one of the Burmese doing the same. It transpired that he was the only one left alive, and even he had a broken leg. We were too dazed for a time to think what to do about him; but eventually the guards threw him a rope and he was persuaded to wrap himself round in a thick blanket, seize the rope and allow himself to fall out of the window so that he could be hoisted up on our side of the rock slide.

Meanwhile Barnard was shaking his head. 'I just don't see how we go about shoring this lot up. I think that shot tapped the main chute. I mean, for every ton we take away, another ton will probably fall in its place. So don't anybody expect to be going home for Christmas. It's going to be tough enough getting these poor dead bastards out.'

Conway typically was more concerned about Warlock than about himself. The old Canadian was bruised and winded, but not much more. 'Don't worry,' I heard him say, gesturing at Lorenz, whose whimpering reverberated along the tunnel. 'At least you've got yourself a surgeon of sorts. I daresay he's been struck off every medical register in Europe, but Shangri-La can probably find a use for him. They'd better, because it'll be a long time before he sees his little green suit again.'

I don't know how Conway survived the shock of that afternoon. He did, but for a long time he was both sad and speechless. Eventually he climbed with assistance into his wagonette and we began the journey back, passing our reinforcements from the valley, already eager to help in the work of excavation. As we reached the tunnel opening a shaft of sunlight broke through the cloud, and from the valley below there rose the distant, delicate sound of children singing to mark the end of school.

18

Nicholas Brent's Postscript (1986):

'THE WORLD IS NOT YET READY'

It took many months for any semblance of normality to return to Shangri-La, or to the Valley of Blue Moon, after the attempted invasion. Thoughout that winter, as we conversed with each other on the terraces, our eyes were not on each other but on the far horizons, our ears strained for any unusual sounds. The mood passed eventually, and the extra guards were reallocated to other work. With great difficulty, and not a little danger, we retrieved the bodies from the tunnel and buried them in our ice cemetery. Slowly, intending to omit nothing of significance, I compiled the report you have just read. By that time, I suppose, most of the inhabitants of Shangri-La had put the recent tragic events as far behind them as they would go, and we all began to look to the future.

When the spring came it seemed sensible to think about augmenting our supplies, so we sent out a band of volunteers by the still difficult northern route, their instructions being to establish a secret depot near the China Highway, and to set up a chain link system to keep it supplied. They were gone for months without a word – I myself must have stood for days on the mountain shoulder overlooking the old trail – and towards the end of the summer Conway agreed with a sigh that I should speak to Gentry about using the helicopter, which the millionaire had shown no inclination to repair. Nor, indeed, had he set any time limit to his visit; having divested himself of all responsibility, he seemed to give himself up absolutely to the pleasure and inspiration which the Valley of the Blue Moon provided in such abundance for those able to abandon themselves up to the concept of Shangri-La. During a mountain stroll I took the opportunity to ask whether he hadn't been tempted to patch up the damaged landing foot and at least make a few exploratory trips while his petrol lasted. He told me an old story about a Jew who mislaid a hundred-dollar bill and looked for it in every pocket except one. The reason for this omission, said the Jew, was that if he looked in the final pocket and the money wasn't there, he'd have no hope left and would feel obliged to shoot himself. Similarly, said Gentry, he was blissfully happy in Shangri-La while the landing-foot needed attention; if on the other hand he mended it, he'd have no excuse to stay.

I suggested to him a plan by which this moral dilemma would not rear its head. Even without the foot, two of us might fly as far as the desert, where the landing would be soft. There we could pick up the Land Rover and head for Myitkyina, bringing back supplies and information; and the big bird, as he called it, would deliver us to the soft soil at the foot of Shangri-La's mountain. The self-deception in this scheme appealed vastly to Gentry's sense of humour and so one fine morning we did take off, the pair of us, rising nobly from the lamasery terrace and floating gently southwest over the valley. Unfortunately not more than a minute had passed before we both heard a nasty clicking noise above our heads. Gentry glanced up and swore under his breath.

'I should have checked the rotor blades,' he said. 'Looks as though one of them has cracked near the tip: the frosts must have got to it. I can probably put down all right, but it'll be more from luck than good judgement.'

I could see already that he was unable to control our direction. Most 'copters dip towards the ground, but we were more vertical than horizontal, and only our seat straps held us in. At this crazy angle, and with a blade which was now clearly hanging by a thread, we teetered over the village settlements, afraid more than anything of crashing into an occupied building. We managed to stay in the air until every house was behind us, and finally came to earth, with more of a plop than anything else, in the marshy land beyond the rapids. There the machine still sits, with one blade dangling, and how it can ever be salvaged without another helicopter to lift it piece by piece is beyond my imagination.

On the day after our adventure, the supply column arrived from the north, with news that a regular link had been established.

What else? Well, poor Sir Arthur never did regain his full faculties. At his best it was like talking to the ghost of the man I once knew, and despite the most careful nursing by Elizabeth (plus some more reluctant attention from Dr Lorenz) his relapses increasingly outnumbered his periods of comparative lucidity. He died quietly in the November of 1984 and is buried at the highest point of the ice cemetery, on the row normally reserved for lamas. As for Lorenz, I can't say that he makes a very cheerful or positive addition to our numbers; but after some months of fretful sulking, no doubt aggravated by guilt, he began to see that he had only Hobson's choice, and that for the sake of his own well-being he had better make the best of things. Since we all made a show of bearing no malice, he eventually found himself performing whatever medical duties were required. Prime among these was some attention to Conway's knee. It was a relief to all of us when we learned that so far as Lorenz could tell there was no malignancy; he performed a simple cartilage operation which reduced the pain to no more than an occasional irritation.

Even the presence among us of a qualified doctor had been unable to prevent the deaths of two lamas and a postulant since our arrival, so the balance is only just being maintained. But one of the dead had recently celebrated his one hundred and seventieth birthday.

Warlock and Gentry and I are now on the full regime, and feeling fine. We keep ourselves busy on a variety of projects which we see no reason to rush to a conclusion. After a few months it was suggested that we might move across the terrace to the lamasery proper; but instead of joining the three other female postulants, Elizabeth chose to stay where she was, in the so-called Master's Lodge. This came as no surprise to me. I have no idea what discussions took place between her and Conway, but from our first days in Shangri-La it was clear to me that they were a pair, and I never brought up the subject of our old relationship except to demonstrate my happiness for her in her new one. I could scarcely have any other feeling, for she is as radiant as the sun, and such constant good humour is infectious. Having lost Sir Arthur, she has found another leader whom she can help and inspire – and that kind of role I could never have filled. As for Conway, his old eyes blaze these days with the enthusiasm, confidence and leadership which I had always imagined in him, but which on our arrival had seemed so diminished. By my calculation he is now ninety-six years old.

During the early summer of last year, an avalanche high on Zarnak was followed by heavy rains. The turbulent waters found an unexpected means of escape, straight down the mountainside of Salabir and into our blocked tunnel. From our vantage point at Shangri-La we watched the flash flood in progress, and I was reminded of my terrifying day in Titus Canyon: it seemed at one point that the whole mountain could be swept away. Yet when the sun shone once more, and we went to inspect the damage at close quarters, we were amazed to discover the happiest of circumstances. The raging waters had cleared a way right through the tunnel, which, as my readers will remember, slopes down towards the desert. This exhibition of natural force had not only taken with it the rubble which six years ago saw the end of Ralph Abel; it also prevented any danger of further roof falls at that point by clearing out an enormous amount of soft rock to leave a huge natural cavern with a high roof which according to Barnard is in no danger of collapse. Alas, our old Land Rover, unused for so many years, had taken the full force of the elements; but most of its working parts were recoverable, and there is still petrol in the cans, so Barnard is working on a scheme for a simplified vehicle which may one day take a party along the desert floor as far as Myitkyina. At present we still fear to venture in that direction in case we put more greedy men on our trail; but Conway has been persuaded that we should make maps of the territory which surrounds us, and I have volunteered to lead the first expedition. I shall take these papers with me.

We continue to receive, by radio and newspaper, accounts of the world outside our valley. In none of us do they inspire any wish to return to the old life. Not only is there so much to do here, in the sense of cataloguing the glories of the past: we remain convinced of the wisdom of Shangri-La in remaining aloof from the endless struggles of Arab and Jew, Iraqi and Iranian, Catholic and Protestant. We await the time when all such foolish passions are spent. For the moment, we hope that whoever reads these pages will profit from them silently, for we would not welcome the spotlight of publicity on our innocent activities. We require no rescue, but inquiring visitors are always welcome, providing that they cover their tracks rather better than we did. The world is not ready to hear of the reality of Shangri-La; but from what we have learned this year about the scourge of AIDS and the disaster of Chernobyl, the time may not be far off. We must all hope that the Valley of Blue Moon can remain uncontaminated.

Nicholas Brent
Shangri-La
December 25th 1986

Epilogue (1987):

IN ST STEPHEN'S TAVERN

'Well, well, Pemberton,' said Twigley as he skilfully dissected a *sole portugaise*, 'you'll be pleased to hear that not only did I read to the end of your remarkable narrative – '

'At last,' grunted Pemberton.

' – but I also got the research boys busy. I set our Canadian friends on to tracing Irving Warlock, and it seems he's always been considered a bit of an eccentric, which isn't too good for your case. Nothing specific, you know, just a harmless crank.'

'I believe some people made remarks of that kind about Jesus Christ. And you'd certainly say it of Gentry if he weren't so rich.'

'You're quite right. Millionaires *are* beyond criticism, in my book. But as for Elizabeth Battersby, it's a matter of public record that she had a bee in her bonnet. No denying that she and her brother and this fellow Brent did go on an expedition, and failed to come back, but the remote parts of the world are full of the bones of explorers who should have known better.'

'And Brent's signature?'

Twigley shrugged. 'I could give you a longish list of handwriting experts whose evidence has been totally discredited.'

'At least you can't prove that the typescript *isn't* genuine. And don't too many things fit together for the story *not* to be true?'

'Only if you *want* it to be true,' said Twigley. 'Personally I've always been wary of wishful thinking.'

'But it's too much of a coincidence if it isn't me. After all, Gentry and Warlock and Ralph Abel all disappeared mysteriously. It's a matter of record.'

'Brent or whoever is masquerading as Brent, could have read accounts in the papers and adapted them to his purpose.'

Pemberton restrained his irritation. 'So, in your view, what action should we take? Send another expedition to check out the story, with instructions to be discreet? And where do we apply for finance? Home, foreign, diplomatic? Perhaps Scotland Yard or even Interpol? I'd value your serious advice, old man, I really would.'

Twigley made careful use of a toothpick. 'I do see your problem. If the whole thing turned out to be fiction, perhaps we could charge it to the Arts Council.'

Pemberton called for coffee. 'I can see you're not going to be helpful.'

'I just think it's something you may have cause to be sorry you started.'

'But that's such a negative attitude. Doesn't the story excite you? Wouldn't *you* like it to be true?'

'Ah, yes, absolutely. I'd also like to see pigs fly. Besides, if it *should* turn out to *be* true, I can imagine every kind of awkward complication. For a start, if Dearden and his junior *are* still alive, or in the junior's case lived until a few years ago, think of the fifty-odd years of salary stroke pension they can claim. I shudder to think what that would add up to at compound interest, especially since they were both kidnapped on active duty; that must bring an added liability. And I hope you've realized that you'd be poking your nose round the Iron Curtain: the Burmese are not the easiest people in the world to talk to. Sort of thing could start a Third World War if it went wrong.'

'I see. You'd rather not be involved. I suppose I shall have to take the advice of my DDS.'

'Mmm. And I can guess what his first remark will be, with economy the watchword of the day.'

'I know: we can't afford it. He's not overkeen on me as it is: suspects me of having had something to do with the Bassingbourne leak.'

'Mine hasn't spoken to me since the affair of the Yugoslavian butter.'

'I don't know anything about that.'

'And you're not going to hear it from me.'

Silence prevailed while both men stirred their coffee. Pemberton said at length: 'So what do you really think I should do? What would *you* have done if the thing had dropped on *your* desk?'

'Oh, I can tell you that. I'd sit on it.'

'Till when?'

'Till the cows come home if necessary. Look here, you've more than enough on your plate at present, and it's definitely not my pigeon. But if it's worrying you, let me make a suggestion. Think about it for a week – till our next lunch. My extra turn.'

'Can't do next week, I'm in Brussels.'

'Two weeks then. After all, it isn't as though anyone's pleading to be rescued. You're actually doing them a favour if you leave them where they are. *If* they're where they say they are. I mean, you could scarcely avoid letting the press in, and old Dearden clearly wouldn't care for that.'

Pemberton waved for their usual brandies, and heaved a deep sigh. 'I suppose there *is* a chance that by following this up I could bring a disaster on everybody's heads. I certainly don't want to be too precipitate. After all, if Shangri-La has existed for more than two hundred years, it will still be there in a couple of weeks, I quite see that.

A couple of months, come to that. Perhaps I might at least leave it until Katherine and I come back from California.'

'What a good idea. Your sister's at Carmel, isn't she? You can lie on the beach and think about it.'

'I suppose there *is* a beach?' murmured Pemberton vaguely. Thoughout his long association with Twigley, he had invariably been the one to lose an argument, and that state of affairs seemed unlikely to change, however long he groped around for a conclusive point.

Twigley seized the opportunity to reach into his brief-case. 'Here,' he said, 'take my copy back right now, and put them both on deep freeze.'

'What about Sir Bruce Thomson?'

'Tell him the whole thing has been classified top secret. It has, by us. He won't rock the boat, he has a lordship in mind.'

'I suppose I might get away with that. After all, it's not as though we were brushing the thing under some tatty bit of office carpet. I shan't forget that a decision has to be taken. It's simply a matter of reaching the right one before we formulate a plan.'

'Exactly. And while you're in California, you could even research a few of Brent's facts.'

Twigley bit his tongue before this sentence was fully uttered, but it was too late. 'Of course,' said Pemberton, with fresh enthusiasm in his eyes. 'I could easily do that. My sister has actually suggested a weekend trip to Yosemite. If we extended that by a couple of nights, I'm sure we could spend the night at Stovepipe Wells: it can't be more than a day's journey. And from there I can easily do the Titus Canyon trip and look for the ruins above Leadfield.'

Twigley shook his head. 'And if you find them?'

Pemberton smiled ruefully. 'If I find them, I shall

probably come back with the bit between my teeth and book a ticket to Rangoon. So, just in case, I think I'll leave these documents on hold, locked in my middle drawer. For the time being . . .'

The two men sat and looked through the window. Their eyes were on a number 29 bus which happened to be passing, but what they saw, one more clearly than the other, was a group of oddly designed buildings on a distant moonlit hill.

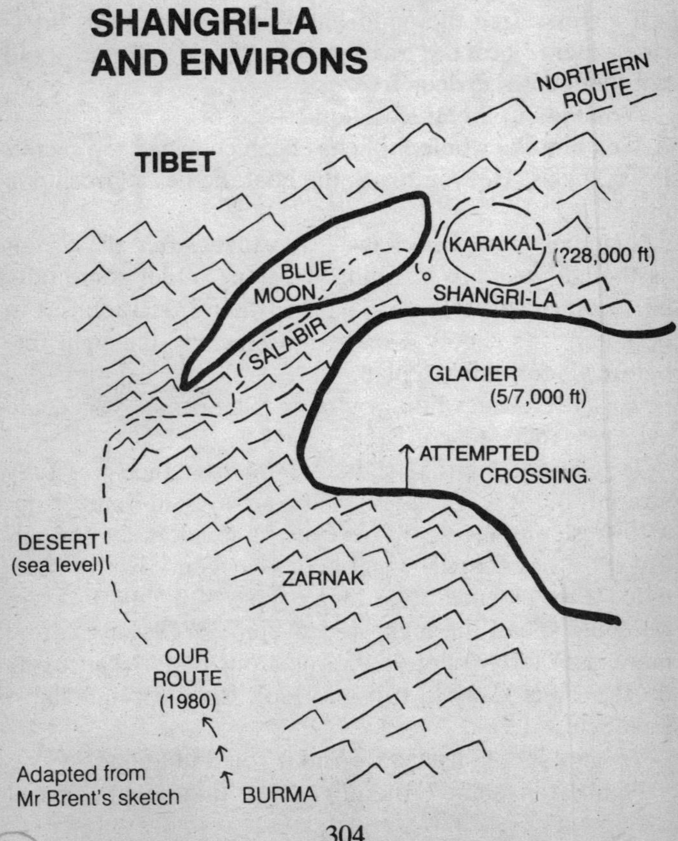